HERO COMPLEX

What Reviewers Say About
Jesse J. Thoma's Work

Wisdom

"I like Jesse J. Thoma's writing style and the topic of drug addiction and health problems she addresses is interesting and still an actual problem all over the world. ...Drug use, addiction, and in this context safety and health are perennial issues that every mayor of any city has to deal with. Obviously, this is an important topic for the author, and she writes it very well. All in all, this was an entertaining political story."—*Lez Review Books*

"Every time I read a book by Jesse J. Thoma, I remember how much I enjoy the way she combines heavy topics and light writing. Despite being book 3 in a series (after *Serenity* and *Courage*), this book can be read as a standalone. ...This book is an interesting blend of instalust and slow burn. Sophia and Reggie start flirting on their first meet and almost never stop. The sparks are everywhere and it's all very exciting. All the edging and sexy talk are pretty damn hot too."—*Jude in the Stars*

Courage

"Thoma writes very endearing characters, extraordinary people in normal lives. ...A slow burn romance with plenty of sparks and chemistry."—*Jude in the Stars*

"Set in the same universe as *Serenity*, Thoma has again done a great job of exploring difficult, relevant topics in an accessible way, whilst also managing to include a believable romance and some much needed elements of humour."—*LGBTQ+ Reader*

"I love a serious police procedural. Add in an enchanting romance with beautiful characters, and you have the perfect novel. That is exactly what I found in Courage by Jesse J. Thoma. I was hooked on page one, and was sad to leave this tale when I reached the end."
—*Rainbow Reflections*

"*Courage* is a slow burn romance with plenty of sparks and chemistry. You can always count on Jesse J. Thoma to write solid but tender stories."—*Rainbow Literary Society*

"I LOVED that Thoma addresses the issues of police reform, Black Lives Matter, and 'defund the police' in a non-political way. She brings these issues into the story in a way that makes SO MUCH sense."—*Love, Literature*

"Jesse J. Thoma brings two stories to life in parallel, one being the work and dynamics of the new ride-along program and how the two protagonists deal with it, and the other the romance between the two. I loved both parts. ...Highly recommended for anyone looking for a good cop/social worker story who enjoys angst and tricky situations."—*Lez Review Books*

Serenity

"*Serenity* is the perfect example of opposites attract. ...I'm a sucker for stories of redemption and for characters who push their limits, prove themselves to be more than others seem to think. This lesbian opposites attract romance book is all that, and well-written too."
—*Lez Review Books*

"I really liked this one. I liked the pace, the stakes, and the characterizations. The relationship builds well, there are likeable supporting characters, and of course, you're rooting for Kit and Thea even as your heart breaks for both of them and their situations. It's a sweet romance, and I appreciated that a lot of the issues Kit faces have nothing to do with her sexuality in a predominately male-driven, sexist profession."—*Kissing Backwards*

The Chase

"The primary couple's initial meeting is a uniquely amusing yet action-packed scenario. I was definitely drawn into the dynamic events of this thoroughly gratifying book via an artfully droll and continuously exciting story. Spectacularly entertaining!"—*Rainbow Book Reviews*

Seneca Falls—*Lambda Literary Award Finalist*

"Loneliness and survival are the two themes dominating Seneca King's life in Thoma's emotionally raw contemporary lesbian romance. Thoma bluntly and uncompromisingly portrays Seneca's struggles with chronic pain, emotional trauma, and uncertainty." —*Publishers Weekly*

"This was another extraordinary book that I could not put down. Magnificent!"—*Rainbow Book Reviews*

"...a deeply moving account of a young woman trying to raise herself from the ashes of a youth-gone-wrong. Thoma has given us a redemptive tale—and Seneca isn't the only one who needs saving. Told with just enough wit and humor to break the tension that arises from living with villainous ghosts from the past, this is a tale woven into a narrative tapestry of healing and wholeness." —*Lambda Literary*

Pedal to the Metal

"Sassy and sexy meet adventurous and slightly nerdy in Thoma's much-anticipated sequel to *The Chase*. Tongue-in-cheek wit keeps the fast-moving action from going off the rails, all balanced by richly nuanced interpersonal relationships and sweet, realistic romance."—*Publishers Weekly*

"[*Pedal to the Metal*] has a wonderful cast of characters including the two primary women from the first book in subsidiary roles and some classy good guys versus bad guys action. …The people, the predicaments, the multi-level layers of both the storyline and the couples populating the Rhode Island landscapes once again had me glued to the pages chapter after chapter. This book works so well on so many levels and is a wonderful complement to the opening book of this series that I truly hope the author will add several additional books to the series. Mystery, action, passion, and family linked together create one amazing reading experience. Scintillating!"
—*Rainbow Book Reviews*

Visit us at www.boldstrokesbooks.com

By the Author

Tales of Lasher, Inc.

The Chase

Pedal to the Metal

Data Capture

The Serenity Prayer Series

Serenity

Courage

Wisdom

Other Romances

Seneca Falls

Hero Complex

HERO COMPLEX

by

Jesse J. Thoma

2023

CREDITS
EDITORS: VICTORIA VILLASEÑOR AND CINDY CRESAP
PRODUCTION DESIGN: SUSAN RAMUNDO
COVER DESIGN BY INKSPIRAL DESIGN

Acknowledgments

First and foremost, thank you to Sandy and Rad and the BSB team. Superheroes don't get work done alone and this book wouldn't have seen the light of day without the amazing support at BSB. Sandy especially provided her usual insights and guidance, and I'm grateful.

To Vic, we started with bounty hunters and ended with superheroes and had a pretty good run in the middle too. I cannot thank you enough for making me a writer. I'm even thankful for your voice in my head scolding me when I'm writing a sentence I know you'd hate. This book would have been significantly worse for wear without your guidance. Thank you.

To my kids, thank you for saying you want to be a writer when you grow up because it "looks like a really easy job" and thank you for sharing your book ideas with me, even if they're mostly about unicorns and dinosaurs. I could not love you more.

To my wife, I could not ask for a better supporter, cheerleader, and partner than you. I will never write a story that comes close to what we have together, but it's fun to try.

Finally, to the readers, thank you for picking up this book. Whether it's your first of mine or you've read every one I've written, it's an honor to write for you. I've loved superheroes long before they were cool. I hope you enjoy this book as much as I loved writing it.

Dedication

To Alexis,
Love rocks and I only want to rock with you.

To Goose, Bird, and little Purple Martin,
I love you yesterday, today, and tomorrow too.

Chapter One

B ard Verstrand studied the monitor. She squinted and leaned closer trying to make out the images from the discreetly placed surveillance camera in the corner of the science lab.

"This is live, correct?" She jabbed at the screen and turned to the group of her employees standing aimlessly behind her.

No one answered.

"I asked if this was live."

"Yes, ma'am. She's, uh, Dr. Scales is in the lab now. It's a live feed from our camera."

Bard studied the monitor again. She found the spying distasteful, but she had no choice.

"Antonio, how close is she?"

Now that he'd been summoned, Bard's right-hand man stepped forward and leaned over the desk, mirroring her own position. "She's almost completed her work. Our window of opportunity likely closes at the end of the day. You know what needs to be done."

Sweat materialized on Bard's palms and her mouth felt dry. She scrubbed her hands on her outrageously expensive pencil skirt to rid herself of the outward sign of her unease.

Antonio put his hand on her shoulder and spoke so only Bard could hear. "I know you've been unsure about taking this path, but trust yourself. Your father left the company to you for exactly these moments. He trusted you to find the innovations that would steer Verstrand Industries into the future, and you have. It's time to take what's yours."

Bard nodded as she once again watched Bronte Scales. She was a brilliant scientist who'd rented lab space in her building for years. The science might be above her head, but she prided herself on understanding people and she'd known the moment Bronte had set foot in the building she could one day help her fulfill her legacy.

"I don't have much choice, do I?" Bard could hear the regret in her own voice. What was her act of self-interest, her act of survival, going to cost Bronte?

"If she's as gifted as you say, there is more out there for her to discover." Antonio stood, ready to give the order for his men to move on Bronte's lab.

Bard hesitated. Was she so afraid of disappointing her father that she was ready to ruin a woman's career? She'd never thought herself a coward. She considered the feeling of sitting in front of her father and telling him Verstrand Industries had nothing new to bring to market for the foreseeable future because she didn't have the ovaries to confront one unarmed, unsuspecting scientist.

"Let's move." Bard stood so abruptly her chair skittered back, slamming into the man standing at attention behind her desk. "I'm coming with you."

"Ma'am, you don't have to do that. You can watch here." Antonio pointed to the monitor.

"I'm coming. I want to ensure all the data and materials are secured. There's a lot riding on this operation." Bard headed for the door forcing her men to scramble to keep up.

Antonio fell in beside her barking orders into his radio, coordinating the raid they'd been planning for weeks.

Once outside the door to the lab, Antonio silently directed the men into their final positions. Bard had watched these maneuvers on other operations via the emotionally distanced video feed Antonio dutifully provided, but it was altogether different participating in the action herself.

Her heart pounded so aggressively as she watched Antonio silently count down that she could feel it in her neck, her temple, and her fingers. No one around her looked the least bit uneasy. Were they not frightened? How did they keep their nerves at bay?

Before Antonio finished his countdown and Bard could worry herself into an ulcer or into rushing the door before the rest of the team was ready, someone called out from within.

"It's unlocked. No need to break it down. Come in when you're done posturing in the hall."

Bard clenched her teeth and grabbed Antonio by the front of the shirt. "That's her. How does she know we're here?"

Antonio looked to the door as if it might provide the answers he clearly didn't have himself.

"If she knew we were coming she's probably in there destroying the data or hiding it well enough we'll never find it. Get your men in there and secure what we came for." Bard let go of Antonio's shirt and shoved him toward the lab.

Despite Bronte's assurance the door was unlocked, one of the men broke it anyway. Bard shoved her way in after the first three entered. She was dismayed at the scene that greeted her.

A trash can stood in the middle of the room engulfed in flames. The fire suppression system hadn't engaged so Bronte must have disabled it before setting fire to the bin. Beakers, pipettes, and test tubes were smashed in the sink and on the floor.

"Sorry for the mess, boys." Bronte casually leaned against one of the lab benches, her hands in the pockets of her white lab coat. "Although I guess you aren't concerned about that." She nodded at the door lying on the floor.

Bard balled her fists. Her wrists were like iron and her face was on fire. She stormed to Bronte and stopped inches from her. "How dare you destroy what was mine."

"None of this was ever yours." Bronte pushed off her perch nearly colliding with Bard.

"Everything and anything I need to make Verstrand Industries successful is mine."

Bronte reached behind her, grabbed her laptop which was still open on the bench, and stepped around Bard. "If you say so. The thing is, here in the real world there are laws and rules, and general human decency. You and your ten armed goons have a look around if you want. Put out the fire when you're done and fix the door. I've got nothing to say to you."

Bard grabbed Bronte's arm as she walked past. She took a deep breath. She'd made her angry so she'd not been concentrating but she was now. First, the laptop. Bronte wasn't leaving with the laptop. She pointed to the computer and one of the men stepped forward to retrieve it.

"I really wish you'd let me walk out the door. I worked hard on this project." Bronte looked regretfully at the laptop before voice-activating the device and requesting "last resort."

Bronte threw it along the floor across the lab to the point farthest from where they stood. Bard pointed at the computer and two men started after it.

"I wouldn't do that." Bronte made an explosive motion with her hands.

Bard could see the smoke coming from the laptop. She waved the men back in time to see electronic debris, guts, and parts fly in every direction. Everyone ducked to avoid the shrapnel.

As she shielded herself, Bard noticed Bronte's right hand return to her lab coat pocket as if she were protecting something. She was hurriedly moving toward the door while the rest of the group was trying not to die by laptop.

"Antonio, her pocket. Whatever's in her right lab coat pocket, bring it to me." Bard stood and followed Bronte and Antonio, both of whom had exited into the hall.

Before she made the door, she could tell an altercation was in progress just beyond her line of sight. Human bodies smashing into walls cannot be done quietly. As Bard exited the lab, Antonio and Bronte crashed to the floor, fighting for the upper hand and the contents of Bronte's pocket.

Bronte delivered a well-timed blow to Antonio's left eye, stunning him long enough for her to kick him off her. Bard watched helplessly as she removed a syringe from her lab coat, plunged the needle into her thigh, and injected the contents into her body.

An angry shriek filled every nook and cranny in the hall, and it took a beat or two before Bard realized the sound was coming from her. What were these feelings? How was this woman bringing them to the surface? Rage? Fear? Exhilaration? She grabbed the gun from the holster of the nearest man and ran to Bronte, who was kneeling with one hand against the wall, sweating and gasping for breath.

"I told you, anything I need for the success of my company is mine, you bitch. Now I need what's in your blood, so you're mine too." Bard raised the gun and brought the butt down on the back of Bronte's head. She landed unconscious at Bard's feet.

Antonio stumbled to his feet and pointed to three men who'd joined them in the hall. "Bring her to the hospital, sub-level, and clean up this mess. As of right now, Dr. Bronte Scales never existed."

❖

Bronte tried to open her eyes, but either they were uncooperative or she was in the dark. She was having trouble focusing. It felt like her brain had been dropped in a frying pan and someone was stirring it into scrambled eggs.

She took stock of what she could. Pain. Heat. Motion. Voices? The voices sounded far enough away that she wasn't sure they were real.

The intensity of the pain increased. Was she being violently assaulted at a cellular level? Reflexively she tried to pull her legs to her chest and curl protectively around herself, but she encountered resistance. She couldn't move her arms either. Her rate of respiration increased, and her heart began to pound. She tried her arms again. They moved but there was resistance. Why was she restrained? She fought harder.

"Easy now. You're not going anywhere."

She recognized the voice but couldn't pull it from her memory. Her brain was too foggy.

"What do you want from me?" Bronte tried opening her eyes again. She was aware of her lashes scraping against something this time. Fabric? Why was she blindfolded?

"I want everything from you."

Bronte tried to rewind and remember how she'd gotten here. Her lab. Her work...Her work. She'd destroyed her work. Bard Verstrand had tried to steal her work. She was the one speaking.

Pain shot through her again. She arched, straining against her bindings. She was sure she was being burned from the inside. How was Bard doing this to her? What did she want?

The pain subsided and she remembered. She hadn't destroyed everything. She'd saved one sample of the zeptobots she'd managed to create after years of work. Or, more accurately, she'd tried to save that sample. Instead of letting her technology fall into Bard's hands she'd injected the entire sample into herself.

"Ms. Verstrand, we're having trouble getting an IV started. Every time we try her skin turns to…well, it seems to turn to metal."

Bronte tried to focus on this new bit of information, but whatever was happening to her, and she suspected it was the result of the zeptobots, was overwhelming her ability to remain conscious.

"What do you mean metal?"

"We've snapped three needles already, Ms. Verstrand. It's almost like it's protecting her, somehow."

"Doesn't matter. We've got plenty of time to get what we need. Keep trying."

She started to lose consciousness. Plenty of time? Only if the zeptobots didn't kill her quickly.

CHAPTER TWO

One Year Later

Each of us exists in triplicate. There is no single story of our lives. We all have a story of ourselves we create for our eyes only. It's who we tell ourselves we are, or one day will be. We also create a version of ourselves we present to the world created from only those stories we want the world to hear. Finally, stories are told about us by friends, family, strangers, and colleagues which forms another version of each of us. We can't control that version of ourselves or the stories that create it.

What does it mean when our three selves converge? What happens when they diverge? Most importantly, which is real and where do we go to find our true selves?

Athena Papadakis groaned as she pushed open the door to Dunkin and saw the length of the line. One of these days she'd learn to leave on time, but then she'd have to give up something else she crammed into her morning, and she wasn't willing to do that. This morning had brought the delightful discovery of a new social media star in the form of an ancient pug who could predict the quality of her day. He'd said this day was going to be great so who was she to complain about a long line?

Despite pug prognostications, Athena tapped her foot while she inched closer to the counter. Nothing was catching her attention as she scrolled on her phone. She wasn't annoyed at being where she was so much as more interested in being where she next needed to be.

"Athena, honey, the usual?"

Doris LaRue's voice cut through Athena's preoccupation.

"Yes, ma'am. I appreciate you, Doris." Athena saluted the four-foot-ten firecracker behind the counter.

"Sweet-talk don't pay the bills, darlin'. Leave it in the tip jar." Doris smiled and turned back to her work.

Despite there still being six people in front of her, Athena knew when she reached the register her order would be complete and ready for her. She had no idea how, but Doris knew every regular customer by name and order. In fact, if you visited more than once she remembered what you'd had the time before and was ready to make you the same. One of these days she was going to switch things up just to blow Doris's mind.

"Big day for you today, isn't it?" Doris handed over Athena's large coffee with two sugars and cream and a glazed donut. "New job starting. Cutting it a little close getting there on time, aren't you?"

"It's a little creepy when you do that, you know."

"I can see how someone caring about a wild spirit like you would be annoying. Don't mention things to me if you don't want me to bring them up. Steel trap, remember?" Doris knocked her knuckles against her skull.

Athena leaned over the counter and kissed Doris on the cheek before heading out the door. She called out, "Don't ever change," over her shoulder on the way out.

She rushed through the door of the hospital balancing her coffee, donut, and her purse as she searched for her new badge. Although she'd worked for the hospital for five years as an emergency department nurse, the new position had necessitated a new badge, which despite being bright orange, she couldn't find. Only those who worked on the sublevels could access those floors.

Once she finally found the elusive badge, she slipped between the closing elevator doors, pushed the button for the sublevel, and swiped her credentials to prove she belonged. Was that a tremor in her hand? She pulled her hand back quickly, balled it up, and shoved it in the pocket of her scrub shirt. She was *not* going to be anxious about this. So what if there were rumors about human experimentation and disfigured test subjects there? She'd worked in the emergency department and relished the chaos. Whether or not the rumors were true, whoever was on the sublevels needed her help, and nothing scared her. She was Athena Fucking Papadakis, super nurse extraordinaire.

When she stepped off the elevator, she was almost disappointed to see a regular, boring hospital wing waiting for her. Except for the Mount Everest-sized men in suits parked outside the two rooms she could see. And the abandoned nurses' station. And the silence. Where were the other nurses? Was it so busy they were all in patient rooms? Why wasn't there more noise? Hospitals were always loud, but this floor was eerily silent. Even the sounds of beeping monitors and carts rolling along polished floors were missing.

"You must be Athena? The new nurse?"

Athena nearly jumped out of her skin. She turned and took in the tall, slightly disengaged looking woman sporting a lab coat and an amused expression.

"Sorry to sneak up on you. I could tell you have some questions so I thought we should get to it. Most people are a little freaked out the first time they see security here or how quiet it is. You weren't. That's interesting."

"How do you know that?" Athena took a step back, needing the distance to find her balance.

"I'm good at reading people. My name's Dr. Galen Ford. I'm in charge down here officially, but we all know the nurses really run the show, so I guess that makes you in charge." Galen extended her hand.

"What do you mean, 'that makes me in charge'? Where are the other nurses? Are you the attending doctor?" Athena shook Galen's hand and looked around hoping to spot someone else, anyone other than the masses of muscle standing stoically on duty.

"Yes, I'm the attending physician technically, but that sounds fancier than it needs to be when it's just us. Just us, sort of. It's easier to show you and I'd hate to ruin the surprise." Galen started walking. She looked back over her shoulder and motioned Athena to follow. "Buster, the other nurse, was here overnight but he left right before you got here. He's got a new baby so I sent him home. I knew you wouldn't be long. I could tell you'd gotten your coffee and were on your way down."

Athena stopped short. The squeak from her sneakers sounded like the shriek of a thousand airhorns in the quiet hallway. "How the fuck did you know that? And don't say you're good at reading people."

"I wouldn't insult your intelligence with that bullshit. We both know I wasn't at the coffee shop with you. Would you care for a tour?" Galen set off down the hall again and looked back over her shoulder.

Athena shook her head and let it go. She smiled despite the batshit crazy start to her shift. There was a reason the sublevels had a reputation. She'd assumed it was rumors gone wild. No one would believe her if she assured them it seemed to be as crazy as everyone assumed and the only one she'd met was the doctor. It occurred to her the doctor might be the reason this place had a reputation.

"What about them?" Athena pointed at one of the stoic men standing guard outside the door Galen entered. She looked down the hall. There were guards outside *all* the patients' rooms. Why was that?

"They're like the guards at Buckingham Palace. You can do whatever you like to get a rise out of them, but they stand there and stare straight ahead all day. They're here to guard, not chat. I assume they wear diapers since they never move. I've tried every question I can think of, but they never answer. Not even a smile. I've tried looking for an off switch, just in case they're robots, but I haven't found one yet." Galen said the last part behind her hand as if the men couldn't hear her if they couldn't see her lips moving.

She could be wrong, but Athena was pretty sure the door guard shot Galen a less than pleased look. Not robots after all. She paused before she followed Galen into the first patient room. She looked back the way she'd come. The elevator she'd exited had deposited her in front of the abandoned nurses' station which she could now see stood like a ship's figurehead. Patient rooms branched off around the perimeter of the space on both sides.

What Athena had assumed was a hallway she now could see was a wall of patient rooms and some type of semi-transparent barrier that looked like it continued to the end of the row of rooms and turned the corner. Athena guessed it formed an inner ring around the floor. It stretched from floor to well above her head, but clearly hadn't always been part of the floor plan. It resembled a cattle corral.

"What's past that wall?" Athena caught Galen's attention and pointed at the barrier.

"Where a bigger surprise comes from and a place we're not allowed to go." Galen waved her into the patient room.

"I figured it would be different down here, but you've really outdone yourself." Athena let the door close behind her.

Galen turned and smiled an unreadable smile. It made Athena's insides squirm uncomfortably. What else did Galen have for her? Was she in over her head already? She took a breath and turned her attention to the patient in the room they'd entered, the one thing she was sure to understand.

The room was dark despite the large window looking out into the hallway. It took a moment for her eyes to adjust. A single adult man was lying in a bed in the middle of the room. He appeared unconscious. Athena was once again struck by the stillness of the room. No monitors or IV poles. No signs of medications or medical equipment of any kind.

"Tell me about him." Athena moved to the man's bedside. Once she moved closer, she saw three-pronged electrical cords snaked between his middle and ring fingers on both hands. A second glance confirmed the cords originated *inside* his body. Now that she was near, she could also see what looked like computer chips under the first layer of the skin on his face and arms. It was like looking at them under murky water, but she could see well enough to be confident in what she was looking at. Who was this man and what were they doing to him?

"There's nothing to tell." Galen's expression closed. "He's alive and it's our job to keep him that way. He's fed and watered via supplements given to him orally at various times of day. That's all we have to do."

Athena crossed her arms. "He's unconscious and in the hospital. Why is that? I can't care for a patient I know nothing about. Do we have to plug him in?" She gestured to the cords. "Why are those there?"

"He's here for…testing. That's part of it. I don't ask too many questions and I suggest you don't either. He's breathing just like everyone else on this floor. We keep him that way and we keep our jobs. If you can't handle the job, I'll tell the higher-ups you want to go back upstairs and you can forget you ever saw anything strange here. Otherwise, let's go to the next room." Galen looked impatient as she held the door for Athena.

"I'm going to need more than that, Dr. Ford."

"No. You don't." Galen gave Athena a pleading look. "Trust me."

Athena let it go. For now. Hopefully she'd gather more information the more patients she met.

When they exited the first room Athena scooted quickly behind Galen, tapped her on the shoulder and said as quietly as she could. "What the flying frittata is that?" She inclined her head toward the clear barrier in front of the large room on her left, not wanting to point.

Galen barely glanced in the direction Athena was indicating. "I knew you'd like them. I call them the basilisk." She stopped and looked Athena directly in the eye. "The only rule on this floor is don't cross the basilisk."

Athena started to make a joke, but Galen shook her head slowly and mouthed, "don't cross them," before moving to another patient room. Athena held back and studied the two creatures Galen seemed afraid of. They were huddled together and as of now seemed unaware of her presence.

Upon closer inspection she could see they were in fact humans in elaborate suits that gave them a mystical appearance. Their serpent-like heads were nearly obscured by the suit and some kind of screen. The rubbery suit covering their bodies tapered behind their heads, eventually giving way to a long black air hose. The hose connected to an oxygen tank built into the suit halfway up their backs. Or at least that's what Athena assumed, although it was tucked beneath the suit that covered the entirety of the person's body, giving them a strange hunchback appearance.

Perhaps the strangest features of the basilisks were the lack of definable facial features and the bright color of each suit. Of the two closest to her, one was decked out in an aggressive yellow, the other in bubble gum pink. When she looked beyond them into the center space, she saw quite a few more basilisks in various vibrant hues.

"Why are their suits so bright?" Athena ducked into the patient room Galen now occupied. This one had a window that looked into the room with the basilisks.

"They're color-coded based on the reason they're here and what privileges they have. What better way to ensure no one steps out of line than to make sure everyone's dressed like a highlighter?"

Athena tracked the movements of the basilisks milling about the middle of the space. Their numbers seem to have multiplied. What were they all doing? What was this place?

"I knew it was worth keeping them a surprise. Aren't you glad I waited so you could see them for yourself?" Galen joined her at the window.

"I love surprises. Like getting the wrong coffee order and discovering it's delicious or your best friend dropping off flowers for no reason. This isn't a surprise; this is the stuff of nightmares. What are they doing?" Athena glanced back at the patient behind them, but he, like the first patient, was free of any monitoring equipment, IVs, or indication of illness, except for the fact that he was unconscious and had what looked like radio antenna of varying sizes and lengths poking out of his skull. It didn't seem likely Galen would provide any more answers than she had in the first place, but the restricted floors were proving even more disturbing than the rumors alluded to.

Athena wasn't any more comfortable in this room than she had been in the first given the patient's condition and her lack of information, but she could spy on the basilisks without fear of interruption.

"What are the basilisks doing? Science experiments. Rehearsals for a real-life nightmare parade. Practicing for a flash mob. Whatever the hell they feel like. Whatever they're told to do. Don't ask questions." Galen shrugged and headed for the door.

Athena grabbed her arm and stopped her. "And that's okay with you? What about your oath as a doctor? You said the first patient was here for testing, but the two patients we've seen can't consent to anything. Is everyone here like that?"

"I'm not breaking my oath to this patient or the last one we saw. Does it look like I'm doing harm?" Galen pointed at the unconscious man behind them.

"It doesn't look like you're doing anything. Wouldn't he rather spend his days above ground living his life?" Athena looked around for a chart so she could put a name with the man, but there was nothing identifying in the room. "Wouldn't he at least like a name?"

Galen sighed. "His name no longer exists. He'll be assigned a new one once the testing is complete. We aren't supposed to know that and I'd appreciate it if you kept it to yourself. If you're down here long enough, you overhear things. The orange basilisks are gossipy bitches if you can get close enough to them."

Athena opened her mouth ready to unleash any of the hundreds of questions that were swirling in her mind.

Before she could, Galen stopped her. "I used to feel that fire you've got burning in your belly. Look, we all have a role to play. The patients on this floor aren't like other people and we aren't like other doctors and nurses. Especially me. You don't have to like it, you just have to do your job. Don't cross the basilisks, okay? Let's go meet Spero and his roommate, maybe that will help. Spero is interesting."

Help what? What kind of help could she give patients who were unconscious while also worrying about upsetting beings called basilisks? There were two guards in front of the final room on the floor. Galen stopped her before she entered.

"These two are a little different. They're not part of the same program as the others. They have names, for one. Spero, the gentleman on the right? Avoid looking him straight in the eye, okay? That's the other rule in this place."

"How am I supposed to treat a patient if I can't look at them?" Athena frowned.

"Trust me." Galen strode into the room. "Spero. How are you today, man? Piss anyone off? Make anyone fall in love?"

Athena followed Galen into the room. She let her eyes adjust to the dim lighting. Unlike the other rooms, there were two occupants in this one and this time, one of them was conscious. Spero was turned away from her when she entered. He turned as soon as he realized she was there.

It took everything in her power to keep her expression neutral and not shout, "*what the fuck.*" A full third of his face, including his right eye, cheek, and half his nose was covered by a computer screen fragment. It looked like a piece of screen had been violently fused with his face.

The screen was blank and despite Galen's warning, she couldn't look away. She saw his remaining eye register her presence. Suddenly the screen came to life and a green smiley face appeared.

Pure, unadulterated joy filled her. God, she loved her job. Who cared that it was weird and there were weird snake people roaming the halls doing who knows what to people, likely without consent? Maybe she should sing. That would liven the place up. What a great color they painted the walls in this room. Wasn't life fantastic?

"Spero." Galen's voice was much too harsh for this beautiful day. "Knock it off."

The screen went blank again and the Technicolor joy that had filled her was dulled to regular definition real life. Before Athena could make heads or tails of the burst of euphoria, the screen came to life again, this time flashing a sad face.

Overwhelming sadness gripped her, filling her chest, making it hard to breathe. Her eyes welled with the kind of tears that came with sobbing. She would not cry on her first day of work. What was wrong with her?

"Spero, enough." Galen stepped between Athena and Spero. "Athena, look at the floor for a moment and everything will be back to normal."

Athena did as she was told. She heard Galen admonishing Spero, but she didn't dare look for fear of the screen. What had he done to her? It took a moment for her emotions to come back under control. The jubilation and sadness were now replaced with anger. She was confident that belonged solely to her. She'd worked too hard for too long to get control of her emotions to have them so easily manipulated.

While Galen continued talking to Spero, Athena moved across the room to the other patient. This bed was occupied by a woman, who despite seeming to be comatose like the others on the floor, was restrained. Also unique, she had a chart hanging from the end of her bed. According to her chart, she'd been comatose for nearly a year.

Athena leaned closer to the woman and examined her skin. She couldn't tell if the skin was made of metal or covered in it, but it was striking, and it appeared to cover her entire body, including her face. The metal wasn't monochromatic but had the swirling iridescence of a rain puddle contaminated with car drippings. The only section of recognizable human skin was a six-inch-wide swath around her elbow where an IV was inserted. Directly above that spot was a device Athena didn't recognize. It was clamped to a pole that was bolted to the bed and the donut-shaped device floated two inches above the woman's arm, just above the IV.

"This is Bronte Scales. Sorry about Spero. As I'm sure you surmised, he can use that screen of his to manipulate emotions. It's a trick he loves to pull out any chance he gets. There aren't many newcomers around here so he doesn't get to brush off the dust all that often."

Athena nodded. "I'll be more careful from now on. Why is she restrained if she's unconscious? And what's that above her arm? It looks like it's burning her." Athena reached out but stopped short of touching the skin exposed on Bronte's arm.

"It's a powerful magnet with a polarity designed to repel metal. They set it up so they could get past the defenses her body threw at them." Galen pointed at the rest of Bronte's skin. She sounded sad. "Look carefully at the edges. What do you see?"

Athena leaned over and took a moment to examine the border where Bronte's human flesh met metal. The patch of skin wasn't an even outline. The metal had been pushed back but looked like it was encroaching unevenly toward the IV. In some areas it was quite close.

"The magnet doesn't seem to be keeping it at bay."

"Very good. Her body keeps adapting. They've had to increase the strength, add other measures. That's why you're starting to see burn marks. I'm not sure there are any measures they won't go to in order to keep her under." Galen placed her hand on Bronte's forehead and then turned to check her chart.

"You're her doctor, why don't you stop it?" Athena crossed her arms. "Are you a doctor at all? Or are you a Doctor Strange kind of doctor and I'm going to find out you're really a sorcerer?"

"Doctor Strange was a doctor first, then a sorcerer so you can't rule out either with your question, but yes, I'm a real doctor. To answer the question you really want answered, you'll learn nothing's simple. Nothing's as black and white as it seems." She hitched her thumb toward the door and made a slithering snake motion with her hands. "Besides, I don't have as many employment options as some." Galen turned back to Athena and put the chart down gently. Her eyes were sad. "Shit." Galen pushed past Athena quickly.

Spero was out the door and planted in front of one of the guards. His screen was lit and the guard was agitated.

"Everyone else is medicated to oblivion, but he's allowed to run wild?" Athena was hot on Galen's heels.

"He's supposed to be sedated too. Allowed to be awake but too medicated to move around. Buster clearly didn't get him his last dose." Galen hollered to the other doormen as she took Spero's arm.

The angry guard was shouting at Spero, at Galen, and at his co-worker. Before the other guard could assist in getting Spero subdued, Athena saw the screen change. The second guard screamed in terror and fell to the floor, pulling his knees to his chest and rocking soothingly.

The other guards slowed their pace and approached with more caution. Athena was caught in the doorway, unsure how to proceed. She'd deescalated dozens of situations with agitated patients and visitors but none of them had the abilities this guy did.

She felt rather than saw the basilisks closing ranks around them. How were there so many of them? And how had they gotten beyond the barrier of the room they were in? Spero turned to one of them. Athena saw a flash from the screen and then there was a muffled scream followed by sobbing. The basilisk fell to the floor and curled into a ball. The others stopped moving, arms at their sides, like they'd been ordered to stay still.

Galen took in the sight for a moment. "Huh, I always wondered if he could affect them what with their whole…" She waved her hand in front of her face. "Guess it's up to us."

Why was it up to them? Why wasn't there a better plan for this guy? Athena tried talking to him. "Spero, let's go back into your room and we can talk about what you need. I'm sure we can figure it out. I'm new here, so maybe you and I can sit together, and you can let me know the things you need for your care?"

She wanted to look at him so he could see she was sincere, but she didn't want to get emotion blasted so she kept her chin to her chest. It felt like a strange bow. It was also why she didn't see him coming as he rushed the door and knocked both her and Galen on their asses in his hurry to get back into his room. She had to scramble to get out of the way before he slammed the heavy door on her leg.

It was eerily quiet as soon as the echo of the door slam petered out. The two guards had recovered and stood dusting themselves off, not looking at anyone, and the basilisks were still standing uselessly and silently uncomfortably close. Athena evaluated all systems after being bowled over.

A crash came from inside the room. Galen scrambled to her feet and ran for the shut door. "Little fucker. Athena, come with me. Don't look at him. Shut the door behind you."

They shoved the door open. It banged against the wall from the force. Athena stole a glance around the room to locate Spero.

He was standing by Bronte's bed protectively, facing out, a stupid, goofy looking happy face on his screen. The magnet machine was smashed at his feet and the IV pole was toppled.

"Did he..." Athena tried to get a peek around him without risking a blast from his screen. The patch of skin had disappeared and was covered in metal like the rest of her. Her breathing was rapid, her metal eyelids fluttering.

"Yes, he did. She's waking up." Galen ran her hand through her hair and blew out a breath. "This is going to be awkward."

Athena nodded a few times and then couldn't help but let out a weird barky laugh. She'd been at work less than half her shift and she'd met a man who could manipulate emotions, a woman whose skin was made of metal, one very weird doctor, an army of snake people, and it seemed like the really crazy stuff hadn't started yet. In a past life she'd have already pissed her pants, but not today. She couldn't decide if the pug had lied about her day or had nailed his prognostication.

"I can't wait to meet her."

And she meant it.

Chapter Three

The first thing Bronte was aware of was a metallic taste in the back of her throat. She lifted her hand, meaning to reach for the location of the blow Bard Verstrand had delivered to the back of her head. The little weasel. Her eyes flew open when her arm's progress was stopped by something she couldn't immediately identify. She tugged harder. No luck.

The room was dimly lit. She was grateful not to be immediately blinded. She strained to look at her arms. Why did her head feel stuffed full of cotton balls? It was making it hard to direct her body and think clearly.

Once she got everything moving in concert, she could see IV tubing twisted around her bicep and restraints holding her wrists in place. Blood dripped along her forearm. Was it her forearm? It felt like it was, but it was covered in some kind of translucent alloy. The hospital wasn't unexpected given how hard she'd been hit on the head, but what was this about? She tried to remember what'd happened after the blow.

"My research." Bronte yanked hard on the restraints.

"Hey, easy. You're safe."

The restraints prevented her from turning her body enough to see the woman who'd spoken, and she couldn't twist enough to lay eyes on her. The sound of her voice however seeped into Bronte's pores. She relaxed.

Bronte closed her eyes when she sensed her approach. What if the woman was Bard Verstrand's twin sister or had a horn growing out of her forehead? Bronte took a deep breath and opened her eyes. Unicorns weren't bad, right?

"I'm Athena, your nurse. I'm getting caught up on what medications you've been on, but it wouldn't be unexpected if you're groggy and a little disoriented." Athena began taking vital sign readings. "I wasn't sure if this would work. Amazing."

Bronte's eyes were still a little unfocused and her head hurt like the devil, but she would have had to be nearly dead not to be struck speechless by Athena. Bronte had been fascinated with Greek mythology as a child and now here she was, meeting an honest to goodness Greek goddess, the most beautiful woman she'd ever seen, and she was strapped to a hospital bed in nothing but a backless gown and hot pink no-skid booties. She wiggled her legs a little to see if she was wearing anything under the gown. Far too breezy for her liking.

"Any chance you can take these off if I promise not to scamper off on you?" Bronte waggled her fingers and rolled her wrists as far as she could.

"Don't know where you think you could scamper to in the condition you're in. Not to mention most people who flee in hospital gowns with their ass hanging out for all to see get hauled back pretty quick." Athena leaned over so she was in Bronte's line of sight. "I'll see what I can do about these restraints though."

Bronte could hear a whispered conversation a few feet away. She lifted her head off her pillow and strained to hear, but with her arms bound she had little room to maneuver. She dropped her head again and swore under her breath.

Oddly, as soon as the rather creative invective was out of her mouth her hearing sharpened, as if by magic, and the conversation happening just out of earshot no longer was.

"We're already going to be on the hook for letting him wake her, you really want to see what happens when you're caught untying her?"

Bronte didn't recognize the other women's voice.

"She's awake now. What reason do we have to keep her restrained? Is she dangerous? Does she have some kind of ability beyond just the skin thing? Because if she doesn't, then there's no reason to restrain her."

Athena was going to bat for her. Tears welled in Bronte's eyes and her chest tightened. The air in the room was too thin. Was she having a heart attack? What the hell were the waterworks about? And why did she feel like crap? What kind of medication had they given her? And what did Athena mean by "the metal thing?"

"Shit, she's close to a panic attack. Who could blame her? We can finish this conversation later."

Bronte tugged on the restraints again. She was desperate to sit. How did the other woman know she was anxious? She wanted to see her. She was helpless and trapped tied to the bed like this.

Before Bronte was able to get out of her bindings or rip off an arm trying, a new woman entered her line of sight. The woman's expression was kind, but she was businesslike and lacking the warmth Athena had in spades.

"Dr. Scales, I'm Dr. Ford. I've been overseeing your care. It's natural that you're feeling anxious and confused. Normally I'd never have woken you in such an abrupt manner after so long, but… the important thing now is getting you comfortable and calm."

"What do you mean 'after so long'?" Bronte yanked on the restraints again. She tipped her head back and stared at the speckled tiles of the drop ceiling. She squeezed her eyes shut and took a breath before opening them again. "What is today's date?"

"I'm taking these off." Athena looked Dr. Ford's way with a look Bronte would never argue with and pointed to the restraints holding her to the bed.

"They're not going to like that." Dr. Ford pointed at something Bronte couldn't see.

"I don't care. She's our patient first and unless you have a reason for her to be tied to the bed these are coming off."

Dr. Ford sighed and slowly shook her head. "Spero, don't let anyone through the door. You started this mess, you don't get to sit on the sidelines."

Bronte heard shuffling from the other side of the room. How many more unseen occupants were waiting to announce themselves?

She didn't try to get a look at Spero. There was no way she'd be able to twist herself into position until Athena freed her bindings. Luckily, she didn't have to wait long. Athena freed her hands while Dr. Ford cut her feet free.

She lifted her arms, rolled her wrists, bent her knees. It was liberating to be able to move her body at will. Her body. Patches of metal slipped away to reveal skin, then reappeared elsewhere like she was some kind of steampunk quilt. She forced the panic away. One thing at a time.

"I'm sitting up now. Keep your eyes off my ass." Bronte gripped the bedrails and pulled herself to a seated position. She immediately felt lightheaded and flopped back.

"How about we go more slowly, together this time. You've been lying in this bed for a year, you can't expect to jump up and sprint out the door." Athena gently touched the crook of Bronte's left arm and frowned.

"Did you say a *year*? That can't be right. Bard hit me on the head, yesterday maybe. The day before? But not a year." Bronte grabbed at her gown, pulling it away from her neck and chest. Too tight. "My work. My research. I have to get it back from her." The metal skin was starting to seep into her memory as something not as odd as it should be.

"Whoa, slow down. Let's take this one step at a time, okay? Step one, sit. Step two, have a sip of water." Athena put her hand behind Bronte's shoulders and helped her slowly rise. She raised the head of the bed to match her new position.

"What's step three? Retrieve my research and stop a maniac from using it in ways it was never intended?" Bronte glared out the large flat screen TV-sized window of her room, but all she could see was a hospital corridor and strange Technicolor robot creatures. Maybe she was still feeling the effects of the medication.

"Let's pencil that in as step ten." Athena handed her a small glass of water. "It's important not to skip any steps so I can make sure we get everything in order before you go out to save the world."

"Which step is the one where I get to put on pants?" Bronte pulled the blanket over her legs, which thankfully now looked like normal, if slightly too thin, human legs.

Cabinet doors banged behind her. She jumped. Her skin tingled, like the feeling you get with a rush of excitement. After it passed she was cool, like the room temperature had dropped five degrees, but she wasn't in a rush to pull the blanket tighter. She couldn't bring herself to look at her body, though. That sense of panic was waiting at the door to barge on in.

She turned to locate the source of the noise. Dr. Ford was standing by the built-in cabinet behind the bed gaping at her, a pair of pants and T-shirt in hand.

"You can turn it on and off? Amazing."

"On and off? What are you talking about?" Bronte looked back at Athena, searching her face for a clue.

She turned her hands over and back examining every surface. She threw off the blanket and looked at her legs and feet. Everywhere there had been soft, pliable skin moments ago, was now hardened and impenetrable. It looked like a solid form of liquid mercury. She touched her face, and the muted clang of metal contacting metal gave her all the data she needed about the state of her face.

"You said this has happened to me before?" Bronte examined her hands once again. Astonishment quickly turned to confusion and anxiety. That panic was forming a tidal wave. She forced herself to focus on the science.

The zeptobots were supposed to work inside the body to seek out and kill cancer cells. Why was she covered in metal? Nothing in her research indicated this was a possible side effect. Was it because she injected so many? Because she didn't have any cancer to seek and destroy? Were they finding their own work? She shuddered at the thought of self-employed zeptobots roaming her body. What else would they do to her?

"The entire time you've been here, in a medically induced coma, you've been metallic," Dr. Ford said.

"Why would they do this to you?" Athena sat on the edge of the bed and put her hand on Bronte's knee.

Why did she want Athena to keep her hand in hers? She'd not had anyone care enough to try to comfort her for longer than she could remember.

"They didn't do this to me." Bronte sighed. "This is why I'm here. They're trying to get this out of me, to steal it. I did this to myself."

Bronte sank back into her pillow and stared again at the drop ceiling, seeking answers in the pits and swirls of the tiles above her. Had Bard managed to get any of the zeptobots from her in the year Bronte had been held captive? If so, what would Bard do with them? Verstrand Industries made electronics, specialty machine components, and other consumer goods. At least those were the legitimate, advertised products. Rumors had dogged the company for years pertaining to illegal sales of guns, body armor, and other weapons. What would Bard be able to do with a metal suit? Bronte nearly vomited.

She looked once again at her hands. She'd wanted to give a gift to humanity and had created something that even to her felt like the best kind of science fiction. But now she was a metal skinned part-human and her technology might be in the hands of the unscrupulous head of a powerful worldwide corporation. What had she done? What had she unleashed on the world?

Chapter Four

A thena must have heard wrong. Bronte couldn't have said the metal skin was self-inflicted, right?

"Tell me what you mean. Why do you think you did this to yourself?" She gently patted Bronte's knee. It was like tapping a bronze sculpture, cool, hard, and smooth.

"I don't think that's the question you really want to ask. I'm made out of metal." Bronte knocked her knuckles against her knee next to Athena's hand. "Nothing can hurt me." She smiled but it didn't reach her eyes.

"Metal maybe, but I suspect there's a very human heart still beating in there. Besides, I asked the question I want the answer to. I have others lined up, but we'll start there."

"Don't you have other patients you have to see?" Bronte looked from Athena to Galen.

Athena looked over her shoulder at the swarm of basilisks pacing the hall outside the room and glanced at Galen. She was pacing too and looked like Athena had felt in fifth grade trying to solve the word problems in math class. It wasn't a pretty, or comforting, sight.

"I have plenty of time." Athena turned her full attention back to Bronte. "Lay it on me."

"Well, you see, it all started when I was a young girl." Bronte leaned back against her pillows and laced her fingers behind her head. She looked a smidge more relaxed and the hint of a smile played at the corner of her mouth.

"Oh, this is how it's going to be. So I should make myself comfortable then?" At Bronte's wry smile Athena dragged a chair to the bedside. She propped her feet on the foot of the bed and indicated Bronte should continue.

"When I was a girl, I fell in love with science. Not a flirtation but a deep, passionate love affair. We bonded for life. Soul mates. I never lost that love, but it's brought me to a strange place today." Bronte frowned as she glanced at her hands.

"So you went from a kid obsessed with her first chemistry set and looking at plants and dirt under a microscope to a woman with metal skin? I like science too, but..." Athena held up her arms and turned them over and back. "Nothing as cool as yours."

"Says the Greek warrior goddess. You wear the name well. What am I now? More tin can than human." Bronte looked at the ceiling, her eyes moving back and forth as though she was reading.

Athena had seen her do that more than once. Was she searching for a higher power or buying herself time?

"And you just called me a goddess, which is hardly human. Thank you, by the way. What if I say your new ability makes you a God?" Athena put her feet back on the floor and leaned forward in her chair, toward Bronte.

"You'd be wrong." Bronte didn't look at Athena.

"Says who?"

Bronte did look at Athena now. "Says me."

"You're just one opinion. I have a different one." Athena propped her feet again. Should she be pushing Bronte's buttons like this? More to the point, should she be enjoying it?

"My opinion is the only one that matters. It's me we're talking about."

"Why? You have one view, I have another. You don't get to be right by default. Haven't you heard the phrase 'she knew me better than I knew myself'?" Athena looked pointedly at Bronte.

"That doesn't apply here. You don't know me." Bronte's brow furrowed. "This"—Bronte indicated the metal on her body—"is not a triumph or a super suit. I'm not proud of it. This is a failure of my life's work. And because of that failure, I have no idea what's in store for me each minute that passes. I've woken after a year to find myself restrained and made of metal, with no idea how to get the hell out of here and get my life back. I find that terrifying." Bronte looked startled at the admission.

"I'll concede the point that I don't know you. That's something I'm trying very hard to change. So, how'd you end up with the exoskeleton? And why are you here, insisting on arguing with me?"

As Athena talked and teased, she watched Bronte not exactly relax, but release some of the pressure Athena had seen building since Bronte had awoken. As she did, the metal receded and her skin returned to its normal pigmentation and human softness. Athena reached out and poked Bronte in the leg.

"Ow. What the hell?"

"I was just checking." Athena leaned closer to Bronte's leg where she'd jabbed. "Whoa. Look at that."

Spreading out from the area of insult was a ring of metal roughly six inches in diameter. As they watched it melted back into Bronte's skin until there was no sign it had been there at all.

"Pretty good defense." Athena's fingers tingled with the urge to touch Bronte again. To conduct another experiment though, right? Not to comfort her and soothe away some of the uncertainty and terror in her eyes.

"It was a little late. Didn't show up until after you poked me. Try again." Bronte looked pensive.

Despite wanting to touch Bronte again, now she wasn't interested in repeating her earlier impulsive act. She squinted and jabbed out her finger. "Ow." She hit metal.

"Yes." Bronte nodded slightly and her mouth crooked into a small smile. "My hypothesis was correct." At Athena's quizzical look, she said, "I invented zeptobots. It was what I was working on when I was, well, when all this happened." Bronte waved her hand in front of her body. "They were supposed to be the answer to curing cancer."

"I'm going to pretend I know what a zeptobot is for a moment. How did they end up in your body and how did you end up here?" Was this how a small child would feel taking college level organic chemistry?

"Bard Verstrand." Bronte's expression hardened and the steely expression was mirrored by actual metal rising through her skin and covering her face.

Before Athena could ask more about Bard Verstrand's involvement Spero was at her side. He put his hand on her shoulder, spinning her to face him. She was caught off guard and didn't avert her eyes in time. His screen was lit with an angry emoji.

A wave of fury threatened to drown her. She couldn't remember being driven by so much rage. She couldn't contain it; she needed to release some of it before the boiling inferno destroyed her from the inside. She needed a target. What had Bronte said? Bard Verstrand had held her captive? That wasn't right. She'd make it right.

"Where is Bard Verstrand?" Athena barely recognized her own voice.

"Spero, you fool. What are you doing?"

Athena saw Galen spin Spero away from her, but it didn't matter. She had a purpose. All that stood in the way were the basilisks. She turned to the door and ran into Galen.

"Get out of my way." Athena tried to push through Galen.

"I can't let you go out there. You'll be back to yourself in a few minutes. They won't be kind to you." Galen braced herself.

Athena's face was hot, and it felt like the blood running through her neck to her head was pulled directly from the surface of the sun. "Last chance, Galen. Get out of the way." She pulled her arm back, her hand in a fist.

When she moved forward to swing, her momentum was halted. What the hell? She whipped around and was face to face with Bronte, out of bed and gloriously shiny.

"I don't know what's going on here, but it seems like the guy with the computer face did something to you and I think you'll regret it if you hit the doc. I don't know what those jelly beans with curling stones stuck on top are, but they look a bit ominous, so it seems like the four of us should get along in here. Okay?"

Athena yanked her hand free. She dropped it to her side. She stalked back to her chair and sat heavily. She took a couple of deep breaths, shuddered, tipped her head back, and closed her eyes. When she opened them, her body was her own again.

"Spero, you asshole. Don't do that to me again."

"Your name is Spero?"

Athena opened her eyes and saw Bronte, now wearing pants under her gown, crossing the room to Spero's bed. Spero was sitting with his knees pulled to his chest, rocking subtly.

Bronte sat on the bed in front of him. Galen moved toward her, but she held up her hand to stop her. "Can I look at your computer? I'm good with technology, I might be able to make it more comfortable. Before I take a look, you have to promise not to do to me what you just did to Athena. Deal?"

Spero nodded, then looked up, his screen blank.

"Good man." Bronte inspected each side of the screen carefully. "I can make some changes to your hardware. Would that be okay?"

Spero nodded again but didn't say a word.

"Are you able to speak or has this screen taken that ability?" Bronte leaned in closer to the connection around Spero's mouth.

Spero made a motion like he was zipping his lips. Athena thought he looked sad.

Bronte nodded and patted him on the shoulder. "I'd also like to get a look at the software, see how you and it have become connected, but I can't do it from in here. I'm the new guy, but it doesn't look like those creatures out there would slide in a toolbox if I opened the door and asked."

Galen barked out a laugh.

"Would you believe this is my first day on the job?" Athena was back on her feet but across the room from Bronte and Spero.

Bronte turned toward Athena and nodded solemnly. "So you aren't attached to the job yet? Excellent. We need to get out of here."

Athena sat heavily on the bed and looked from Bronte to Spero to Galen. Then she took a peek out the window at the basilisks. What the hell did Bronte mean "get out of here?" Out in the hall? Off the floor? Out of the hospital? Was Bronte insane? Athena didn't have to go anywhere. She worked here and could fill out a million pounds of paperwork about what happened today. All she had to do was get Bronte and Spero back in bed.

"I know what you're thinking, Athena." Galen sat on the bed next to her. "They won't believe you. They've seen you cutting off her restraints and chatting like you were on a fucking date. You think they'll really believe you had no part in our escape? We probably don't even have the time to get out, actually."

"How the hell do you do that?" Athena poked her finger into Galen's chest. The fact that she'd said "our" escape was interesting and something to question later.

"Now's not the time." Galen turned away.

Athena stalked away and found a perch away from the rest. She needed this job. That's why she took this weird ass assignment in the first place. The pay was higher than anything she could make elsewhere and she was told she'd still be helping people. But helping unconscious science projects hadn't been in the job description. She looked at Bronte. That was obviously where the adventure would be found. She'd never hesitated to follow the adrenaline and excitement before, why was she hesitating now? Maybe it had something to do with a woman with metal skin and a dude with a computer fused to his face. Skydiving and mountain climbing couldn't compete with that. She was in a different league now and it was giving her pause.

Damn it. Damn it all to hell. She was going to have to look for another job.

Chapter Five

B ronte paced her small hospital room. A sigh escaped before she could squelch it. She scrubbed her face with both hands. Before she pulled them away, she explored the contours of her face with her fingers. It was something a baby might do trying to understand each feature and texture. She had to learn herself anew. Right now her skin was soft and recognizably human. Exactly as she'd known it throughout her life thus far. A short time ago it had been hard as steel, smooth as ice, and if she had to guess, nearly indestructible.

The change from one to the other could happen in the next minute or not again for days. She sighed again. The zeptobots might be her own creations, but at the moment they were maddeningly unpredictable. Her artist parents would love the chaos. As a scientist, she did not. Especially since she'd inadvertently created this chaos despite her careful experiments and engineering. It still didn't seem possible.

She scrubbed her face once again and pulled her hands away with a jerk. Now was not the time for self-reflection or self-pity.

"Doc, have you taken the time you need to consider my request?" Bronte crossed the room to Dr. Ford, who'd been sitting silently against the wall, her chin propped in her hands. Athena was new and it was clear the doctor knew what the hell waited beyond the doors, not to mention who'd be coming after them. It was her that Bronte had to convince.

"If you're asking me to seriously consider this you might as well call me Galen."

"Why would I do that?"

"Because it's my name. Did all that metal sever a few nerve connections here?" Galen tapped Bronte's head.

Bronte swatted her off. She had more she wanted to say but was cut off by a loud bang on the room door. Everyone jumped. Bronte moved to the window to see what made the racket, but Galen stopped her.

"Don't get close to the windows. We need to leave. Immediately. Spero, if they didn't confiscate everything when they transferred you in here, pack it up now." Galen hastened to the windows and pulled the curtains closed roughly.

Bronte turned to Spero, who'd been sitting quietly on his bed watching Galen and Bronte argue. Now he was standing next to both of them, his screen blank, a backpack he'd clearly made himself slung across his shoulders.

"They kept you sedated. When did you have time to gather your stuff and pack, let alone make that?" Galen motioned at the backpack.

"Never mind. Athena, do you have anything you need to grab?" Bronte walked to Athena's side and squatted next to her.

"I'm not going with you. Tie me up if you think that will help make it look like I didn't have a choice about you leaving, but there are other patients on this floor. This is my job. We have a responsibility to them." Athena glared at Galen. "We can't just leave them here."

Bronte thought there was regret in Athena's eyes. She didn't really want to stay.

"We can tweet about what's happening here, or go after Bard Verstrand ourselves, or call the president. I don't care, but I'm not sticking around once the basilisks attack. And there are things about the patients here you don't understand. If they wake up, we're in a world of shit. The two you saw are just the beginning and that's not counting the basilisks." Galen moved to the window again and peeked out.

Bronte joined her. The creatures the others had called "basilisks" were swarming. They looked like ants after an insult was introduced to the nest.

"They're tired of waiting us out. Athena and I are allowed free movement as long as we stick to the same routine. Since that went out the window, they've likely got orders from on high to clean up this mess. The purple ones will lead from the back, but they'll send every last one on the attack. They're going to come in and get you. You and Spero." Galen's face was strained and pale.

"I imagine they won't be kind to you or Athena either." Bronte put her hand on Galen's shoulder. The muscles beneath Bronte's hand were knotted harder than her own exoskeleton had been.

"Probably less kind to Athena. They can buy another nurse, but they can't let go of one who has seen all this. I have skills and vulnerabilities that are harder to find, but even I'm not irreplaceable."

Bronte nodded. Whatever Galen was hinting at could wait. Now that the moment was upon them, how the hell were they going to get out? The clenching and twisting in her gut seemed so at odds with her once cool metal exterior she almost laughed. Almost.

"Spero, you ready to turn on that screen and help us get out of here?" Galen clasped Spero's shoulders.

Spero, silent as always, responded by lighting the screen, but thankfully keeping it blank.

"Those things out there are susceptible to his brand of chaos, right?" Bronte looked at Galen and Athena.

Athena moved to their side. It looked like her curiosity had gotten the better of her. "Yes, I think they're terrified of him. But as I said, I'm not going with you."

"Time for you to suit up too, Doc." Galen waved her hand toward Bronte, from her head to feet.

Bronte took a step back. The room was cool. There was a bead of sweat on her forehead that she felt drip down to her eyebrow. "You can't possibly mean my metal skin. If that is what you're implying, I can't produce it on command. I'll need time to experiment with it, time to figure out how it works and when. I need to understand the repercussions to myself and others."

Galen punched Bronte in the arm. "Son of a bitch." She shook her hand and mumbled another curse under her breath. "When we get out of here, we're going to have to do something about you finding the on-off switch on that. I'm not going to keep punching your metal ass to turn you into a superhero every time we need you."

"I'm not a superhero." Bronte ground her teeth.

"Times's up!" Galen shouted and jumped into a defensive stance, facing the door.

There was another loud bang against the door. The window shattered. The first basilisk, neon yellow and more grotesque up close, pushed through the broken window, arms first. It clawed at the blinds, yanking them from the ceiling. The first was quickly followed by two more. They looked like Technicolor upright vacuum cleaner zombies. The only sound was glass tinkling on the floor and Bronte's own ragged breathing echoing in her ears. Galen slid past them and into the corridor.

Bronte pulled Athena behind her. She pushed the first basilisk back out the window. The creature latched onto her arm. It clawed its way up, silent, relentless. She swung her arm and flung it back to its kind like a bag of feathers. More surged through the window. Bronte punched two more. They flew from her metal fists. She'd never punched anything before. She fought the urge to apologize.

She turned to check on Athena in time to see her kick a basilisk between the legs. He fell to the floor with a groan. Then she dispatched another with an IV pole. Why had Bronte been so worried about protecting the Goddess of War?

Galen popped back into the room. "What's the holdup? There's a swarm out here. We need a battering ram."

Bronte pulled Athena after her to the door. "Come on. I'll clear a path."

They fought their way to the stairs. Bronte led the way. There was nothing the basilisks could do to her. Spero brought up the rear. Bronte could hear cries of terror and rage, peels of laughter, and breath-snatching sobs. He was creating a symphony of emotional wake behind them, leaving them with a thinner mob on their tail.

All four of them were out of breath when they burst into the stairwell, but Galen urged them along at a lung-bursting pace. The basilisks who had initially charged after them kept pace at a greater distance the higher they climbed.

"Why aren't they trying to overtake us?" Bronte spared a glance behind her and nearly missed a step.

"They can't risk being seen up here." Galen was panting but didn't slow. "We're off the restricted floors now. Once we get to the main lobby, they can't follow us, they have strict orders. Don't let your guard down, though. They don't want us getting there."

There was only one flight of stairs remaining. Bronte surged ahead. She waited on the landing for the other three. What was waiting on the other side of the door? When she joined Bronte on the landing, Galen reached for the handle. Athena stopped her.

"She's metal, he's got a computer face. If the basilisks can't be seen, what's your plan for them?"

Galen shrugged. "That's Bard's problem, not mine."

Spero pulled a hood over his head and put his hands out to the sides as if saying "ta-da."

Bronte shook her head. "I suppose I'll serve as the star attraction. Let's move along. Our friends from the deep appear to be regrouping."

As the basilisks rose rapidly Bronte yanked the door open and she and the others spilled into the startlingly well-lit and cheerful hospital lobby. It was bustling with early afternoon foot traffic. Their sudden appearance gave everyone pause, but most continued about their business quickly as if four people stumbling out of the stairwell was perfectly normal. Four out-of-breath people, one of whom was made of metal and dressed in sweatpants and a hospital gown.

Galen pointed to the door.

"I'm not leaving." Athena leaned closer to Bronte.

"I don't think it would be wise for you to be here when upper management realizes we've escaped, and you were kicking those creatures in the balls to facilitate it." Bronte gently put her hand around Athena's bicep and led her after Galen and Spero toward the exit. "And Galen's right. With what you've seen, you're a liability now. You're not safe."

"Fine, but after we're out of the building, I'm going home." Athena pulled her arm free.

Halfway across the lobby there was a commotion behind them. Bronte turned. A yellow basilisk was peeking out the door they'd escaped through. It was pointing at them and screeching.

Two security guards rose from their desk and ran to address the issue. They stopped midway between Bronte and Athena and the wailing basilisk. The guards looked back and forth between them. They said something to each other and one ran toward the stairwell doorway, the other in pursuit of Bronte and Athena.

Bronte needed no further encouragement. She ran, grabbing Athena by the hand, pulling her along. They made it to the door when the guard in pursuit skidded to a halt. Bronte heard the cry that had stopped him. His fellow officer was in trouble. She slowed and turned. The basilisk had the second officer. He was flailing on the ground trying to free himself. His companion abandoned his chase of Bronte and Athena and ran to help his colleague.

Bronte took a step back into the hospital. She should help. Galen and Spero grabbed an arm each and pulled her away. She fought against them.

"He's okay." Galen grabbed her chin and looked her in the eyes. "I promise you, he's fine. He's scared but not in any danger."

There was a loud crack, an eerie silence, and then an explosion. Bronte felt like she was trying to stand still on the sands of an hourglass. The shockwave blew all four of them from their feet. As she fell backward, Bronte heard the tinkling of shattered glass hitting pavement and screams of pain and fear.

Bronte got to her knees, intent on helping those who were injured. She tried to stand but was temporarily dizzy. She leaned forward, resting her hand on the ground to steady herself. She looked around. In the smoke and chaos, she couldn't tell what had caused the explosion or where it had come from. Spero sat, Galen groaned. Where was Athena? Bronte saw her a few feet away. She wasn't moving.

Bronte shook off the dizziness and moved to Athena's side. She checked for signs of life. Athena was breathing. She wasn't obviously bleeding or broken. Bronte leaned closer.

"If I play dead, will you leave me here?" Athena kept her eyes closed and winced.

"I will not." Bronte scooped Athena in her arms and rejoined Galen. "Where's Spero?"

Before she'd finished asking, Spero waved them over to an idling cab and hopped behind the wheel. Galen jogged over and got in the passenger seat. Bronte looked at Athena. She'd closed her eyes and snuggled into Bronte. Bronte's chest seized. Was she more injured than she thought? Galen was a doctor. She lowered Athena gently into the cab and sat next to her.

She'd barely gotten the door closed before Spero accelerated away from the hospital, violating nearly every driving law Bronte could recall. Did the guy have a driver's license? She looked at Athena next to her. At some point in the fight or subsequent explosion Athena had sustained a small cut over her left eye. A thin line of blood had dripped down her cheek and dried there. She looked every bit the warrior goddess. Could the beauty of Athena of ancient writings hold a candle to the one right next to Bronte now? The thought seemed as comical as the basilisks lining up mid fight to dance a Scottish reel.

Whether they died now in a fiery crash or made it to whatever destination Spero had in mind, the escape had been worth it. None of them were in the hands of the basilisks and Bronte had a chance to retrieve her research. That was her first and last priority. Once she did that, maybe she could figure out how to remove the zeptobots and become herself again. Hopefully she could still remember who that was.

Chapter Six

A thena was queasy. It was the kind of queasy she only got in the car. Why was she in a car? She should be at work. She opened her eyes. Bronte was sitting next to her, reflecting sunlight in every direction. Athena sat. Seeing the madcap ride they were on, with Spero at the wheel, did not make her nausea better.

Before she could mount a protest to any number of wrongs, the car screeched to a halt. Spero shut off the engine and exited. Galen followed. Athena looked at the building outside her window. The derelict warehouse looked like something from a dystopian artist's fever dream.

"You're awake." Bronte sounded concerned.

"You kidnapped me." Athena turned from the window. She clenched her fists and her jaw. "I told you to leave me at work."

Bronte sat back. Her eyes widened. "There was an explosion. You were injured. You would prefer I left you bleeding and unconscious? Galen needs to take a look at you. And incidentally, you agreed to come with us. You just said you wanted to go home after, but that's not really an option right now, is it?"

Was that a serious question? Athena gingerly got out of the car and walked toward the horror show of a building she assumed Spero and Galen had entered. It seemed the lesser of two evils. The other option seemed to be contemplating why she'd been happy instead of furious to see Bronte when she'd opened her eyes. Fury should definitely be the right emotion. The fact that it wasn't was extremely irksome.

Athena pushed through the door and stopped just inside. It was hard to conceive why Spero had brought them to this place.

"Is it any better inside?" Bronte asked from behind her.

"No, it's so much worse," Athena called over her shoulder.

The inside of the warehouse was brightened from sunlight streaming in through the few windows not blackened by paint, or grime, or whatever other detritus gathered on glass surfaces in abandoned buildings. The space was cavernous. With the exception of a balcony that circled the room and looked to be about ten feet wide, everything existed on the lower level. Burn marks were visible in multiple locations on the floor. The warehouse walls were covered in graffiti that reminded Athena of a state fair funhouse. She certainly felt like she was on a Tilt-a-Whirl.

Despite some lingering dizziness, Athena squatted to examine the debris covering wide swaths of the floor and every flat surface. Everything scattered around the warehouse was a piece of electronics. More ominously, she also came across several pairs of charred, torn restraints like the ones Bronte had been wearing at the hospital.

"Look at all this stuff." Bronte strode past Athena.

Her face, even through the metal, was alight with joy. It was interesting how the tech morphed to the degree that emotion was still visible, even when it wasn't showing on actual skin.

"Go see Galen. To make sure you're okay." Bronte looked back, concern clear in her eyes.

"I'm fine." Athena waved Bronte off. She considered the "stuff" Bronte was gaga for. It looked like the building had been an electronic storage facility of some sort. She ventured farther into the dim, dank space. In the far corner were hospital beds and medical equipment. What was that doing here? Everything in the building was scorched and thrown about like a fire storm had blown through. Was Bronte sure the explosion she'd mentioned hadn't happened here?

She picked her way across the room to the hospital equipment. It was surprisingly untouched by whatever pyrotechnics had occurred and was more advanced than she expected. There were plenty of cabinets and drawers to open and explore. One bank of file cabinets drew her attention. She pulled open the top drawer. It was full of medical charts. That couldn't be right. She looked around. It shouldn't be right, except she was standing in what looked like one of any number of well-equipped exam rooms that made up the day-to-day of her usual work life. An enormous exam room that had all the walls removed and had been dropped into a post-apocalyptic wasteland.

Athena ran her hands along the charts, stopped near the middle, and pulled one randomly halfway from the drawer. She opened it enough to glance inside. She slammed it back in the drawer and stepped back, her hand over her mouth. What was this place? She stepped to the drawer again and started at the front, pulling chart after chart. The pictures inside were all the same. Autopsy photos of man and computer grotesquely fused. Brain scans revealing metal where blood should have flowed.

She looked to Spero. Was this why he'd driven them here? How far had they driven? She'd be happy to have crossed borders and oceans, but they couldn't have gone far if his records were in this warehouse. She kept looking through the charts. When she came to the "Ls" her hunch was confirmed. She pulled the chart labeled "Spero Lazarus" but didn't open it. She shuddered. Whatever torture he had faced, however that computer had been fused with his face, she was sure it had happened here. Why on earth would he return to the scene of his disfigurement?

Her three companions were spread across the large warehouse, likely doing what she was, exploring, trying to make sense of the wreckage of the warehouse. Spero was farthest away, throwing something she couldn't make out into a large pile on the floor. She took the chart and crossed the room. This record belonged to him. It was up to him to decide its fate. She couldn't leave it with the others when the man she'd battled monsters with was within sight. She approached carefully.

"Spero, I found something that belongs to you. It shouldn't stay unlocked in that cabinet." Athena clutched the chart.

Spero paused his collection of trash and debris. He didn't immediately turn around. Athena saw him draw a deep breath. She could hear him exhale raggedly. Finally, he turned. She raised the chart enough that she could duck behind it if his screen was alight. It wasn't.

"I didn't open it. Whatever's inside is yours."

Spero nodded and slowly opened the folder. He quickly looked away before handing it back to her, still open. He pointed to Athena and then to the side of his face, the point where computer and flesh met.

"You'd like me to look at your face? Of course." She clutched the chart more tightly as her hand developed a tremor. Her insides waffled as well. Damn that screen.

He smiled but it was full of sorrow. His remaining eye shone with unshed tears. He stepped closer and reached for the chart. He flipped through pages until he found what he was looking for and returned it to her.

Athena quickly scanned the page Spero had highlighted. It contained chillingly detailed notes on a complication with the "installation" procedure. The attending physician was concerned Spero likely had continuing high levels of pain in the same location he'd pointed to.

"Pain? You're still experiencing pain here?" Athena leaned closer and took a look at the side of Spero's face.

He nodded. It was the first active communication she'd had with him since they'd met. It was like a win.

"Come with me." Athena picked her way back across the room to the medical area. If there was an exam space already there, she might as well use it.

"Do you mind if I ask Galen and Bronte to join us?" Athena turned to find she was talking to air.

Spero was rooted in place halfway between where they'd started and where Athena now stood. His screen was flashing. She didn't have the chart raised to hide behind, but given the distance it was hard to make out the little emoji faces that were blinking on and off. The emotional waves she was unwillingly surfing weren't as strong as the last time she experienced all Spero had to offer. The sadness, fear, anger, and anxiety were muted, like she was watching an action movie with the sound barely audible, but she was still getting some of the effects. Thank goodness she wasn't closer.

Almost as suddenly as it started, the onslaught was over. Spero leaned over with his hands on his knees and took a few heaving breaths. He turned from her and returned to his trash pile without looking back.

Athena flipped back to the front of the chart. She scanned through the information on the first page.

"Shit." She snapped the chart shut, grabbed a toolkit on the floor next to a crash cart on the far wall, and beelined for Bronte.

"How are you feeling? I should have made Dr. Ford check you when we got here. We should do that now." Bronte looked intently at Athena's forehead.

"What? I'm fine. I'm hungry. I think maybe that and all the adrenaline made me pass out. We're going to have to figure out food soon, but right now Spero and I need your help." Athena grabbed for Bronte's arm, missed, and ended up holding her hand instead. She liked the feeling and that wouldn't do. "You're not metal anymore."

"No, but I may be again soon if you keep squeezing my hand that hard."

Athena practically flung Bronte's hand away. "Sorry." She led the way to Spero. "Do you think that's what triggers it? Being in danger of injury?"

Bronte looked noncommittal. "Too early to say. I need to do more testing. You said you needed help?"

"Yes. Well, actually, Spero does. He's having significant pain where the computer attaches to his face. I remember at the hospital you said you are good with technology. I think he needs medical and technological help. Do you know where Galen is?"

"She said she was going for supplies." Bronte took the toolkit from Athena and set it on the ground near Spero. "Spero, I promised

I'd take a look at your screen once I had a few tools." She pointed at the toolbox.

"I'd like to relieve some of your pain if I can." Athena faced Spero, no chart covering her face or other protection from whatever he decided to throw her way. "I'm sorry I didn't realize the area over there would be traumatic for you. We can stay here if you'd like."

Athena tried not to let Spero see the doubt she was feeling. She was more confident in her ability to teach a flamingo how to use a salad fork than to understand and repair Spero's screen. Nothing in her previous training had mentioned standard treatment protocols for LCD screens purposely fused to vital human systems.

Spero dragged over a large wooden spool that came to just above his knees, flipped it on its flat end, and took a seat. He pointed at the chart Athena still held then pointed to Bronte. She handed Bronte the chart. Then he motioned her forward. She began her exam while Bronte pulled her own spool beside them and read the documents she'd been handed.

It only took a few minutes for Bronte to come to Bard Verstrand's name. Athena had noticed it immediately, but she hadn't had a chance to read enough to know her connection.

"Bard Verstrand's behind what happened to you?" Bronte was on her feet pacing. "Of course she is. Why else would we have been roommates?"

Spero nodded. Athena pulled her hands away, so she didn't do anything to damage the hardware in his head or cause him more pain.

"Hold still, please. Patient first, reading later. Let's help him with his pain."

"Right, sorry." Bronte pulled the tools closer and leaned in to examine Spero's screen.

Athena tried to calm her nerves. Why was she scared of Spero? But she wasn't scared of Spero, per se, she was scared of his screen and what he could do with it. Even blank and dark, the threat of it was powerful.

She forced herself closer. The skin had healed roughly around the screen. How had they gotten man and machine to bond enough for healing to take place?

"I think I see the problem." Bronte ran her finger along the upper edge of the screen.

Spero bit his lip and swatted at Bronte's hand. He squeezed his eyes shut tight.

"I'm sorry." Bronte put her hand on Spero's shoulder. "I think there's too much torque on that side of your screen and it's pushing on one or more of your cranial nerves. I can fix it, but it might hurt while I do."

Spero nodded his consent. Athena took his hand and gave it an encouraging pat. She was amazed at the speed, confidence, and efficiency with which Bronte worked. If she hadn't been a scientist, she could have been a surgeon.

After a few minutes, Bronte stood and inspected her work. "How does it feel?"

Spero nodded once and handed his chart to Bronte. Athena examined the edges of his screen. Parts looked irritated and a trickle of blood pooled on the uppermost corner. Bronte sat to continue reading, but Spero seemingly changed his mind and held out his hand for the chart. Bronte handed it over without a word. Athena gave up on finishing her work. If he was going to continue to wiggle around so much she didn't trust she wouldn't do more damage. He flipped through the pages as he'd done before and finally handed it back to Bronte, pointing to a paragraph partway down the page. Bronte read silently and then exploded to her feet once again.

"My research. She did this to you so she could...I'm going after her right now." Bronte's face was red and her hands had become so much a part of her angry sputtering she looked like a conductor.

Athena sighed. "You will do no such thing. We, all of us, barely escaped her basilisks. What makes you think you can waltz into whatever fortress she's in and steal something she's hell-bent on keeping for herself? I'm guessing, of course, given how little information I actually have, but she sounds like a villain, and that's what they do, right?"

"What can she do to me? I'm a metal robot now." Bronte didn't look quite as sure of herself.

Athena took Bronte's hand in her own and squeezed one of her fingers between two of her own. Before Bronte could pull away, Athena poked her in the arm as well.

"Ow. What was that for?" Bronte shook her hand.

"To show you how dumb your plan is. Look at your hand."

"I am looking at it. You pinched me." Bronte examined her finger.

"Look carefully. Still skin. You'll get yourself killed." Athena pointed to the spool Bronte had perched on prior.

Before she could turn her attention to Spero, the door banged open and Galen stumbled into the building.

"I have supplies. If this is going to be our base of operations, we need supplies." She nearly spilled the bags she carried when she tripped over an unrecognizable scorched piece of electronics.

"Bronte, see if there's anything you can do to help Spero's pain level. I'll be right back." Athena handed Bronte the toolbox and walked over to Galen.

Athena took one of the bags and did a double take. Galen's eyes were unfocused, and her pupils weren't fully dilated.

"Are you high?" Athena couldn't swallow the bite to her words.

Galen snorted. "I'm able to breathe, that's what I am. You can call it whatever you want."

"I'll call it what it is. What's wrong with you?" Athena wanted to throw one of the bags at Galen or throw her out of the building. The last thing they needed was someone who wasn't thinking clearly.

"I've wondered that since I was a child." Galen's expression was deadly serious. "Do you know how hard it is as a small child to feel them all the time? Constantly? It never ends."

Athena stopped and looked at Galen. "What are you talking about?"

"The emotions. What else would I be talking about?" Galen looked perplexed. "Everyone's emotions. Your confusion and disgust. Bronte's anger. Spero's pain. Nearby, someone is in love and someone else is grieving. Hatred, fear, joy, sorrow. It's constant. Wouldn't you dull that if you had the chance?" Galen's shoulders sagged. The last question came out in a whisper.

"That's what was going on at the hospital. How you knew what was happening?" Had a lightbulb appeared above her head?

Galen didn't need to respond. The answer was clear on her face.

"That doesn't explain how you knew I had my coffee. I'm rarely emotional over a latte." Athena crossed her arms and studied Galen.

"Coffee shops have an emotional flavor to them. A lot of restless energy. Plenty of tiredness followed by content. You were easy to pick out of the crowd. You were restless and anxious but also excited and fierce." Galen deposited the bags on a clear spot on the floor.

"Why look for me at all?" Athena didn't uncross her arms, but she did relax her body which she realized was tense enough to trigger a headache if she wasn't careful.

"Sorting through the noise and having something specific to focus on helps when my brain is overwhelmed." Galen squatted and rummaged through one of the bags.

"I have many more questions, but they can wait. Is there food in these bags of supplies?" Athena peeked in one of the two.

"Yes. It's not a bad couple of meals."

Galen meandered to the others. Athena followed with snacks for the group. They pulled two more spools over. Athena directed Galen to sit then took her own place at their strange round table.

Athena assessed her motley crew. They looked lost. She looked over her shoulder at the door, then sighed. "How safe are we here? Does anyone have any idea?"

"I'm guessing, but I'd say we're pretty well hidden where we are. Assuming we avoid unnecessary trips out of the warehouse." Bronte gave Galen a pointed look.

"Hey, metal head, you wouldn't have anything to eat without my *unnecessary trip out*. Show a little appreciation." Galen made like she was going to steal Bronte's snack. Bronte slapped her away.

"Enough, both of you." Athena shot Bronte and Galen a "don't mess with me" look. "Okay. Here's the plan. We're going to eat and then we're going to get to work. Does anyone think it's safe for us to return to our homes?"

Three shakes of the head was confirmation of what she feared.

"All right, that's what I think too. Then if this is where we're going to live, at least for now, we need to remodel. That's our first task. We need to account for eating, sleeping, work, and medical. Everyone on board?"

This time affirmation. And while they ate the mood lightened. The prospect of a task to complete, an outlet for their stress, and the closest they were going to get to home, at least for now, was restorative. How had she gotten to this place? Emotionally lifting and leading three superpowered people she'd just met, at least two of whom had been held captive in a secret facility only hours before. Three people who'd kidnapped her, if she wanted to get technical. And yet somehow when she looked around, they appeared to need more saving than she did. So save them she would, because she suspected without her, they'd be lost and she couldn't let that happen. She'd deal with what it might cost her later.

Chapter Seven

Bard stomped into her office reading a report on the clusterfuck in her hospital sublevel research lab. Antonio was three paces behind her, silently following. Bard wanted to fire him or throw him out the window and watch him fall twenty stories, but she needed Antonio. She always had. They'd been friends since childhood and Antonio had been there for her in a way no one else had. He'd protected her and helped her rise to the head of Verstrand Industries, even when the journey became bumpy.

Bard handed her papers and overcoat to her assistant and made a beeline to the coffee machine.

Her assistant, Decimus, cleared his throat politely. "Good morning, ma'am. Mr. Verstrand is here to see you."

Bard stopped short. She tried to take a breath but found the room lacked sufficient oxygen. She closed her eyes and counted to three. She tried again. She could barely breathe, nothing more than short, shallow breaths, but at least she was able to catch some air. Why was her father here? She could feel his presence in the room now, a granite boulder waiting to fall and crush her.

She continued to the coffee machine and fixed her coffee. Her hands shook so she left the saucer untouched. She willed her hands to still. Had hands ever given a flying fuck about someone's inner pleas? Hers certainly hadn't. "Would you like coffee, Father?"

"I'd like you to explain yourself."

Bard's sip of coffee felt like ice. She finally looked at her father. Ludo Verstrand was sitting in Bard's seat, behind her obsidian desk. Bard had no choice but to stand or take a seat in the visitor chair in front of her own desk.

"You're in my chair." Bard set her coffee cup on the desk and crossed her arms. She was going to make a show of not being intimidated.

Ludo stood, put his hands on the desk, and leaned forward toward Bard. "I put you in that chair and I can remove you at any time. I still hear what happens in this company and fuckups that put the brand at risk will not be tolerated."

Why could Ludo always make her feel so small? She ran one of the most successful companies in the world and yet one visit from him and her insides felt squishy and she wanted to over-explain herself. That wouldn't do. Ludo didn't respect weakness. Especially not from her, the daughter who'd never be the son he'd always wanted.

"I don't know what you've heard, and I don't much care. You left control of the company to me which means I'm busy running it. If you have something specific you'd like to discuss, you can make an appointment, otherwise, I have work to do." Bard was sure he could see her heart about to beat out of her chest and the sweat that felt like a waterfall coming from every pore.

There was a long, uncomfortable minute of silence. Bard scrunched her toes in her Jimmy Choos to keep from outwardly squirming. Antonio cleared his throat. Bard thrilled when she saw Ludo recoil. It was almost imperceptible, but she knew him well enough to see it. Antonio had always scared Ludo. Good, let him see the power she had.

"The path you were on seemed promising. Don't let this incident derail you. And fix it." Ludo collected his coat with the precision and meticulousness he did everything in life. He left without another word or glance.

Bard stood at her desk, back to the door, for half a cup of coffee's worth of time before she trusted that he was gone, and she could relax. She took her seat behind *her* desk and nodded at Antonio. Her right-hand man had, as he usually did, blended into the background while Ludo postured. Bard appreciated how often Antonio stayed hidden in plain sight long enough for most people to forget he was there. He'd helped shift the tenor of more than one meeting when he'd materialized by Bard's side or made his presence known in some other way as he did today.

Antonio dismissed Decimus and took a seat in front of Bard's desk. "I know you didn't wish to appear weak in front of your father, but the escape of our research specimens does represent a complication to our work. We need to recover them."

Bard slammed her fist on the desk. "I am well aware. What are your men doing to re-acquire them?"

If Antonio was surprised or insulted by Bard's outburst, he didn't show it. "Primo and Secondus are in the field. A woman made of metal and a man with a computer for a face will attract attention. Even if they prove elusive, we provided the doctor the drugs she desired. She'll need to get her own now that she's on the street. My men know how to apply pressure to get the information they need."

Despite their years of friendship, Bard knew there were parts of Antonio that would scare her into months of nightmares if she knew the full truth of him and the work he did. She also understood how valuable an asset Antonio was to the company. Bard didn't ask and Antonio didn't tell when unpleasant work needed to be done.

"Keep me updated. We need all three of them back in the fold." Bard sighed.

It had been a year without incident. She was so close to a breakthrough and now her two specimens were in the wind.

Decimus knocked and opened the door. "Gamma is here to see you, ma'am."

Bard frowned and waved the scientist in. He looked nervous.

"Where are Alpha and Beta?" Bard didn't stand to greet her number three scientist.

Gamma shifted from foot to foot. "They were injured in the incident at the hospital. They went to the restricted floor after the elopement, to ensure control of the research subjects was maintained. Some of our emotional response test subjects were manipulated by Subject One. It overloaded the programming of their suits. They attacked Alpha and Beta. The test subjects' suits have been reprogrammed and their enrollment has continued."

"Then you are Alpha now." Antonio looked to Bard to confirm. Bard nodded and scrolled on her computer and made the update.

"But, ma'am—"

Antonio held up his hand stopping further protest. "If you aren't up for the job, we'll promote Delta. Can you be the Alpha? Yes or no?"

"Yes, ma'am, sir." The new Alpha hung his head.

"Excellent. Update me on what the fuck happened at the hospital and where we are with the research." Bard folded her hands and waited.

Alpha kept his eyes on the floor. He shoved his hands in his lab coat. "We required Subject One be removed from sedation so we could test his connection with his device. We needed to see his manual control in real time. He was the only survivor of our Stage One testing. He's been awake for the past week. There were precautions in place. However, he took advantage of the change in routine when a new nurse began her employment. He woke Subject Two. Once she was awake, there was no way to reestablish our research."

Bard didn't move or unclasp her hands. Why hadn't they told her that one of the subjects had been woken? Asking would show weakness. "I thought you'd gotten around the metal skin problem."

"The magnetic treatment we devised only worked in a small area and it was a battle we fought daily. The zeptobots fought back. It wouldn't have been long until they defeated us. However, even if we'd been able to deploy the magnet in larger scale, it was destroyed by Subject One."

Her new lead scientist was still talking but Bard's mind wandered. What a disaster. Would this guy be a good scapegoat if rumors started about what they were doing or was he too valuable to sacrifice? Perhaps the two injured scientists who had once outranked him were better to use as examples. She made a note to speak to Antonio.

Bard held up her hand and cut off Alpha. "Update me on the research. Did you get what you needed from Bronte Scales before she escaped? What about Subject One? His name is Spero, correct?"

Finally, Alpha made eye contact. "Yes, ma'am. His name is Spero. As I mentioned he was the lone survivor from Stage One testing. He's able to control the program we installed on his hardware, but the relationship isn't the same as the one Subject Two has with the zeptobots. He uses his technology, whereas hers are… well, they're part of her. We haven't fully understood it yet."

"Is that because you can't re-create the zeptobots or because our program doesn't work?" Bard stood and moved around her desk. She crossed her arms.

Alpha swallowed audibly. "The program elicits emotional response, ma'am. Subject One is proof of concept and our emotional response subjects are allowing us to fine-tune delivery dose and methods. We've seen less success with the zeptobots, but that's likely because she's been relegated to an inert stage for a year. Had we been able to keep her conscious and do testing—"

Bard picked the first thing her hand landed on, and she launched it at Alpha. He managed to dodge it, and it landed with a thud on the thick carpet. "You've had samples of her blood for a year. What do I pay you for? The program needs to work, and we *need* zeptobots."

Alpha bowed and nodded. "Yes, ma'am. Subject Two is undeniably brilliant. Untangling her work is difficult. It also appears as though the zeptobots are…never mind, ma'am. We will not rest until we break the code."

"You're the Alpha now." Bard pointed at her scientist. "I expect you to deliver results. Make my program work. I can't have an army of computer-faced soldiers marching around the world. I don't want individual human operators like Subject One, who should have been put down a long time ago. Men can be defeated. People see them coming. Fix the zeptobot problem. I'm expecting great things from you."

As soon as the door closed behind Alpha, Bard turned to Antonio. "What would you do about our two injured scientists?"

Antonio evaluated her for a moment. He looked to be weighing his words carefully. "Is your goal to finish your program at the first moment possible or to motivate your scientists to produce for you on this and every project moving forward?"

Bard took a moment to consider. "Find me a way so I don't have to choose."

A smile, the smile that gave Bard goose bumps, spread across Antonio's face. "Then you know what needs to be done. It's the only way. Say the word and I'll take care of it."

Although it made her insides crawl, Bard knew Antonio was right. Antonio was always right about these matters. "Do it. Retire them. Make sure the other scientists know the cost of failing me. Give the ones remaining a pay raise to offset the consequences and keep them in place."

Antonio left to carry out her orders, leaving Bard alone with her thoughts and her guilt. She opened her lower desk drawer and pulled out Bronte's melted laptop. She still didn't know why she'd kept it. Perhaps it was a trophy. Bronte had given up everything and Bard had thought she'd won. Now, was she so sure? Where was Bronte? Bard needed more time. Once she was ready to bring her own version of zeptobots and her program to market, Verstrand Industries would be the most profitable company in the world, and she would be the one being feted for her accomplishments. Even Ludo couldn't take that away from her.

Chapter Eight

B ronte held her hands loosely in front of her, scrunched her eyes closed, said a little prayer for the first time in her life, balled her fists, and thrust her hands out assertively. She opened her eyes. Her shoulders slumped. Her hands were as non-reflective and fleshy as they'd been when she closed her eyes. Was there a password she was missing? A ritual? A sacrifice? She'd said "please" multiple times. What would it take to get the zeptobots to the surface?

Although she'd created the zeptobots and knew every design spec, code, and tiny piece of hardware, they were foreign to her now. She'd wanted the zeptobots to be a cutting-edge cancer treatment, not a metal super suit. Nothing in her years of development and testing had hinted at them behaving as they were now. How was she supposed to communicate with something she'd conceived of but no longer understood?

She picked up the wire crimpers she'd found in the toolbox and stripped the plastic sheathing off a length of wire on her workbench. It had taken a few days of hard work, but their warehouse was transformed into something that almost passed as livable.

"I'm going to stick this wire into my thumb. It's going to hurt like hell." Bronte held the wire above the pad of her thumb. "An exoskeleton would be nice." She rolled her eyes. She'd resorted to talking to herself. Was it herself? Were the zeptobots "her"?

She or they gave no response.

"Last chance to save us." She jabbed the wire into her thumb. "Ow. Son of a bitch. What the fuck. I thought we were on the same team." She removed the wire and stuck her thumb in her mouth. The metallic taste of blood was ironic enough to make her laugh.

"What are you doing to yourself over here?" Athena pulled on Bronte's arm until she allowed Athena to see her injured thumb.

Athena deposited the first aid kit she'd been keeping with her on Bronte's workbench. She handed over antibacterial cream and a Band-Aid.

"I don't have an unlimited supply of this stuff and I have zero doses of tetanus shots. Self-inflicted injuries are going to be triaged pretty low when I have to ration Band-Aids. Don't say you haven't been warned." Athena took the Band-Aid when she saw Bronte in danger of fumbling it without the use of one thumb.

"Galen jabbed me to get the exoskeleton to appear before we fought our way to freedom. I thought if I threatened to injure myself I could make it appear as well." Bronte held up her bandaged thumb. "Experiment failed. Hypothesis disproved."

"Not a failure then. One question answered, a few hundred more to test. Isn't that how science works?"

Bronte smiled. "I didn't know you cared."

Athena returned the smile. "So what if I do?"

"I would like that very much." The words were out before Bronte could sensor. "Won't anyone miss you?" she said quickly.

"Miss me?" Athena looked confused at the abrupt shift.

Bronte pointed toward the door. "Out in the real world. Friends or family? You went to work one day and then disappeared. You're the one who said we kidnapped you. Won't someone wonder what happened to you?"

Athena looked toward the door and smiled. She was clearly lost in a memory Bronte had no part in. "No. They'll think I took off on an adventure. No one will worry for a while longer. It wouldn't be the first time I quit my job and left for a few weeks to parts unknown."

Bronte took a step back. Her chest tightened at the thought. "Adventure? You used to go on extended trips with no planning? That sounds simply dreadful."

"It's not. It's freedom and exploration and a thrill I can tell you've never experienced. This is its own kind of adventure, don't get me wrong." Athena indicated around the warehouse. "But not the kind I'd choose for us. When we're done with whatever this is, I'll come up with something much nicer. You'll see. It'll be fun."

Bronte doubted that very much. "We'll see." That was as much as she was willing to concede, no matter how beautiful Athena looked when her smile reached all the way to her eyes. "I have more work to do."

"Uh-huh." Athena removed one additional Band-Aid from her kit and slid it across the workbench to Bronte. "That's all you get for the rest of the day. Use it wisely."

Bronte chuckled as she turned back to her work. It was harder than she expected not to turn and watch as she heard Athena walk away.

"Lord as my witness, I will get that sexy scientist to unwind a little before this is all said and done."

"I heard that," Bronte said over her shoulder.

"There's no way you could have heard that." Athena sounded alarmed.

Bronte turned. Athena was across the warehouse in their newly designated kitchen with a water bottle halfway to her mouth. Athena was right; the distance was far too great for Bronte to have heard and yet heard she had.

"Can you hear me now?"

"Yes." Bronte held her arm aloft showing a thumbs-up in case Athena's ears weren't as sensitive as hers seemed to be.

"What the fuck. Off-key singing in the shower, swearing under my breath, commenting on your ass, will nothing be private around here?" Athena's hands were on her hips, but Bronte could hear the laughter in her voice. "Seriously though, we might need to get you earplugs." Athena was more serious now.

In the hospital, she'd experienced something similar but hadn't been sure if it had been her imagination. Now there was no doubt her hearing was enhanced. Was this also a result of the zeptobots? And what triggered it?

"Now you decided to come out and play?" Bronte scowled at her hands as if that was where the zeptobots gathered when they needed to have a face-to-face chat with Bronte. Not that they ever seemed to be so inclined.

Athena made her way back over. "You know this makes you a legit superhero now, right?"

Bronte cocked her head. "I was illegitimate before?"

"Yes. A bastard superhero. Fewer than two powers. It's in the bylaws. But now? Now you're legit. Super hearing and metal skin sneaks you in the door."

"I'm relieved we cleared that up. The only hiccup I see is I'm not interested in being a superhero." Bronte folded her arms across her chest.

"That's because you don't have a name and a costume yet. We'll work on those later and if you can still resist the hero urge, we'll talk about it. Right now, let's see what else you've got. Do you think you have super speed? Or strength? Can you lift me with only your pinky?" Athena took Bronte's pinky between both of her hands and held on tightly.

Where had this excitable fangirl come from? It was endearing and damn cute. It was true Bronte had no intention of being a hero to the masses, but if this was the reaction she got from Athena maybe she should reconsider being a hero. If only Bronte knew how to pull that off.

First, she tried lifting Athena with her pinky. "My strength is the same as always, overworked scientist who doesn't know how to get to the nearest gym. I'm incredibly sore from moving all this stuff around the last few days and my back hurts."

Athena let go of her pinky. "That's okay. Maybe you'll have super strength and speed when you're metal. Do you think you'll be able to fly?"

Before Bronte could ponder that horrible thought, Athena had taken Bronte's science journal, flipped to a blank page, and was writing. Athena was writing in *her* science journal. No one touched her science journal. She tried to snatch it back only to have Athena swat her away.

"I'm pulling from deep in my memory banks here, all the way back to Mrs. Fenderwick's eighth grade science class where we learned nothing but the scientific method. To test your hearing we need a hypothesis, a methods section, and results, correct?" Athena turned the notebook so Bronte could read what she'd written.

Bronte looked at the notes Athena had scribbled. There was more there than section headings. She'd developed the outline of a scientific plan. Bronte filled in the rest of the details. They'd test her hearing at multiple points around the warehouse. If Bronte was being honest, listening to Athena talk wasn't a hardship. By the end of the experiment they'd have multiple data points to better understand the strengths and limitations of her enhanced hearing.

Athena pulled over one of their makeshift chairs and pointed Bronte to sit. She counted off ten paces and made a note in the science journal. Bronte was impressed with Athena's scientific attention to detail. But then, a nurse had to pay attention to detail too.

"What about your family and friends? Why didn't I see your face all over the news? Haven't they missed you over the past year?" Athena continued taking notes as she talked.

Bronte sat straighter in her chair. She fought against the wave of melancholy that always crashed through her when a stray thought of her parents swept through.

"You could simply ask if I can hear you." Bronte barely needed to raise her voice to be heard.

Athena shrugged. "What fun is that?"

"This is science, not fun." Bronte squashed a smile.

"Pardon me, I wasn't aware they were mutually exclusive. You answer the questions and I will make sure not to enjoy myself." As she was saying it, Athena giggled. "Oops. From now on, serious of purpose."

No more giggles escaped although Bronte could see Athena trying hard to suppress a smile. What the hell? They were living in a warehouse, and she was testing a newly discovered superpower that would apparently ensure she was legit. At least in the eyes of someone whose opinion she realized she valued. Why did this particular experiment have to be serious as long as they collected good data?

"To answer your question, it's unlikely anyone noticed I was missing. Those that did either didn't care enough to follow up or didn't know enough about me to file a report." Bronte hung her head. What must Athena think?

Athena paced off more distance between them and recorded it. "Why wouldn't everyone want to know you? I haven't known you long at all and I want to know far more."

Heat rose from Bronte's neck to her cheeks. Why was she blushing? She needed a safer topic. "I lived and breathed my work for years. That didn't leave me much room for anything outside of it."

"You're going to have to speak up. I'm lacking one or two superpowers." Athena pointed to her own ears and shrugged.

Bronte cupped her hands around her mouth. "Married to my work. No social life. Hang on." She looked around until she found the walkie-talkies she'd spotted earlier. It was convenient they'd holed up in a warehouse full of electronic debris. She turned both on. Thankfully, the batteries were still good. At least now she'd be able to answer Athena's questions without shouting across the warehouse. She wasn't sure she needed Galen and Spero listening to her side of the conversation.

Athena circled ninety degrees to Bronte's right. "Next question. Do you come from a long line of scientists determined to make the world a better place?"

Bronte paused. One beat, two, three. She knew she needed to answer but wasn't sure how. Or if she wanted to.

"Can you hear me?" Athena sounded confused.

"Yes. I heard you." Bronte turned so she was facing Athena. "I'm the only scientist in my family. They're embarrassed by me."

Athena looked like a cartoon character with her mouth hanging open practically to the floor. "Didn't you say you hoped the zeptobots would be a cure for cancer? Your family is embarrassed by that?"

"They're artists. They see the world entirely differently than I do. Pursuing a career that doesn't allow your brain the creative freedom it deserves is a waste of human potential, according to them." Bronte clenched her jaw as she spoke. She consciously relaxed each muscle as she counted to ten. They weren't worth the tension headache she would cause herself.

Athena rotated again and looked ready to ask a follow-up question.

Bronte interrupted her. "My turn to ask a question. Why have you stayed? You could have left at any time. We wouldn't have stopped you, despite our kidnapping you initially. I protest labeling it as such, for the record."

"I'm not sure." Athena looked around the room. Her gaze finally rested on Bronte. She smiled. "You three have all the flashy powers, but it seems like you might need a little saving yourselves. And what bigger adventure am I going to find than you three and a case of stolen research being sought by a bad guy who will gladly kill at least one of us and imprison the others?"

"I thought it was because there isn't anywhere safe outside the doors." Bronte wasn't sure she liked the idea of needing saving.

"That too, I suppose." Athena moved again. "I'm certainly not staying for the amenities. We're running out of cash and food, and I don't have any clean clothes. What's your favorite color?"

Bronte furrowed her brow. She was worried about the things Athena mentioned as well.

"Focus, Doc. Favorite color?"

"Color? Green, why?" Bronte craned her neck to look at Athena.

"For your costume, of course." Athena pulled a different, smaller notebook from her front pocket and jotted something inside.

Bronte shook her head vigorously. "No. Nope. No costumes. Absolutely not. You might be cute, but you're not sweet-talking me into spandex and spangles."

Even from halfway across the warehouse Bronte could see the mischievous smile on Athena's face. "Could I sweet-talk you out of them is the question. Since I'm so cute and all."

Bronte came close to falling out of her chair. "What are you doing?"

"Flirting. Or trying to, although if you have to ask I must not be doing a very good job." Athena moved farther away. "Can you still hear me?"

"Just barely over my thudding heart." Bronte didn't depress the walkie-talkie button.

"Did you say something?" Athena held her walkie-talkie and gave it a shake. "I can't hear you, remember."

"I said, yes. I can hear you." Bronte squeezed her hands together until her right index finger turned an unhealthy shade. Her palms were sweaty. "I don't know how to flirt." The words escaped in a rush, like schoolchildren released on the final day before summer vacation.

"Do you want to? Flirt, I mean?" Athena's voice was kind and comforting. She wasn't teasing or flirting now. She was giving Bronte the space to speak her mind.

Bronte didn't need to think it over. "Yes, of course I do. With you. Not generally."

The static from the walkie-talkie felt like an accurate representation of the status of her thoughts. Jumbled, nonsensical, and loud.

"Then we're going to be fine."

Athena was as far away from Bronte as she could get in the warehouse, but Bronte felt connected to her. She liked it almost as much as it scared her. She'd never let herself form attachments to others before. It got in the way of her work. What did a connection between a "legit superhero" metal robot human and a goddess like Athena even look like? Why would Athena want it? Maybe Athena was enjoying the adventure now, but there were other women outside the warehouse to catch her eye. Other "normal" women, without metal skin and super hearing. Besides, wouldn't she need to know who and what she was before she asked someone else to know her?

At least they had data from the hearing experiment. When everything else confused her, she could fall back on science. Less comforting was the sight of Athena holding her science journal and the jolt of pleasure that shot through her as she approached. She wasn't going to be able to science her way out of this one.

Chapter Nine

Athena jumped when the warehouse door slammed open. Galen filled the doorway, her arms loaded with bags. Athena closed and locked the door, then relieved Galen of some of her burden. She peeked inside one bag. It contained clothes, food, and other badly needed supplies.

"Where'd you get all this?" Athena tried to keep the suspicion from her voice as she followed Galen to the kitchen.

They deposited the supplies and unpacked. Athena nearly wept at the sight of fresh fruit and clean clothes for all of them.

Galen unwrapped a lollipop and popped it in her mouth. "My habit of carrying a lot of cash finally paid off. I'm out now though. I slipped IOUs into everyone's pack of underwear. I charge interest. And we need to figure out how we're going to get more money."

"Do you think Bard's men are still looking for them?" Athena nodded toward Bronte and Spero.

"Not just them. Us too. She won't give up until she finds us. Spero was smart to bring us here, but I'm shocked we haven't already been found." Galen looked calmer than her dire warning suggested she should be.

"What happens if they do?" Athena bit her lower lip.

Galen pulled the pop from her mouth and looked her in the eye. "You really want me to answer that?"

That was a simple question to answer. "Fine, then we need to get them in better shape. I could use your help. How did you know to punch Bronte in the shoulder back at the hospital to make her turn to metal?"

"Lucky guess." Galen turned and walked away.

"No, it wasn't. I need your help." Athena put her hand on Galen's shoulder to stop her.

Galen turned and pointed back to the kitchen. "I got food and supplies. I did my part. If you want to play superhero with those two, go ahead, but I want no part of it. I want to keep my head down, my mind uncluttered, and survive."

"Don't you think they're our best chance of surviving?" Athena crossed her arms over her chest.

Galen laughed, a hoarse, unhopeful sound. "The minute you show her how to control that metal skin she's going to walk out the door and into Bard's office, demanding she return her research. How long do you think we'll survive after that?"

"So that's a no on helping?" Could she get away with slapping her? "What kind of doctor are you? You let them stay locked in that torture chamber. You helped keep them there. How is that doing no harm? Why were you down there in charge of it all? Did you know Spero was in pain and chose not to do anything about it?"

Galen looked at the ground and kicked viciously at a piece of wire. "I had my reasons and they're none of your business. You don't know what it cost me. You assume what you say is the whole story. As for Spero, of course I knew. I could feel it every day. There wasn't anything I could do. He needed an engineer, not me. He needed her." Galen pointed across the room at Bronte.

"I guess it's lucky he woke her then and she was able to help him." Athena wasn't ready to play nice. "If I don't know the whole story of your time on the sublevels, then tell me. What am I missing? Maybe you're right and there wasn't anything you could've done for any of the patients, but you can help Bronte and Spero right now."

Galen glared at her. "You're not listening. I *can't* help, and you can't hide your fear from me, even though I wish you could. You can't tell me you're not scared of Bronte too. Especially what she could mean for the rest of us." Galen rubbed her temples.

"What the hell does that mean? What I am"—Athena put her hands on her hips—"is pissed off. Is your sensor picking up that emotion?"

Athena resisted the urge to flip her off as Galen snorted and walked away.

"Everything okay?" Bronte picked an apple and her eyes lit. "I tried not to, but I overheard you and Galen talking about me."

"Like I said before, we need to get you earplugs." Athena dug the heel of her palm into her forehead.

"I won't do anything to endanger any of you." Bronte gently lowered Athena's hand and raised her chin. "I'd never put you at risk." She cupped Athena's cheek and then removed her hand as if she suddenly realized what she'd done.

"But you're going after your research." Athena sighed. It was unspoken but she knew it was true.

"I don't know what they're up to, but you've read Spero's chart. You saw what they were doing at the hospital. You saw the basilisks and the other patients we had to leave behind. They're using my work and manipulating something that was supposed to be pure and good. What would you do?" Bronte looked pained.

Athena leaned her head back and looked at the ceiling. "Ugh. I don't know if I'm mad at you for being a stubborn ass who's going to get us all caught or if I'm impressed at your single-minded nobility." She took the apple from Bronte's hand and set it down. "Get Spero. We have work to do. But I'm telling you this, for the record. If you get me killed, I will never forgive you."

Spero looked annoyed when he followed Bronte to the corner of the warehouse Athena had secretly started calling Superhero U. His screen lit.

Athena held up her hand and raised an eyebrow as she looked at him. "No. Not yet."

Spero raised an eyebrow of his own. He dimmed his screen.

"I want to see how much control you have of that thing." Athena waved in the direction of his screen.

Almost before Athena could react, Spero's screen lit and emojis flashed by so quickly she wasn't sure she'd have been able to keep up even if Spero had been facing her directly. As it was, he'd turned away from her, so she didn't feel any effects.

"Are you done showing off?" Athena made a show of checking her nonexistent watch.

"What's your plan for us?" Bronte was clicking a pen cap on and off rapidly.

Athena plastered on her most confident smile. "I've secretly always wanted to train a superhero. You're going to turn to metal and, Spero, we're going to see if there are any limits to what you can do. I've watched all the movies and every television show. I know exactly what to do. We have to break you down first, then build you back up. We'll figure out all your powers and what the limits are. Are you two as excited as I am?"

Bronte slammed the cap on the pen and shoved it in her pocket. "Movies and TV are about fake heroes without any powers. I've been running experiments to turn metal for days. What makes you think I'll be able to do it now on command?"

"Because now I'm the one commanding you," Athena whispered. She patted Bronte on her rapidly reddening cheek. "What were you feeling at the hospital before Galen punched you and you went superhero?"

Bronte looked like she was rewinding a low-definition video in her mind. "Fear. Anger. Like I wanted to protect you and Galen and Spero. I knew the basilisks would hurt any of us they could. Once Galen punched me, I felt pain."

Athena shivered. That day was still fresh down to her marrow. She didn't need much to relive it. "Can you focus on those feelings and how your skin feels when it changes?" She took Bronte's hand. That probably wasn't necessary for this to work.

Bronte closed her eyes. She squeezed Athena's hand. The pressure was like a warm wave that rolled through Athena's body, finally breaking with a fluttering crash in her stomach. She tried to pull her hand away, but instead Bronte reached for her free hand as well. The double hand hold wasn't helping her stomach calm. She glanced at Spero, who made a kissy face. She stuck her tongue out at him.

"I feel like I'm back in that tiny hospital room. Can you feel my palms sweating?" Bronte's voice hinted at her discomfort.

Athena looked at their joined hands. A silver shimmer was creeping from Bronte's fingers to her hands toward her wrists. Athena stroked the back of Bronte's hands. "Keep going. It's working."

"It is?" Bronte opened her eyes and dropped Athena's hands. The metal receded.

"It was." Athena blew out a breath. "Should we try again?"

Bronte shook her head. "How far did the metal go?"

Athena indicated three-quarters up Bronte's hand.

"That took most of my concentration and I didn't even cover my hands. It has to be faster. If I ever needed it that would never work. A bad guy's not going to wait five minutes for me to slowly get ready. Spero, I need your help to test a hypothesis." Bronte shook her arms and legs and rolled her neck like she was preparing for a title fight. "I need to be scared. Try not to traumatize me though. Short blast maybe?"

"Actually, this is good. Spero, I want to see if you can change the volume. If we use a five-point scale, can you give Bronte a level three?" Athena took a big step back. "Are you sure about this?" She turned to Bronte.

"Not at all but we need to solve this. Hit me, Spero." Bronte bent her knees like she was expecting a physical blow.

Spero's screen lit and the emoji that appeared was smaller than usual. Athena watched Bronte's face change rapidly from nervous to fearful. Even a level three from Spero was producing a strong reaction. Bronte backed away. She shrunk inward. Her eyes were frantic. And suddenly she was metallic from head to toe. Her hair disappeared under the metal covering and her face lost some of its definition and expression. Spero's screen went dark.

Bronte held up her hand and examined it. "What a terrible power. I have to be terrified to get it to work?"

"We don't know that yet." Athena tried to put a comforting arm around Bronte's shoulders, but it was like hugging a statue. She pulled away awkwardly. "Do you remember how it felt when you went metallic? Can you make it recede now?"

Bronte frowned. No one said anything for an uncomfortably long time. Athena tried not to clear her throat, ask questions, or squirm. She was the one who asked Bronte to do this, it was okay if she needed time.

Eventually, Bronte dropped her hands to her sides with a clank. "I don't have any more idea how to make it go away as I do to get it to appear."

Athena tapped her chin. "That's because you're not thinking like a scientist. Do you mind if I try something?"

"Go ahead. I've failed, repeatedly." Bronte looked disgusted. "Which proves your point. Science is all about testing hypotheses and being wrong fairly often. Why I'm not able to handle failure with this is frustration on top of annoyance."

"If you were advising me, as a scientist, what to do to get the zeptobots to disappear, what would you say?" Athena rocked back on her heels and waited.

Bronte looked contemplative. "Well, fear brought them out and they don't seem to care about sweet-talk or threats from their host. Maybe they respond to the emotions of the host? Or physical stimuli. That would explain Galen's punch." Bronte muttered to herself a few minutes longer. Athena couldn't follow her words or thought process. Abruptly, Bronte stopped talking to herself. "I'd advise you to feel an emotion on the opposite side of the spectrum as fear."

Athena nodded to Spero. "You heard the lady. Happy, relaxed, something the opposite of scared." Athena stepped back so she wasn't in line of sight of Spero's screen.

Spero rubbed his hands together and a love emoji appeared on his screen. Bronte's shoulders lowered, her breathing slowed, and she smiled contentedly. Most impressive, her metallic skin receded rapidly.

She turned to Athena, her eyes soft and shining with emotion. "Have I told you how beautiful you are?" She stepped forward and put her hand on Athena's cheek. "I think I love you."

Athena gently lowered Bronte's hand and stepped back. Maybe, if the touch had been genuine, she'd have considered leaning into the caress, but not like this. "Spero, enough. What are you playing with? I said happy, not this."

He shrugged and made another kissy face pointing between the two of them. Athena waved the implication away. He pointed to a nearby pile of electronics that weren't charred beyond recognition that they'd stacked but not inventoried yet. She nodded as he walked away. She'd get back to his powers soon.

Athena returned her attention to Bronte who seemed her old self again. As if by mutual understanding, neither of them commented on Spero's manipulation. "You designed the zeptobots to protect people from cancer, right?"

"That's right. They were supposed to work inside the body to destroy cancer cells without the side effects of current treatments. At least that's what I thought. Metal skin is a rather inconvenient side effect. I never saw any sign of this in any of my testing. I worked on them for years. I don't understand what went so wrong." Bronte looked at her hands.

"What if nothing went wrong? I think the zeptobots are doing their job. I think they're protecting you when they come to the surface. Have you tried talking to them?" Athena said it casually and confidently. No reason to give away that she thought it sounded mildly insane.

"Yes. I've asked politely. Begged. Spoken sternly. Nothing's worked." Bronte's shoulders drooped. "I worked on this project for years. I shouldn't be reduced to having a coffee date because we know nothing about each other. This isn't speed dating. I designed them. I built them. Why don't I know a damn thing about them?"

Athena pushed Bronte into a chair. She moved behind her and put her hands on her shoulders. "You designed and built them, but what if they're something different now? What if they took the best of what you gave them and borrowed the best of you over the past year? What if they're better than what you created? Let's try one more time. Tell them what you need. This time don't treat them like invaders. Assume they're here as friends." She gave Bronte's shoulder an encouraging squeeze. At least she hoped it came across as encouraging.

"Okay. Zeptobots, it's me, Bronte Scales. I created you. We live together now and I need us to get along. If I say 'suit up' I need you to give me the exoskeleton. 'All clear' means you can go back to your checkers game or whatever you do all day when we're not suited up together." Bronte looked over her shoulder at Athena. She looked unsure. "This is ridiculous."

Athena nodded. She was pretty sure this wasn't how Batman or the Flash figured out their superpowers, but whatever.

"If you agree to this arrangement, turn my hand to metal. Please." Bronte looked at her hand.

They both stared at Bronte's raised hand. Nothing happened. They waited longer. Still nothing.

"Maybe they have to take a vote? How long should we wait?" Athena knew her voice was much less confident than it had been.

"They don't have ears; they can't hear me." Bronte lowered her hand. "I'll have to figure it out on my own."

Athena squeezed Bronte's shoulder. Hard. "No, you won't. Look."

From fingertips to wrist, Bronte's hand was shimmering silver.

"Holy fuck." Bronte turned her hand forward and back. "Okay. I guess we're a team. 'All clear.'"

Her hand immediately returned to its usual fleshy tone.

"Why don't you practice a few times?" Athena urged Bronte to her feet and moved the chair. "I'm going to catcall and whistle over here while you do."

Bronte looked a little shell-shocked but took a wider stance and raised her arms slightly like she was ready to fight if needed. "Suit up."

She was metal before she finished the words. Both she and Athena let out whoops of excitement. They were loud enough to startle Spero. Even Galen looked over from her perch across the warehouse. It looked for a moment like she might join them, but she quickly returned to whatever it was she was engrossed in.

Bronte shifted her position and stood in a ready pose with her arm outstretched. "Can you blast that pile of junk over there?" Bronte thrust her hand forward. Nothing happened. She stood like that for a few seconds, then stood and shrugged. "It was worth a try."

Athena laughed. She hadn't expected this playful side of Bronte. "It doesn't matter, you can suit up whenever you need to. You have a ready-to-wear exoskeleton and all you have to do is ask for it. Nothing is cooler than that."

Bronte surprised Athena by scooping her in a hug and spinning her around in a full circle. Almost as soon as it started, Bronte seemed to change her mind and all excitement was gone from her face.

"Thank you, Athena. For helping me better understand the zeptobots."

Spinning in Bronte's arms, hell, being in Bronte's arms felt good. A little too good. Athena's stomach clenched. She didn't get tied down. She lived for the moment and the next adventure. Was adventure something she could still have in her life or was this warehouse all there was? Who was she kidding, what life was she talking about? Everything she'd known had been blown to shreds in the past couple of days. Her job, her safety, her free movement in society.

This wasn't the time for developing feelings for anyone. That's not what this was though, right? She and Bronte were bonding over a challenge overcome and an obstacle conquered. Surely that's all it was. She'd never be stupid enough to entertain the idea of finding an unwilling superhero attractive. Too late for that, she conceded, but that's where it ended. There'd probably be plenty of adventures to be found in her arms, if she was playing devil's advocate. Athena shook her head. Since when did the devil need an advocate? She'd keep her head turned toward the angel on her shoulder, thank you very much, no matter what her heart had to say, now or in the future.

CHAPTER TEN

Bronte was sure she was walking on air. She could control going metallic. How insane was that? The entire situation was nuts if she stopped to think about it, but for now she was riding the high of being able to make something work exactly as she wanted, when she wanted. Since she woke in the hospital, nothing had felt in her control. Until the day Bard kicked in her door, everything in her life had been orderly and prescribed. She followed the scientific method at all times, since all she did was work. At least now there was something she could point to as hers, something that made sense. As long as she set aside the fact that having superpowers was a bat shit crazy place to try to build a house of normalcy.

She flipped through Spero's chart as she made her way to her workbench. Her metallic hands reflected the warehouse lights. She'd been metallic for hours since she'd mastered changing back and forth. It seemed the fastest way to learn more about moving in that state. She'd been up all night, but now knew she could change the sheen of her exoskeleton from a matted dull finish to bright and shiny. That was handy when her roommates were trying to sleep. Apparently, no one wanted the bunk next to something as bright as a neon sign advertising cheap cigarettes at a twenty-four-hour minimart.

Spero was waiting when she arrived at her workbench. She nearly dropped his chart.

"You scared me, man. Were you trying to sneak up on me?" Bronte wagged a finger at him.

He tapped his ears and pointed at her.

"I know I can hear better than anyone here. But only if I'm paying attention." She muttered the last part under her breath as she tossed his chart on the bench. "I've been looking over your chart trying to figure out what they were doing to you and the others. Do you know?"

Spero pointed at his screen then at himself.

"They wanted to fuse you with the screen? That's pretty obvious, buddy. Do you know why?" Bronte flipped to another page in the chart. It mentioned "human operators." "They're obviously interested in emotional manipulation via technology, but we need more information. We need a look at their data."

Spero nodded. He picked up a weird looking piece of equipment at his feet and placed it heavily on the bench. Bronte examined it carefully. The longer she studied the less she believed what she was looking at.

"Did you build a computer from the scraps you found in here?"

Spero held his arms out to his side as if saying "obviously."

"Is there a way to get online without being detected? If you're good with computers are you any good using them? Maybe using them to get into places others would prefer you don't go?" Bronte resisted the urge to cross her fingers.

This time Spero rolled his one visible eye. Bronte took that as a yes although with Spero you never could be sure. She didn't know why he didn't seem able to speak. She added it to her mental list of things to look into. She hadn't finished reading his chart, maybe that would provide the answers she sought.

Before she could spend more time thinking about his vocal capabilities, he pulled a neatly folded sheet of paper from his pocket and handed it to her. She unfolded it and found a list of electronics, tools, and materials. Most of them were common and easy to come by but one or two weren't the types of things you could buy just anywhere, and at least one was very expensive.

"You want me to get these for you?" Bronte indicated the list.

Spero nodded and pointed to the computer.

"I don't know if you remember, but we have a lot of people after us and we don't have any money." Bronte tried to hand the list back to Spero.

He pushed the paper back to her and handed her another sheet. This one contained detailed directions, that seemed to be not far from the warehouse they were in. There were crudely drawn paths through the abandoned industrial park they now called home, the woods, and far from roads. Where it led, Bronte could only guess. At the bottom it said, twenty thousand dollars.

"Is this for real?" She knew she sounded skeptical. Strike that, disbelieving.

By way of answer he pointed at the list of directions, double tapped on the dollar figure, then pointed to the list of items he wanted. Finally, he pointed to the kitchen, then Athena.

"Now you want me to endanger Athena too? Is that what all the pointing and lists are about? Sending us out there?" Bronte was talking to Spero's back. He was walking away, retreating to his own workspace across the warehouse. "This is a terrible idea." Bronte made her way to Athena. "How would you like to set out on one of those adventures you mentioned you like? I don't remember the details, so this might not qualify, but I'd love the company and I could use your help."

Athena looked suspicious. "You said they sound awful."

"Trust me, I haven't changed my mind. Special request from Spero. I think. He built a computer and needs some supplies to get us online. I'm not entirely sure what he's asking if I'm honest. It's hard to tell with him, but we do need more food and other basics." Bronte heard the papers crumpling from her tightening grip. "Where's Galen? Should we bring her too?"

"She's been curled in a ball in bed most of the day. Something about the full moon and too many emotions." Athena looked worried as she glanced toward the bunks.

"Is she a werewolf?" Bronte whispered behind her hand.

Athena playfully batted at Bronte's shoulder. "You remember there are people after us, right? They can track us if we start checking our email, and in case you forgot, we don't have any money." Athena ticked things off on her fingers.

"Are you coming or not?" Bronte grabbed a hooded sweatshirt she was thankful Galen had purchased and headed for the door.

"Of course I am. Someone's got to look after you." Athena fell into step next to her with her own sweatshirt. She rapped her knuckles on Bronte's head. "All clear."

Annoyingly, the zeptobots retreated and her exoskeleton disappeared. "I'm the one in charge. Don't listen to the backseat driver. Hell, she's not even in the same car." Bronte still wasn't sure how to talk to the zeptobots so she continued talking to her hands. She pulled her hood over her head and as low over her face as she could as they exited the warehouse. "Don't you think my metal suit might come in handy out here?"

Athena adjusted her own hood but not before Bronte saw her shake her head and smile ruefully. "If we want to call as much attention to ourselves as possible, yes. If we need you to suit up, do not waste even a second getting all shiny. For now, let's be two people out shopping for whatever's on your list with our pretend money. That will make this trip strange enough. We don't need to add a metal woman to the mix."

Bronte unfolded the directions Spero had given her. "I haven't even told you the weird part yet."

Athena laughed. "Oh good, because I've been waiting for all of this to get weird."

Bronte turned and caught Athena's eye. They stayed that way, caught in each other's gaze. Inhale. Exhale. Bronte's stomach fluttered. Maybe the zeptobots were practicing rhythmic gymnastics?

Bronte and Athena smiled, then laughed. Not joyous laughter but pressure relief laughter like the quick steam release from a pressure cooker.

"Have to find the humor where we can, right?" Athena reached for Bronte's arm but pulled her hand back before she made contact. "Knock my socks off with the newest oddity."

"Spero gave me directions to what he says is a twenty-thousand-dollar stash." Bronte pointed to the right, past a long row of warehouses in similar disrepair to their own.

This slice of town had once been the beating heart of the city when manufacturing was how a living was made. Now the buildings remained but the soul of the place was long gone and no amount of political arguments had arrived at a suitable use for the old buildings. Meanwhile nature waited on no man and was slowly retaking the land.

"Do you think it'll be there?" Athena's eyes twinkled. She didn't look nervous or timid. She looked confident and fearless.

Athena belonged at the helm of a pirate ship or leading an expedition in search of long-lost treasure. Adventuring suited her. Bronte wished she knew what suited her, especially given all the recent changes in her life.

"One way to find out." Bronte clung close to the shadows of the buildings although she noticed several security cameras hanging broken from the roofs. Even those that were working probably weren't being monitored anymore. She scolded herself for not being more nervous. It was hard not to get caught in Athena's infectious smile and the thrill of the chase. Maybe robot Bronte would consider an adventure now and then.

They followed the directions silently until they approached the target. They'd traveled cautiously, but it had still only taken them thirty minutes. Spero had directed them far from well-traveled roads and through areas with plenty of hiding places. It would be hard to track them even if someone had been looking.

"Why does Spero make us play charades constantly if he could carry around paper and pen to tell us what he's thinking or wants?" Athena looked over Bronte's shoulder at the directions.

Bronte shrugged. "If you figure out why he does anything he does, let me know." She tapped the paper. "It says we need to go into that cemetery." Bronte pointed across the street to an old looking cemetery tucked in among ancient trees. "Then we find plot nine hundred seven. The name on the marker is TLEC."

"Then what?" Athena scooted closer. She was practically draped over Bronte's back. "Is that right? We dig? I'm not digging up Spero's great-great-granddaddy no matter how much money's buried there."

"Are you scared of old bones? I thought you liked adventures." Bronte didn't want to move because then Athena wouldn't be so close.

"Not the kind that might summon old ghosts. I draw the line at apparitions and spirits." Athena shuddered. "We all have limits."

"Good to know." Bronte finally broke the contact but took Athena's hand. The jolt of heat made her subtly check to make sure she hadn't developed a new fire power or something else unexpected. It was only their joined hands that was making her skin feel aflame and her fingers tingle. Were the zeptobots doing that too? She gently released Athena's hand.

"It wasn't just you. I felt it too." Athena smiled at Bronte.

"Okay. Good. That's good. Wait, are you reading my mind? I thought that was Galen's thing." Bronte stopped walking.

"No need. Your poker face is shit. And Galen senses emotions. She can't read minds."

"Oh. I guess I should work on that. Maybe when we get back. Right now though, what if Spero's place is a secret stash or a dead drop? You know, like you see in spy movies." Bronte took Athena's hand again. Bronte looked left and right to check for cars and bad guys before stepping out of the shadows of the large nondescript building they'd been using as cover. This section of town was also industrial but hadn't been abandoned. There were security cameras and regular patrols by hired guards. She felt exposed as soon as the sun hit her skin.

Athena must have felt the same because she squeezed Bronte's hand tightly and made a run for the cemetery. Bronte stumbled, then found her footing and kept up.

"Why would Spero have a dead drop or secret spy stash?" Athena pulled them to a stop once they were safely in the cemetery and began looking at the plot numbers. She pulled Bronte along one of the curving paths that led farther from the road.

"Why does Spero supposedly have twenty thousand dollars buried in a cemetery?" Bronte was winded but wasn't going to give Athena a reason to drop her hand. She dutifully panted along with her.

They found the plot and marker before either of them could come up with an answer that made sense. They stared at the ground in front of the grave marker. It was unadorned except for "TLEC." No dates or sentiments were written on the marker. The grass was neatly trimmed despite the cemetery's age. It didn't look like many of the adjoining sites received frequent visitors.

"Now we dig?" Bronte knelt in front of the marker and reread Spero's directions. They lacked critical details she would have liked to possess. "How deep? How far from the marker? What size object are we looking for? What do we use to dig?"

"You're too much of a scientist. Use your gut." Athena moved her hand along the ground from the middle of the marker about ten inches. "Here." She dug her fingers into the earth and pulled at a chunk. Then she stood and looked around. "Do you see anything we can dig with?"

Bronte sighed. Was she really about to talk to her hands again? "I don't need full body metal, but my hands would be great. I need to dig a hole. Can you read my mind?" Bronte pictured what she needed while saying "tool" silently. She almost jumped out of her skin when her hands nearly blinded her as they reflected the sunlight.

"No way. You have claws." Athena grabbed one of Bronte's hands and turned it over and back.

Sure enough, there were half-inch-long claws, with a diameter just shy of a pencil at the base protruding from the end of each finger. Bronte scooped at the dirt over the spot Athena had marked. Her clawed metal hands were like the bucket scoop on an excavator. If Spero's great-great-granddaddy was buried here, these paws were more than capable of digging him up. Not that she had any interest in doing so. If Spero was lying about the money he'd gone to a lot of trouble to send them here. But why did he know about this pot of gold? What kind of person buried money in a cemetery?

Five scoops in and they both heard the unmistakable clang of metal on metal. Bronte sped up her digging. Despite the inefficiency, Athena elbowed her out of the way and took over for the final bit, clearing off a three-foot-square box. She didn't pull it out of the hole before finding the latch and popping the lid.

Bronte peered over Athena's shoulder. They stared, speechless, at the contents. Money wasn't the only thing the box contained. There were passports, driver's licenses, what looked like marriage, birth, and death certificates, and a disturbing variety of weapons.

"Do we take anything else?" Athena poked at a handgun. "As a nurse, it feels wrong to take something I could hurt someone with."

"I'm a scientist. I can tell you about combustion and velocity, but I've never fired a gun. I'm unwilling to carry one." Bronte lifted the stacks of twenty-dollar bills out of the box. There were ten stacks held together with violet paper straps. "If there are one hundred bills in these stacks then Spero was right."

Athena shook her head looking shocked. "I have some questions for that man when we get back. I'm grabbing some of these passports too. They might come in handy." She put the money and passports into a sling pack she'd fashioned out of material from the warehouse.

Bronte hastily closed the lid and shoveled the dirt back on the box. They'd been here too long. "We should go. It feels too exposed."

"I agree. The hairs on the back of my neck are standing, like something's out there after us. I guess there is though." Athena rubbed the back of her neck and followed Bronte back the way they entered.

They made it nearly back to the road when Bronte heard something that sounded out of place. She couldn't locate or identify the sound, but her instantly thudding heart and electrified feeling told the only story she needed. She took Athena's hand and pulled her behind the closest tree. She heard the bullet whistling their way seconds before it impacted the tree, sending shards of wood into the air.

"I guess I should have given my neck hairs more credit." Athena closed her eyes and breathed deeply. "You and I are going to have to work on a definition of adventure. Mine don't usually involve bullets."

"Good to know. And this is why I don't like adventures." Bronte peeked around the tree. There were three men she could see. "Suit up." She whispered the command.

"Do you know if the zeptobots are bulletproof?"

"I chose a metal that can withstand the harsh conditions inside the human body indefinitely." Bronte again peeked around the tree. The men weren't advancing. She looked at the distance to the road and the cover of the hulking buildings and maze of warehouses, some of which were busy doing whatever real warehouses did. It looked like the space between the eye of a hurricane and an umbrella drink in a tropical paradise. In theory geographically close but in reality, miles of shitstorm apart.

"So you have no idea if those bullets will kill you." Athena looked worried.

"No, I have no idea. But I know for sure they'll kill you. So I'll make a scientifically sound judgment and stay between you and the projectiles. Do you think you can make it back to the buildings?"

"Yes. We can't go back to our starting point though, you know that, right? Until we're sure we've lost these guys, we're on our own. And your plan to step in front of bullets for me? It's a shit plan. I don't like it." Athena peeked around the other side of the tree, picked up a rock, and chucked it as far as she could in the opposite direction to where they wanted to go.

As soon as the rock hit the ground Athena took off. Bronte was caught flat-footed, but she caught up quickly. They made it halfway to the road before the men started gaining ground. Bronte dug deep and ran faster. The wind was blowing through her short hair. She focused on the goal in front of her and assumed Athena was still by her side.

"Bronte, I can't keep up. Please wait for me." Athena sounded desperate.

The sound of her fear stopped Bronte. She pivoted and was floored at how far she'd run ahead of Athena. The three men were close on her heels. They weren't firing their weapons. It looked like they intended to take Athena alive. The shot earlier must have been a warning shot.

Bronte raced back to Athena. Seeing her approach, the men raised their guns. One of them shouted for her to stop and not come any closer. Bronte was surprised to see their faces tense with fear.

One of the men's hands was shaking, making his gun wobble. She didn't stop. She needed to get to Athena.

As Bronte reached Athena one of the men yelled "stop" again. Bronte wasn't sure which one fired their weapon, maybe the shaky handed one. It didn't matter. All that mattered was keeping Athena safe. She draped herself around Athena's back and wrapped her tightly in her arms. Bullets pinged off her back. The impact was uncomfortable but seemingly harmless. Without thinking, she scooped Athena into her arms and started running again.

She could hear the men pursuing her. They were shouting at each other, angrily debating the merits of continuing to shoot at her. She knew she was worth more to them alive, but dead was probably better than in the wind. She didn't slow to give them a chance to come to a consensus.

"I knew you'd be stronger and faster in your super suit." Athena was so close it felt like she was whispering in Bronte's ear.

Bronte shivered and nearly dropped her. That wasn't true, right? It was adrenaline that was allowing her to carry Athena while running at a full sprint. She glanced over her shoulder. Their pursuers were falling farther and farther behind. She wasn't running anywhere close to super speed, but she was running faster than she could ever remember moving.

Once they were safely back in the maze of buildings Bronte found a place relatively well hidden with good lines of sight and easy escape routes for a moment's rest. She set Athena back on her feet. Athena's knees appeared as unsteady as Bronte's felt.

Those men had to work for Bard, right? Maybe they knew about Spero's stash too and were waiting for him to show up? Could Spero have sent them into a trap? No, Bronte didn't believe that. It didn't make sense. The question now was what did they do about Bard's men? They couldn't go back to the warehouse and risk exposing their base of operations and their friends. Bronte looked at Athena. At least she wasn't alone. At least she had Athena. Being with Galen or Spero wouldn't be as comforting. It had to be Athena's unique adventurous spirit, right? Or her nursing bedside manner? Anything other than the fact that Bronte longed to spend more time with her, even though they'd met all of forty-eight hours ago. But Athena was alive and capable and so beautiful. Bronte, on the other hand, had a symbiotic relationship with seemingly sentient robots and she could turn her hands into digging machines. She had functionality and modes. What did she have to offer Athena except a menu of useful tools? Her life's work, her hopes and dreams, had turned her into the thing her parents had most feared. She was an automaton, a robot, devoid of the creative spirit and freedom that were necessary ingredients of the human soul.

CHAPTER ELEVEN

A thena dragged a final armful of branches to a fallen tree she and Bronte had discovered in a thick stand of woods not far from the cemetery. Athena was fairly certain these woods were part of a sprawling state park, but being shot at and their subsequent attempts to stay hidden had muddled her sense of direction.

She dropped her branches next to the tree and whispered Bronte's name. She was gratified when Bronte emerged from the makeshift shelter they'd built. She'd been completely hidden as Athena had approached even though she'd known where to look. With luck, no one would find them overnight even if they got close. They'd debated finding a building to sneak into, but they'd timed the frequency of security patrols and counted cameras and didn't think the risk was worth it. They'd both agreed disappearing into the woods that bordered the cemetery was safer. Bard's men had found them somehow and they couldn't rule out it had been from the security cameras in the occupied buildings.

Bronte's face lit up when she saw Athena. "Come on in. It's not five star, but it could be worse."

Athena added the last branches she'd collected to their lean-to and crawled inside. Bronte was right, it wasn't bad. "I've definitely camped in worse."

"You should put that at the top of one of your adventure posters." Bronte helped Athena into the shelter.

Athena shook her head. "My headliner will be 'better than Bronte's. No gunshots, guaranteed.'"

"Oh, come on. You can't guarantee something like that. What if you happen upon stagecoach robbers? Or it's high noon and a duel is scheduled on the street you're crossing? What about pirates? Plenty of folks have black beards these days." Bronte shifted and grimaced.

"You're awfully cute when you're being a pain in the ass." Athena motioned Bronte closer. "What's hurting you?"

"It's nothing." She looked surprised when Athena gave her a "don't fuck with me" stare. "My back is uncomfortable. It's not a big deal. Probably not used to lying on the ground."

Athena crawled over Bronte's prone form in the small space. The side closest to the tree afforded more headroom. She instructed Bronte to roll over and tried not to let her mind wander to places it shouldn't when she was initiating a medical evaluation.

Nothing was obvious on Bronte's exoskeleton. Athena took a moment to admire it. Currently Bronte wasn't shiny and blinding. The liquid mercury look was matte, full of depth, and stunningly beautiful. Much like its wearer.

She banished those thoughts to a dusty corner of her mind. She could revisit them when she had nothing else to do, maybe when she was decluttering her mind or doing some light spring cleaning of the stray thoughts she no longer needed.

"I don't see anything obvious. Can you take off the suit?" Athena rapped her knuckles gently on Bronte's shoulder.

Bronte raised up on an elbow and looked over her shoulder at Athena. "Are you sure that's a good idea? Given all this." She indicated their hiding spot.

"You can suit up again if we need you. Show me what you've got." Athena urged Bronte to get on with it.

Bronte sighed and the metal receded. As it did, bruises about the size of a nickel appeared. They dotted her back. Athena tried to count them, but tears welled blurring her vision.

"Anything?" Bronte looked back again. "What's wrong?" She sat as best she could in the confined space and pulled Athena into her arms.

"I should be comforting you. You have bruises all over your back. You stopped all those bullets that were meant for me, and every impact is written all over your skin." Athena wiped the tears away aggressively.

"Hey." Bronte cupped Athena's cheek. "First, they were shooting at me, thank you. And I'm fine. I'll take some bruises to the alternative any day. Besides, now we have another data point to add to our understanding of what I can and cannot do."

"Bulletproof, sort of, isn't much of a data point." Athena stretched out on her side facing Bronte and propped her head on her hand.

Bronte mirrored her position. "It'll do for now." She furrowed her brow and almost instantaneously the exoskeleton appeared.

"You're getting really good at that."

Even in the dim light of the late evening and their darkening night's dwelling, Bronte beamed. It was the first real stress-free smile Athena had seen since they'd been ambushed in the cemetery.

"When do you think it'll be safe to go back to the warehouse?" Athena inched ever so slightly closer to Bronte. She wanted the comfort her solid presence provided.

Bronte rolled onto her back and whooshed out a breath. "I don't know. We probably could have gotten back without being caught tonight. If someone was following us, I'd think they'd have moved on us by now, but better to be cautious. Maybe tomorrow we can try. I'm worried about Spero and Galen. I don't think we were followed, but how did they know we'd be at the cemetery? We'll need to be careful getting back, for them and for us. It isn't good that they're aware we're still in the area."

Athena considered. She reached for Bronte's hand but couldn't quite bring herself to grasp it. She settled for resting her palm on Bronte's forearm instead. "We don't have the things Spero needs yet. Leaving again would be risky. I think we should try to complete his list before we return. And hope for the best that they're okay."

Bronte seemed to have no objections to taking Athena's hand. She rolled back to her side and intertwined their fingers. She squeezed gently and then released their grasp. "Are you always so brave?"

Athena couldn't help the strangled laugh that escaped. "Oh no. As a child I was scared of everything. My anxiety crippled me. Years of therapy and hard work means I can live in harmony with it now. Most of the time. Today was quite a stress test."

"And the adventures? Taking a job on the restricted floor at the hospital?" Bronte's eyes were filled with understanding.

"I missed so much life in my early years. My greatest anxiety now is reverting back to my childhood self, the one who watched life from the sidelines. Stasis doesn't work for me." Athena's throat tightened and her heart rate had increased. Her stomach was churning.

"Hey, breathe with me. It's going to be okay. Lie down. I'm going to cover our backs while we get some sleep. I promise to keep you safe tonight." Bronte wrapped herself around Athena's back until they were spooning.

The smell of the fresh forest floor and the feel of Bronte's strong solid arms around her was more powerful than all the meditations and aroma therapy in the world. She relaxed into Bronte's body and drifted. Her own superhero would protect her tonight. All she had to do was sleep.

Bronte shoved the last package into their hiding place from the prior night and stepped back to make sure everything was hidden from sight. She stepped to the left and right. It would be nearly impossible for their stores to be discovered accidentally.

"Is that everything from the list?" Bronte wiped the damp earth from her hands.

Athena ran her finger down the list and nodded. "Spero owes us for this. I don't care how much money he has hidden around the city, next time, *he* goes on one of these scavenger hunts. My feet hurt from traipsing all over town chasing his list and I have a headache from thinking every other person is going to shoot at us."

The cash had helped them acquire the most obscure items. Sellers were less discerning when they could walk away with the money in hand. Even Venmo had flaws. They'd been vigilant about staying in the shadows and watching every person who was nearby, but the three men from the night before hadn't appeared. Bard likely had an army at her disposal though, so anyone they passed could be on her payroll. Since they weren't dead or captured, they were either being watched, or the guys were looking somewhere else.

"We need to refill our basic necessities before we go back. I know the longer we're out the more the risk, but the other two don't have any money and I doubt there's much food left." Athena tucked Spero's list back in her pocket and swung her pack over her shoulder. "If we really want to push our luck, there's someone I want to drop in on. She might be able to provide us with some information."

"Are you sure that's a good idea? Is it safe?" Bronte rubbed her wrists where restraints had once tied her to her hospital bed. Like a phantom limb situation, sometimes they still chafed the skin and made it hard to breathe.

Athena shrugged. "Don't know. Guess it's a good thing I'm bringing my own personal superhero."

Bronte rolled her eyes. "I've told you, I'm not interested in being a superhero."

Despite saying that, she was having a hard time forgetting the feel of Athena in her arms. Bronte the scientist wouldn't have been holding her last night. As soon as Bronte had told her she was safe, Athena had practically melted into her and fallen asleep. Dumb and cliché as it may be, Athena ceding protective duties had made Bronte feel pretty super. Was that what being a hero was all about? Making others feel safe and in the process yourself heroic? Bronte didn't care about being seen as heroic but *feeling* heroic meant it was possible she was more than a host for the zeptobots. Feelings were human and wonderful and comforting. She'd never tell him, but she didn't mind getting zapped by Spero because it meant she could still feel. Until she figured out what she and the zeptobots were now, that confirmation was deeply comforting.

"Let's keep moving. Staying still this long is giving me the willies." Athena linked her arm with Bronte's and led her from the woods.

After purchasing and stowing their groceries, Athena took the lead weaving them through back alleys and side streets. "I think Spero would be proud of us. Now we've got our little hidden stash. Maybe we should draw him a map and make him come collect his toys."

"Do you think he has more repositories like that one hidden nearby?" Bronte crashed back into a wall when Athena stopped abruptly and shoved her back. "Everything okay?"

Bronte wasn't suited up. It was hard to blend in when you were metallic, but since the cemetery incident she felt like she was in a room filled with dynamite, in a suit covered with motion activated sirens, sitting next to a sleeping dragon.

"Stand down. We're fine. We're also here." Athena cautiously looked around the corner and then pulled back next to Bronte. "It's busy but not as bad as it would have been a couple of hours ago."

"Where are we?" Bronte looked around Athena. Her heart rate increased so dramatically her vision dimmed.

"Put that away. All clear, little bots. Jesus." Athena knocked on Bronte's head. "You want to get us caught?"

Bronte took a deep breath, then another. She wasn't aware she'd called the zeptobots and her metallic exoskeleton. "Why did you bring us back to the hospital?" Her breath was ragged.

Athena's features softened. She put her hand on Bronte's chest, above her pounding heart. "I didn't bring us back to the hospital. I brought us here." They looked around the corner at the coffee shop. "Say a little prayer that Doris is working today."

"Who's Doris?" Bronte barely got the question out before she was running after Athena across the street, against the light, dodging cars, along with four other caffeine-starved patrons. Most importantly she was running away from the hospital that had upended all of their lives.

"Our eyes and ears, hopefully." Athena pulled Bronte into the long line snaking through the shop. She stood on her tiptoes and scanned the employees behind the counter. "She's here. I have to talk to her. If anyone from the other side comes in, can you hold them off long enough for me to have a couple minutes with her?" Athena whispered the last request.

Jesus. Who was this woman? She sure as hell didn't act like a nurse caught up in life-and-death madness. She should be the superhero; she was better at it than any of the rest of them. Bronte watched her more closely as they slowly moved toward the counter. The one Athena had identified as Doris was a revelation. She was calling out orders and greeting people by name, seemingly from memory. She seemed to be doing ten things at once without faltering or even missing a beat in the conversations she was carrying on with numerous people at once. She caught her breath when she realized that not long ago she would have described Doris as a "robot" and meant it as a compliment. It didn't feel much like a compliment now.

Long before they reached the counter Doris spotted Athena. Her eyes lit in recognition and she hollered over to them. "The usual, hon? Haven't seen you in a while. Was starting to worry about you."

"No, my friend here says I should try something new. I'll take a small coffee, black." Athena had to stand on her tiptoes to be seen over the tall man in front of them.

Doris narrowed her eyes at Bronte and hollered over her shoulder. "Frank, I'm taking my ten." She came around the counter and made her way straight to Athena, then took her and Bronte by the arm and dragged them out the employees only side door.

As soon as they were outside, she rounded on Bronte and jabbed a finger in her chest. "Start talking. Explain why my Athena is ordering black coffee in my shop and telling me it's your idea she try it? Moment you walked in I wasn't sure I liked the look of you. Not for her, at least. Start talking or I start dialing." Doris pulled out her cell phone and waved it menacingly.

Bronte tried to take a step back, but Doris followed until Bronte was against the wall with nowhere else to go. She'd been pinned in less than a minute by an angry sub-five-foot barista. Yet more proof she wasn't hero material. "Does she not like black coffee? I don't know what you want from me. Athena, help me out here."

"I don't know. You did kidnap me." Athena seemed unable to contain a smile.

From her work apron Doris produced a retractable truncheon and smacked Bronte on the shoulder. "Next time's harder unless I get some answers."

"Ow." Bronte shook her arm. The familiar chill of the exoskeleton spread from her neck to her fingers. *Shit.*

"Doris, wait. She also saved my life. We need your help." Athena moved next to Bronte and took her hand.

"Oh, I can see that well and good on my own. You." Doris pointed to Bronte and her neck where the metal had now receded. "I didn't believe all the chitchat about you from those black-suited folks who come through here, but now I've seen it with my own eyes. You've got a bit of a condition there, don't you?"

"You won't—"

Doris interrupted before Bronte could finish. "No one will hear a thing from me, Metal Lady."

Bronte frowned. "My name's Dr.—"

"Dr. Zepto," Athena interrupted her.

"Okay. Nice to meet you, Doc. Since I don't have to break your kneecaps, not that I suspect I could if I tried, what can I do for the two of you? I've got five minutes left on my break and I haven't eaten or gotten a smoke. Don't suppose you remembered the tip jar this time either?" Doris looked pointedly at Athena. "You said you needed my help?"

"You said people have come in talking about Dr. Zepto. What have they been saying?"

Doris smiled and wagged a finger at Athena. "You want me to keep your friend here a secret but spill everyone else's coffee dregs?"

Athena stared at her blankly. "Yes."

"Well, okay. When you put it like that." Doris looked taken aback but gathered herself quickly. She took a moment to light a cigarette. "I heard just enough to piece together that there was some sort of disturbance over there at the hospital. Everyone knows about the explosion of course. There's been whispered conversations about how to get rid of pictures of some kind of, I don't know, sea creature from the sound of it, that was spotted above ground? And a woman made of metal. Sounds like a bunch of hash if you ask me. But then some people came in, all serious and official looking, and asked if you'd been around. You *or* her. You hadn't, so I said as much. Not that I would have told them if you had. Suits with questions never take care of the tip jar and they'll turn on you quick as look at you."

Bronte looked at Athena who nodded her understanding. Doris was hearing more than she knew.

"Has the name Bard Verstrand ever come up?" Bronte hoped her voice was calm even when her insides felt like a soda can that had been shaken by an overtired toddler.

"Not here, but my auntie talks about her all the time. She signed up for one of her research studies at the hospital. Come to think of it, it wasn't that long before the explosion and rumors of you existing that she finished. Came out talking about puppy bears whispering to her through her television. Now, hon, don't take this the wrong way, but she's always been a bit eccentric, so I didn't pay her no mind. Now that I've seen you and your jazz hands I may have to stop by for another visit."

"Doris, you're a peach. Thank you for your help." Athena handed her a fistful of Spero's money. "Something extra for the tip jar. But don't share it. No one else in there is half as good as you." Athena kissed her cheek.

"Sweet-talk and a little something green to back it up. You do know how to turn a girl's head. You two need me to keep tabs on the rumor mill for you?" Doris tucked the money in her bra.

"That'd be great. We'll swing back by as soon as we can and check in." Bronte took Athena's hand. "But be careful. These people aren't playing around."

"Oh, one more thing. I don't know if you know that lady doctor who went missing around the same time you two disappeared. I've seen her around a few times. She's always with a crowd that's nothing but trouble. She was in just before you today. They headed that way." Doris pointed away from the hospital.

Bronte and Athena thanked Doris and stuck to the shadows as they moved away from the hospital. They found cover in an alleyway a block from the coffee shop. Bronte had a pretty good idea what Galen was up to, given her emotional instability, but she was still on their side, wasn't she? But where was she getting the money for the drugs she needed to dim her so-called gift? Was she holding out a cash store she hadn't told them about?

"We can't leave her out here alone. She doesn't know Bard's men found us." Athena sighed. "Let's collect her and our other supplies and see if we can make our way back. If not, I guess it's another night spooning under the stars." She winked.

Bronte felt the heat rise from her neck and cheeks. Her fingers tingled as she remembered the feeling of waking with Athena pressed into her. Robots probably didn't get sensations in the places awakened by Athena's ass pressed into her all night. That had to count for something.

It didn't take long for them to find Galen. She was two blocks over in the direction Doris had directed them. Unfortunately, she was also at the bottom of a four-man pile and on the losing end of what looked to be the finish line of an ugly street fight.

"Oh my God." Athena clapped her hand over her mouth. "They're going to kill her."

Bronte froze. Her mind was screaming to help Galen, but the mind-body connection seemed to have been severed. She couldn't will her body forward. "You're a scientist" and "You don't know how to fight" repeated over and over in her brain.

"One of those men is from the cemetery, Bronte. They're Bard's men." Athena took off running toward Galen and her attackers.

"What are you doing?" Bronte's voice sounded small and pathetic to her own ears.

She watched Athena jump on one of the men's back and hit him in the back of the head. Of course the Goddess of War knew what to do in a fight.

The man reached behind him and threw Athena to the ground. He stood over her and raised a boot above her chest. Bronte heard a roar but didn't know if it came from her, Athena, a lion escaped from the zoo, or some other creature. She did know she was no longer rooted in place. The force propelling her into the fray didn't feel entirely under her control, but she hoped it hurt like hell when she drove her shoulder into Athena's attacker and took him roughly to the ground.

Bronte turned her attention to the three remaining men. Two were still pummeling Galen. One was stalking her way. He raised his fists as she stood. She mirrored his stance, not knowing what she was doing. He swung and howled in pain when he made contact with her metal jaw. She swung wildly, landing a glancing blow to his ribs. She heard the breath whoosh out of him. Another wild swing. This time she connected with his jaw and he stayed on the ground.

"Little help, mate." Galen gasped for breath.

"Get off her." Bronte grasped a large man by the back of the pants and flung him from Galen. She swallowed an apology when he landed with a groan thirty feet away.

Galen stumbled to her feet and limped to stand at Bronte's left shoulder. Athena stood on her right. Bronte took a step toward the final man. He reached behind him as if moving for a weapon.

"Really?" Athena sounded incredulous. "You think you have a chance against her?"

The man paused, looked at Bronte, lowered his hands, and ran.

"I think that's our cue. Let's get out of here." Athena took Bronte's hand.

Bronte looked at their joined hands and then from Galen to Athena. It was probably good her legs were coated in metal because she wasn't sure human flesh would hold her, they were shaking so badly. Her stomach felt like an out of control roller coaster, and her feet like lead.

"Not the time to fall apart." Galen slapped Bronte hard on the back. "Hold onto her hand like a lifeline if you need to, but pull it together. They're scared of you now, but they won't be if you start blubbering in the middle of the street."

"She saved your ass. Mind your manners." Athena stared daggers at Galen.

"You should have left me for dead." Galen started up the street, seemingly unconcerned about being attacked again.

The sight of Galen defeated and alone spurred Bronte into action. "Come on. We can't let her walk us all into a trap. Let's get our supplies and get home."

Galen was badly bruised, but she insisted she was fine. She repeatedly refused to allow Athena to look her over. They had no choice but to carry on. With three of them, carrying the supplies they'd stashed was a much easier task. They took precautions making their way back to the warehouse. Was their home still a safe sanctuary given their latest encounter with Bard's men? How long until they were discovered? Galen assured them no one was following them. Bronte wasn't sure how she could be so certain, but she was exhausted and ready to be safely back inside the warehouse, so she was willing to believe her. She couldn't hear anything or anyone nearby, but the range of her enhanced hearing did have limits.

Athena seemed willing to trust Galen as well. Once they made it back and deposited all they'd collected, she changed out of her dirty clothes and crawled into her makeshift bed. Bronte changed her own clothes as quietly as possible so she didn't disturb Athena.

She lay back on her bed and stared at the high industrial ceiling. She held her hand in front of her and watched as she turned it from flesh to metal and back again. She looked to Athena sleeping a few feet away. She could picture Bard's man raising his boot to slam on Athena's body. Tears rolled down her cheeks.

Athena loved to tease her about being a superhero, but when it counted she'd been unable to do anything to help her friends. Even when she finally got off the sidelines she wasn't sure she'd been in control of the decision to jump into action. What did that make her? Was she a host body to an artificial intelligence? A half human, half machine? Would there come a day when the zeptobots no longer needed her? And as a human, was she the kind of coward who would watch people she cared about get hurt?

Her shirt felt too tight and the air too thin. She practically flew out of bed. Was flying something else she could do now? Sitting with the fear wasn't going to do her any good. She set off to find Spero. Work had always been a balm. Her parents had always accused her of being a single focus machine dedicated to science. If only they could see her now.

Chapter Twelve

Bard leaned her head back against the hot cedar planks of her private sauna and closed her eyes. She heard the door open but didn't bother pulling a towel over herself. If her guests were offended by her nakedness they could wait outside.

Someone cleared their throat. Bard didn't open her eyes right away. They could wait. She heard the nervous shuffling of feet. When did she begin to crave the ability to manipulate others? She could string along her guest's discomfort or end it instantly. It was heady.

Bard smiled and opened her eyes. Her three top scientists, Alpha, Beta, and Gamma, stood sweating before her. One of Antonio's men, a new hire, waited stoically by the door.

"You have good news." It wasn't a question.

"Yes, ma'am." Alpha looked nervously from one colleague to the other. "We think we do. No, we do. The program works. The one initiated in Subject One has been refined."

"Explain." Bard retrieved her towel and sandals. The scientists scrambled after her as she exited the sauna.

"It's autonomous and undetectable. We can launch it on any device, and it runs in the background inertly until activated." Alpha looked more confident the longer he spoke.

"You've eliminated the need for human operators?" Bard pulled on underwear and pants.

"Yes, ma'am. Once it's installed, which can be done remotely, we can control it like any other piece of software." Beta pushed his glasses up his nose with shaky hands.

A thrill of energy moved from Bard's toes to her chest. She felt like a live wire. "Have you solved the targeting problem?" She finished dressing and headed for her office. The others scrambled after her once again.

"We can pick anyone from anywhere and manipulate their emotions until they do exactly what we want them to do. And they won't even know they're being played." Gamma's eyes gleamed like Antonio's.

Bard shivered. She knew what they were doing, but she preferred euphemisms and insinuation. "I do not reward overconfidence. Tell me, Gamma, have you delivered a working zeptobot prototype as well?"

Gamma swallowed visibly. "No, ma'am." He didn't make eye contact.

"Would you like us to commence with a test run to show proof of concept to our investors?" Alpha stepped forward. He glared at Gamma as he did.

Bard nodded. "Bring me proof of a twenty percent increase in consumer purchases in the product areas we identified."

"Very good. Two thousand should give us plenty of data. Will that be all?" Alpha started to back away.

"No." Bard crossed her arms. "Zeptobots, Alpha. You've had more than enough time. Septimus is going to stay with you. Perhaps he can provide the motivation you're missing." Bard waved to the man, whose muscle-to-man ratio didn't look possible.

Septimus pointed to himself and then trotted across the room to Bard's side. "I'm still getting used to the name. Until a week ago I was Kevin."

"That life is done now. You work for me, Septimus. Do you understand the job?" Bard turned on her newest employee. It was annoying she had to crane her neck to yell at him.

"Of course, boss. I'm your go-to, number seven." Septimus clapped Bard on the shoulder. "You need me to scare these scientist fellas? Whatcha say, boys, shall we get to work?" Septimus flung his arms around Alpha and Beta and pulled them into a tight embrace.

Bard wasn't sure she liked Septimus's disregard for authority, but his intimidation game was on point. Bard shooed Gamma after the other three. After they left she asked Decimus to find Antonio. She didn't need to wait long for her right-hand man to appear in her doorway.

"Is it ready?" Antonio had never been big on small talk.

"They're starting the commercial testing on the emotion program now." Bard poured two drinks and handed one glass to Antonio.

"And what about the other?" Antonio looked at Bard over the rim of his glass with a raised eyebrow.

"Getting housewives and men looking for their lost youth to max out their credit cards will make us rich and keep our investors happy. It might even keep my father out of this office for the rest of his life, but it's not what I really want. I want control." Bard swirled her drink and took a sip.

"Control comes from fear." Antonio took a seat in one of the armchairs by the fireplace.

"Then we'll tell them what to be afraid of." Bard joined Antonio and clinked glasses. "And we'll be ready, as the only saviors from the things that scare them most."

Antonio looked impressed. "You're starting to sound like me. I wasn't sure you had it in you. It will be a pleasure ruling the world with you. Once you get my zeptobot enhanced soldiers, you'll be untouchable." Antonio downed the last of his drink and left as quietly as he'd come in.

Left alone with her thoughts, Bard gave Antonio some thought. Had she become the same as him? Maybe she was worse. She knew the crippling fear that stole reason and rational action. She'd felt it as a child when she thought of disappointing her father. What would that child think of her actions now? She pushed that thought aside. It didn't matter. She was doing what must be done, for the company and the world. Better for the world to see all there was to be scared of and turn to her to ease their burden. She would, after all, be a benevolent ruler. Unbidden, a fleeting thought of Bronte Scales entered her mind. She poured another drink. Even grand masters had to sacrifice a few pawns in pursuit of the end goal, and if killing everyone who'd escaped from that lab was necessary, so be it. Alone in her office, she let her own fear wash over her. She played out every catastrophic scenario she could think of.

"No." She slammed her glass on her desk. "My plan is perfect."

But in the back of her mind, like a skipping record, she heard... what if, what if, what if...

Chapter Thirteen

Since they'd returned from their two-day extreme camping trip, Athena was at loose ends. The warehouse felt more like sharing space with four strangers than it had at any time since they'd moved in. Galen was still recovering from the assault and spent most of the day resting. Despite her objections, she'd finally allowed Athena to examine her. She'd been more bruised and battered than broken, but she was hardly in fighting shape. Athena also suspected she hadn't been successful in procuring the drugs she'd likely been after and was now suffering from emotional input overload and possible drug withdrawal on top of her physical ailments.

Spero had been working day and night using the materials she and Bronte had brought him. He barely stopped long enough to eat let alone interact with anyone else in the group, although his interactions were tricky at the best of times, so Athena wasn't sure if she was relieved to not have to worry about the screen. And then there was Bronte. Since they'd returned, she was as emotionally impenetrable as that metal exoskeleton of hers.

Bronte had made her feel safe and cared for in the scariest circumstances of her life and now she was as distant as if they barely knew each other. This from a woman who had held her all night like Athena was the only thing that mattered. The same woman who had thrown a man through the air like a rag doll because he'd been threatening Athena harm. The same woman she barely knew.

Athena didn't expect the pit of loneliness that had encroached on all the warm, fuzzy feelings she'd started to associate with Bronte. Feelings anchored you in place and stagnation wasn't something she tolerated. But that was before she'd been kidnapped and her life had turned into a high-wire act orchestrated by a tutu-clad armadillo. That was before Bard and superpowers. Now she didn't know what she could and couldn't tolerate because she'd been shot at and was living in a warehouse with three people she barely knew.

She wanted to be pissed at Bronte for pulling away and shutting her out. She would have traveled that road if not for how lost Bronte looked. Whatever was haunting Bronte's thoughts had her wading through some murky waters. As a nurse, Athena knew a thing or two about thinking through thorny issues and sorting through information overload. If only Bronte had reached out instead of pulling inward, maybe she could help. Athena didn't know her well enough to push, but she realized she'd like to know her better, despite her current frustration.

"Enough already." Was talking to herself a bad sign? She shrugged. Too late now. "You three, time for a family meeting." She walked toward their meeting area.

No one turned around or paid any attention. Athena whistled. It was a skill she'd learned as a child, practicing for hours in her room. It seemed like the kind of skill a brave, adventurous girl would have and so she'd developed it in case she was ever that kind of child. Today it was everything she needed and more.

"I said, family chat. Move your asses."

This time she had everyone's attention. Whether they were interested in what constituted a family chat or were hoping to avoid another ear-piercing whistle, she didn't care. They were headed her way. She pointed everyone to the spools they'd been using as chairs. She thought of this as the command center and it was time for a planning session.

"It's time we talked. We can't stay hidden here forever. Spero, are you making progress over there?" Athena forced herself to look him in the eye and not give in to her fear of his screen.

Spero nodded, looking bored. He didn't always do things the way Athena would have liked, but he was consistently true to himself. She liked that about him.

"Bronte and I learned there was other research happening at the hospital. Those participants were enrolled and allowed to leave at the end of their time. We heard someone came out of a study saying something called a 'puppy bear' was talking to her through the television. Galen, any idea what that means?" Athena turned so she had a better look at Galen sitting next to her.

Galen looked at the floor. "Yes."

The room was completely silent and everyone stared at Galen.

"You want to expand on that?" Bronte's voice was hard.

"You and Spero weren't the only ones on that restricted floor as you saw, and that floor wasn't the only one used as part of the research division of the hospital. Verstrand's developing a program. It fucks with emotions." Galen fidgeted with something on the ground with her shoe.

"Like what Spero can do?" Athena looked warily at Spero's screen.

Galen looked at Spero as well. "Yes and no. I don't know all of it. I only know my part. Think of it this way. When Spero blasts you and you're angry or scared, you act and think in certain ways, right?"

Athena and Bronte nodded. Spero still looked bored. Maybe he knew this already.

"Imagine if what Spero does was more subtle and happening all the time." Galen looked from Bronte to Athena.

"She could get people to do whatever she wanted." Bronte balled her metallic fists. "Why did she need Spero and why did she need me?"

Galen sighed. "I don't know how you fit in. I honestly don't. Spero was a human driver for the original prototype. It couldn't run without human operators. But they needed a certain kind of person. Brilliant, creative, morally flexible, and not uncomfortable with the idea of hurting people for the greater good."

All eyes turned to Spero.

"Who the hell are you, man?" Bronte put voice to the question swirling through Athena's head. "You've got cash and weapons stashed in a cemetery and you were picked for this project."

Spero pulled a notebook from his pocket and wrote quickly. *I'm nobody. I don't exist.*

"You'll have to do better. You exist to me." Bronte clapped him on the shoulder and turned back to Galen.

Athena didn't think Bronte saw the look that crossed Spero's face, but she did. His screen was blank, but the part of his face that was visible was full of emotion. Appreciation maybe. Awe, happiness. When was the last time that someone insisted he was seen? Based on his reaction it had been a while. Bronte had given Spero a gift, even if she had no idea. Superhero indeed.

"You said you had a part in Bard's program." Athena gently prodded. They could circle back to Spero. It was best to let him process for a minute before they pushed.

This time Galen looked skyward. "You know how I can 'hear' emotions?" She looked at Athena with a pleading look.

Was she hoping Athena understood? Could fill in the blanks? Would absolve her of something? Offer forgiveness?

Athena nodded. "You can sense others' emotions. They overwhelm you sometimes."

"Well, can you imagine how valuable that skill is when someone wants to manipulate emotions? Especially if they don't want anyone to know they're being manipulated? I was forced to sit in on thousands of hours of research visits while they perfected their program. I'm the reason it works." Galen dropped her head into her hands.

"Can you fill in a few more details?" Athena looked around the circle at each face.

"If they wanted someone to feel joy after watching some stupid commercial and be more likely to buy whatever it was selling, they couldn't ask the person if they felt happier than they should. So they used me. I could feel them fucking with every feeling those poor bastards had." Galen wrung her hands.

"What was in it for you? Why would you agree to be part of that?" Athena sat straighter.

"The research volunteers weren't forced. That part was above board. I doubt the consent form asks them to be part of an evil asshole's plan to fuck the world, but they weren't like Spero and Bronte. I asked to be in charge of the restricted floor. Another doctor couldn't tell if the patients were in pain, or scared, or dying. I intervened where I could, when I could without being caught by the basilisks. It was the least I could do. And for me, do you really want to know what I got out of it?" Galen crossed her arms.

Athena didn't need Galen to say it. She'd alluded to the special circumstances of her employment back at the hospital and explained why she sought relief from drugs. It made sense that Bard would supply her with easy access. It kept her under her thumb. What Athena didn't know was whether now that she was on her own, Galen posed a risk to the rest of them.

"What was she trying to accomplish with all the testing?" Bronte looked thoughtful.

Galen shrugged. "All the tests I saw had to do with shopping or making healthy choices like wearing sunscreen. But I can tell you, I hear a lot of emotional turmoil in the world and Bard's not going to make people feel good if she wants real power."

"That's awfully cynical," Athena said.

"Doesn't mean it's not true." Galen looked at Athena. She looked sad. "I'm sure she's excited to make a lot of money, but I'm willing to bet she has something else planned for all the mind games. She's incredibly smart, seems to have embraced her villain side, and is hotter than fuck."

Athena sat straighter. "What does her being hot have to do with anything?"

Galen cocked an eyebrow. "I'm painting a picture. She's an evil skinbag, but the packaging is nice to look at. It'll make it easier for her to roll it out."

"Not my taste." Bronte looked toward Athena. "We need to figure out what the rest of her plan is." She got to her feet and paced behind her chair. She was pulsing metal to skin and back again. It was beautiful. "And how the zeptobots fit in. And the basilisks. Who were they? Do you know?"

"Research subjects, I think. At least some of them. I think there were more security guards mixed in, or maybe some of Bard's muscle. Whatever they were, they didn't seem to act of their own accord. Those screens they looked into? I saw one go haywire one day. That poor basilisk was hooting like an owl, trying to do backflips, attacking any green basilisk it saw, and sobbing loudly. The real security was down there fast and took the poor bastard away. I don't know what happened to him. I also never figured out what the neon purple ones were. They might have been robots or spies, for all I know." Galen shrugged.

"Two things are true here, Galen. Bard saw an opportunity with you and took advantage and you made the choices you made, and they're done. The program doesn't work because of you. Did you have a part to play, yes, but it would have been perfected regardless. You said Bard's brilliant." Bronte leaned over and patted Galen's knee. "There's one villain and she's not in this room."

"Not letting me completely off the hook?" Galen cocked an eyebrow.

"You were my doctor while I was sedated against my will for a year." Bronte shrugged.

Galen picked at one of her fingernails. "Fair enough. I am sorry about that. You too, Spero."

"Okay, so where does this leave us?" Athena slapped her hands on her knees.

"I'm going after Bard. I'm getting my research back." Bronte stopped pacing and looked at Athena. She was all metal now.

"No." Athena and Galen echoed each other. Spero shook his head.

Bronte threw her hands up. "You heard Galen. She's planning something terrible. She wanted my blood and the zeptobots for something, and we can damn well bet it isn't for curing cancer. We have to stop her."

"Do you even know how to fight? Cause when Bard's men were kicking our ass you didn't look like you'd ever thrown a punch." Galen snorted.

Athena slapped Galen's arm.

"What? It's true. Metal skin isn't going to do her any good against Bard's men if she's unconscious because she swings her arm like a wet noodle. Bard's protected by the Ten Romans. Their leader is a very scary dude named Antonio." Galen shuddered. "And the fact that they know we're still in the area isn't good. They'll double their efforts now, and that guy won't stop. Besides, what research are you going to retrieve? She's had it for a year. It's been copied, multiplied, modified, and stored in ways you can't anticipate. She has it. It's done. Time to move on."

"I'm pretty sure Antonio and I have met. He was there the day they took me from my lab." Bronte looked angry and defeated. "Are we done here?" She didn't wait for a reply before walking back to her workstation.

"What's wrong with you?" Athena rounded on Galen.

"Please, even from under my sweaty man pile I saw the way she froze when we were out on the street. If she goes after Bard she'll get herself captured or killed and probably the rest of us too. A few hurt feelings are better than a body bag." Galen stalked off too.

"You have any salt you'd like to rub in any of the open wounds?" Athena looked at Spero.

He walked off without looking at her.

"That went well." Athena ran her hands through her hair and stared at the three empty seats.

She wasn't sure which of the three she was most annoyed at. It wasn't great timing for Bronte to be considering going lone wolf. It was true Bard Verstrand needed to be stopped, but none of them were capable of doing it on their own. The question was how did she get the others to see what was plain to her? They needed each other, and in all likelihood, the world needed them.

CHAPTER FOURTEEN

B ronte sat hunched over her workbench writing every detail she could remember about the building she'd shared with Verstrand Industry headquarters. Her research still had to be in Bard's office there, she hoped, and if it wasn't, a computer on that network could tell her how to find it. All she needed was a plan to get in. She didn't care what Galen said, there had to be a way to retrieve her work so that it was out of Bard's hands. If it came to it, she'd destroy it rather than let it stay with Bard. She was willing to sacrifice almost everything, even herself if it came to it, to keep Bard from misusing what she'd created. The thought of another bout of hand-to-hand combat turned her stomach given how she'd fared in the last one, but if that was the price, then she would pay it. Maybe she'd get lucky and sneak in and out undetected.

Usually Bronte was more organized during her data collection phase, but she was pressed for time and she was acting as both researcher and subject. She scribbled more notes. Her shoulders hurt. How long had she been working? She tried to get a sense of the time, but the clock was too far away to see. She'd given up wearing a watch after the first time she went metallic. Something about the alloy frizzed out her watch. She'd been careful with all other electronics since.

"You planning on stopping for dinner?" Athena leaned against Bronte's workbench.

Bronte looked to Athena and was lost in the way the light in her eyes danced like the stars reflecting off the ripples on the ocean.

Unbidden, thoughts of relationships and love crowded into her thoughts. It was foreign and spooked her. She'd never had anything resembling a relationship and the only thing she'd ever loved was her work. What must it feel like to be loved for who you are?

Athena smiled at Bronte. It was a smile she'd not seen Athena give either of the other two. What must it feel like to be loved by her? Bronte shook her head to rid herself of those thoughts.

"What did you ask?" Bronte tried to refocus.

Athena rolled her eyes, but Bronte could see she wasn't angry.

"Even when I try hard to avoid it you drive me...You're impossible." Athena took Bronte's hand. "Come with me."

"What were you going to say? Where do I drive you?" Bronte looked at their joined hands. She liked the way it looked.

"There are so many possibilities, aren't there?" Athena swung their hands and pulled her along.

"You're not going to tell me, are you?" Bronte tried to suppress a smile, with minimal success.

"I am not." Athena winked.

She led Bronte across the warehouse to the far corner where the medical suite was located. They passed the beds and equipment and tucked against the wall was a makeshift table and chairs. It was secluded enough that Spero and Galen probably couldn't see them once they sat.

"What are we doing?" Why was her stomach turning on her? Which emotions were setting her aflutter?

"Eating." Athena released Bronte's hand and pulled a bag of food from under the table. She set about laying it out. There was even a handmade battery-operated contraption that sort of resembled a candle if you squinted and used your imagination.

Bronte took a step back, away from the table. "Is this a date?"

Athena started to smile but quickly returned her expression to just shy of neutral. "You can call it whatever makes you happiest. I'm going to call it dinner if that works for you?"

Bronte nodded far too long. She probably looked silly. "Sure. Dinner is good. Why aren't the others eating with us?"

"Would you like me to invite them?" Athena looked amused.

"No." Bronte sat. "I'd rather eat with you."

"Good. Me too." Athena set the last of the food on the table and sat across from Bronte. She turned on the candle-like object with a flourish. "Spero left this on my pillow. I assume it wasn't a token of his affection."

"I wouldn't blame him if it was." Bronte ground her teeth.

"I'd prefer tokens from someone else, but she's been distant lately and buried in her work." Athena raised an eyebrow and held Bronte's gaze a beat longer than usual.

Bronte hung her head. "I shouldn't have treated you that way." She felt her face flush. She looked at Athena. "I'm sorry. I shouldn't have assumed you meant me. I can talk to Galen if you want."

"Oh good Lord, Bronte, I didn't set up all this to have dinner with her. Of course I mean you. Where have you been since we got back home?"

"I don't understand. I've been here." Bronte cocked her head to the side.

"Don't fuck with me, Dr. Zepto. The woman who held me all night so I was safe did not walk back into this warehouse." Athena looked hurt.

Bronte looked at her hands and fidgeted. Her voice was barely above a whisper. "I don't know who you're picturing me to be, but that woman doesn't exist. I'm not capable of keeping anyone safe. I'm sorry I pulled away. I'm ashamed I let you down. You've worked so hard to make me a hero."

Athena looked shocked. "What are you talking about?" She reached out and took Bronte's hand. It had turned to metal. "All clear little bots. She's in no danger."

The zeptobots retreated. "How are you able to communicate with them so easily?" Bronte stared at her hand.

"They're part of you and you and I can talk to each other just fine, so why would they be any different?" Athena rubbed her thumb across Bronte's knuckles. "You haven't let me down. Just the opposite. I was scared out there, which is a feeling I hate, and you chased that away."

Bronte shook her head. "I froze when those men were attacking you and Galen. The zeptobots took over. I did nothing. And my metal skin was what protected both of us while we slept. That wasn't me either."

Athena intertwined their fingers. "You and the zeptobots are one and the same. They're not a sentient being living in your body controlling your actions. You did those things. You made me feel safe. You fought off those men."

"Says the woman who just spoke to the zeptobots and expected them to respond. You're not a scientist. You don't know how they're working in me any more than I do." Bronte tried to pull her hand away, but Athena held tight.

"I don't care. You are still the hero of the story. Batman to their Robin."

Bronte pushed her plate away. "I appreciate what you're saying, but I know what happened."

"So do I. I was there too. You have your version of the truth, I have mine. Galen probably has yet another perspective. So who do we believe?" Athena let go of Bronte's hand but scooted her chair around the table to be closer.

"Mine. It's me we're talking about." Bronte poked at the food on her plate.

"Nope. I'm not conceding that. Until you believe in yourself, you need to trust in me. I believe in you enough for both of us. Do you trust me?"

Bronte searched Athena's face. "I trust that you believe what you're saying, even though I know you're wrong." Bronte smiled, despite herself.

Athena's face lit up. "That's okay. You don't realize you've already lost this argument. You might as well concede now."

"Is that so?" Bronte's shoulders relaxed and the knot in her stomach loosened. Athena didn't say anything, but the look on her face made Bronte's stomach do flip-flops. She decided to move to safer topics. "Why did you become a nurse? With your thirst for adventure, I'd have guessed skydiving instructor or alligator wrestler. Nursing seems too tame for you."

Athena rested her elbows on the table, her chin on her hands, and leaned forward like she was about to tell Bronte a juicy bit of gossip. "If you think nursing's tame, you should swing by the emergency department on the weekend of a full moon during the summer."

"Now I'm picturing you battling werewolves and vanquishing demons under a blood moon." Bronte started to reach across the table to wipe a smudge on Athena's face but stopped herself. She handed her a napkin instead, her hands a little shaky.

"It's not so different than that." She took the napkin and caressed Bronte's hand as she did so. "But you asked why I became a nurse. I did it for my uncle, Vasileios." Athena's gazed looked far away, looking upon a moment of sadness.

"Was that what he wanted for you?" This time Bronte was courageous enough to reach across the table. She took Athena's hand.

Athena shook her head still looking burdened by unshed tears. "He wanted me to see the world. Of everyone in my family, he understood me the best. He'd sit for hours with me in my room and tell me stories of adventure and excitement awaiting me on the other side of the door while I was too anxious to set foot outside. He never judged me or made me feel weak or stupid. Every time he left he'd say 'Someday, Athena, you and I are going to see the world together.' We never did get the chance."

Bronte squeezed their joined hands. "What happened to Uncle Vasileios?"

"He got sick. Terminal cancer. He should have had years to live, but things spiraled quickly. There are two things that stand out to me about that time, aside from loving and losing him. The first was that my love for him was more powerful than my anxiety and I was able to visit him every day whether he was at home or in the hospital. The second was his nurses. One of them found out about his plan to travel the world with me, so they brought the world to him." Athena paused and wiped at a stray tear.

Bronte scooted her chair around the table and sat next to her. Athena took her hand and leaned her head on Bronte's shoulder.

"The nurses brought him food from different parts of the world, magazine articles, books, videos, podcasts, anything they came across. In the end, I guess we saw the world together, because of them. I thought, giving someone a life, no matter how close to death, is more challenging, meaningful, and fulfilling than any other job I could think of. And if I were to ever get bored, there's always the werewolves and ample vacation days which I put to very good use." Athena smiled shyly at Bronte.

"Werewolves or metallic robot women who love the dimples you get when you smile."

Athena blushed. "I don't need to be bored to seek out your attention. I'm glad you know about Vasileios. Not many people do, he's always felt too important to share, but we've battled monsters and bad guys together, so perhaps nothing's off limits." Athena made a show of looking Bronte over from head to toe. She raised an eyebrow and gave a wicked grin.

This time it was Bronte's turn to blush. Why didn't the zeptobots protect her from that embarrassment? Would the metal turn pink if she were suited up? Athena saved her from spinning into a world of questions with a quick kiss to the cheek and pulling a box of donuts from the bag of food she'd prepared for their dinner. They didn't talk about Bronte's powers or zeptobots the rest of dinner, but it wasn't far from Bronte's mind. She thought about what Athena had said too, about life being challenging but meaningful. Wouldn't retaking her research and crippling the work Bard was doing help restore the lives her friends had led? She had to retrieve her research and stop Bard from using it to hurt people. Athena may never forgive her, but at least she'd be safe.

CHAPTER FIFTEEN

B ronte opened the outer door a crack. The cool air hit her and filled her lungs. It felt like the first hint of spring after a long winter. She didn't realize how stale it got in the warehouse. She opened the door a little wider and slipped out into the still, dark morning. The others were sleeping, and she took one last look at Athena, curled up in her bed, before she closed the door behind her. She was the only one who needed to put herself in danger at the hospital. The others had to stay as far from it as they could. She would keep them safe.

Their section of town wasn't lit with welcoming streetlamps and friendly porch lights. Occasionally there was the harsh glare of an industrial motion sensor light flashing on, but most had been destroyed long ago, and for any still working it was easy for Bronte to blend in with the shadows. She turned her hand to metal and experimented with finishes. She'd mastered shiny versus matte, but she wasn't sure if she could change the color from liquid mercury to obsidian. She asked the zeptobots silently. Her hand changed to a dark gunmetal gray. She whispered, "Thank you."

She set off at a run toward Bard's building. Two miles in she realized she wasn't gasping for breath. The fresh morning air felt like fuel for her lungs, and she loped easily away from the warehouse and into populated areas of town. She couldn't remember ever having run two miles in her previous life, let alone at the pace she was now setting. Another data point to record for later analysis. She covered the roughly five miles in under fifteen minutes. An unexpected wave of emotions hit when she was confronted with the building she'd spent years in, perfecting her zeptobots, expecting to produce something for the good of the world. Now, here she was, ready to break in and try to steal it all back, to prevent it being unleashed on the world. If she did, she'd prevent Bard's plot and she and the rest of the group would be free. She thought of Athena. She'd be free to resume the life she seemed built for, helping the world and finding time for adventuring too. And Spero…what would happen to him? There didn't seem to be a good path forward for Galen, who would always be overwhelmed by the excess of the world around her. Bronte ignored the melancholy that followed. Maybe life could never be normal for the three of them again. But Athena could have a chance at getting her life back. That was something.

She took a deep breath and shook out her arms. "You guys ready?" She looked at her hands. Would there be a time when that didn't feel silly? She didn't get a response, not that she was expecting one. "Okay. Let's go."

Bronte moved among the shadows to the building. She knew there was a little used door that led to the basement and only locked with a key. A key that a couple of the housekeeping staff stashed under a false rock so they didn't get locked out when they came out for illicit smoke breaks. It was insanely against the rules and all protocol, and she was grateful for their flouting of the rules.

She found the rock and the key and let herself in. Now she needed to find a networked computer. She'd borrowed a few of the supplies Spero had requested, but as soon as she hacked in the threat would be detected. Her time would be limited. She wasn't worried about being discovered. Athena had told her she was a hero. She could fight her way out. She had to. There was a lot depending on her success.

If she wasn't able to get back to the warehouse, she'd left a note for the others. Her plan was to leave any data she recovered in a safe location for them to retrieve, assuming she didn't get caught before she could hide it. Spero would be able to take the next steps without her. She thought of Athena and the possibility of never seeing her again. She shook her head to banish those thoughts. Now was not the time for distractions.

Bronte checked doors until she found an empty office. She locked the door behind her and booted up the computer. She plugged in Spero's thumb drive which overrode the password lock. She started searching files quickly, counting silently in her head. She figured at best she had a couple of minutes before she was discovered.

It was difficult to control the mouse because her hands were shaking so wildly. Her heart was thundering so loudly in her ears she was convinced someone was banging on the door multiple times. Her enhanced hearing wasn't helpful when her own nerves were drowning everything else out.

After what felt like hours, she found what she was looking for. The folders were labeled "The Program" and "The Army." Not terribly imaginative, but clear. She scanned them while she waited for the files to transfer to the external hard drive. Bile rose in her throat. Bard didn't intend to use her technology to sell more cell phones and dietary supplements. She was planning full-scale world domination and raising an army to do it. Using Bronte's technology. What the files contained was vomit worthy. Bronte had to stop her. She had to tell the others.

As soon as the files transferred, she deleted them from the system on the off chance this was the only copy, collected her things, turned the computer off, and peeked out the door. Three of Bard's men were running toward her. She threw the door open, hitting the closest one in the face, and ran in the opposite direction. She turned a corner and two more men awaited. Bronte lowered her shoulder and barreled through them. Her breathing was ragged. Her heart seemed to have begun beating everywhere in her body. The men tried to grab her, but her metallic skin was slippery and difficult to grasp. She burst free and kept running.

As she ran she tried to remember where the exits were. Keeping calm while being chased like a rat in a maze proved challenging. Her brain was fuzzy. Her eyesight focused down to only what was in front of her. She banged off a wall as she took a corner too quickly.

Enhanced speed wasn't an asset in a small space with tight corners. She skidded round another corner only to face two more of Bard's men. She changed direction and took a quick right down another hall. How many of them were there? Galen had called them, "The Ten Romans." Were these them? If so, she'd met seven.

Somehow she made it into the lobby of the building. It was still early so there wasn't much activity. She dropped the metal skin and walked quickly across the large space toward the door. She glanced over her shoulder. None of the seven men she'd encountered were following.

"Bronte Scales. So nice to see you again."

Bronte turned slowly. A shiver ran along her spine.

"I have nothing to say to you." Bronte stood as tall as she could. She recalled her metal skin.

"Quite a magic trick. It won't save you." Bard looked bored.

"You shouldn't have come back here." The man called Antonio was standing next to Bard. He waved his hand at something behind Bronte.

Before she could turn to see what he had indicated, a ferocious blow landed across her shoulders. It knocked her off balance and she fell to her knees. The external hard drive flew from her hands and skidded across the floor. Bard stopped it with her foot.

"And now that I have this as well as you, you've failed completely." Bard smashed the hard drive with her expensive looking snakeskin heels. Plastic shards scattered across the floor.

Bronte lunged forward and grabbed the damaged drive. She rolled away and got back to her feet. "Now what do I do with it?" She said it under her breath, but as soon as it was out of her mouth, the metal on her hands began to move. She was so surprised she almost dropped the drive. She watched in amazement as her exoskeleton expanded, enveloped the drive, and then returned to its previous shape, molded to her body.

She turned her hand over and back. Where did it go? She didn't have time to think about it before another blow hit her shoulders and another stuck her in the legs. This time, she didn't go down. She turned to face her attackers. Two more of Bard's men. Nine of ten. They each had long sticks and were swinging them expertly at her. She swung wildly as one aimed at her head. She missed. The strike clanged off her ear, bringing her once again to her knees. Once she was off her feet the two men moved in and rained down a torrent of attacks. Although her metallic skin protected her, Bronte wasn't able to get back to her feet or fend off the blows. She tried unsuccessfully to swat them away and mount a counterattack. It was painfully obvious how inept she was at hand-to-hand combat. What had she been thinking?

She fell with her face against the cool floor after a particularly brutal series of strikes. Then, as suddenly as it had begun, the assault stopped. Bronte gingerly returned to her feet and faced Bard and her attackers. She took up what she hoped was a fighting pose.

"I don't know if I admire or pity your insistence on prolonging the punishment." Bard waved something forward. "I'd like you to meet the latest product of your creation. This is Septimus, in a prototype suit. It won't be long until we've perfected your incomplete work and the suit won't be necessary. We'll inject people just as you injected yourself, and then use the program to make certain they do as they're told. And unlike you, they won't be virtually useless in a fight."

Septimus stepped into Bronte's line of sight. He was wearing a metal suit of armor that looked like next generation military tactical gear. He pulled a shield over his face that was a screen of some sort. When she looked closer there were screens on his shoulders, chest, and knees.

"Do you think you're worthy of the powers you have now?" Bard sneered at her.

Septimus's screens lit. She was overcome with doubt. It doubled her over and left her gasping for breath. She saw her hands return to their human skin. The next attacks sent searing pain through her ribs, her shoulders, and back.

"What gives you the right to wear that suit? Who are you? You're no one." Bard squatted in front of her and lifted her chin. "You're going to get the others killed. Their deaths will be your fault. It's only a matter of time before we find them."

Bard held her face toward Septimus. Bronte was powerless to stop her. The screens changed and the guilt that swept through her was more overwhelming than the doubt. Bard wasn't saying anything Bronte hadn't already thought. Of course she was right.

"Surrender now and I promise Antonio will go easy on them when he finds them. If you're cooperative, maybe I'll even let the hot little nurse go." Bard stood.

Antonio kicked Bronte onto her back. "Or maybe I won't." Antonio smiled at Bronte. The darkness in his eyes made her skin crawl.

Bronte wasn't sure whether it was the kick, the disconnect from the intensity of the screen, or Antonio's threats that got her moving again. She didn't care. She scrambled to her feet. Another blow landed hard on her shoulder. She swallowed a cry. She couldn't seem to summon the zeptobots. Had they abandoned her?

She saw one of Bard's men swing at her again. She lifted her arm to deflect the strike and this time the clang of metal on metal rang out through the lobby. She pulled her arm back and saw the familiar metal retreating as quickly as it had appeared. Another blow, another pop-up shield. She said a silent thank you and hoped the zeptobots could hear her.

Before she made it halfway to the lobby door she was knocked off her feet and she slid across the freshly waxed floor. She refocused in time to see Septimus stalking toward her with his fist cocked. Apparently fucking with emotions wasn't the only thing his fancy suit was good for.

"I really need to get out of here." Bronte scooted backward on her butt. "I need your help. I can't look at this guy or we're both screwed. Can I put you in the driver's seat?"

"No matter what you do, it will never be good enough." Bard strode toward her. "You aren't going to cure cancer and I'm going to take credit for the zeptobots. You're alone in your life and always will be."

Shame and sadness filled her. She hadn't been fast enough to avoid Septimus's screens. There were too many of them. Tears streamed down her face. She wiped at them angrily as she scrambled to get away from Septimus's pounding fists and vicious kicks.

"Help me." Bronte held up her hands.

"Are you surrendering?" Bard sounded delighted.

Bronte's legs stiffened and she was forced to her feet. She caught Septimus's next punch, twisted his arm, and threw him to the ground, where he lay stunned. She felt like a playable character in a video game.

"I wasn't talking to you." Bronte flipped Bard off as she sprinted for the door.

Once outside, she ran. She ran and kept running as far from Bard's office as she could. She passed the hospital which provided an extra surge to keep her moving. She was still miles from the warehouse and she didn't think she could make it back. The adrenaline was wearing off rapidly and as it did the pain intensified. Her field of vision started to go dark. Her limbs were fluttery, like the one time she'd passed out in middle school.

She slowed and took stock of her surroundings. She wasn't sure who had been driving their high speed sprint, but either she or the zeptobots had brought her to the coffee shop she'd visited with Athena. "All clear." As soon as the metal skin fell away so did her ability to stand. Blood flowed into her eyes and her body screamed with pain. She stumbled for the coffee shop but couldn't make it to the front door. The alleyway behind was closer. Maybe she could rest there long enough to regain some strength. She made it as far as the dumpster and collapsed. The last thing she remembered before the world went dark was the slam of a door and someone's cry of alarm.

Chapter Sixteen

Athena paced. Her jaw hurt from clenching her teeth. Her fingers ached from how tightly she'd been balling her fists. There should have been a groove from the path she paced from Bronte's workbench to the kitchen.

On this pass she slammed the note she'd found on Bronte's pillow hard on the workbench. She'd been clutching it since she discovered it this morning.

"What the fuck was she thinking?" Athena wanted to rip something in half or scream. The note seemed like a good candidate, but it was her only tie to Bronte who might be dead or have completed her mission and abandoned them.

Galen was draped across the bench. She'd been watching Athena pace for the last hour. "You know what she was thinking. If you're honest with yourself, you knew she was going to do this."

Athena opened her mouth to spit back a retort but closed it again. She turned her back on Galen and resumed her pacing.

"It's not your fault. You couldn't have stopped her if you tried." Galen pushed off the bench and stood, her arms crossed.

Athena spun around again. "Wait, you knew she was going to leave, didn't you? She had to have given some emotional clue."

Galen shrugged. "So what? There wasn't anything I could do to stop her."

"You could have told us. You could have warned us. Now we're all in danger. He could have done something." Athena pointed to Spero.

Galen jabbed a finger in Athena's chest. "I did warn you. I told you this would happen when you started playing superhero. And what did you want him to do to her? Leave her simpering in the corner for the rest of our time here? Emotionally compromise her so badly she couldn't walk out the door of her own free will?"

Athena took a stumbling step back. "No, of course not. I'd never do that to her."

"Then there's nothing any of us could have done. She set her mind and you're not allowed to use other people's...*gifts*, to control her behavior. That would make you as bad as Bard. If you're religious, pray she makes it out alive and doesn't get the rest of us killed." Galen stomped off leaving Athena alone with a storm of uncomfortable emotions.

She sat heavily at Bronte's workbench and reread the note she'd left. It was succinct and unflinching. It told them where she'd gone and left instructions in case she didn't make it back. Athena shivered. She was mad as hell, but beneath the anger she was scared. Scared and more than a little hurt.

Athena dropped her head into her hands. The flirtation and superhero university had been all well and good, but now real feelings were inconveniently bubbling up uninvited. She took a deep breath, then another for good measure. Of course she was worried about Bronte. They were friends. Good friends. Friends who felt things for each other. Bronte was a friend she wouldn't mind kissing. That happened sometimes with friends, surely. It didn't have to mean anything, right? When all this was over, she'd be free to carry on with her freewheeling life, seizing the next adventure waiting just over the horizon.

She thought of her scavenger hunt with Bronte and her stomach clenched. "Pull it together." She stood so quickly she nearly knocked the stool over. She cast around for a destination to take her mind off Bronte past and present. Spero caught her eye. She headed his way.

"Anything I can help with?" Athena put her hand on Spero's back as she looked over his shoulder. He looked nonplussed but took half a step to the side so she could join him anyway. "This is the computer you've been building, right?"

Spero nodded. He pointed to the list he'd made for them. He'd crossed two things off the list. He pointed from the list to the computer and made a face.

"What happened to those?"

Spero pointed across the warehouse to Bronte's workbench. It didn't escape Athena's notice that he pointed with his middle finger.

"You think Bronte took them?" She looked at the list again. A thumb drive and an external hard drive. Exactly what you might need to store data you planned to steal.

Spero ignored her question.

"Why don't you write to us more often instead of playing this inefficient game of charades?" She still didn't get an answer. Spero had returned to work on the computer.

"Are you almost done?" She leaned closer and pretended she knew what he was doing.

He held his thumb and index finger a hair away from each other. He never looked at her.

"That's good. I'm not exactly sure what we'll be able to do with this once you're done, but you seem to know what you're doing. What can I do to help?" Trying to figure out Spero's unique communication method was already making it harder to focus exclusively on Bronte's well-being.

Spero pointed to a toolbox a few feet away. He didn't give any more indication which tool he needed. Athena guessed. She was wrong. She tried again. Spero glared. Third time was not the charm.

"Do I need to start asking for hints? Save us both some time and point me in the right direction." Athena crossed her arms.

He stared at her for a long time. Finally, he smiled and mimed the shape of the tool he wanted.

"Was that so hard?" Athena handed him what he needed and pulled over a stool to watch him work.

They both jumped when what sounded like a cell phone rang. The sound filled the quiet warehouse. As far as Athena knew, none of them had cell phones. The fact that one was ringing now set her on edge. The noise was coming from their sleeping quarters, and given how startled Spero looked, it wasn't his.

Galen ran toward the sound and rummaged through a bag next to her bed. Athena felt like screaming at her. Phones could be traced. How could Galen be angry at Bronte for endangering them when she'd had a cell phone under her pillow? Galen answered the phone cautiously. She listened intently for a few seconds, then hollered to Athena. "It's for you."

Athena pointed to herself. "For me? Who's calling for me?" Her heart rate rose so fast she was a little dizzy. Why did anyone know she was here? Why would they call Galen's phone looking for her?

Galen waved the phone. "Says her name's Doris and it's an emergency."

Athena made it across the warehouse so quickly perhaps she had superpowers herself after all. "Doris, what's wrong?"

"Hello to you too, hon." Doris's voice was quiet and strained on the other end of the line. "I hope it's okay I called. I heard that you went and rescued your lady doctor friend so I thought she might be able to get in touch with you. I had to bribe some of the friends she sees about pharmacologics to get a moment on their phone. I didn't know how else to get in touch with you. But there's plenty of folk around me, so I should be quick."

"I'm glad you called. What can I do for you?" Athena wanted to jump through the phone and speed things along. She didn't care how Doris got Galen's number.

"Well, I think I have a personal item that belongs to you. Seems you misplaced it." Doris's voice dropped even lower.

Athena didn't say anything for a few beats. "I don't know what you mean."

"Hon, I think you lost something, and you need to come and collect real quick. It's shiny and metal. I'm sure you'll recognize it when you see it."

She couldn't help the sob that escaped. "Oh my God, she's there. Is she okay?" How could she be if Doris was the one calling her for help?

"Well, your item seems to be a bit damaged, and you know how heavy it is, so if you've got someone who can help you carry it, I'd suggest you bring them along. You'll be owing me extra for the storage fee of course. I know it's not worth much, but I suppose it means a lot to you." Doris's voice was soft with understanding.

"Thank you, Doris. You really are a peach. The doc and I will be there as soon as we can." Athena waved Galen over. Suddenly her stomach lurched. "Oh, and, Doris, she's alive, right?" The words nearly clogged in her throat and choked her.

"Just barely, hon. At least from what I can tell. I wouldn't spend too much time taking in the sights."

As Doris signed off Athena could hear her yelling at whoever it was she'd borrowed the phone from. Likely some of the drug dealers Galen frequented.

"From your excitement and worry, I assume there's goodish news? Do I need to put my ass on the line to clean up a mess I had nothing to do with?" Galen was calmly eating an apple.

"Get over yourself. Bronte put her ass on the line to clean up *your* mess when she could have left you to get beaten in the street, since you so kindly helped keep her sedated for a year. Grab your kit, she needs us." Athena took the apple and threw it in the trash. Galen grumbled but followed her. Athena called out their plan to Spero who grunted but didn't look away from his work.

"If someone's coming to hurt us, can you sense that?" Athena tossed medical supplies quickly into a bag to bring with them.

"Maybe. Probably." Galen was spinning casually on a medical stool. "Attackers usually have heightened emotions. Nervousness, excitement, anger, that kind of thing. Most of them stand out from the crowd."

"Good. Even more reason for you to come with me." Athena swung the bag over her shoulder and pointed to the door. "And you owe us."

"Owe you for what?"

"Being a terrible doctor, that cell phone, sneaking around and putting us all in danger, your terrible attitude. You pick." Athena held the door for Galen.

Galen stared at her for an uncomfortably long time. "Fine. I'm driving."

Athena stopped short. "Driving? Driving what?"

"Does it matter?" Galen strolled out the door like she wasn't a wanted woman. "How were you planning on getting her back here?"

"I hadn't figured that out yet, but we managed before." Athena scrambled to keep pace as they went around the back of the warehouse. She glared at Galen's back. "Have you always been such an asshole?"

Galen's steps faltered. Her shoulders slumped. "No." As quickly as she'd paused, she righted herself. She stopped and pointed to what was apparently their ride.

"Then why now?" Athena hesitated next to the car. It didn't look like it would hold together in a strong breeze much less actually carry people anywhere. She didn't ask where she got it, nor why she hadn't mentioned it before. She doubted Galen would answer.

"I've been subjected to every nearby person's emotions since I was a child. I never asked for this." Galen started the car and floored it away from the warehouse.

"And now you have drugs to keep the feelings away. What do you think will happen if you let them come back?" Athena braced on the dashboard as Galen rounded a corner. She was driving on the way back.

"I don't have to guess. I know." Galen squeezed the wheel tightly.

"And that scares you." Athena wasn't asking.

"It would scare you too." Galen looked at Athena. Her eyes were full of fear and pain.

"Maybe people would surprise you after all this time."

Galen snorted. "About as likely as you and I making babies together. I still get glimpses, remember? I can't shut it all out."

From Galen's amused smile Athena hadn't been able to hide her displeasure at Galen's baby making suggestion.

"Why did you become a doctor if you dislike people so much? You're around them all the time." Athena braced herself again as Galen turned hard around another corner.

Galen paused so long Athena was sure she wouldn't answer. Finally, she licked her lips and blew out a breath. "I can't be the only person like me in the world. The chances of that are infinitesimally small. Nobody was there to help me as a child, but maybe I can help others like me. Bard and people like her collect misfits and abnormalities and use them. She used me, but I was using her too. She brought me Spero and Bronte. The other patients weren't like them, like us. They signed up for those modifications, but if I could have helped them too, I would have."

"You're still a mystery to me." Athena studied Galen carefully. "You expect the worst from people but there seems to be a heart beating in there still." Athena pointed at Galen's chest. "I have hope for you yet." She softened her words with a smile.

"More evidence of the worst of humanity awaits us, I suspect." The car screeched to a halt and Galen pointed to Doris peeking around the corner from the alley behind the coffee shop.

"Let's go." Athena was out of the car and running for Doris and Bronte.

"'Bout time you showed. I'm none too popular around here. Won't let anyone out for a smoke break. I told them someone used our alley as a latrine, but that's not going to keep anyone from their nicotine much longer." Doris glanced nervously at the coffee shop back door.

"Where is she?" Athena heard her voice crack. Before long she was sure all of her would shatter.

Doris led Athena into the alley. "She's mumbling about Shakespeare taking over the world and some kind of robots. That condition she's got seems to be on the fritz, but she's alive."

Athena looked at Galen who mouthed, "Bard."

Bronte's feet were the first thing Athena saw poking out from between two ripped trash bags sitting next to the dumpster. "Oh God." Athena dropped to her knees next to Bronte. "What did she do to you?" She didn't try to stop the tears.

The zeptobots were appearing and disappearing in sporadic patches all over Bronte's body. When the metal faded from one area, bruises and blood emerged. Her face was swollen around her left eye and she had a large gash on her forehead. Athena shuddered when she thought of what else was hidden beneath Bronte's clothes.

"Let me check to make sure she's okay to move." Galen put her hand on Athena's shoulder. Her voice was soft and her touch reassuring.

Athena was incapable of doing anything to assist, and she stumbled back to make room for Galen to check Bronte over. She hated feeling helpless. It made her feel trapped. She'd been here before, watching from the sideline as everyone else was brave and capable and alive.

Fuck this. You're never scared of what you'll find under your stethoscope. Athena took a deep breath and a wobbly step closer to Bronte. Who was she kidding with that pep talk? Her legs were shaking, and her heart felt like it was being crushed by a monster truck.

"Over the next few days, she's going to lean on you. She trusts you and you're a hell of a lot stronger than any of us. Don't forget it." Galen patted Athena on the shoulder then stood. "I think we should be safe to move her. Looks like the car will fit back here. And if not, it's not my car anyway."

Athena decided now was not the time to inquire as to the true owner of the hunk of junk they'd risked their lives in on the way over. As long as it transported them back, she would happily remain ignorant.

She took Bronte's hand. "Come back to me, please."

Bronte's eyes fluttered. Athena squeezed her hand tighter.

"That's it. You're safe now. You're safe with me."

The metal patches were still appearing at random on Bronte's skin. They were larger than before and staying in place for longer periods before disappearing. Athena put her hand over one that formed on Bronte's cheek.

"I'll watch over her now. You've done well. You must need to heal too." Athena fought the urge to jerk her hand away when the metal extended away from Bronte's skin and partially covered her hand. Were the zeptobots testing her? Confirming her identity? The zeptobots turned her hand so her palm was to the sky. As the metal withdrew, she was left holding Spero's external hard drive. "What the fuck?"

Athena didn't have time to question the zeptobots further, not that they would answer. They retreated completely, revealing the full level of violence from Bronte's encounter with Bard. Athena reached out and ran her fingers along Bronte's cheek tracing a path free of blood and bruising.

Bronte's eyes scrunched and then opened slowly. She looked around wildly but calmed as soon as her eyes locked on Athena's.

"I'm so glad you're alive. I've been worried." Athena took Bronte's hand once more.

Bronte laughed and then grimaced. "I feel half dead. You're not mad?"

"We'll get to that. First let's get you home." Athena pointed to Galen's car backing down the alley. She helped Bronte to her feet.

"I seem to have a habit of ending up unconscious and waking to your face."

"Should I start calling you Snow White?" Athena got Bronte settled into the back seat and ran around to the other side. She waved to Doris, who quickly disappeared inside.

Bronte made a face. "I'd rather be a dwarf."

"I don't remember any of them being woken by a kiss." Galen glanced over her shoulder before flooring it out of the alley. "If you're into that sort of thing of course."

"I am." Bronte said it quietly. Almost too quietly for Athena to hear. Her face, the parts not covered in evidence of battle, reddened and she looked away from Athena and out the window.

"I'll remember that if you knock yourself out for a third time." Athena couldn't help but tease.

"Seems treacherous for just a kiss." Bronte looked disappointed.

"You're a scientist used to solving tough problems. I'm sure you'll devise something better." It seemed strange to be joking after the emotions of the day, but she and Bronte would be flirting and joking if Bronte hadn't nearly gotten herself killed. The banter, even more than looking at her face to face, made Athena believe Bronte was alive and coming back home.

Bronte leaned her head back against the seat. Athena wasn't sure if it was from frustration or pain. She took her hand. "Pain?"

"It's manageable. We're almost there, right?" Bronte inhaled sharply as they hit a pothole.

That told Athena more than Bronte seemed willing to share. She was worried about what Bronte wasn't saying and what Galen might have missed in her quick assessment. Their limited medical supplies also concerned her. Although they had a medical exam room and more supplies than was normal for a partially torched warehouse, it was far from a fully stocked clinic. If Bronte needed critical care intervention, they were in trouble.

Bronte had her eyes closed and was gripping the door armrest so tightly her knuckles were white. Her face was pale and strained. Athena didn't want to fret. She didn't want to feel the panic and heartache, but her emotions seemed completely outside her control. She could fool herself by saying she'd be worried about Galen or Spero too if they were injured, but deep down she wouldn't feel like this. The problem was she didn't want this. Flirting and fun, sure, but not feelings real enough to leave her helpless when confronted with an injured Bronte. Caring that much meant settling. It meant stasis. It meant giving up on the little girl who'd longed for adventure and courage. No one was worth that. She looked at Bronte again. No one was worth that, right?

Chapter Seventeen

Bronte was tired of recovering. She'd been spending her days mostly in bed, the pain from her defeat deterring her from long stretches of movement. She was also ashamed of getting her ass kicked by Bard and her men and for going it alone when her friends had warned her against it. Now here she was, beaten and broken in more ways than one. Hiding in bed seemed a better option than facing the others, even if the pain had receded a little.

Even the zeptobots seemed mad at her. She'd tried to call them a few days after her confrontation with Bard and metal had only covered her middle fingers. Her human roommates had been more subtle, but she knew they were equally displeased, especially Athena.

Something sharp poked her in the right butt cheek. She squirmed onto her left side. The same sensation hit her on the left side. She gingerly got out of bed. "What the hell?" She tried to look behind her but her ribs were still too sore for twisting. Another sharp pain, this time on the right side. She spun instinctively and rubbed the tender spot. It was covered in metal. "Is this some kind of punishment? I thought we were on the same side."

Bronte was about to get back in bed when Athena caught her eye. Her spin from the last painful jab had brought Athena directly into her line of sight. "Are you meddling? We're going to have to talk about boundaries." Her answer came in the form of two quick jabs to both ass cheeks. "Enough. You made your point. I'm moving. Now put on your headphones or something. I don't need you listening to everything."

She approached Athena cautiously. Since she'd returned to the warehouse Athena had been polite, professional, and caring, but in a way you'd expect from a nurse. Bronte missed the flirting and connection they'd had before her misadventures.

"Hi. Do you mind if I join you?" Bronte didn't immediately sit on one of the overturned crates they'd made into kitchen chairs.

"You're up." Athena's face was inviting before she seemed to remember she was angry and shuttered her expression closed. "The kitchen's available to everyone. Have a seat."

Bronte's mouth was dry. She licked her lips. "I'm sorry I went against Bard alone. I know none of you wanted me to. It was stupid and reckless."

"Yes, it was." Athena nodded but her expression remained unreadable.

"What can I do to make it up to you? I miss you." Bronte didn't like the desperation she heard in her voice.

"I've been with you every day since I found you half dead in that alley. I've made sure you didn't end up dead-dead. What more do you want from me?" Athena's eyes were full of fury and pain.

Bronte leaned away from Athena's intense emotions. "I want things to be like they were before." She said it quietly and looked at the floor.

"And yet, you come over here and apologize for being reckless. Do you know what apology I want to hear?" Athena stood and folded her arms around herself.

Bronte shook her head.

"I want you to apologize for making me worry. I want to hear that you're sorry for leaving me to wonder if you were dead or Bard had you buried in a deep dark hole running God only knows what experiments on you. I want to know that you thought for one second how I would feel because I'm not used to caring so much about someone else. You were all I could think about when I didn't know if you were okay. But you're sorry for being reckless and probably that you didn't succeed." Athena turned away from Bronte. Her breathing was ragged.

Bronte didn't say anything for a few beats. Finally, she stepped forward and put her hand on Athena's shoulder. "I'm sorry I scared you. I should have been more considerate of your feelings. You're all I thought about. I wanted to get my research back, yes, but I also hoped if I did, we'd all be free. Then you could go on the adventures you love so much. You wouldn't be trapped here."

Athena looked to the ceiling and sighed. She didn't pull away from Bronte's touch. "The only time I've felt trapped since we got here was when I found you in the alley, unconscious. I was so worried about you that I wasn't able to help you. That's not who I am. That's not who I want to be."

Bronte pulled her hand away from Athena. Why did her body feel too heavy to carry? "You don't want to be someone who cares?"

"I don't want to be someone paralyzed by fear. I spent too much of my childhood too anxious to do anything. I can't go back there." Athena turned and put her hand on Bronte's face.

"Then don't. Be here. With me. We don't have to decide what that means or what it looks like tomorrow or the next day." Bronte put her hand over Athena's and intertwined their fingers.

Athena looked conflicted. "I can't even ask you not to scare me like that again because you're…" Athena indicated Bronte's body with her free hand. "You're all of this. It's part of your damn superhero job description." She freed her hand and snaked it around the back of Bronte's head. She pulled her close and kissed her.

Bronte quickly got over her surprise. Athena's lips were soft and insistent. Bronte wrapped her arms around Athena's waist and melted further into the kiss.

"Just to clarify, I'm not a superhero." Bronte mumbled against Athena's lips.

"Shut up." Athena smiled.

Athena ran her tongue along Bronte's upper lip. Bronte's small gasp of pleasure seemed to be all the encouragement Athena needed. When their tongues met Bronte pulled Athena tighter. Athena shifted so she was straddling Bronte's thigh. She let out a quiet moan as their tongues met again and Athena's sex connected with Bronte's leg. Bronte could feel the heat of Athena's center. She fought the urge to pull Athena against her and urge her to go further. Bronte didn't have a lot of experience with kissing, but she couldn't imagine it being better than this.

She was feeling it everywhere, and the longer they kissed the more blood flow her body seemed determined to direct between her legs. She moved her hands lower down Athena's back until they were resting on her ass. Her arousal shot through the roof. She hoped she didn't embarrass herself by coming here in the kitchen solely from kissing this Greek goddess.

"Jesus, you two would drown out the emotions of a city block. Have some consideration for the lonely and horny among us." Galen pushed through Athena and Bronte forcing them apart. Despite her dick move her smile betrayed her true feelings on the matter.

Athena winked when she caught Bronte's eye. "How does breakfast sound? We can take it back to your bed if you're still in too much pain to stand."

"Oh, for fuck's sake." Galen rolled her eyes.

"Enough out of you." Athena pointed at Galen. "You know as well as I do she's in no shape for what you're implying. I wouldn't do anything to jeopardize her recovery and I certainly wouldn't want you watching or listening in the way you do."

Galen laughed and waggled her eyebrows.

Athena flipped her off but didn't look angry.

"I'd like to try staying up a little longer. Is our table still set?" Bronte tried to keep the hopefulness from her voice. If they were alone maybe she could steal another kiss. She'd had one, now she didn't want to stop.

"Yes, all set, but I have a better plan. You get back in bed and I'll pull a chair over and keep you company for a while. Kissing is no reason to wear yourself out."

"Seems like a pretty good reason to me." Bronte grimaced as she tried to cross her arms. Her ribs were still painful.

Athena pointed toward their sleeping area. Bronte grumbled but acquiesced. She walked gingerly to her bed and lay down. The pain relief was immediate. Athena had been right, as she usually was.

"You look like you're thinking deep thoughts." Athena pulled a chair next to Bronte's bed. "This brings back some memories."

"As long as we're not invaded by the basilisks. Although I'm tired of being the one flat on my back in bed."

"Is that so? I'll tuck that away for the future." Athena raised an eyebrow.

"That's not what I meant." Bronte tried to sit but slouched back when pain shot through her shoulder and chest.

Athena gently pushed her back. "It's okay. I like a woman confident enough to top me. Now stop hurting yourself or I'm going to have to leave." Athena kissed Bronte's cheek.

"Holy hell, woman." Bronte knew her face must be fire engine red. It felt like it was an inferno.

"Something I said?" Athena got a pillow from her bed and helped Bronte prop herself up.

"Thank you. Not sure I want you to be able to see my blushing, but I like looking at you." Bronte repositioned carefully so she could see Athena more easily. "When you're not in scrubs or wearing clothes Galen buys for you, what do you wear? What does your life look like outside of this warehouse?" Bronte almost slapped herself on the forehead. "Not that I'm only interested in what you look like. That sounded really shallow. I want to know everything."

"I'll tell you, but only if you reciprocate. Deal?" Athena's eyes sparkled. She clearly liked this tit for tat.

Bronte nodded slowly. Why was she agreeing? Her life was so boring, Athena would never find it interesting.

"Let's see, despite my insistence my life is full of adventure, most of the time it's pretty boring. I love being a nurse which means long, intense hours. But when I'm not at work I love a little black dress and a pair of killer heels." Athena smiled, looking like she was drifting into a memory.

"I guess Galen forgot those on her last shopping trip." Bronte was proud her voice didn't crack like a turned-on teenage boy.

"Hard to run or fight bad guys in the heels I own. Galen did okay."

Bronte nodded. She knew Athena was teasing her and from the look of it was enjoying herself, but she couldn't help the way her body was reacting. Was it possible her insides had hijacked her circulatory system and rerouted the blood flow anywhere that ensured she remained hard and wet throughout this conversation? Now that the image of Athena in a form-fitting black dress had been introduced, it was all she could think about. Athena's classic Grecian skin and dark curls would complement the ensemble. What kind of jewelry did Athena prefer?

"Come back to me, Bronte." Athena looked like she knew full well what daydream had captured Bronte's attention. "Your turn. Spill." Athena put her elbows on her knees and rested her head in her hands, giving Bronte her full attention.

"Well." Bronte got lost in Athena's gaze. She couldn't remember anything about her life. "I'm a scientist. That's who I am and what I do."

"I bet you look hot in a lab coat. Do you ever do your experiments wearing nothing underneath that white coat?" Athena winked.

Bronte frowned. "That would be terribly unsafe."

"Never? Not even around the house? Too bad. So what does non-work Bronte wear? What do you do for fun?" Athena scooted her chair closer.

"I work. I don't think I know how to do anything else. If I'm not in the lab I usually wear jeans, a T-shirt or Henley, and boots. I don't pay much attention to fashion." Bronte looked at the small pile of clothes Galen had secured for her. They were probably more fashionable than what she had in her own closet. "The only thing I'm religious about is a haircut. What you see now is appalling. My hair is always neatly clipped. This is one year's growth. I need a pruning."

Athena had her eyes closed and a small smile on her face. "I'm taking a mental snapshot. I like a Henley, jeans, and boots. I can't wait to see you in them with your short, sharp haircut. And if you work as much as you say, I'll have to find a reason to lure you away."

"I take my work very seriously, so you better think of something good." Bronte tried for a stern look.

"Your seriousness of purpose is one of the things I like most about you. Now rest. Nurse's orders. I'll check on you in a while." Athena stood. She squeezed Bronte's hand before collecting her chair and walking away.

Bronte watched her go, missing their connection as soon as she was out of touching distance. How had they gone from barely speaking to kissing in the space of a morning? She wasn't complaining but it left her confused. She liked Athena, really liked her, but she was scared of letting her down. How could she ever be enough for a woman like her? And what if she wanted something Athena wasn't interested in? Bronte took a deep breath. No use getting so far ahead of herself. There were plenty of things to worry about but a hypothetical future involving Athena wasn't one of them. Things would work out. Or at least that's what she kept trying to tell herself. If only she was willing to believe it.

Chapter Eighteen

A thena was bored. Bronte and Spero were working, Galen was off doing things Athena didn't want to think too hard about, and she had nothing to do. No one needed a Band-Aid or a chest tube removed. There wasn't need for medication dispensing or any of the millions of other things she was confident in performing in her day-to-day as a nurse. Bronte insisted she was healed and no longer required her care. At least not medical care. It had been less than a week so either she was lying or the zeptobots were showing off.

Athena didn't like feeling useless, but whatever Bronte and Spero were working on was beyond her skill set and she wasn't interested in going on drug runs with Galen.

She pushed off her bed and stomped across the warehouse to the side door behind the medical suite. She glanced back at her roommates hard at work. They'd been tinkering with Spero's computer. As far as she knew, it wasn't operational yet, so they hadn't had a chance to look at the data from the thumb drive. Neither looked when Athena pushed out the door. Galen had told them there weren't any cameras for a block in any direction out this entrance, so they'd begun using it to soak in the sun or stand in the rain. Athena thought of it as the "patio."

Once outside she leaned against the warehouse wall and tipped her face to the sun. Before all this nonsense she'd listened to meditations instructing her in an oddly demanding yet soothing voice to imagine the sunshine flowing through various body parts in order to relax. She'd never been able to do it and that failure had stressed her out more than whatever had prompted her to turn on a meditation in the first place. But now, standing here, face to the sun, she understood. She didn't need to imagine. She could feel the sunlight dripping through her body inch by inch, releasing tension as it went.

Her ankles and feet were about to relax into a loose guitar string when the warehouse door banged open and the sunlight magic was gone. She opened her eyes and balled her fists, ready to swing at whoever had interrupted her moment. In that instant she didn't care if they were friend or foe.

Spero stood calmly, out of punching distance, staring at her.

"Are you looking for me or the sun?" Athena unclenched her fists.

He glanced at her hands. His unreadable expression never changed. He pointed at her then toward the door.

"You need me in the warehouse? Is everything okay?" Athena's heart rate increased. What if Bronte had had a setback in her recovery?

Spero patted the air with his hands in the universal sign for "calm the fuck down." He pointed at the door again.

"Why now? I was enjoying a moment." Athena looked skyward. A cloud had covered the sun. "Damnit. Your timing is terrible."

Athena waited for a reaction from Spero, but he seemed content to wait out her temper tantrum. She took one more glance at the shrouded sun, sighed, and opened the door for Spero. It wasn't that she minded the warehouse or her roommates' company, but it had been nice to have a moment for herself without any expectations.

Spero led her to his corner of the warehouse. It was still filled with a pile of what looked to Athena like junk, his DIY computer, the materials she and Bronte had collected for him, a printer, which was a new creation, and a few new things she didn't recognize.

He pointed her to a seat then turned the computer toward her so she could see the screen. On it was a photo of her and a list of demographic characteristics she didn't recognize. Apparently, he and Bronte had gotten it working.

"Who's Katrina Stevenson?" Athena leaned closer to get a better look.

Spero pointed to her, then back to the computer. He grabbed one of the passports she and Bronte had brought back from his cemetery stash and pointed between the screen and the passport.

"I don't understand. Why do I need a new name and passport?" Athena's palms were sweaty.

Athena followed Spero's glance at the door nearest his workspace. He wrapped his thumbs around each other and flapped his hands the way Athena's father had done when making a shadow bird when she'd been too scared of the dark to sleep. Spero nodded toward the door again and then tapped the passport. He tried to hand it to Athena.

"Are you saying I'd be free?" Athena tentatively reached out for the passport but didn't take it immediately.

Spero nodded. He pushed the document toward her again.

She took it and opened it. Katrina Stevenson, who looked like her, but wouldn't be anything like her, stared back. Was it that simple? Was Spero skilled enough to erase one life and create a new one so she'd be free?

"An identity is more than a new passport." Athena closed the cover on Katrina and looked at Spero.

He rolled his eye and looked offended. He handed Athena a piece of paper with more directions written out neatly. At the bottom the words "fifty thousand dollars" were circled and underlined. Before she could ask about that eye-popping sum, he returned her attention to the computer. He scrolled through page after page of driver's license, bank accounts, birth certificate, and other documents she'd need to become Katrina.

Athena wasn't much of a judge, but it looked like he'd convincingly created a person out of thin air using a computer he'd built from a scrap heap.

"Why should I go?" Athena looked from Spero to the computer screen containing the promise of freedom from Bard and danger. "You think I should leave?"

Spero's screen lit and before Athena could look away she was filled with intense joy. It only lasted a minute, but even in that short time she realized how much she missed the feeling of unfettered happiness.

"You want me to be happy and free?" Athena searched Spero's face.

He nodded. He handed her the directions and wrapped her hands around the passport. He tried to shoo her away.

Athena didn't move. Could she walk away? She tried to hold on to the feeling of peace she'd gotten standing in the sun and the joy Spero had shown her. She couldn't. Whenever she grasped for those emotions guilt trampled them and overrode everything else.

She looked at Spero who'd returned to work on his computer. How long had he worked so she could be free? He'd not afforded himself the same opportunity, although, admittedly, his screen made it hard for him to hide. Despite not having the chance to free himself he'd thought of her happiness. She turned and studied Bronte across the room. Bronte was at her workbench, but her body was tense and still. Athena realized she'd likely heard everything Athena had said to Spero. Athena's stomach churned when she considered what Bronte must be feeling. She hoped it was the same as what Athena was feeling when she pictured walking away and likely never seeing Bronte again.

Athena knew, despite the appeal to get her life back, she couldn't leave. She cared too much for these three. They'd started out as strangers but now felt like a kind of family. Perhaps a weird, possibly dysfunctional one, but they were hers. She couldn't leave them to face what was coming alone. She couldn't leave Bronte. Not after the alley. Not after they'd kissed. Not yet. Not until she knew the other three were no longer being hunted. Maybe, when everything was settled...

"I'm not leaving you." Athena said it so quietly she wasn't sure Bronte would hear her, but when Bronte's shoulders dropped from their position around her earlobes, Athena knew she had.

Athena turned back to Spero. "I can't leave."

Spero turned quickly. He looked shocked. He held his arms out to the side as if asking for an explanation.

"I don't have words to tell you what it means that you did this for me." Athena surprised both of them by hugging him. She stepped back and shoved her hands in her pockets. "Like I said. I really appreciate what you did for me. But I can't leave you, or Bronte, or Galen by yourselves. I know there are three of you and you have powers I don't, but we're a team now. At least, I think so. A square without one side is an open box. Who knows what could get in? So, I'm staying, and we'll defeat Bard together. Hopefully, I won't need that new identity after all."

Spero studied her for a long few moments. Then he smiled. It reached all the way to his eyes. His screen flickered, but instead of the usual yellow, this time it was green. Athena had never seen a genuine smile or the green screen before.

"What was the green screen?" Athena tried to catch Spero's eye. "Was that what you were feeling? Can the screen communicate that? I didn't feel anything when it lit."

Spero shook his head vigorously. He tried to turn away, but Athena put her hand on his shoulder and stopped him.

"Hey, I'm sorry I upset you. You've never shown much emotion before, it was nice to see. Does this"—Athena waved her finger around the screen on Spero's face—"take over your emotions too?"

For a while it didn't seem like Spero was going to answer. Very slowly he shook his head. He spun in his chair and grabbed his medical chart from under a pile of picked apart electronics. He flipped to a few pages in and handed it to Athena.

She read the section he pointed to. It was background information on Spero. Galen had hinted at the fact that Spero wasn't bothered by the outcome of Bard's experiments possibly resulting in harm to others, but what Athena was reading painted a much darker picture. Spero wasn't just ambivalent to the potential for harm, he'd inflicted pain and death himself as a covert operative for the government.

She read and reread one passage to be sure she understood.

Mr. Lazarus was told as an operative he needed to walk in the darkness. His emotions were no longer relevant and should get lost in the blackness of midnight. In response he said, "I am the dark that sucks all light from the midnight hour." Despite the poetic nature of his response, he has managed to shut down any emotional response to his work, no matter the necessary actions. His dedication has resulted in his becoming one of our elite operators.

"You've been trained not to show emotion." Athena was holding back tears. She couldn't reconcile the killer described in this file with the man who offered her a path to freedom.

Spero nodded slowly. He wasn't making eye contact.

"But that doesn't mean you're incapable of feeling, right?" Athena wasn't sure why she kept pressing.

By way of answer, Spero grabbed a piece of paper and scrawled out, "Why does it matter?"

Athena paused. She looked at the chart again. "Because this isn't the man I know." She held up the chart. "A man with no ability to feel wouldn't have offered me a path out of here. He wouldn't have woken Bronte or been hell-bent on stopping Bard. Your actions set everything in motion. I want to know because I want to know you."

Spero went still. He stayed like that for a long while. Athena waited him out. Finally, he shook his head.

"No what? No, you can't feel things? No, you wouldn't share them with me?" Athena let the frustration creep into her voice. Spero was entitled to his privacy, but he seemed like he wanted to share… something, with her.

He pointed again at the chart. Athena closed it and threw it on the work bench. "Screw the chart. I don't care what it says. It's words on a page. I don't know that man. What do you want me to know about you?"

Spero's screen lit, yellow this time. Athena didn't look away in time and was overcome with fear. She closed her eyes instinctively. The fear abated. "Do you want me to be scared of you or are you telling me you're scared?" Athena opened one eye a crack. Spero's screen was still lit. She shifted so she was facing ninety degrees away from him.

"Knock it off. Communicate with me instead." Athena took a chance and glanced at him again. His screen flickered off. "Much better. Thank you." She searched his face. "You can trust me, you know. Nurse confidentiality if you'd like. Which is it? Do you think I should be scared of you or are you afraid?"

Spero grimaced and looked unsure. He looked at her intently then his shoulders sagged in what looked like resignation. His screen blinked once, then twice, and finally came to life. The emoji that appeared was the same Athena had just seen but this time it was unmistakably green. It had no effect on her.

"Thank you for trusting me." She reached out and took his hand. "There's no reason to be scared of your emotions."

Spero snorted and his screen went blank. He turned and returned to his work. Apparently, their conversation was over. Athena respected his need to retreat. She patted him on the shoulder before walking away. The fact he'd shared as much as he did was remarkable.

Athena meandered to the kitchen and pulled ingredients from their stores. It was her turn to cook. She thought about what she'd said to Spero and whether she followed her own counsel. She couldn't help but look over to Bronte. Their eyes met and Bronte smiled. Athena was a bit weak in the knees. She was definitely not abiding by her suggestion to Spero. Her emotions scared the hell out of her, at least when it came to Bronte. Maybe Bronte could be her greatest adventure, or maybe she'd be as trapped as she feared. The question was, how was she supposed to work it out before she was too far down one path to retrace her steps if she chose wrong? She hated her indecisiveness. She glanced at Bronte again. Could she really walk away and be satisfied with never seeing Bronte smile again? Could she stay and risk seeing her broken and beaten? If only she had superpowers to help her know what would ultimately make her happy.

CHAPTER NINETEEN

Bronte slammed her hand on her workbench and swallowed a stream of curse words that she'd be embarrassed to say out loud but accurately captured her frustration. She startled when someone wrapped their arms around her from behind. She was instantly metal.

"Down boy. It's me." Athena put her chin on Bronte's shoulder.

As always seemed to be the case, the zeptobots responded to Athena. Bronte didn't mind. She loved the feel of Athena's touch. It wasn't the same with a metal barrier.

"Whatcha working on that's got you banging your fists and looking like an angry bull?" Athena moved next to Bronte and quickly kissed her cheek before looking expectantly between Bronte and the workbench.

"If I tell you, can I have another kiss?" Bronte knew she sounded too eager but she didn't care.

"I guess you'll have to give it a try and find out." Athena winked. "Start talking."

Bronte laughed. When she was with Athena it was almost possible to forget about the problems waiting for her outside the warehouse front door. "I'm trying to modify the zeptobots to see if I can enhance Galen's and Spero's powers. I don't have the ideal equipment, but even without that I'm running into problems. It's like the zeptobots don't want to change."

"That's good though, right?" Athena looked hopeful. "If you can't figure out how to modify them, Bard wouldn't be able to either."

Bronte considered. "Spero's still working on the hard drive. Bard did a number on it when she smashed it, but he seems to think there's retrievable data. From what I saw, she hasn't cracked them yet either. She's made modifications at least on paper, but I'm not sure to what end. I'm sure she hired smart people and bought cutting edge equipment, but from what I'm seeing, it would be a huge challenge to force those modifications onto the zeptobots."

"I'm going to take that as good news. For your problem, talk to the zeptobots. I'd be resistant if someone tried to change me too."

"You've told me to talk to them before. It feels strange, you know." Bronte looked at her hands, then glanced at the table where the sample of zeptobots from her blood stood.

"It was solid advice then, still is now. They're clearly able to listen, and if I'm not mistaken, they even think for themselves. It's like you've got a roommate in your body." Athena jumped so she was sitting on the workbench facing Bronte. She crossed her legs slowly, ensuring Bronte had a good long view. "Do you still want to talk about your work?"

Bronte shivered. The innuendo in Athena's voice and having her perched sexily on her workbench was replumbing her circulatory system. Less blood was flowing to her brain than felt healthy, but the increased flow to her center and breasts was a welcome tradeoff. "What conversation topic did you have in mind?"

"Come here and find out." Athena uncrossed her legs and pulled Bronte between them by her shirtfront.

Bronte stumbled and gasped when Athena dug her hands into the hair on the back of her head and kissed her.

"How about this?" Athena said against Bronte's lips.

Unable to form words, Bronte nodded, then deepened the kiss. She wrapped her arms around Athena and moved closer. The heat coming from Athena's center radiated across Bronte's stomach and shot her arousal up another level. How could she have that effect on a woman like Athena?

Bronte could have stayed at her workbench kissing Athena forever, but they were startled apart by a loud bang on the bench. Bronte jerked away from Athena and stood protectively in front of her, metal exoskeleton in place.

Spero was standing casually by the bench, a pipe in hand. He looked between Athena and Bronte and smiled. Bronte didn't detect anything but sincerity in his expression.

"What the hell's wrong with you? Couldn't you see we were busy?" Athena hopped off the bench and stood next to Bronte. She wrapped her pinky around Bronte's little finger.

Spero shrugged. He looked indifferent. He pointed the pipe at Bronte and then pointed across the warehouse. He walked away, clearly expecting Bronte to follow.

"I'm not going with you because you threatened me with a pipe. I thought we were friends, man." Bronte stepped in front of Athena again as she moved a couple steps closer to Spero.

Spero looked to the ceiling as if asking for patience from the heavens. He moved back to Bronte and held the pipe out to her. She took it automatically. He nodded his approval. He pointed between the two of them then moved into a fighting stance. Once he was ready for combat, he pointed to Bronte.

"You want me to fight you?" Bronte looked at the pipe in her hand, then at Spero. "I'm not doing that."

Bronte tried to hand the pipe back, but before she could, Spero launched a rapid attack. He moved so quickly and efficiently Bronte was disarmed and on her back before she processed the initial offensive.

"What the hell. First you interrupt, then you attack? What's going on? I want another chance to defend myself. I wasn't ready." Bronte slowly got back to her feet.

Spero looked to the ceiling again. Bronte saw him take a deep breath. He came to stand next to her and resumed his fighting posture. He looked at Bronte and pointed to her, then his eye, and finally to himself.

"You want me to watch you?" Bronte shook her head. "Why?"

"I'd like to point out again, we were busy." Athena took the pipe from Bronte and handed it back to Spero.

He refused the pipe and his screen lit. He didn't put anything on the screen, but his meaning was clear. He expected them to listen.

"Don't even think about it, mister. You don't get to bully or manipulate either one of us. You need or want something, ask. Enough with the histrionics." Athena took Bronte's hand and pulled her around Spero to the kitchen. "Her ribs are barely healed. You shouldn't have put her on the ground."

Bronte looked back at Spero. He looked stunned. "I don't think he's ever met anyone like you. I haven't either." Bronte lifted Athena's hand and kissed it quickly.

"As long as he doesn't start kissing me." Athena got them both a glass of water.

"Maybe that's his plan?" Bronte nodded toward Spero. He was stalking his way over.

Athena shook her head. "He's a good guy. Single-minded perhaps, but a good guy."

Spero stopped in front of both of them and sighed. Once again, he pointed between himself and Bronte. He held his fists as if getting ready to fight. Then he pointed to Bronte and the warehouse door and made the fighting pose again.

Bronte scratched her head trying to understand. "So you want to fight me so I can go outside and fight?"

Spero nodded then cocked his head and slowly shook his head. He held his hands out to the side and shrugged his shoulders.

Athena's eyes got wide. "You want to teach her to fight. Is that what you're trying to say?"

Spero nodded enthusiastically. He pointed at the pipe Bronte still held. Then he looked over his shoulder and pointed at a small pile of junk on the floor a few feet away. Bronte could see a length of chain, a trash can lid, and a few other things that may or may not belong to Spero's stack.

"Fine." Bronte pointed the pipe at Spero. "I need the lessons. But next time you do not interrupt kissing. You understand? If you do, you'll regret teaching me anything." She knew there was less bite to her words than she wished.

Spero mock saluted and waved Bronte after him. She followed slowly. She looked over her shoulder hoping Athena was coming too.

"Don't worry, I'm not missing this. But, Spero, remember her injuries." Athena hollered across the warehouse to Galen to tell her what was about to happen.

Galen grabbed a seat and dragged it after her. They all followed Spero as he led the way to the patio. Their relaxing haven had been turned into an obstacle course for extreme warriors. There were scrap metal barriers to hide behind, heaps of junk that could be used as weapons, and crates and other sturdy boxes, short and tall, that could be used as hiding places or high ground. Bronte looked around. What the hell was she supposed to do out here? What did any of this have to do with fighting?

"What about getting caught? Aren't we going to be conspicuous out here?" Bronte glanced up and down the alley.

Spero pointed in both directions and covered his eye.

"Blind? I know there aren't cameras right near us, but did you blind all the others?"

He smiled wickedly.

"You and that computer are a little scary." Athena and Galen sat against the warehouse wall. They'd brought out snacks like they were settling in for a movie. Spero looked thrilled to have an audience. Bronte was anything but.

Bronte stood across from Spero and arranged her body in what she hoped was a decent fighting posture. She held her fisted hands in front of her. She could semi-imagine punching someone from this position. Spero looked at her and shook his head. What was she doing wrong?

He took his own fighting stance and raised his eyebrow expectantly. He pointed between them. Bronte tried to mimic his pose. He shook his head. She tried again. Finally, he came over and forcibly adjusted her body position until she'd been turned around so many times she'd never be able to replicate it.

Spero took her fist and pulled it forward in a punching motion. He showed her how to rotate her wrist as she moved through the punch so her knuckles were facing the sky as she made contact. He demonstrated snapping her hips to get power into the punch. He continued his silent lesson for at least thirty minutes.

Athena and Galen hollered out encouragement from time to time. Galen catcalled when Spero needed to be particularly close.

Abruptly, Spero stepped back and resumed his fighting posture. He pointed at Bronte and before she could set herself, he moved toward her, lightning fast, unleashing a barrage of blows.

Bronte stumbled back, trying to avoid the attack. The zeptobots came to her defense but even if she wasn't in danger of physical injury, she wasn't interested in getting her ass kicked. She stumbled over a pile of crates and ended on her ass on the other side. She scrambled back to her feet. Spero was advancing quickly.

"Come on, Bronte, you can do this." Athena's voice lacked conviction.

She noticed the crates, the angle of the sun, Spero's fists, his blank screen. Her thoughts were too fast and jumbled. She watched Spero's hips. From what he'd shown her no punch could be thrown without engaging the hips.

Bronte saw his hips twist to generate power. She tracked the next strike as Spero swung. She stepped out of the way which bought her enough time to set herself. Instead of waiting for him to attack again, she took a swing at him. It didn't feel like the perfect punches Spero had taught her, but it caught him in the ribs. His sharp exhalation gave her one data point that perfection may not be necessary when it came to fighting.

"Give him hell." Galen raised her glass in salute. "Oh shit."

Spero regrouped and ducked under Bronte's next offensive. The swing was wild and her follow-through was long which left her vulnerable to his counterattack. Now she knew why he'd insisted her arm extend and snap right back in place like it was connected to a rubber band.

Bronte adapted the longer they fought. It was a physical exercise but it was also force, acceleration, torque, and pattern recognition.

She could master those aspects. The rest was muscle memory. They chased each other around the patio, scrambling and ducking over and under obstacles. Bronte wouldn't have gotten a decision in the bout, but she didn't fare as poorly as she'd feared.

Spero was dripping with sweat when he stepped back and held up his hands. Bronte put her hands on her knees, gasping for breath. Athena appeared by her side with water and a towel.

"Can I towel you off, champ?"

"I don't think metal can sweat." Bronte stood and gulped the water.

"Maybe not, but should I rub you down anyway?" Athena licked her lips.

Bronte swallowed awkwardly and coughed. "I'm going to survive him only for you to kill me."

"I think you'll live." Athena kissed Bronte lightly. "Fight club beckons once more."

Bronte took one more swallow of water and reluctantly returned to the makeshift training ground. As she walked away, she heard Galen and Athena whispering.

"Am I going to walk into the warehouse one day and see you two fucking in the corner?" Galen asked.

Athena laughed. "You'll never be that lucky. No visitors allowed."

Galen groaned. "Can't blame me for hoping."

Heat shot from Bronte's face to the furthest reaches of her nervous system. She didn't know if it was the way Athena assumed they'd have sex or Galen's desire to watch.

Spero punching her in the stomach was like a swimming pool of cold water. She stumbled back and glared at him. "No warning? I wasn't ready."

"Bad guys don't announce when they're going to hit you, mate," Galen hollered from her perch, her mouth full of something crunchy.

Spero nodded and pointed at Galen.

"Fine. Let's go." Now Bronte knew. The question was, how could she keep her mind on Spero and fighting when Athena was so close? She had to hope Galen didn't mention fucking again.

This time Bronte was comfortable sparring with Spero. He sped up and slowed down the ferocity of his attacks and she matched his pace. She was even confident enough to initiate her own offensives. There weren't any lingering problems from her ribs, and during one particularly theatric dive and roll she actually felt a bit heroic. Was she a badass now?

She hadn't expected to learn so quickly, but there were times it didn't feel like she was in charge of her body. Could it be the zeptobots were doing as much learning as she was?

Spero called time and they both caught their breath. After a minute he indicated Bronte should ready herself again. This time he didn't step forward to fight. Instead he flashed his screen and Bronte was overcome with anger. It churned through her and felt like it was eating her alive.

He was doing this to her. He was the reason she felt like this. Why was he making her fight to exhaustion? She lunged at Spero wildly. Her punches were out of control and he avoided them easily. He shoved her back and turned off his screen. She gasped for breath as the anger receded.

"Why did you do that?" Her anger was her own now.

Spero tapped his forehead forcefully. Then he touched his chest above his heart and shook his finger.

"Head, not heart?" Bronte put her hands on her hips. "But you're messing with my head."

He pointed to his head again and raised his fists. Cautiously Bronte did the same. Before she could look away, Spero's screen flashed again. Fury shot through her. Why was he doing this to her again? She'd show him how well she could use her fucking head when she smashed it into his nose. She grabbed a pallet and held it above her head, ready to fling it at Spero.

"Think, Bronte. Fight through it." Athena's voice seeped into her thoughts, past the anger.

Bronte stepped forward, still intent on knocking Spero out cold and ripping the screen from his face. She hesitated. Could she use the anger? She lowered the pallet a little. No, he had no right. He had to pay. She raised the wooden weapon again, ready to strike.

"Don't let him win." Athena's voice was closer now.

Bronte dropped the pallet and dug the heels of her hands into her temples and closed her eyes. She sank to her knees. The fury abated. A comforting arm snaked around her shoulders. She leaned into Athena's touch.

"Bard's going to try the same thing that worked before. You're stronger than she is. Don't let her win." Athena helped Bronte to her feet.

"Let's go again. I was close to shutting you out." Bronte kicked the splintered wood to the side and raised her fists. She gestured for Spero to start over.

This time, when the anger came it felt like a visitor, not a part of her. She pictured it as a furious red ball moving through her brain, trying to infect anything it touched. "Zeptobots, can you take care of that?"

Bronte said it jokingly, but as soon as it was out of her mouth the red sphere was surrounded by a swarm of pinprick lights and was consumed. The small lights increased in intensity and Bronte got a surge of energy. She stalked toward Spero and calmly and methodically parried every punch he threw and found every weakness in his defense. The sparring was over in less than a minute and he admitted defeat.

She looked at Spero, then at Athena and Galen. They all looked shocked. Galen had a chip halfway to her mouth.

"You started glowing." Athena recovered first. "You actually started glowing. There wasn't anything Spero could do to stop you. You became like, a super fighter." Her smile looked like it might crack her face in half. "That has to go on the list as another superpower."

"I glowed?" Bronte looked at her hands. The metal looked the same as it always did.

"Yeah, mate. Like a life-sized robot night-light." Galen finally popped the chip in her mouth.

"I think it was from what Spero was doing to me." Bronte turned to Spero who still looked in shock. "Can you try another emotion?"

They continued for hours. Spero manipulated Bronte's emotions over and over. Like with anger, it took a few tries for Bronte to fight through the initial wave. Once she did though, the same thing happened. She pictured a ball of light and the tiny dots destroyed and absorbed it. She apparently glowed each time and her fighting became powerful and skilled.

Bronte pointed to the pipe and chain Spero had pointed out hours ago. "Can you teach me how to use those?"

Spero nodded but indicated he was tired.

"Tomorrow?" Bronte didn't want to stop now that she'd made a breakthrough.

After the fight training dispersed, Bronte stayed on the patio. It was dusk but the patio was in shadow and nearly dark. She held out her arms in front of her and tried to make herself glow. Nothing she did worked. She pictured the glowing balls and tiny dots attacking and destroying them. Were those the zeptobots? Was she seeing what was happening in her brain? How was that possible?

Bronte slid down the wall and sat in the dark. She didn't know what had happened during the training or how. What she did know was she'd felt more like the superhero Athena kept insisting she was than at any point since she gained all these powers. But what did that mean? She'd always lived a solitary life. Superheroes couldn't do that; people depended on them. Was she ready to be seen by so many? And did she want to be seen as she was? Who and what was she? Galen had called her a robot night-light. Was that far from the truth? Being seen and being accepted weren't the same things. Bronte didn't have answers and couldn't find them hidden among the stars. What she did know was if she chose to live a less solitary life and was rejected, she might never recover. The question was, how would she decide if it was worth the risk?

CHAPTER TWENTY

Athena watched Bronte doing what she could only assume were complicated incantations until her curiosity got the better of her.

"Are the spells working?" Athena leaned against Bronte's workbench.

Bronte frowned. "What spells?"

"You look like a frustrated wizard trying to work out how to turn a superhero into a glowworm. Am I close?" Athena stifled a laugh at Bronte's utterly perplexed look.

"I'm not a glowworm. And I'm not a wizard." Bronte crossed her arms.

"Ah, but you didn't deny the superhero part. I'm wearing you down." Athena took Bronte by the hand and pulled her along. "Come with me." She led Bronte to the patio and then out into the alley and away from the warehouse.

"Where are we going? It's not safe out here." Bronte tried to pull Athena back.

"That's why I brought you." Athena turned and patted Bronte's cheek. "I also checked with Spero about his camera outage range."

"What about Bard and her men? How long can we stay hidden, especially if we're wandering around in the open?" Bronte surveyed the empty street.

"Spero may have shut off the cameras for everyone else's use, but he can still access them. He's got an entire network of eyes. At least with the cameras that still work. Plus, he gave me this." Athena held the device Spero had given her that morning. It looked like an upside-down lollipop. "I call it the 'panic pop.' If there's danger, he'll let me know."

Bronte nodded although she still looked unconvinced. "So now what?"

"I don't know. If this were a normal night and we were two people who weren't trying to stop a shit pickle from unleashing hell on the good people of Earth, what would you want to be doing tonight?" Athena wanted to take Bronte's hand, but she waited. She wanted to give Bronte space to answer in whatever way she chose.

"That's easy. I'd want to ask the most exceptional woman I've ever met on a date." Bronte took Athena's hand.

"Well, shoot. Who is she? I'll start my training with Spero and we can go a few rounds for your affection." Athena squeezed Bronte's hand,

Bronte stopped walking, pulling Athena to a stop as well. She looked serious. "I was talking about you, Athena. Only you. I would never lead you on and then tease you about someone else. I hope you know me better than that."

Was it possible for a heart to melt hot and sweet throughout your chest? "I know that, sweet woman. I was teasing you."

Bronte started to say something in response, but Athena cut her off with a kiss. She kissed her like she'd wanted to, like no one was watching, like they needn't hold anything back. She buried her hands in Bronte's shaggy hair and wrapped her left leg around Bronte's calf. Bronte held her tight, one arm around her waist, her hand on the small of Athena's back, the other hand on Athena's ass.

When they broke the kiss, Athena wasn't eager to let Bronte go. Bronte seemed to feel the same way, as she kept Athena tightly in her arms. Athena rested her cheek on Bronte's chest. "What am I going to do with you?"

Bronte kissed the top of Athena's head. "Anything you want."

Athena leaned back in Bronte's arms and raised her eyebrows. "That certainly leaves open a lot of possibilities."

Bronte looked like she'd just realized how her words could be interpreted but she didn't retract them. "I mean it. I'm scared of a lot of what's happening right now, but I'm not scared of you. Although perhaps you should be scared of me."

Athena pulled all the way out of Bronte's arms and put an arm around her waist. They kept walking. "Why would I be scared of you?"

"Ta-da." Bronte stopped walking and turned to metal. "Not exactly girl-next-door material."

Athena frowned. "Have I ever given you the impression that girl next door is my thing?"

Bronte smiled crookedly. She looked relieved.

"How about you let me decide what scares me?" Athena set them on their way again. "Were you trying to make yourself glow back at the warehouse?"

Bronte hesitated then nodded. "I have a hypothesis about how it works, but I can't replicate it. When I was fighting Spero and he was messing with my emotions, it was like I could see the emotions, and then something attacked them and absorbed them. Then I felt powerful and you all said I glowed."

"That had to be the zeptobots, right?" Athena could hear how goofy excited she sounded.

"Maybe? I don't know if I was seeing something that was even real." Bronte wasn't nearly as excited.

Athena poked Bronte in the ribs. "So ask them."

"You keep saying I should do that, but I don't know how." Bronte blew out a breath, pulled her hand free from Athena's, and ran both hands through her hair.

"Come with me." Athena motioned Bronte to a fire escape on the side of a building that didn't have much more curb appeal than their warehouse. Athena looked at the ladder, gave it a shake, and then started climbing. She looked back at Bronte. "Are you coming?"

"You know flying isn't one of my powers, right? When that thing falls off the building, we go with it."

"Have a little faith." Athena wasn't religious but she considered crossing herself. Couldn't be too careful, right?

Their leap of faith was well worth the heart palpitations. The fire escape led all the way to the roof and from the top they had a spectacular view. Athena had found it difficult to orient herself and the warehouse in relation to other landmarks in the city, but from here she could see where she was in comparison to everything else. They were on a hilltop on the edge of town with the rest of the small city spreading out beneath them.

"It's beautiful here. Almost worth the near-death experience to get here." Bronte smiled at Athena adoringly.

"That fire escape is at least the tenth scariest thing we've done since we met." Athena ticked things off on her fingers silently.

"What a terrifying thought. And you wonder why I don't want to be a superhero." Bronte pointed at two lawn chairs that had definitely seen better days but still looked like they had a few days left in them.

"Galen was the one who told me about this rooftop. Must be hers. Before you ask, I don't know and am not interested in who she entertains here." Athena pretended to put her fingers in her ears and closed her eyes.

They each took a chair and were content to hold hands across the short distance between them and watch the clouds pass by overhead. Athena had never been content sitting still, but she had no desire to be anywhere else at the moment. The feeling was so foreign it unnerved her if she thought too much about it, so she didn't.

"Did you know Spero offered me a way out?" Athena turned her head so she could see Bronte's reaction.

Bronte nodded slowly. "I heard. I wasn't trying to." She quickly tried to explain.

"Next shopping trip we're going to get you earplugs." Of course Bronte had heard. Nothing was out of earshot of her.

"Why didn't you go?" Bronte still had her head resting on the back of the chair and her legs stretched out, but Athena could see her body was tense.

"You must have overheard what I told Spero. I couldn't leave you three. We're a team. We all need each other." Athena looked at her hands. "And I couldn't leave you."

"Oh. Okay. That's good then." A grin slowly spread across Bronte's face. "That's very good. I'm glad you didn't leave. I would have missed you. A lot."

"Me too." Athena sat on Bronte's lap. She leaned her head against Bronte's strong chest.

"Much better." Bronte slid her arms around Athena's waist. "Will you tell me how to talk to the zeptobots? They listen to you and you seem to understand them. Better than I do even though I created them." Bronte sounded frustrated and a bit sad.

"I have more distance. Maybe I can see things you can't. Maybe science skills aren't what you need. Maybe you need a nurse." Athena took Bronte's hand.

"Tell me." Bronte shifted so she and Athena were looking at each other.

Athena studied Bronte's face. It was as it always was, chiseled and beautiful, but her eyes were giving away her frustration and worry lines were creasing their corners. "From my perspective, you see the zeptobots as separate from you. Maybe like you're their host or they're a parasite?"

Bronte frowned. "That's not how I see them. Is it?"

"I don't know. Only you can answer that. But it seems like they've proven over and over that they have your back. And if what you suspect about the emotions and your glowing is right, then when you work as a team, you can do amazing things. They are you and you are them. But you're also separate entities in some way, because they clearly think for themselves to some degree." Athena squeezed Bronte's hand. She waited for an indication Bronte was annoyed. She'd given her this advice before.

"Next you're going to tell me to talk to them, aren't you?" Bronte smiled and kissed Athena's hand.

"You're getting to know me pretty well." Athena leaned in for a real kiss. "And yes, that would be my advice. They seem to have some good ideas. You created them and you're brilliant so it makes sense they are as well. I'm sure you'll have a lot to talk about."

"Zeptobots, is there more we could be doing together? More powers I don't know about?" Bronte looked to her hands like always.

Athena shivered against the cold as they waited for an answer. The sun was setting and as it did the temperature was dropping quickly. Without warning Bronte pulled her close and let out an excited exclamation.

"What are these?" Bronte held out her arms. "Wings?"

"Hey, I'm cold, wrap me back up, I was warmer with your blanket arms." Athena took both of Bronte's arms and pulled them around her again. She had a thin metal film from her wrists to her armpit to her waist. She looked a little like a bat.

"Is that what they are?" Bronte craned her neck to get a better look at her strange new look. "Zeptobots, was this your idea? Can you give me a sign if that was you and not a thought of mine you're acting on."

Almost instantly, her left hand was reflecting the setting sun. They both nearly fell out of the chair.

"I guess that answers your question." Athena pulled Bronte's arms around her tighter. She wanted the warmth, but she also craved the feel of her. How would she ever leave this safe and protective cocoon?

"I could sit like this all night. The cold will probably force us back inside, but I don't want this moment to end." Bronte rested her chin on Athena's shoulder.

Apparently, she was a mind reader now. Athena sighed in contentment. She felt warmer from the glow of her happiness. She paused. No, she was warmer because Bronte was warmer. What was happening?

"Are you heating up?" Athena pushed Bronte's arms away and felt the blanket wings. They were warm to the touch, like stones left under a summer sun.

"I guess I am. I don't know how that's happening." Bronte looked startled.

"Zeptos, I get you want to show off, and I'm impressed, but too much. All that you are her and she is you stuff is true, but wait for her to ask for your help with stuff between the two of us, okay? No surprises, even ones you know I'll like. Make her work for it a little." Athena was looking at Bronte but scolding the zeptobots. Even she was a little confused.

"Hey, you told me to team with them, now I have to do everything on my own?" Bronte was pouting.

"No, but this can't be a Cyrano situation either. Trust me, I'm worth a little extra work." Athena was blustering. Bronte created a blanket from her armpits. How could Athena compete with that?

"I know you are." Bronte's voice was quiet and her expression was sweetly earnest.

Athena couldn't help thinking how easily she could fall for Bronte. She didn't want to be thinking those thoughts. Not when Bronte was getting more powerful by the day and Athena's real life was waiting once she was done playing superhero.

"Bring back the heated blanket arms. Let's watch the sunset."

Athena pulled Bronte's arms back around herself. She leaned against Bronte again. The sense of calm and safety returned. She wanted to be annoyed but couldn't. Bronte was remarkable. If she were interested in settling down, there couldn't be a more perfect candidate. But she wasn't, obviously. That was ridiculous.

"Athena?" Bronte sounded like she'd been working up the nerve to speak. "I know you're like a tumbleweed, beautiful and wild and free, but I sure do like watching the sunset with you. If you ever decide to pick a permanent direction, I hope you'll consider mine."

If Bronte wasn't holding her so securely or she wasn't so content right where she was, maybe Athena would have been more panicked about Bronte's tentative declaration. As it was, she couldn't bring herself to care about anything but this moment, this woman, and the natural beauty lighting the sky in front of them. That had to mean something, but she was too happy to puzzle it out. Maybe tomorrow she'd reexamine. Or maybe she'd kick the can further down the road. It was hard to argue with where that had gotten her so far.

Chapter Twenty-one

A fter the freedom of the fresh air and vibrant colors of the rooftop with Athena, the warehouse was stifling. Bronte knew she'd been storming around the place for the past few days, but stagnation was setting in. She'd tried to take the fight to Bard and got her ass handed to her. Now she was hiding in a warehouse, learning to fight, for what exactly? They had no plan, no way to storm the castle and crush the usurper.

She stomped over to Galen. "Can I talk to you for a minute?"

Galen kept rooting around in the food storage bin. "Am I in trouble for something?"

"Have you done something wrong that I should know about?" Bronte frowned and inspected Galen more carefully.

"Nope and you're not my daddy." Galen popped a cracker in her mouth and walked out of the kitchen. "Unless you want to be, but that's a whole different game."

"Hang on." Bronte grabbed Galen's arm. "I don't care what trouble you're getting yourself into." Bronte hesitated. "I care a little. But that's not what I want to talk to you about."

Galen looked mildly interested.

Bronte rushed on before Galen changed her mind. "What are we doing here?" She indicated the warehouse. "What's our plan?"

"We're not dying, Bronte. That's the plan." Galen started to walk away again.

"Wait. There has to be more than that. Don't you want to stop Bard? We can't do that if we're hiding here." Bronte jogged around in front of Galen, forcing her to stop again.

Galen looked at the ceiling. Finally, she spoke. "Bard tortured you with her shitty experiments, but you were asleep. That doesn't make it okay, that's not what I'm saying, but what she did to me, I had to be there, every day. I had to participate."

"You participated in my care too, I recall. Thanks for that."

Galen shrugged off Bronte's outburst. "I saved you from much worse. Believe me or don't. I'm not going to defend myself."

"What do you mean by that?"

Galen paled. "You got a taste of it when you went lone wolf into Bard's office. If she hadn't been able to get the magnet to work she would have tortured you until your exoskeleton fell away and she could take what she needed. Keeping you under kept you from all that. I wasn't given a choice, but I knew the alternative would make your life hell."

Bronte nodded. "I'm sorry for what you went through, but I'm still not sure they're the same."

"It's not just that. You can turn your weird ass power on and off. You want to be a human magnet collector one minute, great. Then you can shed that skin as easy as you put it on. I can't ever turn off my 'gift.' It follows me everywhere. Even into my dreams. You're right we're not the same. I'm addicted to drugs, I'm distrustful, and a loner. I'm selfish and sometimes a liar. You on the other hand are a fucking Boy Scout."

"You can trust me, if you let yourself." Bronte started to say again that she was sorry, but Galen cut her off.

"I don't want your pity or your sorrow." Galen looked disgusted. "You don't need to feel sorry for me."

"Might need to run a diagnostic or you've run into some static." Bronte tapped Galen's head. "I can feel bad for a friend without pitying you. As for what I need? I need your help."

"You *want* my help. There's a difference. I want to stay here. Purgatory is better than hell. And at least here I'm only surrounded by a few people's emotions. Out there…" Galen stepped around Bronte and walked away.

"Is there anything I can do to change your mind?" Bronte called after her.

"Show me an actual plan and I promise to consider it." Galen turned enough to look at Bronte and then continued across the warehouse.

That seemed fair, if only Bronte had anything close to a plan. Athena was busy in the medical corner inventorying their supplies and adding things to the shopping list, so Spero was her man. He was, as usual, at work on his computer. She clapped him on the shoulder. "What are you working on, Spero?"

He wheeled around wildly, his body tense. His screen was lit and his eye wide. Bronte didn't have time to react before she was overcome with sadness. Tears welled and she fell to her knees. As quickly as the sensation began, it was blunted. A face shield dropped over her eyes and although she could see through it, she could sense the power of Spero's screen was muted. That had never happened to her before. Was it the zeptobots? At the same time she felt, rather than saw, the same energy absorption and once again became powerful beyond measure. She had no intention of attacking Spero, but when she looked at her hands, she could see for herself the phenomenon her friends had described. She was indeed glowing.

She looked at Spero who had dimmed his screen and looked contrite if a little annoyed. Bronte apologized. She didn't mean to sneak up on him. He spun back to his computer with a loud grunt.

"I came to ask you a question, not scare you." Bronte stepped next to him but kept her hands in her pockets. She was disappointed that they were no longer glowing. "Have you had any luck with those files I copied?"

Spero looked at her and rolled his eye. He clicked a few times and file after file opened on the computer screen on his desk.

"So that's a yes, then?" Bronte tried to read bits and pieces as the files opened but the rapid opening of each one made it difficult to digest. "Okay, quick summary. How screwed are we on a scale of 'not as bad as we thought' to 'humanity's doomed, time to book a flight to Mars.'"

Spero turned back to his computer. He held up three fingers as he did.

"Option two. I have an unreasonable fear of being in space so that's not going to work for me. I think it's the lack of sound, or maybe an aversion to vacuums." Bronte shivered.

Before she could continue and embarrass herself further, Spero spun and glared at her. He pointed at a crate nearby and then at his computer. Bronte took the hint and dragged the crate next to him and sat.

"If it's as bad as you say, then how do we stop her?" Bronte leaned forward and examined the document Spero displayed on the screen.

Spero had compiled a list of resources Bard controlled. They were human and physical resources. Bronte's insides jittered like they were made of a bowl full of worms when she saw the Ten Romans listed. She continued down the list even though she felt like the name of Bard's personal soldiers of doom was a threat in and of itself.

"There, what's that?" Bronte pointed at the name of a building and letters of the Greek alphabet.

A few clicks and the plans for the building and a list of personnel appeared on the screen. It was Bard's main laboratory. Human subject research may be happening at the hospital, but the other laboratory science was apparently happening offsite. Bronte looked back at Spero's list. Bard had the main offices of Verstrand Industries, where Bronte had worked and where she'd stolen the data from. The hospital where Bronte and Spero had been unwilling test subjects and this separate research laboratory were also under Bard's control. There were twelve other buildings on Spero's list, some in other cities, some out of state, one out of the country. It was impossible to say whether they were being used for legitimate Verstrand Industry business or Bard's plans for world domination. Bronte ignored Bard's buildings outside of their city. It didn't make sense to spread her illegal activities so far away from her control.

"That's where we should strike." Bronte pointed at the laboratory on Spero's list, then leaned back on her crate, nearly tumbling off in her excitement.

Spero looked at her in confusion.

"You, me, and Galen. I can't do it alone and we have to stop Bard. You and Galen told me getting this data wouldn't stop her, but destroying her lab might slow her down. I already said I can't move to Mars." Bronte hoped her expression was resolute and encouraging.

Spero wagged his finger in Bronte's face. Was it something she said?

"Look, I'm not interested either. I want nothing to do with this." Bronte turned to metal. "But I *can* do it and I don't want a bunch of Bard's men being able to as well. The three of us can complement each other. Especially now that you taught me how to fight. At least I won't upchuck and hide behind you."

Bronte didn't like the way Spero cocked his head from side to side as if trying to decide if he believed her. She was eighty-two and a half percent sure she wouldn't vomit. Spero turned back to the computer and drew an "x" across the screen with his finger.

"Why not the laboratory?" Bronte wanted to argue but held her tongue. At least he wasn't automatically sidelining himself. At least she didn't think he was. It would be so much easier if he could talk. "I might be able to get a sample from the work there and see how far they've come toward reverse engineering a zeptobot. Or we could blow up the damn thing."

Spero shook his head again. He put his hands together and wove them through the air like they were a snake.

"The basilisks? She has them at her lab too? How many of those nightmares does she keep hidden around this town? If kids knew they existed, they'd never sleep again. Okay, fine. Where can we hit that will show Bard we're not scared, get the information we need, and give us some practice as a team?"

Spero scrolled through additional files and pulled up another document. He pointed, looked at her with a confident expression, and crossed his arms.

"What is that? A supply house? No way. Bard won't give a shit if we attack there, and it doesn't do anything to stop her. She probably has a hundred more." Bronte ran a hand through her hair and blew out a breath. "Find me somewhere that has a blood sample."

Spero nodded. He held his two hands, palms facing each other, closely together. Then he moved them apart a couple inches, then a few inches more. He continued until his arms were stretched wide and his hands were as far apart as he could reach.

Bronte grumbled. "I get your point. Start small. How long exactly does your plan take? Is there a world left by the time we attack a target that means something?"

Spero nodded toward his computer. He put his two thumbs together palms down, then overlayed his left hand with his right, so the fingers formed a crisscrossed network.

"I get your point; the lab is a bad idea and computers share the same network so the supply house is no different from Bard's office. Am I interpreting that correctly? If that's the case, then going to the supply house doesn't gain us anything because I've already chatted up Bard's network. We need to try for a blood sample."

Reluctantly, Spero reexamined the list. Finally, he pointed to a different supply house.

Bronte started to argue until she read Spero's notes. "Negative eighty Celsius freezers? Why would those be there? Unless…"

Spero raised his eyebrows, then turned back to his computer.

"But why would they store biospecimens outside the lab?" Bronte leaned close to the computer to get more details on the supply house, but Spero had moved on.

Spero waved her off. He looked behind her at Galen across the room. He pointed to her, then Bronte, then himself. He shrugged then put the tips of his fingers to his mouth and kissed them executing a perfect chef's kiss. He shrugged again. This time he pointed to the three of them and mimicked an explosion with his hands before shrugging again.

Bronte looked from Galen to Spero. He raised his eyebrow. "You're right. We have no idea how we'll do. Let's see if we can get Galen on board and we'll take a swing at the supply house. I'll see if Athena wants in on this madness. I need to know how far Bard's gotten with the zeptobots."

Spero nodded toward Galen and headed her way. Bronte clapped her hands on her knees and stood. Her legs were leaden. Even though none of this was her fault, Bard had wanted her zeptobots. Without that, they'd all be safe. Now they might never be. That was a heavy weight to carry. She searched the room for Athena. When she caught sight of her and their eyes met across the warehouse, some of her burdens seemed lighter. Was it Athena or her feelings for Athena that had done that? And if it was the latter, would they one day become a burden of their own when Athena inevitably left? Bronte couldn't entertain those thoughts now, not when she desperately needed confidence she didn't feel and a lighter load. In this moment, Athena's welcoming smile was providing both. She didn't dare dream past the present.

CHAPTER TWENTY-TWO

A thena couldn't believe she was sitting in front of Spero's computer monitor watching Bronte, Galen, and Spero stalk down the street like she was playing a first-person video game. They were about a mile from the warehouse with another mile to go, but given how detached she felt from what was happening on the ground, they might as well have been across the country.

Bronte was wearing a body camera and they all had earpieces. Athena wasn't sure where Spero had gotten those. She didn't ask. Athena had been joking about superheroes and saving the world so long it had actually seemed like a good idea. Watching them walk into danger now was causing her to reevaluate. She'd been outvoted when she'd said she wanted to go with them. Given that she was the only one without some kind of extra power, she finally had to back down.

"Athena, you there?" Bronte sounded nervous.

"Wouldn't be anywhere else." Athena's leg bounced wildly under the desk.

"I appreciate that. More than you know."

"Save it for later, you two. Are we on some weird foreplay stroll or are we out here to go after Bard's blood supply?" Galen stuck her face in front of the camera and glared.

"What I think you were asking, Galen, is whether the building you're targeting still looks good, right?" Athena stuck her tongue out even though Galen couldn't see her.

"Sure, whatever." Galen moved out of camera range. "How're we looking?"

Athena looked at the other window open on the computer. It was a traffic camera feed across the street from the supply house. Spero had reviewed the footage he'd recorded since this time yesterday and unless someone was inside that never left, there were only three of Bard's men in the building.

"Unless I'm missing something, no one has come or gone from the building." Athena checked and rechecked the screen. She stared at it until she saw a car drive past so she knew the picture wasn't frozen.

"Are you missing something?" Galen sounded less annoyed and more scared.

"Hey, lay off." Bronte on the other hand sounded pissed. "We're all a little scared, no need to take it out on Athena."

"I can tell you're scared. He's his usual blank slate. My emotions are my own business."

Athena could see Galen again on the camera. She looked agitated as she pointed to Bronte, Spero, and herself. It was an odd perspective to follow the three of them on the traffic cameras and other CCTV feeds along their route while also seeing Bronte's body camera view.

"Are you two done bitching at each other?" Athena cut in. "This might be your first mission or operation or walk in the park, but anyone want to show a little professionalism? For the folks who do this sort of thing for a living?"

"I think those folks only exist in comics, babe." Bronte chuckled.

Athena's mouth went dry. Had Bronte casually called her "babe" in the middle of the most stressful thing they'd ever been a part of? Athena banished all endearments, terms, acts, and whispers now and in the near future from her thoughts. She had other areas that demanded her attention. Like comic book characters.

"Those folks were only in the comics. Now there's you three. Do 'em proud." Athena was glad they couldn't see the sweat beading on her brow or how often she had to unclench her jaw.

"Yes, Arm Fall Off Lad, the Whizzer, and Fruit Boy have set a high bar." Galen looked directly into the camera again.

Bronte swatted her away. "Dude, it's weird that you keep staring at my chest."

"No, it's not," Athena and Galen said together.

"Can we focus please?" Bronte cleared her throat a couple of times.

Galen popped back on camera one more time. "She's bright as a strawberry."

Athena could picture it. Bronte's easy blush was adorable even if she'd never tell Bronte. She refocused. "You three ready? Go over your assignments one more time for me."

Spero looked back at Bronte and flashed his screen. He lifted his middle finger in what Athena could only assume was extra emphasis of his preparedness.

"I'm emotional surveillance. If I sense anything squirrelly, I'll alert the others. I'm also in charge of getting into the building and stealing as many blood samples as I can from inside once the two big lugs here start hitting people." Galen sounded less nervous than she had before. "I wore my freeze-proof underwear so I can shove it all in my drawers."

"I guess I'm one of the lugs. Spero and I will draw out Bard's men, subdue them, and buy Galen time to get inside and get the samples. I really hope nothing goes in her underwear. She's free to steal anything else after that. When she's done, regardless of what she finds, we'll plant the spyware Spero built to infect the rest of the network and destroy everything else at the storage facility." Bronte sounded like she was reading a price list for spare lawnmower parts.

Athena's body was weirdly amped up and deadly calm. Her legs and stomach were doing the jitterbug, her heart was thumping out a loud bass beat from a hip-hop hit, and her brain seemed hellbent on playing improvisational jazz. She took a couple of deep breaths and shook out her hands.

"Okay, I'm your benevolent overlord. I'm going to walk you through the tricky bits. You guys can do this. Hold on. Don't turn that next corner." Athena leaned closer to the monitor as if she could pluck the group of men she saw gathered a few hundred feet from her friends and fling them away. One of the men was part of the group that attacked Galen.

"Bard's men. They're around the corner. You have to hide." Athena's voice was calmer than she expected. Her friends couldn't see the whole picture, but she could. Bard's men, nearly fifteen of them, were checking buildings and looking carefully in alleyways. They weren't leaving any stone unturned as they searched. Athena could guess what they were looking for. Her friends needed her to get them home.

"What do you mean?" Galen leaned into camera view on Bronte's body camera. Every line, strain, and grimace on her face gave away how she was feeling.

"I'll get you home, but you need to hide. Now." Athena knew some of her own worry seeped into her voice.

The body camera footage moved wildly. She could see on the other camera feed that Bronte was scrambling to squeeze behind a dumpster. Galen and Spero were similarly trying to disappear from sight.

Athena stifled a scream when she realized they were too late. The group of men turned toward them like hunters after prey. Spero and Bronte seemed to come to the same understanding. They exited their hiding places and looked ready to fight. When Bronte turned in Spero's direction, Athena could see his screen flashing menacingly.

"Where's Galen?" Athena searched the monitor for her. Finally, she saw her, partially hidden behind a trash can, doubled over, holding her head in her hands. "Galen, what's going on?"

"We're right by a strip mall. I can see two fast food restaurants from here. There are too many people." Galen fell to her knees, still holding her head.

"Well, what do we have here?" One of Bard's men sneered at Galen on the ground. "We were just looking for you. Where's the little nurse? She's the last piece we need to collect."

"You'll stay the fuck away from her." Bronte lunged at the man, but she was sent flying by an unidentifiable wave or blast or field coming from short metal sticks wielded by each of Bard's men.

"Tell us where you've been hiding and I might consider letting the little hotty go. Bard won't of course, but I'd at least consider it." The man laughed. It was a cruel laugh.

Athena watched as Bronte crawled to Galen. Spero was still on his feet, and he moved protectively in front of them. Bronte jabbed Galen's shoulder and pulled her back to standing. "Come on, Galen. All hands on deck. We're in a bit of a pickle here." Bronte sounded one notch below panicked.

Spero glanced over his shoulder then flashed his screen as he turned back to Bard's men. He caught one of them looking and sent him to the ground in a pool of tears.

"Galen, listen to me." Athena leaned close to the screen as if that might help her get through to Galen. "This is like a noisy bar. When you're in a bar you can always pick out the voice of the hottest girl in the room, right?"

Galen nodded almost imperceptibly but Athena was willing to take that small step forward.

"This is the same thing, except we're not looking for hot women, you're looking for the safety of your friends and what they're feeling right now. All you have to do is look for their unique emotions. Focus on looking for those instead of tuning out the others. I know it's like a fire hose for you and it's overwhelming. Can you sense Bronte and Spero? Focus." Athena was standing now, her nose practically pressed to the monitor.

Athena watched Galen stand on wobbly knees. "I think so. I feel like I'm drowning."

"You haven't seen anything yet, Doc." The seeming ringleader of the group of men nodded to the others and they closed in around Bronte and Galen. Their advance forced Spero to retreat until the three of them were back-to-back in a desperate triangle.

Athena watched helplessly as the first punches were thrown. The fight looked like a video game because she was safely here, in the warehouse, away from harm. Galen was crouched again, barely deflecting the blows coming her way. Bronte's metal skin was fluctuating in and out. She was fighting back but was clearly distracted by the zeptobots.

"Bronte, work *with* the zeptobots." Athena sat and pulled close to the desk. She was not going to let her friends die out there. The calm she depended on as a nurse settled in, allowing her to focus through the panic.

"I'm trying. What are they playing at?" Bronte grunted. The camera shook wildly. Athena assumed she'd been hit in the torso.

"Last time you were in a fight, they had to take charge. Don't fight each other. You're more than capable now but you need their help. Let them know that. Work together." Athena turned her attention to Galen. "Galen, listen to me. You can't sit there and get the shit beat out of you. Either start swinging as well as you throw verbal jabs or get off the ground and run."

Galen didn't move.

"Galen! On. Your. Feet." Athena used her most commanding nurse voice.

It did the trick. Galen shot off the ground and started swinging madly at anyone within range. She almost took Spero's head off in the process, but she connected solidly with a few of Bard's men as well.

"Spero, can you help get some of these guys off our back?" Bronte was back to full metal and dispatched one guy about ten feet away with a punch.

When Spero turned, his screen lit and his eye caught the sun, Athena thought he looked like a wolf caught in the midst of the hunt. He shook his head and turned back to his next foe. Athena watched as Spero fought him.

"Bronte, Spero can't make use of his screen with anyone not in his direct line of sight. Most of Bard's men are avoiding facing him, which means they know who and what he is. His best weapons right now are his fists." Athena wanted to throw something. This wasn't how today was supposed to go. Instead of toasting a victory later she was hoping they wouldn't be pouring one out for a fallen friend. "Can you regroup and retreat? You were ambushed and there's no way you'll have any element of surprise now. No blood sample's worth any of you getting captured or killed."

She could see only half the men who'd started the assault were still in fighting shape, but that still outnumbered her three friends. Even on the grainy surveillance video she could see Galen's surge in energy was flagging. It likely wouldn't be long until she was swamped by the onslaught of emotions once again.

Spero signaled "one minute" toward Bronte and the camera. He fought his way to Galen, grabbed the small container she'd brought for the blood sample, and he sprinted away. Three men followed after him, but he never slowed.

Bronte started to follow. Athena reached for the screen as if she could hold her back. "No, Bronte, you have to stay with Galen. There are too many of them and I don't know for sure if more are coming." Swallowing felt difficult, like she was trying to get past her heart stuck in her throat. What she wanted to do was tell Bronte to run back to her, to get to safety, but she couldn't ask her to leave their friends. Athena's job was to sit safely in the warehouse and watch her friends succeed or fail, possibly even die, without being able to do a damn thing about it. It was a shit job.

She chewed a fingernail as she watched Bronte turn back to Galen in time to engage two of Bard's men. At least the zeptobots seemed to be working with Bronte a little more consistently.

Time passed slowly as Athena stared at Galen's mostly internal, occasionally external battle, and Bronte taking on all comers, until Spero finally returned. Bronte swung around in time for Athena to see Spero grab Galen by the shoulders and flash a joyful emoji on his screen. The change in her was instantaneous. She socked a guy in the nose singing a song from the B-52s at the top of her lungs.

"Did you get what we need, Spero?" Bronte turned to Spero.

Before he could answer the camera looked like it was floating and then was facing skyward. One of Bard's men came into view from above.

"We've heard all about your games, metal head. You were stupid to come out of your hidey-hole. Ms. Verstrand will always be ready for you. She'll always be better than you."

With that the man unzipped his jacket to reveal a flexible screen across his chest. It was already lit and flashing words, pictures, and emojis. Athena stared at the screen, unable to look away. She expected to feel the effects, but felt nothing. She heard Bronte cry out.

"Don't like that, do you?" The man pulled a remote from his pocket. He clicked a few buttons. "How about this? Better?"

New images flew across the screen. Bronte moaned.

Athena squirmed in her chair. Her stomach contents flipped and flopped like a small boat in a large storm. Why had this guy waited so long to torture her? Was he waiting for Spero to return so they'd all be together when he incapacitated Bronte? Did he have a plan for Spero too?

"Bronte, listen to my voice." Athena knew she sounded desperate. "You're stronger than he is. Let the zeptobots take care of this. Remember what happened when Spero was training with you." No answer. "Galen, Spero, can one of you help?"

"No can do. We've got a bit of a situation ourselves." Galen sounded like she was in pain.

Athena couldn't tear her eyes away from Bronte long enough to check on Spero or Galen. "Bronte, you can do this. Listen to my voice. Focus. You're stronger than he is. Do the thing you did when you were training." Athena stood and gripped the side of the desk until her fingers were white and cramped.

Finally, Bronte answered. Her breathing was short and ragged. "I am stronger."

Athena watched Bronte's glowing fist rise in front of the camera and connect with Bard's man. He flew back as if hit by a bus. Athena was a bit motion sick as Bronte got back to her feet and the camera swung crazily.

Bronte's offensive was over in a matter of minutes. Bard's men were groaning on the ground as Bronte, Spero, and Galen sprinted away.

"Where did you go?" Bronte sounded annoyed as she turned to Spero.

Athena watched Spero wiggle the storage bag a little. He lowered it again and kept running.

"You really got a blood sample? Seriously?" Bronte didn't sound like she believed him. "You didn't do anything else insane like wire that storage facility to blow, did you?"

Athena's stomach dropped at the look on Spero's face. It was a cross between glee and resolution.

Bronte stopped and turned back in the direction they'd come from. "There are people in there, Spero. I don't care if they're Bard's men, I'm not letting them get blown up."

Something stopped Bronte from running back into danger. Although Athena appreciated her morals, she was glad Bronte wasn't running headlong into yet more chaos. She wasn't sure her nerves could take much more. Not to mention her tooth enamel, if she hadn't already ground it all off clenching her jaw.

Bronte turned back and Athena saw Spero patting the air in the universal sign for calm down.

"So you didn't rig the place to blow?" Bronte sounded skeptical.

Spero held his index finger and thumb an inch apart. Then he waved Bronte forward as he took off running again.

Bronte didn't follow right away. Finally, after Spero and Galen were half a block ahead, Bronte followed. She muttered as she took off after them. "No one better die."

Athena kept tabs on the surveillance cameras as the three made their way back to the warehouse along the path Spero had charted for their return trip. They stopped frequently to check for tails and doubled back often if they suspected anything amiss. Athena provided a wider range view. Bard's men had spread out. Some, those limping or staggering, had retreated in the opposite direction. A few had hopped in a nearby car and were slowly moving street by street, but Athena had the advantage of steering her friends clear.

The rest of the men were on foot, once again searching buildings and alleyways in the direction Bronte, Spero, and Galen had run. Spero's route had taken them initially away from the warehouse before doubling back so Bard's men on foot were methodically searching in the wrong direction.

The closer her friends got to home the more Athena was able to relax. So many emotions started bubbling up she felt like Spero was toying with her. She didn't expect to feel elated and scared and on the verge of tears. Would that have happened even if she hadn't been watching someone she cared about as much as she did Bronte out there fighting?

She should have anticipated this side effect of letting herself care. She'd been so worried about getting tied down and how that would impact her wild, carefree ways, she didn't think about how wild Bronte's life was about to get and what that would mean for her. Being the one watching from the sidelines was hard and brought her back to her younger days when she watched every other kid living their lives without her. Except she wasn't that kid anymore and she wasn't watching someone else live the life she wanted. She was a part of the team and she got to decide for herself if she wanted to stay or go. Could she see herself happy in this life? What about a life with Bronte the person, not just Bronte the hero? They weren't the same and she had to be okay with both if she wanted a future with her. That's what scared her. She'd never pictured domestic bliss for herself. What if she could only say yes to one?

Chapter Twenty-three

B ard poured three glasses of champagne and slid two across the desk. Antonio picked up his glass immediately. Alpha hesitated.

"It's not poisoned, Alpha. If she wanted you dead, you and I wouldn't be sharing drinks." Antonio handed Alpha the drink and then clinked glasses.

The look on Alpha's face was too much for Bard. His expression looked like a combo of a man with duct tape over a mouth full of glass shards and someone with a bursting bladder at the end of a two-hundred-person bathroom line. "He's right, Alpha, but no need to piss yourself. We're here to celebrate the work you've done. I wasn't sure you could pull it off when I promoted you, but I'm impressed. The pilot test of the Program is exceeding our expectations."

Alpha still looked like he was waiting for the other shoe to drop. "I checked the numbers before I came here. Our targeted consumer products have all seen substantial increases in units sold since the Program went active."

"And what about the pharmaceutical data points?" Bard put her glass down and stared at Alpha. She knew the answer but wanted to hear Alpha explain.

"Well, those are a little harder to measure. For one it takes longer to see the effects. Two, there are alternate treatment options. Not everyone who is depressed or anxious chooses medication. People who want a new TV aren't going to buy a basketball." Alpha squirmed.

"I don't care about therapy or yoga, Alpha. Those don't make me money." Bard came around her desk and stood towering over Alpha. She'd always enjoyed her height and the fact that it kept her on an even playing field with the men who comprised the majority of those who surrounded her.

"Ma'am, doesn't it matter that we're making people feel terrible?" Alpha looked at his shoes.

Antonio grabbed Alpha's chin roughly and forced him to look Bard in the eye. "No. If she gave a shit about that we wouldn't fuck with their emotions in the first place. Your job is to build what she tells you to. She decides what's best for this company. Understood?"

Alpha swallowed audibly and nodded.

Bard took Alpha's champagne and poured it out. Antonio showed him to the door.

"You think he's going to be a problem?" Antonio poured himself more champagne and flopped back in his seat.

"If he is, you'll deal with it for me." Bard returned to her seat behind her desk. "Tell me about the break-in at our biospecimen storage facility. How did Dr. Scales know about it at all?"

"Unclear how she obtained the information. You destroyed the drive she attempted to smuggle out and we don't think she downloaded much information even if it hadn't been smashed. We either have a leak or she has someone with computer skills advanced enough to break through our security. If I had to take a guess, I'd say Subject One is responsible. We chose him because he's brilliant and doesn't have respect for rules." Antonio spun the stem of his glass between his fingers.

"He was there, correct?" Bard put her own flute down. She didn't feel like celebrating anymore.

Antonio nodded. "The doctor, too."

"Either of them effective?"

"Minimally. Subject One has limited impact given the narrow field of his screen. Our men were able to avoid coming face-to-face with him thereby neutralizing his effectiveness. The doctor has never done well above ground." Antonio's eyes glinted in the way that made Bard's skin crawl.

"Minimally effective doesn't usually mean stolen data and I quote 'explosive destruction of our non-networked computers.' Your report also says Dr. Scales is getting more powerful." Bard shuffled papers around until she found the report Antonio had written about the incident.

Antonio scoffed. "More powerful compared to the sniveling weakling who thought she could attack you and live, sure. That's a low bar to crawl over."

Bard slammed her fist on the desk. "A weakling does not singlehandedly incapacitate fifteen of your men. Don't underestimate Scales, Antonio. If she's learned more about the zeptobots and how to use them, then I want her back in the lab like the lab rat she is. I don't want her or the other two getting in the way of my plans. I don't care how unlikely you think it is." A bead of sweat slid along her spine. "And I sure as fuck don't want her coming at me."

"None of my Romans were there. If she wants to get to you, she'll have to come through us. Once Alpha and the nerd brigade finish their work, nothing they have can compare to my Romans. Doesn't matter how much she's learned, only pain awaits her on that path." Antonio stood and deposited his glass in the sink across the room.

Bard nodded. "Music to my ears. Phase two begins tomorrow. The election is approaching. It's a perfect test of our control. Our candidate knows his script, right?"

"I've made it clear to him the consequences of failing us." Antonio grinned like he'd be okay with success or failure.

"You've always said you and I aren't that different, Antonio. I never believed you, but maybe you were right. You use fear your way, and now I'm going to use it mine. I don't care about selling more televisions or antidepressants. I want control. People are controlled by telling them what to be scared of and presenting the solution they think they want. With the Program we can increase people's fear so much they'll buy anything I sell them." Bard moved next to Antonio and put her hand on his shoulder.

Once upon a time, Bard had been unsure about her path forward. She'd been scared herself, of whether she had what it took to lead her company and move out from under her father's shadow. She didn't doubt herself anymore. She controlled fear now and she'd use it to manipulate anyone she needed to get what she wanted. The world had always been hers, she finally saw that, and she was ready to take it. She didn't want to stop and think about what that made her and whether that was ultimately what she should be afraid of.

Chapter Twenty-four

B ronte climbed the fire escape to the rooftop where she and Athena had watched the sunset together. She was alone tonight, but sulking was usually a solitary activity. Everyone had been asleep when she'd slipped out of the warehouse and made her way here. She'd been unable to sleep and hoped some air would help. She'd thought to leave a note for Athena in case she woke so she didn't worry.

Once Bronte made it to the roof she dragged one of the chairs over to an exhaust vent and propped her feet up. She leaned her head back and looked at the stars. They reminded her of the tiny dots of light she saw when the zeptobots destroyed Spero's emotion attacks.

"What happened to us out there against Bard's men?" Bronte didn't bother talking to her hands. If the zeptobots didn't know she was talking to them then their connection was in greater peril than she thought.

She didn't expect an answer but a quick sharp pain on her left earlobe made her reconsider.

"Was that you guys?" She sat straighter.

The pain zapped her again.

She rubbed her ear. "Ow. Okay. Is my ear the problem with our relationship? No, that's dumb. Ears, hearing, listening. I'm not listening. Is that it?"

Bronte's thumb and wrist turned metallic. The metal hardened forcing her thumb upright into a thumbs-up position.

She slumped back in the chair. "I'm sorry I'm not listening to you. If I'm being honest, I don't know how to listen to cohabitating tiny robots, but I'll try harder. I've done everything on my own for a long time."

Bronte sat staring at the stars again for a long while before she had another question. "I didn't program you to do any of the things you're doing now. How are you learning and giving me all these powers?"

There was no answer for so long Bronte thought the zeptobots were done talking to her. Finally, her head started to tingle.

"I have to figure it out on my own?"

A zap to the temple.

"Okay, no. I already know the answer?"

Another zap.

"My brain?"

More tingling. Bronte thought of the possibilities. She'd created the zeptobots so in some way they had her brain, but she didn't think that was right. That wouldn't explain their adaptation. It was like they had a brain of their own and were thinking.

"Are you using my brain to think?"

Her head tingled so much she had to scratch it to get it to calm.

"Yes, yes! Okay! Easy on the nerve stimulation, please. I don't need a short circuit. We might need to talk about boundaries. I'm not sure I want you roaming my gray matter. Can you read my thoughts? Some of those are personal." Bronte knew she was blushing but why? The zeptobots couldn't see her.

Another zap to her temple. At least they weren't reading her mind. Made sense, they probably had better things to do. Important tiny robot work. Whatever that was.

Bronte turned her attention back to the reason she was here in the first place. She was throwing herself a world class pity party. She'd planned the raid on the supply house, convinced the others to join her, and it had gone to shit. Even the blood sample she thought Spero had gotten had turned out to only be more data on a hard drive. He said there was blood sample data there that hadn't been on the main network, but she'd wanted a sample she could analyze herself.

Galen must have felt similarly because she'd quit the nascent team they'd built as soon as they'd gotten back to the warehouse and was barely speaking to her. She was pretty sure she'd been high ever since. Spero hadn't left his workspace except to eat and go to the bathroom and he threw things at anyone who approached. The mood in the warehouse was tense and it was her fault. The only one who still seemed to like her was Athena but even that relationship was different. There were far fewer stolen kisses and she missed them.

She replayed the fight as she'd done over and over. Galen was immediately overwhelmed. They should have turned back then. Spero was largely ineffective since his screen was easily avoided. And she fought the zeptobots to the point of nearly getting beaten to incapacity, again. If Athena hadn't pulled her out of her own head...

The zeptobots had come through for her. The face shield they created had been enough of a barrier to break the emotional manipulation. She'd been able to think clearly and get back under control. The face shield. Was that the answer?

"Bots, hypothetically, would you be able to adapt to a new host?" Bronte did talk to her hands this time.

By way of answer her hand turned metallic palm toward the sky.

"You don't know?"

Everything returned to her natural skin except for her thumb and wrist.

"I have an idea, but it will take us working together to test it. I'll get started tomorrow." Bronte thought about heading back now and getting to work, but it was peaceful on the rooftop and she wasn't ready to return to the stress of the warehouse. She closed her eyes and listened to the sounds of the night.

A noise that didn't belong to the peace and quiet startled her awake. She was disoriented which scared her more than the strange sound. She tried to place her surroundings and the noise. She was on the rooftop. She'd fallen asleep. The sound was someone climbing the fire escape. She suited up, ready to fight if needed.

Athena came into view and Bronte relaxed. Her heart pounded, not out of fear but elation, as it always did when she first caught sight of Athena.

"What are you doing here? It's the middle of the night." Bronte gave Athena a hand the rest of the way onto the roof.

"I could ask you the same thing. You scared me half to death. I wish you could fly because I'd shove you right off this roof just for the satisfaction." Athena had her hands on her hips and a scowl on her face.

"I guess I needed some air. It's a little stuffy in the warehouse right now." Bronte nudged a clump of something indistinguishable with her foot.

Athena didn't say anything for a long time. Bronte finally looked at her. Athena's head was cocked to the side and she was studying her intently.

"You know what happened out there wasn't your fault, right? Your plan didn't include getting ambushed on the street by fifteen of Bard's soldiers. What's happening in the world is also not your fault. That's her doing." Athena moved closer, into Bronte's space.

Bronte took a step back. "You're wrong. The fight was my fault. I could have gotten both of them killed. I'm the metal one. I should have protected them better. That's the second time Bard's gotten the better of me."

Athena stepped forward again. "But she didn't, sweetheart. For one, she wasn't there. And you kicked everyone's ass and helped your friends. You did exactly what you needed to do. Spero got a new hard drive to break into that will give you data on Bard's work on the zeptobots, and you all made it back in one piece. That was mostly the point of why you went, so it was actually a success."

Bronte wanted to back away again, away from Athena's kindness and beautiful eyes, but she got the sense Athena would chase her all over the rooftop if needed. "I only did what I did because of you. If I was on my own who knows what would have happened."

Athena took Bronte's hand and led her to the chairs. She gently pushed Bronte into one and sat on her lap like she had when they'd watched the sunset. "But you weren't alone. We're a team, remember. It feels weird saying that since you three knuckleheads kidnapped me to start us off."

"Best decision I ever made, even if it wasn't made consciously." Bronte pulled Athena closer.

"So you admit it." Athena turned to Bronte. They were only a confession away.

"I'd never deny you your freedom or ability to make your own decisions." Bronte was the one to move closer this time.

"Good answer." Athena tangled her fingers in Bronte's hair and kissed her.

Athena clung to her tightly and Bronte realized both of their cheeks were wet. She pulled back and wiped the tears rolling down Athena's cheeks. "Why are you crying?"

Athena wiped angrily at her tears and rested her head on Bronte's chest. "Because I'm scared, and I don't like it and I care about you and don't want to."

"Oh," was all Bronte could think to say.

"When I was a kid, I was scared of everything. I was so anxious I spiraled myself into panic attacks over the smallest things. I missed out on so much of my childhood because I was too scared to enjoy it. I watched it go by outside my bedroom window or heard about it from friends. I swore to myself thousands of times I wouldn't be like that forever and I haven't been as an adult. Therapy is a wonderful thing. I haven't been scared again like that until you." Athena looked at Bronte. She didn't bother wiping the tears anymore.

"I don't want to cause you distress." Bronte was sure her ribcage was suddenly four sizes too small.

"It's because I care about you so damn much." Athena put her hand on Bronte's cheek and smiled.

Bronte frowned. "You said you didn't want to care about me."

Athena sighed. "I did say that. I do want to care about you. It makes me happy. You make me happy. But it scares me too. I've always sworn I'd never settle because then I'd miss out on the thing just over the horizon. I have so much to make up for from all I missed out on as a kid."

"Is that what we're doing here? Building a quiet life, white picket fence, considering a golden retriever?" Bronte laughed. Athena joined her.

"Tease all you want. I watched you on that screen, far away, unable to help and was terrified I was in danger of losing the chance at something I never knew I wanted. It was like I was back in my childhood bedroom watching everyone else outside, except this time I was watching you, fighting and getting hurt." Athena's tears started in earnest again.

Bronte pulled her close. "You're the bravest person I've ever met, but I don't ever want to do anything that upsets you. I won't go again. We can leave together tonight. I can keep us both safe and we can be free. Spero can make me a new passport too, and we'll go."

Athena shoved off Bronte's chest and glared at her. "You think I'm going to stand for that?"

"But, I thought…" Bronte trailed off.

"I know what you thought. I'm sending mixed messages. But you should know me better than to think I'm going to put my own needs above thousands of others. Bard is going to hurt a lot of people if you don't stop her. The world needs you and I know it will curdle your insides if you walk away and watch what she does with your technology." Athena kissed Bronte lightly.

"Some things are more important than all of that." Bronte ran her hand through Athena's hair and over her back.

"No, I'm not." Athena shook her head. She took Bronte's hand and kissed it. "Whether by accident or fate, you have these powers. You and Bard are forever linked and you're the one who can stop her. I know you've said you don't want to be a superhero, but most of us can't do what you can so we need those who can to step up for the rest of us."

Bronte looked at their joined hands. Was it possible she'd swallowed a hurricane? "Is that all I am now? A tool for the greater good? A metal creature others need but who isn't like them?"

Athena squeezed Bronte's hand. "You listen carefully, Bronte Scales. You are not a tool or a creature. You're not a robot or a machine. You are a beautiful woman with extraordinary gifts. Something *you* created lives inside you, works with you. You are brilliant and powerful, and you take my breath away. The zeptobots haven't made you less human. You've got to stop listening to that poisonous voice in your head."

"I know you see things one way, but I'm struggling to see it the way you do." Bronte looked skyward.

"Then don't try. Trust what I'm telling you. Trust me. Your version of yourself is no more accurate than mine, so believe in the one that's going to bring you strength." Athena kissed Bronte's cheek. "I believe in you."

"How can you say our two versions are just as accurate? Don't you think I know myself better?" Bronte knitted her eyebrows.

"We've talked about this before. We all have blind spots. And even if we didn't, friends and strangers create their own ideas about who we are. Who's to say whether they're right or wrong? People lie about themselves and others all the time. All I'm asking you to do is trust me. What I see is a woman, full stop. A heroic, gorgeous woman."

Bronte sighed. Athena was asking a lot. "I can't do it alone. Galen and Spero are barely speaking to me, and you already said how hard it was to watch from afar."

Athena raised Bronte's chin so they were looking eye to eye. "I'll be wherever you need me to be. I've got your back." She made a show of looking Bronte over. "Maybe your front too."

"I don't think that's going to help my concentration in a fight." Bronte's mind was full of thoughts unrelated to Bard or super-heroing.

"Might give you some motivation to return to me in one piece though." Athena returned to her reclined position in Bronte's arms. "As for Spero and Galen, you have to convince them to join you. Whether you like it or not, you're the leader of this team. We all need you to show us the way. They're scared but they won't be if you show them how to control it."

"I've got an idea about that. I have no idea if it will work, but I'll start working in the morning. But no one's fooled by your pep talks, which are extraordinary by the way. You're the leader of this group. When someone needs something, they'll always turn to you."

"I knew I could count on you to have a solution at hand." Athena kissed along Bronte's jaw line.

Bronte tried to control her breathing, but Athena was making it hard for her to focus. "Do you want to go back home and get some sleep?"

"If it's all the same to you, I'd rather stay here. If I crawled into bed with you back home Galen would probably try to join us. That's not something I'm interested in. I want you all to myself. And when we finally get to enjoy each other fully, I want it to be in a bed, just the two of us, not running from anything or anyone." Athena whispered in Bronte's ear.

Bronte held Athena close and kissed her possessively by way of answer. They stayed that way, wrapped in each other until the sun peeked over the surrounding buildings. Bronte would have happily stayed on that rooftop all day, but she knew they needed to get back. As if by silent agreement, she and Athena stood, stretched, and descended wordlessly. They walked back to the warehouse hand in hand. Bronte had a spring in her step and a hopeful tune in her heart. Athena did that for her. She helped her see the hope and the light. She also made her happy. But what did she give back to Athena? She looked at Athena, beautiful, brave, and bold in the morning sunlight. Would Bronte be enough when the world didn't need saving? She couldn't remember wanting anything more.

Chapter Twenty-five

Spero bumped into Athena on his way across the warehouse. His arms were full of wires and electronic guts. He looked like he was barely holding on to the load.

"Do you need help, Spero?" Athena picked up two long pieces of wire that fell as he passed.

He waved her after him and she followed, collecting what he dropped all the way to his workstation. When they arrived, he dropped the pile next to what looked like a four-foot-tall, upside down birdcage. The wires were woven together in a tight mesh, and it was big enough for a person to sit underneath comfortably. Spero pulled pieces from the new stack and began weaving them into the sculpture.

"Anything I can do?" Athena wasn't busy and Spero's construction project looked well worth her time.

Spero stopped what he was doing and looked like he was weighing his decision carefully. Finally, he pointed to the pile of wires and then back to himself. Athena took that to mean she should pass them over. She sat on the floor and sorted through the wires as Spero continued adding to the cage.

It didn't take long until Galen and Bronte noticed what they were doing and joined them.

"Are you building a Faraday cage, Spero?" Bronte examined the cage closely.

Spero quickly nodded. Bronte looked impressed.

"A what?" Athena had heard of Faraday the man but didn't know what a Faraday cage was.

"It's a metal cage that keeps electromagnetic signals from getting in or out. There are all kinds of uses for them. There are Faraday cages in everyday objects like USB cables and airplanes and more specialized ones like MRI machines and some evidence collection bags." Bronte was still looking the cage over closely.

"What are you going to use it for, mate?" Galen pulled over a chair and crunched a chip from a just-opened bag.

"Are you ever not eating?" Athena mock scowled at Galen. "Wait, don't answer that. It might give me a reason to really be annoyed with you."

Spero looked at them, not trying to hide his frustration. Whether he was annoyed at their joking or the noise at his worksite, Athena wasn't sure. She refocused on the job she'd been given. Spero nodded her way. She took it as thanks.

Bronte squatted closer to the cage and tested the width between wires. "I'm impressed. Nice work. It seems bigger than you need for your computer."

Spero pointed over his shoulder. Athena, Bronte, and Galen all looked in the direction he pointed. The hard drive he'd removed from the storage facility sat on the edge of his desk.

"This is for that?" Bronte examined the hard drive. "If it had a tracker wouldn't we all be screwed already? Maybe when you plug it in the tracker will activate? Or are you worried it will jump on the network you created for your computer and we'll have a big flashing arrow over our heads?"

"Bronte." Athena took her hand on her next pass by. "Give the man a moment to answer."

"I know. I know. I've wanted to know what's on here since we brought it back a couple of days ago." Bronte sat next to Athena and set the hard drive near the cage.

Spero ignored Bronte's flurry of questions. He put the last wire on the cage and grabbed the hard drive.

"Now what can we do?" Athena stood, ready to help.

He lifted one side of the cage and motioned her to get the other. They lifted carefully until it was high enough that he could slip underneath. He lowered it as soon as he was inside the cage.

Athena's fingers tingled and her chest tightened uncomfortably. She had a feeling she wasn't going to like what was about to happen. Sure enough, Spero sat, set the hard drive on the floor next to him, and pulled a cable and a knife from his pocket.

"Whoa, what the fuck, mate. What's happening in there?" Galen moved to lift the cage, but Spero's screen lit menacingly, and Galen backed off. "No need to get your panties in a twist. Don't do anything stupid is all I'm saying."

Spero reached for the knife and used the reflective blade to examine the top of his screen. He felt along the ridge and marked a spot with his finger. Before Athena or anyone else could do anything to stop him, he sliced a three-inch gash across his scalp where the screen and his skin met.

Athena lunged forward ready to throw the cage to the side and tend to his wound. Spero waved her off. He produced a washcloth from his pocket and held it over the wound.

"Let us stitch you up." Athena crouched in front of Spero. Her knuckles were white she was gripping the cage so tightly. "Whatever you're doing doesn't have to happen this way."

Spero looked at her and pulled the cloth away from his head. It was still bleeding but the flow had decreased significantly. He pulled back the skin far enough to reveal a port at the top of the screen. He lifted the knife again and using it as a mirror cleaned off the port. He inserted the end of the cable and attached the other end to the hard drive.

His body stiffened as soon as the hard drive connected. His face went blank, and his one eye moved back and forth rapidly as if reading a long text at one hundred times speed. Athena could see his pulse pounding on his neck and he was sweating profusely.

"Galen, he can't take much more of this." Athena wanted to get to him, but she held steady.

"Give him a minute." Galen moved next to Athena. Her focus was entirely on Spero as well. "If his pulse and breathing aren't regulated in ninety seconds, we go in."

It took more than a minute, but Spero's breathing slowed and his countenance returned to its normal impassive state. His one eye blinked like he was waking up. He wiped the sweat and blood from his face and took a deep breath. He waved off questions barely formed from those outside the cage. He scooted to the edge of his enclosure and faced them. His screen blinked on. Instead of displaying emojis as usual, this time schematics, formulas, operations manuals, and detailed plans flashed across the screen.

Athena tried to take in the images as they flashed by. She couldn't read everything fast enough and she couldn't process those she was able to read. Bard had more capabilities than they thought, and she was planning to use them soon. Maybe she'd already started given how much the outside world seemed to suck suddenly. Her stomach churned. Were they too late to stop her?

"We have to give all this to the police." Galen sat heavily on the floor. She ran her hands through her hair and left them there, holding her head in her hands.

"What are they going to do?" Athena couldn't take her eyes off the information Spero was speeding through. "We stole all this."

"What other choice do we have?" Galen sounded defeated. "Someone has to stop her."

Bronte looked pensive. She was still watching the information flitting across Spero's screen. "I can't read fast enough to be sure, but I haven't seen Bard's name on any of these documents. Spero, can you tell if anything here can connect back to her?"

Spero shook his head and held his hand in the shape of a zero.

"How is that possible?" Athena felt like someone had poured concrete in her brain and her nerves were firing through the quickly hardening mess. "Isn't all of this her company? How could it not tie back to her?"

"My guess, none of this is being done officially by Verstrand Industries. She can wreak havoc and then say someone stole her technology or it was a rogue employee misappropriating her work." Bronte slammed her metal fist into the floor. The concrete cracked

"Stop it there." Athena pointed to Spero. "What's that?"

Spero's eye scanned back and forth like he was reading the document on his screen. When he was done, he motioned to his screen then behind him to his computer. He then pointed from his screen toward Athena's head before making a motion like he was buying something.

"Are you saying they're using her program to make people buy things?" Athena recoiled in disgust.

Spero nodded. Then he made as if he were scanning a list and checking off one item. Next, he put one hand in front of him palm down and held his right hand in the air about shoulder height.

"What are you doing now? Are you taking an oath?" Bronte looked confused. "Wait, politics, you were voting, right? If they can influence shopping behavior, why not voting behavior too."

Spero pointed to Bronte and nodded.

"Doesn't that already happen? With focus groups and targeted ads?" Athena must be missing something.

Once again, Spero nodded. This time he put one hand palm down close to his chest level. He moved his other hand as high as he could reach. There was a roughly two and a half foot gap between his two hands.

"Okay, Bard's doing a lot more. I don't want to see a world where Bard is picking our elected officials." Galen shuddered. "I wonder who she'd pick? Someone evil and powerful like her or dumb and compliant?"

"Are you picturing her in bed?" Bronte physically recoiled.

"What?" Galen spoke a little too loudly for someone completely innocent. "No, of course not."

"Focus please." Athena didn't want to think any more about Bard's sexual proclivities.

Spero scanned through a few more pages of documents before stopping and then pointed to his screen.

They all read what turned out to be a military contract.

"Fuck. She's contracted with the Department of Defense to develop next generation uniforms and wearable psychological weapons. That's what one of her men was using on me during that fight. Like Spero's screens, only more advanced because it can be worn instead of attached to a single unit." Bronte looked disgusted. "She has free rein to build whatever she wants. She can create as many prototypes as she wants and what are the odds she'll never deliver a single thing to the military? Meanwhile she has fully operational suits at her disposal."

"I know you wanted me to be a superhero, Athena, but this is getting into some weird-ass comic book shit." Galen shook her head. She had a crooked smile on her face.

Athena couldn't help but laugh. "Good. The bad guys always lose in comic books. Look, I'm not sure the police can help. Didn't the last paper you brought back say something about the police union endorsing one of the candidates? Who's to say that's not part of Bard's plan? So, if the police can't help, how do we stop her?"

"We don't." Galen stood. "It sounds like a comic book but it's not. We tried playing superhero and all we got was our asses kicked and that hard drive that shows us we're way out of our depth. I don't need to see what happens next time against the really scary bad guys. What would have happened if those guys had been the Ten Romans?"

"We don't have a choice." Bronte stood too and addressed Galen. "We can't let Bard win." She pointed back toward Spero. "Look what she's capable of. I didn't see anything about zeptobots yet, but I know it's in there. If she creates those and combines them to create a cross between me and Spero, everything is lost."

Athena found the energy crackling off Bronte and Galen intoxicating. It was like she was standing in the rain listening to thunderclaps overhead and lightning striking the ground around them. It was exciting and dangerous and impossible to walk away from.

Galen got in Bronte's face. "You can do whatever the hell you please. You have a suit of armor to cover you and protect you. When I leave here, I'm vulnerable. I'm exposed. You're asking too much. I said I quit before and I'm not signing on again now."

Bronte looked to Spero. He shrugged and shook his head.

"What if I can make it better for you? What if I can fix the problems we had before?" Bronte sounded desperate.

"If there was a fix for what I have, don't you think I'd have found it by now?" Galen pushed past Bronte and strode away.

"No, because you didn't have what I have," Bronte called after Galen.

Athena wanted to knock sense into both of them. They needed to quit bickering and figure out how to stop Bard, but as she'd told Bronte, she had to bring the team back together. They already trusted her or they wouldn't have let her watch the cameras and lead them. What they needed was to trust each other, and to do that they needed someone to take charge and help them all feel safe. Galen wouldn't do it and Spero's moral flexibility excluded him. It had to be Bronte.

Bronte looked to Athena then to Spero. "Are you okay helping him?" She pointed to Spero.

Spero unplugged the hard drive and crawled out of the Faraday cage. He looked like a creature from a horror movie with the blood streaking down his face.

Athena hooked an arm under his shoulder and helped him to his feet. "Let's get you cleaned up. You're going to need stitches." Bronte was hovering a few steps away, clearly wanting to be somewhere else but not wanting to leave when Spero was such a mess. "Go, we're fine. I'll whisper if I need anything."

Bronte laughed. "I do try not to eavesdrop you know, but I don't complain about being able to hear your voice anytime you're speaking."

"Save the sweet-talk for a time when I don't have a patient." Athena shooed Bronte away.

Spero made a kissy face, as he often did around the two of them, but the effect was somewhat diminished when he had to stop to wipe blood before it trickled into his mouth.

"Come on, tough guy. Why didn't you plug that thing into your computer instead of into your head?" Athena led Spero to her medical corner.

He pointed at his own head and his screen. Athena knitted her brows. She didn't understand him.

Spero tried again. He mimed trying to remember something and then having an idea. Then he pretended to scroll back through something with his hand until he found what he was looking for. He pointed to his head again.

"Are you saying that all the files you showed us are now stored in your head?" Athena worked hard to keep her mouth from falling open. This crew she'd fallen in with was never boring.

He tapped his screen. It lit and the files she'd read earlier flashed rapidly, page after page.

"So you have a little computer in your face. I guess that makes sense. You'd need more than a screen to do what you can do. Were any of Bard's men able to do what you do? I know they don't have embedded computers, but could you tell if they can control the screens they had the same way you do?" Athena put her hand on Spero's back and led him to an exam table. Spero still didn't like coming over here, but he'd allowed it once before and she needed the supplies.

Spero hopped onto the exam table. He looked around warily but stayed relaxed. He pointed at his screen and raised one finger.

"You're the only one. Do you know why? Bard did this to you, right? Why can't she do it again?" Athena cleaned some of the blood off Spero's face so she could get a better look at his wound.

Despite what must be considerable pain, Spero didn't flinch or show any sign of discomfort. He looked at her and shrugged one shoulder. Bard's motives were a mystery to all of them it seemed.

Athena tended to his wound as best she could. He initially refused to let Galen stitch the port closed under the skin. Eventually Galen and Athena were able to convince him the risks of infection and wound healing complications far outweighed the potential benefits. They'd gotten his pain under control from the prior procedure, she didn't want to introduce another point of discomfort.

Earlier in their relationship Spero likely would have flashed angry or frustrated emotions on his screen and directed it toward one of them. Or perhaps he would have chosen something to make them more compliant. Now however his screen remained dark. Athena placed her hand on his shoulder and gave it a squeeze. He frowned but didn't shake her off.

"I care about you too, but I won't tell anyone you told me." Athena leaned close and whispered so only Spero could hear.

A true smile threatened the corner of his mouth. What did his laugh sound like? Since Galen had the suturing under control Athena left the medical corner. She thought about visiting Bronte, but she was hunched over at her workbench. She looked like she was lost in whatever project had her sprinting away from the group earlier.

Even if she would probably be in the way loitering by Bronte's workbench, she took a moment to admire her unobserved. Bronte's intellect and moral compass were the things that drew her most passionately, but she wasn't complaining about all Bronte had going for her physically either. The woman was gorgeous. Athena liked her women tall, dark, and handsome and Bronte checked all the boxes.

"I know you're busy over there, but I'm enjoying the view of you bent over your workbench. You have a very fine ass, Dr. Zepto," Athena said quietly.

Bronte looked up quickly before locking eyes with Athena.

She blew Bronte a kiss. "Get back to work, hot stuff, but come find me when you're done. It's been a while since I kissed you."

Bronte leaned her head back and looked at the ceiling. She was too far away for Athena to hear anything if she spoke. It was fun teasing her. Bronte's super hearing came in handy at times like this. She blew Bronte another kiss and pointed to her workbench. She turned and sashayed away. When she peeked over her shoulder Bronte was exactly where she'd been, watching Athena's departure.

Athena rooted through their makeshift pantry for something to eat. Their stores were getting low again. One of them would have to make another trip to the store. That was starting to feel more and more risky the longer they stayed here and the more times they confronted Bard's men. But they couldn't stay here forever, could they? They'd made it a home, but it wasn't a real home. She looked at Bronte again. She made it feel like home.

The chip Athena was about to eat never made it to her mouth. Home. How was that possible? That couldn't be true, right? Except it was and she knew it. She'd told Spero the truth about liking him, but as a friend. She did not feel the same way for Bronte. How could Bronte elicit so much more when she wasn't sure she wanted her to? When Spero and Galen were in danger she'd been worried for them. When Bronte had been in danger it felt like a vice was slowly squeezing her insides until nothing worked right. The question now was what was she willing to do about it?

Chapter Twenty-six

B ard slapped her hand on her desk. Her cheeks hurt from the huge smile. Smiling was a strange sensation after so much growling and spitting fire lately. Actually, it felt nice. She looked at the poll numbers on the paper Decimus had handed her as soon as she'd gotten to the office this morning. She slapped the desk again and laughed. That was too strange. She stopped. Smiling was as far as she could go. For now.

"Decimus." Bard shouted instead of using the intercom.

Antonio walked through the door instead of Bard's assistant. "Were you looking for me?"

Bard adjusted her skirt and collected herself. "Yes, actually. Were you sitting outside my office this whole time?" The thought was both comforting and terrifying.

"No. You have better things for me to do than watch Decimus work all day. I came by this morning after I talked to research and development. The suits are done, and the injections are as good as they're going to get. They're not as good as Subject Two's creation, but Alpha assures me they will serve us well. My Romans have been fitted. And for the rally, our boys are ready to roll. We talked about deployment today. Are you ready to step out of the shadows and claim your rightful place in the sun?" Antonio extended his hand to initiate the complicated handshake he and Bard had created as children.

Bard looked at Antonio's offered hand and took it. She was ready. "Extend the reach of the Program. I want everyone who's going to that rally today to have a reason to be on a device we control before they get there. Vacations, blow jobs, crypto. I don't care what you have to dangle to get them to open their computers or phones."

Antonio's eyes gleamed. "And our boys?"

"Activate them. Someone has to be ready to clean the mess and play the hero." Bard pictured the day minute by minute.

Her plan was perfect. After she manipulated the emotions of the attendees of a political rally for the opponent of her candidate, they'd arrive amped and on the edge of control. All a tinderbox needed was a spark, which she was happy to provide. Once chaos broke out, her soldiers would swoop in to restore order and save the day, showing off the new uniforms she'd designed in the process. All she had to do was make sure the opposition candidate was caught in the melee and Bronte Scales and her band of misfits stayed away from her fun.

"I want some of your Romans at the rally today." Bard stopped Antonio before he could make the door.

"Why? There won't be anything at the rally our soldiers can't handle." Antonio looked insulted.

"Not for the rally. I want them there to deal with Dr. Scales and the other two if they dare show their faces. I'm tired of them buzzing around like a mosquito at a picnic. Deal with them for good but keep their secret until we're ready for the world to know." Bard looked at Antonio long and hard until she was sure the message was delivered. The enhanced abilities the Romans now possessed from her version of the zeptobots needn't make its way to the public's consciousness.

Antonio smiled his creepy smile. "Understood, boss. It will be my pleasure."

Bard shuddered. She knew it would be. Poor Dr. Scales. If only she'd been smart enough to get the hell out of town. Whatever fate befell her wasn't on Bard's conscience. Bronte had had plenty of time to run far away. She'd had no choice but to unleash Antonio. If she didn't, there was a tiny chance Bronte could ruin her plans, and failure wasn't an option. What would her father or the board or the world say then? Fear was a powerful motivator, something she knew about firsthand.

Chapter Twenty-seven

B ronte peered through her brand new microscope and a jolt of excitement shot through her. The microscope had been a present from Galen after her last trip out to replenish their food. Bronte didn't ask where Galen had gotten it since it was making her work easier by a factor of one thousand and some things with Galen were best left unspoken.

She looked through the eyepiece again to make sure her eyes hadn't been playing tricks on her. They hadn't. She'd successfully modified the zeptobots, and unlike all of her previous attempts, this time they'd accepted her modifications and were staying in their new form. The zeptobots didn't behave like ants or bees with a queen and subordinates, but she was confident they all communicated instantaneously and worked together toward a common goal. Her exoskeleton was one example, but even when she didn't need them, they seemed to be learning and adapting. With prior iterations she'd adapted one zeptobot and when it was reintroduced to the larger sample all the others rejected it.

This time she'd done what Athena had suggested from the beginning, she'd talked to the zeptobots. It was certainly the first time she'd ever had a conversation with one of her experiments, but in the end it was worth it. Once she explained what she was trying to do, the zeptobots worked with her until they were all satisfied with the outcome.

If her hypothesis was correct, then these new zeptobots were going to be game changers for Spero and Galen. At least once she finished her work and created the custom equipment she had in mind for them. Right now though she wanted Athena. She wanted to tell her about her accomplishment and share her happiness.

Bronte scanned the warehouse but didn't see Athena. She tried the patio. Athena was sitting in a chair they'd made out of old pallets, face to the sun, eyes closed, feet crossed at the ankles. She looked every bit the Greek goddess she was named for. Bronte couldn't move. She was sure time stood still as she stared at Athena and took in her beauty. Bronte's mouth was dry as the desert sand. Looking at Athena, with the sun shining off her hair and making her skin glow, was the first time Bronte truly understood the consequences if Athena walked away when this was over. The thought made her heart rip apart ever so slightly.

The invading thoughts were enough to kill Bronte's high and make her turn back to the warehouse and her work. None of it seemed nearly as exciting now.

"Why are you leaving? You came out here sounding like you were skipping and now you have a rain cloud overhead." Athena propped on one elbow. She looked concerned.

"I was thinking about how beautiful you look, enjoying the sunshine." Bronte hesitated and then sat on the ground against the wall next to Athena.

"And that made you glum? I need a bit more explanation." Athena sat and propped her elbows on her knees, head in hands. She looked expectantly at Bronte.

"No, of course not. Well, sort of. I was thinking about how I'll feel when you leave." Bronte tugged at a small weed that had managed to grow through the concrete. It was honest and maybe a little blunt, but what was the point in beating around the proverbial bush?

Athena knelt in front of Bronte and took her face in her hands. "We're taking on a threat to the world and we're facing it together. I'm here right now and have no plans to leave. Let's tackle one problem at a time, okay?"

Bronte nodded. She could do that, totally, probably. Why was it so damn hard? Before she could fall further into the rabbit hole of questions without answers, Athena kissed her again. It was a kiss of possession, like Athena was marking her territory. Bronte was happy to be claimed.

During their frantic kissing they both lost their precarious balance and tumbled over. Bronte landed on top and wasn't in a hurry to move. She looked at Athena whose dark curly hair was haloed around her. Her eyes were inviting and she smiled like this was the only place she wanted to be. Bronte kissed her again. Athena wrapped her arms around her, holding her tight. Athena moved her ankle up Bronte's calf.

It was a challenge to pull coherent thoughts from her brain while lying on top of Athena, held close and kissing her. She was throbbing painfully and fighting a strong desire to rip Athena's clothes off.

She broke the kiss and took a breath. Athena trailed her nails along the side of Bronte's torso, stopping just below her breast. "Have mercy."

"Begs the woman between my legs." Athena bit Bronte's ear as she whispered.

"I knew I'd walk in on you two fucking one day." Galen whooped loudly and crouched next to them.

"We're not fucking." Bronte squirmed to change her position, but Athena held her tight.

"I lost my balance and took Bronte with me. Happy accident." Athena flicked Galen on the nose.

Galen moved out of the line of fire. "I get it, you tripped and her cock landed inside you. Look, it happens."

Bronte finally wiggled free and helped Athena to her feet. She could feel the heat on her face and knew she must be beet red. She wished she could turn to metal and hide her embarrassment.

"When that day comes, I think I've already told you, there won't be any extra tickets sold. Private performance." Athena took Bronte's hand. "You wanted to show me something?"

Bronte's head was spinning from the kissing, the feel of Athena under her, and Galen's terrible timing and teasing. "Yes. Yes, I did. Actually, Galen, you should come too."

Galen snapped her fingers dramatically. "So nothing naughty then?"

Athena glared at her and opened the door for Bronte. "Behave yourself or I'm going to lock you out here."

Galen pretended to zip her lips and followed them into the warehouse. Bronte slowed her pace as they approached her workbench. The nerve-firing arousal of a few minutes ago was now replaced with annoying, boring nerves. What if they both thought the work she'd done was a waste of time or an affront to science? She'd worked on the zeptobots for years, testing each step meticulously in a pristine lab. This iteration had taken her a couple of weeks of stolen time between everything else they'd been doing during their time in the warehouse, including trying to stay alive. The entire plan for the new zeptobots had been conceived in the warehouse that had seen better days, if she was being generous.

"All right, here you go." Bronte slid a capped, sealed Petri dish across the bench toward Galen.

Galen peered at the dish. "What the fuck is this, mate? I thought you had something more than an empty dish for me."

Bronte took the dish back and slid a prepared slide under her microscope. "It's not empty. Take a look."

Despite her obvious reservations, Galen stepped to the eyepiece. She jumped back immediately.

"What's in there?" Athena looked curiously toward the dish, then to the microscope.

"I don't know for sure, but if I were to guess, they're zeptobots. What are you playing at, mate? You can't just leave those lying around on a table like they're last night's pizza box."

"I'm not playing at anything. I think they can shield you from emotional overload. When I was being bombarded with too much emotion, the zeptobots created this face shield-type thing. It dampened the emotional input. I think they could do that and more for you. They could replace the drugs and you could be free to live.

Isn't that what you said you want? I don't care if you walk out of the warehouse and never speak to me again. I worked on this because I think it will help you."

Galen shook her head. "How do you know they'll work like you say? You thought the ones in you would cure cancer and now you cosplay as the Silver Surfer."

Bronte chewed her lower lip. "You're right, I can't guarantee. But I'm pretty sure. The zeptobots and I talked it over."

Galen stood blinking at her for a very long time. "I must have misheard you, mate. I thought you said you came up with something you want me to put in my body by talking to tiny robots that accidentally gave you superpowers."

"I did. They know themselves better than I do, and I know what I needed them to become for you and Spero. It will work." Bronte's wrist and thumb turned metal, forcing a thumbs-up. She showed Galen. "See, they agree."

"You're insane, you know that? I'm not snorting or drinking or injecting those things. For all I know I'll get your special hearing and I'll get to feel my neighbor's angry sex *and* hear it too."

"I thought you were a bit of a voyeur. Keep an open mind and think it over." Athena moved next to Bronte and took her hand.

While Athena was talking Spero sidled up. Galen's histrionics probably drew his attention.

"I'm glad you're here, Spero. I modified some of the zeptobots for you too." Bronte was off balance but found her footing when Spero arrived. She pointed at another dish on her bench. "I think they'll help amplify your abilities and solve the problem of needing someone to be looking directly at you for your powers to work. They should also be able to help you with your screen. If you want, I think they could remove it, but if you don't want that, they were pretty confident they could heal any remaining damaged tissue. It should get rid of any remaining pain."

Spero looked skeptical. He peered into the microscope and then back toward the dish with his name on it. Galen was looking at her dish like it would leap off the table and bite her.

Bronte was about to try a new tactic when a screeching, screaming alarm sounded from Spero's corner of the warehouse. Everyone jumped. Bronte was metallic which felt like the only thing holding her heart from thundering out of her body.

"What is that?" Athena had her hands over her ears.

Spero ran across the room without answering. The rest of them followed. Spero flew into his desk chair and started typing furiously.

"Have we been discovered?" Bronte began planning an escape that would ensure Athena's safety.

"Do people know who we are?" Galen's foot was tapping wildly.

"Is it Bard?" Athena seemed remarkably calm.

Spero silenced them with a wave of his hands. Everyone shut up but leaned in closer. Spero flew through security and surveillance camera live feeds at breakneck speed. They were all glued to the screen. Bronte wasn't sure what they were looking for, but she couldn't look away. She knew he'd slowly been hacking security footage around the city, but his reach was remarkable. From what she could see, he had nearly the entire city covered. What she didn't know was what his alarm was for or who'd set it off.

Suddenly, a grainy black-and-white image appeared that made her blood run cold. "Stop."

Her demand was echoed by Athena and Galen. They all stared at the live feed. Bronte's stomach churned. She watched as camouflage-clad men with flexible screens sewn into their uniforms attacked, rounded up, and harassed civilians. From what Bronte could see, it looked like the violence was taking place at a political rally.

"Spero, is that what your alarm was? Were you looking for violence in a crowd?"

He shook his head and pointed at one of the uniformed men.

"You were looking for them?" Bronte had never seen the uniforms before. How did Spero know to look for them?

Spero tapped her on the shoulder as she stared at the computer monitor. She looked at him and saw the Department of Defense contract displayed on his screen. There, halfway down the page, was a mockup of the uniforms she was now seeing fully realized.

"Where is that? I have to try and stop it." Bronte looked around the warehouse desperately, hoping there was something useful she'd overlooked in the weeks they'd made it their home.

Bronte whirled around when she felt a hand on her shoulder. It was Spero. He pointed to her workbench and motioned like he was giving himself an injection.

"This could be a trap. Bard's cunning and ruthless. She'd love to eliminate all three of you. Have you thought about what you could be walking into?" Worry lines creased Athena's face.

"It might be, but if it's not, I can't sit here and watch. You told me that I have to use this power I have to protect those that don't. I'm not living your expectations of me if I'm here while innocent people are getting hurt." Bronte pulled Athena into a hug but let her go quickly. It would be so easy to find a reason to stay. "Spero, let's do it." A wave of relief washed over Bronte as she started across the warehouse. At least she wouldn't be alone. Would the zeptobots work? She had no idea. But at least this time he had say over what experiment he was willing to take on.

Halfway there, Athena slipped her hand in Bronte's. "I want to tell you not to go, but I know you have to, so I'll only ask that you come back to me."

Bronte squeezed Athena's hand. "There is no better motivation to return home than knowing you're waiting."

"All right, all right. Enough with the cute stuff. Save the world, then propose." Galen dramatically rolled her eyes and made a gagging noise. "Get two shots of your special serum ready, hot stuff. If the world's ending, I might as well go out doped up on some experimental robot drug that will probably turn me into a fire breathing armadillo."

"That's the spirit. Welcome back to the team." Athena hugged Galen, much to Galen's chagrin.

"Athena, can you get two syringes from your kit?" Bronte took a deep breath then started collecting what she needed as fast as she could. Speed was important but so was care. She might have injected herself in the middle of a fistfight, but she didn't want to hurt her friends.

When Athena returned with the syringes, Bronte checked under the microscope one last time. "Can you prep them for an injection? Bicep is probably fine. I shoved mine in my thigh through my clothes, so I don't know that location matters all that much." Bronte handed Athena a stack of alcohol wipes.

As fast as she could, Bronte prepped the injections and got them into the arms of her friends. Galen immediately contorted in pain. Spero seemed fine until he vomited.

"How long does it take for this to work, mate?" Galen's face was strained, her body tense.

Bronte looked from Spero to Galen. "I'm sorry. I'm so sorry. I should have considered possible side effects until the zeptobots can conform to your systems. I don't remember this happening. As soon as I injected myself Bard knocked me unconscious. You two should stay here. You can't face what's out there like this. I'll scout the scene and come back for you." Bronte was happy her voice was stronger than her resolve. Her stomach was iffy and if the zeptobots hadn't put a hard metallic shell around her knees she probably would have been on the ground.

"Sweetheart, you can't go alone." Athena pulled her into a hug. "I know you want to stop Bard. That you feel like you have to stop her, but even as strong and brave as you are, what's out there is too much. You promised you'd come back."

Bronte wiped at the tears rolling down Athena's cheeks. "I won't be alone. I'll have you. Will you help me like you did before? I'm sure Spero won't mind if you use his computer."

Spero had lowered himself to the floor and was leaning against her workbench. He shook his head weakly.

Athena looked unconvinced but she didn't argue. She jogged to Spero's desk and returned with the earpiece and body camera Bronte had worn the last time she'd ventured out. "Zeptobots, can you secure this better than we did last time? It was hard for me to keep tabs. The camera swung too wildly."

She stuck the camera in the middle of Bronte's chest and it was swallowed by the zeptobots, which then placed it as securely as a badge on her chest. Bronte shivered when Athena leaned close and whispered "don't die" in her ear.

Athena got the earpiece situated and shoved Bronte toward the door. "Go now before I can't watch you walk out. I'm serious about the not dying part. I'll keep an eye on you and these two. I'll send them along as soon as they're ready."

Bronte took a step toward the door, then doubled back and pulled Athena into a searing kiss. She needed her strength and the comfort of the feelings growing between them. Bronte was scared out of her mind, but Athena believed in her. As she raced out the door to face unknown danger, she clung tight to Athena's unwavering confidence. Only time would tell if it was enough to see her through.

CHAPTER TWENTY-EIGHT

A thena could tell from the moment Bronte arrived at the site of the political rally that she was in trouble. She was one among thousands and the crowd was volatile and unafraid of violence. Every time Bronte engaged Bard's soldiers, she was bludgeoned by members of the public that she had come to protect. Either they had misread the situation or Bard was continuing her manipulation in a way they weren't aware of.

"Athena, anytime I get close to them, I'm attacked. Can you see anything from where you're sitting? Are the soldiers doing something to the crowd?" Bronte struggled to stand and protect herself from another onslaught.

"I need a minute to look at the full park camera coverage. Hang tight." Athena fought the pain of watching Bronte suffer She was sure it was close to pulling her apart at the seams. However, there wasn't anything better she could be doing for her than what she was doing. Losing her cool now didn't serve Bronte or any of the people at the rally. She glanced over her shoulder. Spero and Galen were both prone on the ground, curled into a fetal position. She and Bronte were on their own.

Athena flipped through camera angles and rewound footage. She focused on the group closest to Bronte during the last attack. "Gotcha." She pumped her fist triumphantly. "Bronte, five of the men who attacked you were looking at their phones right before they turned on you. Two women were looking at a screen on an iPad, and one man and three women were looking in the direction of two soldiers, so they may have seen the detachable screens."

"Shit." Bronte was breathing heavily, and she sounded in pain. "How many soldiers are here? Can you tell?"

Athena scanned quickly. "At least fifty."

"Sure. No problem. Fifty soldiers and conservatively a thousand cell phones or other types of screens. One of me. Good thing I'm not a betting woman." Bronte was on the ground again, rolling, as multiple boots came in and out of view of the camera.

"Are they trying to stomp on you? You might have to fight back against the civilians. I know you don't want to, but it's not worth you getting seriously injured." Athena bit her lower lip. She wiped at her eyes and gasped as a boot came much too close to the camera.

"I can't. They aren't in control of their decision making. I don't want to get hurt, but it's not fair if I hurt them for something they aren't doing of their own free will. I just have to figure out a way to get to the soldiers and the main screens. Then I'll deal with the cell phones and other stuff." Bronte was back on her feet and running toward a group of soldiers about fifty feet away.

Athena held her breath as another group of rally goers approached with hatred in their eyes. Suddenly Bronte was above them, seemingly floating through the air. "Holy shit. Can you fly now too?" Athena gripped the edge of the makeshift seat.

Bronte landed hard and the camera shook. "No, I jumped. Quite high. You didn't tell me super-heroing was so rough on the knees." She took a few more steps toward the soldiers and then accelerated rapidly. Her arms flailed in front of her. "I don't know what's happening."

"Bronte. Are you okay?' Athena stood and leaned toward the screen. She wanted to reach through the computer and hold Bronte back. She wanted to pull her to safety.

A few seconds later Bronte crashed into a metal box. Four soldiers leaned down and looked at her, laughing. Athena could see their taunting faces.

"See, the problem with metal, *Dr. Zepto*, is it's attracted to magnets. Ms. Verstrand told us you'd probably show. All alone this time? Couldn't get your loser friends to join you? Just as well considering what's waiting for you." One of the men spit in Bronte's face. "Ms. Verstrand will be here soon. Then you and she can have another chat." The soldier looked at his buddies. "And they didn't think we could handle her. They thought only the Romans could bring her down. She doesn't seem that powerful to me."

Athena screamed with rage. She stood so quickly her chair went flying. Galen and Spero looked over her shoulder. Athena studied one, then the other. She'd been so focused on Bronte she'd forgotten to check on them recently. Thankfully, they looked marginally improved. "How are you two feeling?"

"Fit as roadkill and ready to fight." Galen pointed at the screen. "What happened to our girl?"

"She's been captured. They've used magnets to take hold of the zeptobots in her body. Bard's making an appearance at the rally and then she wants to chat with Bronte." Athena rubbed her eyes.

"How do we get her back?" Galen's usual cocky grin and blasé attitude were gone.

Athena closed her eyes. "I don't know yet. I need a minute to think. Are the zeptobots working for you yet?"

"No fucking way." Galen sounded shocked and not as though she was answering Athena's question.

Athena opened one eye. Galen was wearing an intricately detailed hardhat with a longer visor, a crest along the top, and long scythe-shaped pieces covering both cheeks. It was bronze in color, but not like any bronze Athena had ever seen. It was stunning.

"That's a new look for you." Athena pointed to the helmet.

"Even better, I can barely feel your emotions. They're there, but the volume's been turned way down. Plus, I feel like a badass. Do I look like a badass?" Galen had her hands on her helmet, exploring every detail.

"Total badass." Athena smiled at Galen's enthusiasm and obvious pleasure. Galen's face looked more relaxed than she'd ever seen.

"Whoa, check out this guy." Galen stopped exploring her new headwear and took a lap around Spero.

Athena studied Spero's new look. He was head to toe covered in something Athena couldn't quite put her finger on. It resembled a projector or computer screen, but while it looked like it should be reflective, it wasn't. When she looked at it, it was like looking into deep nothingness. It was extremely unsettling.

"Mate, you look like a walking blackhole. Except gray. I think. What color is that suit?" Galen reached out to touch it, but Spero slapped her away.

He lit the screen still attached to his face and a smiley face emoji appeared. He didn't aim at either Athena or Galen so Athena felt no effects. However, as soon as the emoji appeared on his screen the suit began to change color. Before long it was a vibrant blue sky on a clear day. Despite the circumstances, Athena was overjoyed. She couldn't stop staring at Spero's suit and the beautiful blue color.

"I've never realized how amazing the color blue is. It's so gorgeous." Athena clapped her hands together. "I know things might look a little bleak, but we can do this. How about we go out on the patio and get some sunshine? I couldn't ask for better teammates and we're going to figure out how to get Bronte back. Let's devise a great plan."

Spero turned off his screen and the suit faded back to black hole chic. Athena's mood faded with the color of Spero's clothing. She was close to tears as the weight of Bronte's capture and how damn worried she was returned. Feeling happy despite her pain had been a respite from the emotions crashing like waves through her heart. She wasn't sure if she should be thanking Spero or cursing him.

"It seems like you two are in fighting shape, so it's time to come up with a plan to free Bronte. Spero, can you keep an eye on Bronte or bring the computer with us? There's not enough room over here." Athena went to Bronte's workbench. She wanted to be close to her. Bronte would return. Athena had to believe that. Now she had to figure out how to make it happen. She prayed she was the woman for the job.

❖

Bronte struggled fiercely against the cuffs binding her hands behind her back. Not only were they bound tightly, the cuffs digging painfully into her skin, but she was unable to summon her metal skeleton to her arms and hands. The magnets were clearly repelling the zeptobots and making it impossible for them to travel past her elbows. But her elbows and upper forearms were tingling uncomfortably like she was being jabbed with hot needles. She didn't like guessing, it was too emotional and unscientific, but if she were to guess now, the zeptobots were fighting back against the magnets. "Walk or I will relish the excuse to make this painful for you." One of the two men dragging her forward punched her in the stomach as he delivered his threat.

Although she wanted to ask questions, like what this asshole had against her, demand her release, or fight, she knew she was in no position to dictate the terms of their arrangement. Bronte stumbled along, hoping she would find an opportunity to fight her way out of this predicament. She thought of Athena. Was she watching now?

Bronte bent her chin toward her chest, as close to the camera as she could. She lowered her voice to a pebble drop above a whisper, as low as she dared to go if she wanted to remain audible. "I love you." She got no response to her impulsive declaration.

One of the men slapped her in the back of the head, hard. "Cupcake, I didn't know you cared. You should save your sweet-talk for Ms. Verstrand."

They approached the stage at the front of the rally crowd. It was surrounded by Bard's soldiers standing at attention, screens on, but blank at least for now. Bronte looked onstage and caught a glimpse of overly shiny, expensive sky-high heels and crisply ironed, perfectly tailored pants. She was disappointed in Bard. She expected her to be dressed in full bad guy haute couture to complement her purchased army. Slick businesswoman made her a dime a dozen supervillain.

Her captors dragged her on stage and uncuffed her long enough to give her hope. That glimmer was extinguished quickly when the zeptobots still weren't able to overcome the magnets and she was prodded with an electric shock stick that brought her to her knees. She realized they'd attached armbands above the handcuffs which were still in place. That must be what was keeping the zeptobots at bay.

"That's in case you were thinking anything I wouldn't like." The chatty one of her escorts sneered at her and waved the shock stick in her face.

She was quickly secured again, this time with her arms straight out from her body at roughly ear height. Her feet were spread apart. She was strung up to metal framework built into the stage like a metal statue of the Vitruvian Man. Bronte struggled against her bonds until Bard and Antonio stepped into her field of vision.

"Dr. Scales, I assumed you were tired of losing and yet, here you are. You must know by now the outcome will never change between the two of us. It seems your friends are clear on how this will end, as I see they didn't join you on this foolish exercise today." Bard paused a long time as if waiting until she had Bronte's full attention before continuing. "Since you decided to join me today, you can have the best seat in the house for my speech to my adoring fans. I'm here to explain to them why they should be afraid, terrified actually, and who can help them sleep better at night."

Bronte rolled her eyes. "Let me guess, that someone is you?"

"Of course not." Bard looked horrified. "Why would I want to waste my time babysitting mind-controlled automatons? I have no interest in governing. I want to control him." Bard pointed to a square-jawed, neat haircut in a suit who looked dead in the eyes and overly eager to please.

Bronte recognized Bard's patsy. He was running for governor, and having Bard that close to the levers of power was a ghastly thought. "That's a dumb plan." Bronte tried putting as much conviction in her voice as possible.

"Says the woman whose plan got her tied up on stage." Bard turned to leave. "Out of curiosity, why's it a dumb plan?"

"If you're not smart enough to figure it out, I'm certainly not going to ruin the surprise for you." Bronte winked and hoped her acting skills were good enough to fake out someone confident and overly cocky.

Bard glared at her. "What is she talking about? There had better not be any surprises. If you know anything, now's the time to tell me." Bard seethed at her soldiers.

One of the two men who'd escorted her to the stage-whispered in her ear and pointed at Bronte. She didn't have a good feeling about whatever information he was passing along.

The longer she listened the darker her face became. She stomped back to her. "Where is it?"

"Where's what? I don't have anything." Bronte tried to move her arms and her shoulders wrenched. She stifled a yelp.

"The communication equipment. Probably a camera and earpiece. Am I right? Is that what you were talking about? Planning some kind of escape or ambush? Do you think we didn't anticipate that?" Bard pointed to Bronte's head and one of her men grabbed her by the chin and turned her head roughly.

Bronte's stomach dropped. She hadn't heard from Athena or the others, but she couldn't lose the possibility that she would. The hope that she'd hear Athena's voice and be reassured that everything would be okay was about the only thing keeping her from losing it completely. Right now Bard had only been able to keep the zeptobots from her arms, but what if they got her out of the rest of her suit? What would happen to the camera?

Before the panic blossomed into a full-blown attack, Bronte felt as if someone had shoved hard, thick cotton balls in both ears. Her hearing was diminished but not gone completely. She wasn't sure what was happening, but her instinct told her it was to her benefit. Maybe the zeptobots were figuring out how to work beyond the magnet.

Bard moved to Bronte's right. She could feel her breath on her ear and cheek. Bronte recoiled. Bard moved to the other side. She yelled something Bronte had trouble making out, then Bard hit her on the side of the head. She could have done without that, but as she now suspected that side of her head was metal, it seemed to hurt Bard as much as her.

"Dig it out." Bard looked furious.

One of her men scraped at her ear. After a few minutes, Bard's henchman held his hands up in apparent surrender.

Bard shoved him to the side and called another man forward. "Find the camera."

Bronte was poked and prodded for another ten minutes without Bard finding what she was looking for. Bronte said a silent and very enthusiastic thank you to the zeptobots who she assumed were responsible for keeping the camera and earpiece hidden.

At the end of the search Bard got right in her face. "Antonio wanted to take you back to the lab immediately, but I wanted you to stay for the show. I don't have a magnet big enough for anything but your hands out here, but when he takes you back to the lab, you'll never wear metal again. Enjoy the last bit of time you have with those zeptobots before he rips them out of your dead body."

Bard patted her cheek condescendingly and turned away. She transformed into the smarmy CEO of a multibillion-dollar company and gave a speech in support of her handpicked gubernatorial candidate. It was full of fear, fire, and brimstone. She praised the troops who had bravely fought and captured the out-of-control criminal who'd disrupted the peaceful rally. With a grin that suggested she was playing a game already three moves ahead, she motioned at Bronte.

Bronte was displayed like a trophy. People threw trash, shoes, and rocks. By the time Bard was done and the dumb as a box of rocks candidate took to the mic, he could have said anything, and the crowd would have followed him to the ends of the earth. Seen in action, Bard's program was impressive. Bronte had to get free. She had to figure out how to stop Bard and disable the program the soldiers were using. She didn't have a plan for any of it, and worst of all she hadn't heard a thing from any of her friends back at the warehouse. Did they know she'd been captured? Were they worried about her? Were Spero and Galen okay?

Bronte knew it was time to level with Athena about her feelings. Not just that she loved her and wanted her to stick around, but about the deeper stuff. She'd tried to talk to Athena already about her fears surrounding what she'd become and that she wasn't the kind of woman Athena deserved, but she needed to try again. She needed Athena to hear her. Being captured and threatened with serious bodily harm had clarified a few things. She owed it to Athena and herself to be honest. First thing first however was getting out of her magnetic bracelets and back to full fighting strength. Despite having all the motivation she needed waiting for her back at the warehouse, things were looking bleak. She tugged at the restraints, lacking a better plan. Her shoulders screamed in protest. Bronte had spent most of her life on her own and yet, in this moment, she wasn't sure she'd ever been more alone. At least she had the zeptobots and the hope that her friends were at the warehouse, readying a plan to come for her. Her only solace was that the final pages of this particular comic book were yet to be written. Hopefully, the story didn't include her being back on a lab table, alone and probably dead.

CHAPTER TWENTY-NINE

Athena paced her third or maybe fiftieth lap between Bronte's workbench and Spero's desk. She was like a skipping record glued to the turntable. Hope as she approached Bronte's workbench turned to despondency when she drew near the computer and saw Bronte strung up on stage behind Bard. Spero had pulled every angle of the rally he could find. They had plenty of information even if it was hard to look at.

"Do you think it's safe to talk to her yet?" Athena leaned close to the computer screen. It was hard to make out details about Bronte's health, mental or physical, but she knew her so well, she could tell Bronte was struggling.

Spero shook his head. He pointed at Bard.

Athena groaned. "I know. I don't want her to think we've abandoned her, that's all. Once we have a plan, we'll get in touch. Not a moment sooner, for her sake and ours." She turned and finished her loop.

This time she stopped at the workbench and sat. She picked up Bronte's pencil and pulled over a piece of paper. How long had she been staring at the paper? It was still blank. Athena aggressively ran her fingers through her hair then slammed her fists on the bench. She yelled out in frustration.

"Whoa, little help please. I pushed a button I don't think I should have." Galen sounded panicky.

Athena spun around. She saw Spero bounding over as well. Galen was sitting on her bunk. She stood. Spero took one look at her and screamed. It wasn't a silent scream, but a full-throated, shake the roof panels, scream of terror. Galen and Athena stared at him.

"That's some high quality belting, mate. I expected you might be rusty if your voice ever came back but you went right for the high note. Impressive." Galen gave him a slow clap ovation.

Athena looked back and forth between Spero and Galen. "I don't know which of you to start with. Spero, can you do more than scream? Galen, why are you a half lion, half peacock, zero human?" Indeed, Galen herself seemed to have disappeared. In her place was a lion's head, complete with enormous mane and Galen's features, which then morphed into the body of a peacock, complete with beautiful, multi-colored tail feathers. At the moment they were on full display filling most of their sleeping quarters. The size of the head looked like it should tip the body right over. It was incongruous and disturbing.

Spero looked like he had something very painful in his throat he was trying to spit out. Athena waited patiently.

"Mayb…n…re…z…ots." Spero looked disgusted as well as a little baffled.

Athena hugged him. "Give it time. It sounds like you and the zeptobots are getting to know each other and learning how to become partners. That doesn't happen in a few hours. I, for one, can't wait to hear what's on your mind. I can be patient until that day comes."

Spero hadn't hugged her back initially but squeezed her tightly when she was done talking. When he let go, Athena turned to Galen expectantly.

"I don't know that the *why* I look this fabulous is all that important. The *how* is the interesting bit." Galen looked at Athena hopefully.

Athena rolled her hand to get Galen to move along with the story. It was hard to have a serious conversation with a talking lion head whose tail feathers shook every time she moved her feet.

"I started noticing my kick-ass helmet might be doing some other things. It doesn't seem to only block emotional input. These

zeptobots learn and create things on their own. It's amazing."
Galen shook her head, presumably to focus and her mane shook
majestically. Her tail feathers rustled behind her. "Anyway, this
helmet seems to block the input by absorbing it. And then it's there
for me to use."

"What do you mean 'there for you'?" Athena was having a
hard time not staring at Galen's tail.

"Like tokens for a video game. I think I can use the emotional
energy absorption to turn into anything I want." Galen looked like a
giddy ten-year-old.

"And the first thing you chose to mold emotions into was an
impractical animal combo?" Athena indicated Galen's current state.
"Why?"

"Isn't it obvious? Built in boa and best hair day every day built
right in. Plus, you don't have to lick your own ass since there's no
cat butt to be found." Galen turned around and ruffled her tail
feathers.

Athena dug the heels of her hands into her temples. "How
is this going to help Bronte? We're supposed to be planning. I'm
supposed to be planning. Spero, go back to the computer, please."

Spero shuffled off, muttering to himself. Athena couldn't quite
tell but it sounded like his words still weren't fully formed when
they left his mouth, but it was amazing to hear him at all. He had a
beautiful deep baritone.

"I'm more useful like this, you know." Galen looked at Athena
seriously. "I can turn into anything. That will help us."

"As long as your battery's charged, and you don't decide a
mermaid tail is cooler than two ax hands." Why was she being a
jerk? The stress was getting to her, and she missed Bronte like a part
of her insides was missing but she shouldn't take it out on Galen.

"Hey, I know I tease you two, but I see the way you look at
each other. You don't find that with someone very often. And I want
her back too. I don't have many friends." Galen transformed back
into herself, and it looked fluid rather than painful, almost as though
water was taking shape, sliding and flowing into the person who
was Galen.

"Not working for a villain might be a good place to start attracting some new ones." Athena pulled Galen into a hug too. She hadn't realized how much she'd needed the closeness. "Want to help me figure out our great rescue plan?"

"Thought you'd never ask." Galen shot over to the one seat at Bronte's workbench and claimed it. "Let's get to work. If Spero can talk and I'm a transformer, we might have half a chance. You have any special powers you want to unveil?"

"Nothing to report." Everything she'd been proud of in her life until this moment seemed trivial in this situation. Normal people were bound to feel less-than when surrounded by exceptional ones. She'd have to adjust to feeling mediocre.

"Don't sell yourself short. None of us would have lasted a week without you here. Kidnapping you was the best decision any of us made, but please don't press charges. I wouldn't do well in jail." Galen smiled sweetly.

"Get to work and I'll take it under advisement." Athena rapped the pencil on Galen's knuckles.

"What about..." Galen grabbed the paper and pencil. She shook her head and handed the pencil back.

"How about..." Athena started to write, then erased.

That went on for an hour. Galen brought over snacks. Spero checked on them and gave them an update on the rally. Lucky for them it showed no sign of wrapping up. Bard may have kicked off the speeches, but there appeared to be a long line of political puppets who extolled the virtues of Bard's company and military while blaming the peacemakers for taking away everything good about their country. A bit of xenophobia was thrown in too, probably as a way to prep the country for the eventual international takeovers. Athena went to check on Bronte herself, mostly because she needed to see her, but when she saw how Bronte looked tired and pained, her heart ached. She'd been tied in the same awkward position for far too long now. If only magnets weren't binding her hands. Magnets! That was it.

Athena rushed back to Galen and their work. She motioned for Spero to follow her. "Galen, magnets. I think that's the key. Spero, will that work?"

Spero looked thoughtful, then his eye lit with excitement. He nodded enthusiastically.

Galen looked confused. Spero pulled over the still blank paper and drew a quick diagram. Understanding slowly dawned across Galen's face.

"Magnets, fear, and peacocks." Galen started writing furiously.

Athena shook her head. "It doesn't have to be fear, and peacocks won't get the job done."

"You have no faith in the power of the peacock." Galen looked serious. "You know fear is the fastest way to get what we need. That's exactly why Bard is using it. It's the most primitive part of the brain, the bit that reacts swiftly to protect us. It's going to have to be part of it. At least at the beginning."

Athena nodded. "But no one innocent gets hurt and, Spero, you use it as little as possible."

"We'll do the best we can." Galen looked to Spero, who nodded, before she went back to writing. "You can keep an eye on us from here."

"Not this time. I'm coming with you." Athena had been thinking it over and she couldn't sit this one out. Even if she had to take her place strung up on stage, she was going to make sure Bronte was free.

Galen looked like she wanted to argue, but she didn't say a word.

Athena made sure Galen and Spero were okay finishing the write-up and then made her way to the computer. As soon as they were able, she wanted to talk to Bronte. Her heart ached seeing her hurting and not being able to tell her it would be okay, that she was working on getting her home. That she hadn't forgotten about her. Did Bronte doubt that? Did she trust Athena's feelings?

She paused. She hadn't told Bronte how she felt. She'd been scared of losing a life that had seemed perfect but now looked empty.

If she returned to it at the expense of the woman she loved, she'd be giving in to the same fear that had ruled her life for so long. There was nothing waiting around the corner that could be better or more exciting than what she was looking at on grainy security footage right now. Bronte was the adventure she wanted. It was all so clear now. All she had to do was rescue her girl and tell her how she felt. The normal everyday girl falls for girl stuff. No problem, she totally had this. She said a prayer that was true. It had to be.

Chapter Thirty

B ronte was tired. The speeches were endless, the sun was relentless, and her shoulders were screaming. She was a scientist. She wasn't used to tests of physical or mental stamina, and any physical stuff lately had been down to the zeptobots. She wasn't sure how much longer she could go on.

She was desperate for the sound of Athena's voice, but she'd heard nothing but the delusional ramblings of Bard and her minions. She surveyed the crowd. A few, maybe one out of ten, looked truly engaged and buying in to what was being said. The vast majority looked like robots, only without her shiny shell. She thought about what Athena told her about perceptions. How would those in the crowd define themselves? Probably not as the robots she saw. Who was right?

Bronte looked at the soldiers surrounding the stage. Their uniform screens appeared blank. How was the crowd under Bard's control? She strained to see behind her. She could just make out the corner of a projector screen. That must be how she was holding this crowd in check. But why? There was no fawning media or wall-to-wall coverage. From what she could tell it was a bunch of men getting to the microphone and blustering. There had to be something she was missing.

"Bronte, can you hear me?"

It took all of Bronte's willpower not to weep with joy, call to the heavens, or shake her ass in an embarrassing dance of excitement and relief. "Yes, I've missed your voice." She kept her voice low and tried to move her mouth as little as possible. She realized ventriloquists were more talented than she gave them credit for.

"We have a plan to get you out of your current pickle and stop Bard. We're going to need your help. You game?" Athena sounded energized in a way Bronte had never heard before. It suited her.

"Is the camera still working? Can you see what my 'pickle' as you called it, looks like? Bronte subtly rotated her body as much as she could within the limitations of her restraints.

"We've never taken our eyes off you. I wanted to get in touch sooner but we didn't want to risk Bard going Sherlock Holmes on us and ruining the surprise. I've been worried about you." Athena's voice was lower, and Bronte could hear the emotion.

"I'm okay, but I could really use one of your pep talks and a hug." Bronte sagged against her restraints. It put more strain on her shoulder joints but relieved pressure on her muscles.

"Pep talk first, hug after we finish the job. And I have a few surprises for you when we get there. We're close. You're going to have to get out of those restraints on your own and come help Galen and Spero. I don't pack as much punch as you do so I'm going to run the show from the wings." Athena was back in charge of her emotions and the operation.

"Galen and Spero aren't letting you come with them, are they?" Bronte's stomach churned.

"They're not letting me do anything because I'm not a child or a dog on a leash that needs permission to go where I please. I'm coming along to make sure the right people are in handcuffs at the end of this." The fire in Athena's tone was not subtle.

"That was dumb of me. I should have said, I'm glad you'll be here with us and I can't wait to see you." Bronte wanted to cover her face in shame but that would have been a giveaway that she was talking to someone, not that it was possible in her current situation anyway. "Tell me how I'm going to get out of these cuffs once you arrive. And after I do, what then?"

"Magnets."

Bronte could hear the smile in Athena's voice. She felt like someone had blown a white fluffy dandelion in her chest and it was spreading warmth and sweet, glorious fuzzy feelings near and far. "I'm going to need a little more than that."

"Let me see if I can merge what I know and what Spero imparted. You're being held with magnetic restraints. In the hospital Bard did the same thing to keep part of your arm flesh, not metal, so she could draw blood and keep an IV in." Athena paused as if waiting for the information to sink in Bronte's brain. "The zeptobots were fighting back. I don't think it would have been long before they won."

"Okay. I still don't understand. If the zeptobots could fight this, they would have already. I asked them. We're both stuck here." Bronte pulled her arms against the cuffs again with the same result. "Bard already has magnets and I don't want to become an even bigger one. Everyone's metal pocket contents would fly over and stick to me."

"As much as I'd love to see that, I'm not sure you know how to make yourself into a magnet and I don't want you to waste time trying. I want you to make yourself unattractive." Athena was giggling.

"Excuse me?" Bronte spoke louder than she meant to.

One of the men on stage turned to her and yelled over, "You heard what he said. Grow a thicker skin."

"We might need to talk about the group of friends you hang out with, babe." Athena still sounded amused.

"Can we get back to my attractiveness?" Bronte was trying to concentrate but her time in the sun and the pain in her arms were robbing her of some of her mental capacity.

"There is nothing you could do that would lessen your attractiveness to me. What I need you to do is convince the zeptobots to stop being so attractive. Specifically, they need to reconfigure and make themselves repellant. If they do that, they should repel those magnets and you can break free." Athena was back to business.

"You hear that, guys? It's all up to you." Bronte looked to her hands. Old habits died hard.

"Work on your physical science homework, we'll be there soon. We have to get the civilians out of the park, then we can go after Bard."

"Athena, be careful. The crowd looks strange. Most of them look like brainwashed zombies. She has them under control. I think there's a screen behind me. I don't know how they'll react when they see you three." Bronte's stomach was churning at the thought of Athena among the dead-eyed robot crowd. "Hold on, I heard something."

Before she could see anything, she was able to identify the sound. It was chanting. The chanting of a large group of people and it was getting louder. Suddenly, Antonio snatched the microphone from the latest sap and roared at the crowd. "The enemy approaches. They've come to deny you the right to cast your vote, for what you believe in. We have your back. Bard Verstrand and your next governor have your back. Stand strong. Stand strong."

"You catching all this?" Bronte pulled at the restraints again. "There's going to be a bloodbath. Where are you guys?"

"We're about a block away. Right behind every media station and newspaper in the area. Whatever happens here today is going to be broadcast far and wide." Athena blew out a breath. "We'd better be on the right side of this one in our hearts and public opinion."

"Stopping Bard is the most important thing. I'll take the fall if anything goes pear-shaped." Bronte tried the cuffs again, willing the zeptobots to reverse their polarity.

"The hell you will. Now that I found you, you don't get to run off to jail and show your shiny side to anyone willing to have a look. Get your ass out of those cuffs and come help us. Enough standing on stage like a diva."

Bronte had only meant to protect Athena and the others. None of it would matter if they couldn't show the world who Bard really was. "Come on, zeptobots, you heard the lady. I need you to become a superconductor. Or at least something much less attractive than you are now. Can you help us both out?"

By way of answer, both of Bronte's middle fingers turned metal.

"What? Now you're mad at me too? What did I do?" Bronte let her head lean back. She looked at the clouds passing overhead. That was a mistake because she didn't see the bottle that thudded off her chest and didn't have time to prepare for the blow to her sternum. Apparently, the crowd wasn't done with her yet.

The bottle seemed to be the last straw for the zeptobots too. Bronte didn't have time for consultation or processing. Her wrists and ankles cooled far beyond what she'd normally tolerate, and the restraints flew off. The bent and twisted metal spun and catapulted through the air like latex fragments the moment a water balloon is filled too full.

What happened next distorted in her field of vision and played out in slow motion. Bard screamed in rage and pointed at Bronte, who took off for the edge of the stage and jumped for the crowd. As she started to descend, her footing became semisolid and there was something underneath for her to push off of. She did so and was flung back into the air. She waved her arms wildly, trying to catch her balance. She stumbled when she practically fell from the sky. She was more prepared for the sensations and counteraction the next time. She jumped her way over the crowd, trying her best to avoid thrown objects and obvious recordings and pictures.

Finally, she saw Athena, Galen, and Spero enter the park. She made her way to them and landed a bit more roughly than she intended. Apparently, she still had a bit to learn about sky hopping.

As soon as she was on the ground, Athena pulled her into a crushing hug. "I knew deep down you could fly."

There was so much Bronte wanted to say, but now wasn't the time. The question burning a hole in her brain, however, was whether Athena had heard her impulsive declaration? "Did you hear me when I was being dragged to the stage?"

Athena shook her head. "I was with Galen, I think. Spero, did you hear what Bronte said?"

Spero frowned. His eyebrows knit together. "Assum...fo.... meeeeeeee."

"You can talk?" Bronte knew her mouth was hanging open in disbelief. "Why would you assume I was saying 'I love you' to you?"

A shit-eating grin spread across Spero's face. Bronte wanted to knock it off him. She turned to Athena who looked a little stunned.

"You said that?" She searched Bronte's face.

"I did. I meant it too." Bronte took one of her hands.

"Guys, not to interrupt this lovely moment, but all the saccharine shit isn't going to help us against them." Galen pointed at the large crowd advancing toward them. Behind that group of unfriendlies, the other group had finally entered the park and was drawing a fair amount of attention from Bard's group.

"Let's go. Galen, you're going to need that helmet. Spero, suit ready? And, you, I need you all shined up and ready to go." Athena gave Bronte's hand a squeeze before letting go and switching into full superhero boss lady.

Bronte went metallic and girded herself mentally. She'd never had a successful battle, but they didn't have a choice this time. The team had also upgraded since the most recent failure. She didn't know what Galen's helmet was or about Spero's suit, but she hoped they were from the zeptobots and they were working as hard for her friends as they did for her.

Bronte looked back to the stage and Bard. She was pacing like an angry earwig in a jar, doing the human equivalent of snapping her pinchers and posturing. She still had a microphone and control of the crowd, so she remained dangerous. She could hear her even when she wasn't shouting into the microphone. She waved at her friends to be quiet. She needed to hear what Bard was saying.

"If you're going to stop and listen, we need to do it from somewhere other than here." Galen pointed to the two approaching crowds on a crash course, where the foursome stood almost directly at the meeting point.

"I don't need to hear anymore. I was right about the bloodbath, but that's what she's counting on. Actually, they've planned for it. They're arguing so I can't tell who is the mastermind. She's in control of that group too." Bronte pointed over her shoulder at the oncoming protest group. "They're supposed to come in and instigate violence so that her security forces can crush them."

Athena shook her head, looking horrified. "It plays right into the message of fear she's been stoking. All politicians use it, but I don't think it's ever been weaponized like this. Does she care how many people die today?"

Bronte shook her head. Her eyes hurt with the pressure of unshed tears. "No. And Antonio certainly doesn't either. He said to one of the uniformed men not to worry about a high body count. The higher it goes, the more likely it stays in the news cycle."

"Time for us to get to work then." Galen tapped her head in mock salute and what looked like an ancient battle helmet appeared, covering her head and cheeks.

Bronte must have looked surprised because Galen smiled and pointed at her helmet. "You like? You're not the only game in town anymore, mate. Spero and I have some new tricks we're dying to show you."

New tricks sounded good to Bronte. They'd need them all. As long as everyone followed the one rule Athena had given her, no dying. Bronte looked to her left, then right. The crowds on either side of them were overwhelmingly large. The air crackled with an ugly cocktail of rage, desperation, and frustration. Bronte's heart was heavy. She didn't want to hurt any of them but knew it might come to that. Was there an acceptable number of casualties to save the majority? There wasn't to her, but what if she had no choice? Would she be able to live with herself? She looked at the media helicopters circling overhead. Would the world forgive her?

Athena kissed her cheek and whispered, "It's going to be okay. We've got this."

The metal on her cheek felt warm from the kiss but it didn't penetrate to her internal turmoil. Athena seemed so sure, but how could she be? Bronte hoped she was right because the cost of failure was too high to contemplate.

Athena called out to each of them and gave instructions. They took their positions and soon were surrounded by warring political factions. Bronte was quickly engulfed in the crowd and had no time to think about anything but the tasks assigned to her. The battle had begun.

CHAPTER THIRTY-ONE

A s soon as the crowds converged and the real action began, Athena did as she'd promised and got out of the fray. She scrambled up an embankment on one side of the park which gave her as close to an aerial view as she was going to get.

She'd sent Bronte back to the stage to knock out the projector. Spero and Galen were where she'd left them in the crowd. They were tasked with keeping the two factions from engaging until Bronte could give them back control of their emotions, until Spero got a hold of them to calm everyone down, which he couldn't do until the soldiers' screens had been neutralized as well. There wasn't any way for them to block cell phone signals, but it was the best they could do.

"Bronte, we're having a little trouble with crowd control here. How close are you to the projector?" Galen was out of breath.

"You saw the size of the crowd. I'm doing the best I can. I can't run through people." Bronte had a hint of annoyance in her voice.

Athena could see Bronte fighting her way through the crowd.

"Mate, you can salsa across the sky. You can practically fly. Why the actual fuck are you on the ground?" Galen was well past hinting at annoyance.

"Bronte, if there is a faster way to the stage, now would be a good time to explore that option. Galen, what happened to your helmet?" Athena scanned back and forth from Bronte and Galen and Spero. Galen looked on the verge of panic and she was glancing from side to side as if lost.

"I'm having a little trouble with that, actually." Galen's words were clipped and strained. "It's like it keeps falling off. It was so easy back at home."

"Murph turwoo." Spero let out a groan and a stream of sounds that certainly sounded like impolite language.

Athena watched as Galen and Spero appeared to be swallowed by the angry crowd. Fists rose and fell, and she heard nothing from either of them for seconds that passed like time in an hourglass filled with rocks.

"The helmet's not falling off. You and the zeptobots aren't communicating. You're a team now, neither of you runs the show. Don't fight them. You have to trust them as your teammates like you trust us." Bronte was forceful and confident.

To Athena's great relief, a swath of people fell away from the mosh pit around Spero and Galen and the two of them stood, seemingly unharmed, back-to-back, moving in tandem in a circle. Spero's suit was flickering dimly. Athena couldn't see Galen's helmet.

"I don't trust you a lick." Galen looked in Bronte's direction. "You're like a raptor who's choosing to bounce along the ground like a fucking chicken instead of flying like you were made to do."

"I'm going to assume you meant that chickens look silly when they walk, not that I'm a coward." Bronte sounded amused. "Have a look above the crowd and give the zeptobots a chance before you blow this for all of us."

Athena looked to the last place in the crowd she'd seen Bronte. It was as thrilling as the first time to watch her rise high above human height and run across the air as if she were hopping from rock to rock in a stream.

Bronte was fast, but she was the only thing above the crowd. She was drawing a lot of attention.

"You might want to test your top speed, babe. I think you're about to have projectiles headed your way." Athena flinched when a bottle nearly hit Bronte in the back of the head.

"They have to catch me to hit me." Bronte zigged and zagged her way to the stage as quickly as she could.

Every soldier raised their guns at her, but she was moving so quickly and erratically only a few took shots. Bronte was almost to the projector when the second round of shots rang out. Athena heard the sound of metal on metal and saw Bronte knocked from the sky. She stood and screamed her name, her heart in her throat as her stomach dropped.

Athena ducked behind a boulder when a few of the closer members of the crowd looked her way attempting to locate the source of the scream. She peeked from behind the granite toward the stage. The soldiers rushed up the stairs. Bard stood over something; she assumed it was Bronte.

"Bronte, can you hear me?" Athena took a deep breath and wiped at the tears. "Spero, Galen. How are you two? Bronte gave you good advice. You need to work *with* the zeptobots. Talk to them if you have to."

"I think we've got it figured out. She saved our asses." Galen was somber. "You know if she's down, one of us has to go and finish what she was trying to do, right?"

"Hey, helmet head, stay in your own lane." Bronte sounded strained, but not under attack.

Athena peered back around her rock in time to see Bronte climb back into the air and launch herself through the projector screen. It tore and collapsed. Bronte circled back, grabbed the computer sitting next to the destroyed screen, and sprinted back across the sky toward Galen and Spero.

"Show-off." Galen's attempt at grumpiness was undermined by the clear joy in her voice.

Athena slumped against the rock and put her head in her hands. She closed her eyes for a moment and reminded herself to breathe. The worst was yet to come. The civilian crowds were awful, but they hadn't attempted to directly engage Bard's men.

Watching from the safety of the warehouse was hard, but this? This was something altogether different. She shuddered. The battle was far from over and she'd never abandon her friends, but for a brief respite, she needed the tiny space she carved out for herself behind this rock where the battle didn't exist and all that was in front of her was a beautiful park.

When she'd sought adventure previously, she'd never imagined anything close to this. She opened her eyes and peered around the rock. She found Bronte easily, high above everyone, shining brilliantly in the sun, her face the very picture of heroism. She might never have pictured this, but here was where she wanted to be. She climbed atop the rock and tapped open her comm line again.

Chapter Thirty-two

The plan wasn't working.

Bronte, Galen, and Spero were preventing the warring factions from killing each other, but they weren't getting anyone out of the park. Worse, it wouldn't be long until they'd have to defend themselves more aggressively and innocent people would start to get hurt. Taking down the projector didn't seem to have had any effect. Somehow, people were still being influenced.

"Athena, can you see what Bard's doing?" Bronte looked over to the rock where Athena had been calling out crowd movements and alerting them to breakout skirmishes.

"Hang on, I'm going to get a better look. She's planning something."

Bronte searched the ridge but didn't see Athena among the trees or boulders. She climbed higher in the sky until she saw her fighting the tide of people surging away from the stage. "What are you doing? That's not safe." Bronte's hands started sweating and her knees wobbled.

"You're one to talk. You're thirty feet in the air with angry people all around you trying to knock you back to earth." Bronte started to argue but Athena cut her off. "Don't even start with the superpowers thing." Athena lunged at something in the crowd and then kept forcing her way forward. "I helped myself to a hat, cell phone, and one of these inflatable silver rally sticks. I have a helmet, a screen, and I'm bright and shiny. Three in one."

"That's not close to the same. Be careful, okay?" Bronte gave a quick salute in Athena's direction.

Bronte turned her attention back to the fight on the ground. The crowds on both sides of them looked eerily similar. Although they were displaying plenty of passionate, volatile emotions, there was something missing in their eyes. They looked as if they were watching themselves and trying to discern where the conviction was coming from. They didn't look like their heart was in it even as their bodies marched on.

Spero's suit was orange and the stress level it was creating was obvious. The people closest were afraid and didn't want to come near but were being propelled ahead by the masses behind them. From the sky Bronte could see how close they were to catastrophe.

She landed next to Spero. It was loud on the ground. She had to shout to be heard, even through their comms. "It's about to get ugly. Fear isn't going to work."

"What do you suggest?" Galen had turned into a horse and was galloping back and forth maintaining their neutral zone between the two groups.

Bronte muttered to herself as she worked out the details of a rapidly developing plan. "Spero, try making this forward group happy. Galen, can you help him? Let's see if joy is a stronger motivator than fear." Bronte made sure they understood before she climbed back into the sky.

"Once we start the party, then what?" Galen looked delighted with the assignment.

"Convince as many people as you can to leave the park, that's what. I'll be right back for the fun. I need to check on Athena." Bronte ran through the air, straight for the stage and the soldiers with guns. She'd happily get shot one hundred times more if it kept Athena safe.

As she approached, Bronte saw Athena on stage, inching her way closer to Bard who looked like she was relishing the violence and chaos, and three men who were hunched over a bank of laptops she hadn't noticed before, thanks to them being under a canopy of sorts. Bronte admired Athena's bravery even if she wished she'd be more careful. The least she could do was draw some attention away from Athena's approach.

The closest soldiers drew their guns as Bronte neared. She ran high enough that if they shot the bullets would sail well above the crowd. She made a tight circle and ran along at head level with the guards on the ground. She alighted on the stage briefly and turned her hands to flat shovels and ran long enough to smack every guard she could reach before taking to the sky once again. She made another pass, then another, this time dodging bullets as soldier after soldier opened fire as she drew near.

"I've got what I need, Bronte, get out of here." Athena retreated off the stage.

Bronte made one final turn to head back to safety when something long and hard connected solidly with her midsection. Her metallic exoskeleton did nothing against the abrupt stop midair or the forced exhalation of the contents of her lungs. She landed hard on the stage and slid on her side across the wooden surface.

She scrambled to her feet as a man holding a long pipe approached. He looked vaguely familiar. She tried to go airborne, but the man with the pipe beat her again before she could dash to safety.

"Dr. Scales, or do you prefer Dr. Zepto now? It's not pleasurable to see you. Although I won't mind causing you pain once more."

"I remember you. You and I might remember our last encounter differently. Even without all this." Bronte indicated herself and her exoskeleton. "I still kicked your ass. You ended the fight with no laptop, no serum, and you created a superhuman. It's Antonio, right? Not your finest day on the job."

"We do see things differently, but this time I'll leave no doubt. I'd kill you, just for fun, but my boss wants you alive. No one said you had to be in one piece." Antonio advanced, his face twisted in the creepiest expression Bronte had ever seen.

"That sounds like a nice offer and normally I'd stay, but I don't have time for this right now." Bronte tested her enhanced speed as she cut across the back of the stage, away from Antonio and the others nearby.

She heard Antonio giving chase but no one else could do what she could. She leapt into the air and was soon out of reach. Why had the zeptobots taken so long to reveal this particular power? She was three leaps and bounds from the stage when she heard Antonio ordering the soldiers into the crowd. What made her heart beat triple time was the mention of the Romans and something about double enhancements.

"Something's going on over here. The Ten Romans are here and they might have enhancements now too. How are you doing at getting people out of the park?" Bronte looked in the direction of her friends. She squinted and shielded her eyes. Surely, she wasn't seeing what she thought she was? "I'm hesitant to ask, but is Galen a giant turkey?"

"Peacock, mate. It's all about the tail feathers." Galen turned her impressive posterior in Bronte's direction. She was singing one of the worst renditions of nineteen eighties pop hits Bronte was sure had ever touched human ears.

"I have more questions than we have time for now. Bard and her creepy friend are up to something. The soldiers have moved into the crowd." Bronte climbed higher so she could see all of Bard's men. "I don't like the look of this. Where are we with the crowds?"

"Spero's trying to disable Bard's program with the laptop you brought him. Until that's offline we can't get everyone out of the park because even when we release some of them from whatever spell they're under, the moment they move away from us, they're back under again." Athena sounded worried. "The singing peacock routine is keeping the Montagues and Capulets from killing each other, for now."

Antonio was giving orders again. Bronte strained to hear over the crowd noise. Even her enhanced hearing struggled against the thousands of voices in the park. What she was able to hear made her blood run cold. She'd never understood the phrase before but now she felt like liquid nitrogen was running through her veins.

"Antonio gave an order to agitate the crowd and shoot at the first sign of aggression. I think they're trying to salvage their big hero moment. I have to stop them, or people are going to die." Bronte ran through the air directly toward the nearest soldier.

"Remember your promise." Athena's voice was stern and commanding. "Absolutely no dying over there. Don't even dabble. I'm having none of it. You hear me?"

"Yes, ma'am. Loud and clear." Bronte stopped above a cluster of three soldiers. They saw her but didn't raise their weapons.

"Good, because I'm refusing to say the three words I want to say to you. The three words to describe how I feel, until you get back in one piece. Now, go save the world."

Bronte turned her attention back to the soldiers on the ground. "Hey, boys. I hear you're interested in shooting innocent people. That makes you pretty evil, FYI, and I can't let you hurt anyone."

"What are you going to do about it, metal head? We're the ones with the guns and the screens," one of the soldiers said. And yet, he didn't shoot. There was something behind his eyes, some shred of humanity that was clearly battling with the emotions being forced on him. The other three lit their screens and flashed a quick series of negative emotions across them. Bronte looked around and saw the same on all the soldiers' screens.

"I need those guns," Bronte whispered to the zeptobots. Before she could puzzle out an answer to how she'd make that happen, the three weapons flew out of the soldiers' hands and into hers. More accurately they flew onto her hand and stuck there. "Magnets, huh? I didn't think we knew how to do that. How about a little super conductance again?"

Bronte's hand once against grew uncomfortably cold and the rifles rattled against her palm. Suddenly they shot off her hand with a great deal of force heading back to their owners. Two struck the soldiers clean in the face, the third landed a direct hit to the middle of his chest. All three men fell to the ground in a gasping heap.

Bronte landed and collected the rifles. "Doesn't look like you're in any shape to fire these. I'll hold onto them for you." Before she took off, she pulled out the battery pack sewn neatly into the shirt front of the soldiers' uniforms. She smashed all three and then took to the sky again, seeking out more of Bard's men.

Before she reached the next soldier Athena's voice cracked through the comms. "Bronte, Spero's done. He disabled the Program. We're starting the evacuation now. Galen's heading to you for backup. She has the same rules about dying as you do. Keep your eye on her."

"I can hear you, you know." Galen was out of breath but she still sounded testy. "I'm a grown-ass lady. I don't need a babysitter."

"You're no lady. Flutter your tail feathers in my direction if you get into trouble and I'll be happy to rescue you. I'd never leave a damsel in distress." Bronte refocused on the soldier below her. "When you get here, Galen, we've got to take out as many of these soldiers as we can. The crowd's on edge. The soldiers are starting their emotional attack."

Bronte landed in front of her next target. He raised his gun. She grabbed the muzzle and ripped the rifle from his hands. He shuffled backward, fear in his eyes, but she wasn't letting him go to rearm himself and return to the crowd. She lunged forward and struck hard at his ribs. He attempted to counter but flailed harmlessly at her arms instead. She struck again. Sternum, cheek, uppercut to the chin. He fell to the ground and scuttled away from her.

"You're retired. If I see you back in the crowd, I won't be so kind next time." Bronte removed his battery pack and slung his rifle over her shoulder with the others and went in search of her next fight.

She was halfway to the next soldier when she saw his screens change from the rapidly changing emotional roller coaster to a deep furious red. The reaction from the people gathered near him was instantaneous. From the angry roars all around her it seemed the soldier in front of her wasn't the only one to activate his screen. The soldiers were clearly not working on the same network as that which had been influencing the crowd.

Galen materialized next to her. "This is going to end badly. I took out two soldiers on my way over here, but there are still too many of them."

"Can you make yourself into a gun if you wanted?" Bronte examined Galen carefully. There was so much more she wanted to know about her relationship with the zeptobots.

"I don't know. Probably. But I'm not going to." Galen crossed her arms across her chest, squeezing herself tightly. "What would I be shooting as bullets? My eyebrows? A nipple? An ovary? At the end of the fight would I have to collect my body parts strewn around the field or would I return to myself and have to settle for looking like Swiss cheese?" Galen shivered.

"All right, no gun." Bronte moved toward the soldier she'd identified as her next target. "I'm going to get us one of these uniforms. Take out the soldiers you can. We move as quickly as we can and try to get the civilians to the exits."

She and Galen bumped fists and sprinted into the crowd.

Bronte reached her target and had him on the ground before he saw her approach. "Your uniforms, are they networked or controlled manually by the wearer?" The man didn't answer right away so Bronte picked him off the ground a few inches by the front of his shirt and slammed him back down.

"Networked. They're networked." The soldier tried to shuffle backward, away from Bronte.

She grabbed his leg at the knee and pulled him back. "And if I want to disable all of them, can I do that from yours?"

"I don't know, I swear."

Bronte lifted him again by the shirt front.

"Okay, okay. Maybe. If you short-circuited mine, it might cascade but I'm not tech support."

It was a long shot but worth a try. Bronte ripped the battery unit from the man's uniform and reversed the polarity. With the zeptobots' assistance, as they seemed to have a much better understanding of wiring and tech than she did, she reattached the connections. Bronte's body was vibrating and warming. She was sure a hive of bees had moved in under her ribcage.

Bronte touched both sides of the battery connection and released the supercharge the zeptobots had created. The man's screens shattered and went dark. Bronte could hear the same happening all around her.

"Get this thing off me. You're fucking crazy, woman." The soldier ripped his uniform shirt off and took off at a sprint.

Bronte let him go. She slung the shirt over her shoulder as well as his rifle. The load was getting awkward She needed somewhere to store them, but for now she didn't trust them out of her sight.

As she was about to resume her mission, three rapid gunshots echoed throughout the park followed by a gut-wrenching scream of agony. A hush fell over the park. It lasted a beat. Another. Another. Then the silence was broken by the sounds of panic.

"Where was that, Galen?" Bronte looked around wildly trying to pinpoint the sound.

"I don't know. I couldn't see it. Fuck. I've taken out four of them, but there's so many more." Galen's anger was evident in her voice.

More shots rang out. Hysteria followed. The crowd was running haphazardly, in no particular direction. If anyone fell, they'd be trampled. Bronte climbed into the sky again. Finding the source of the gunshots was all that mattered. It was an easier task when the bullets started flying at her.

She ran through the air directly at the man shooting at her. She recognized him as one of Antonio's Romans. She never slowed when she dove out of the air, feet first into the soldier's chest. His body and rifle went flying. Bronte wasn't immune to the sound of crunching bones beneath her feet as they both thudded to the ground. She heaved but didn't vomit, a small victory.

Bronte scanned the immediate vicinity. Six bodies lay on the grass. She couldn't tell if they were alive. All of them were bleeding in varying degrees of severity. "Galen. I need you. Now. I have injuries."

Galen unleashed a string of curse words that would have made Bronte blush if she weren't so worried about the individuals bleeding in the grass. "I'll be right there."

"I'm coming too. I'm sure I have more field medicine experience than either of you two." Athena's tone left no room for argument. Bronte tried anyway. Athena was unswayed. "Bronte, I'm a nurse. There are injured people who need my help. You can stand by my side and fuss or you can do your job while I do mine."

"What about the evacuation?" Bronte moved between those on the ground checking pulses and assuring those still alive help was on the way.

"Local police are on the way. Paramedics too. We have a team of civilians coordinating the evacuation now. Spero and I are coming to you," Athena said.

Bronte waited until Galen arrived before she climbed back into the air and assessed the scene once again. There were still too many soldiers and vulnerable civilians on the ground. The panic was real now, and the soldiers seemed to have joined the emotional melee. The shooting was coming from The Ten Romans. Bronte was pretty sure the one she took out was dead, but that still left nine. She looked to the stage and didn't see Bard or Antonio. She didn't know if he counted as one of the ten.

She watched helplessly as two Romans fired wildly into the crowd. Some people fell immediately, others tripped in the panic to get away. Bronte raced to them and stood above the soldiers, drawing their attention.

She told Galen and Athena there were more injuries and then shouted at Bard's men. "I'm the one you want, aren't I? Instead of shooting unarmed civilians for the world to see, come and fight me. If you dare." Bronte ran to the stage and landed. She looked around, hoping the soldiers would follow and move away from those trying to escape.

Bard was still on the stage, but under the canopy now. Was she cowering from the very media she'd invited or had her escape routes been cut off now that the crowd had truly panicked and were no longer under her control? Bard sneered at her from across the stage but made no move to draw nearer. Bronte saw the Romans approaching from all sides. She counted nine in total. Their uniforms were decorated differently than the others, with Roman numerals sewn prominently on their chests.

Suddenly, the screens on their uniforms lit brightly and the men turned to metal. How was that possible? Had Bard made a successful replica of her zeptobots? But how were they behaving the same in all the men? The zeptobots had proven to adapt to each host. She looked more closely. The men weren't all the same. One of the men, the one with "IV" on his uniform, had radio antennae protruding from his head. She watched as his screens changed first and the others followed a half second behind. Was he controlling the rest of the group?

Before she could spend more time pondering the science of the interconnected suits, Roman "II" stepped forward with a sword hilt in each hand. The strangest part was the butt of the hilts were plugged in to cords that appeared to come from his hands. That didn't seem possible. Bronte's breathing hitched and her heart raced when he snapped his wrists and metal blades grew from each hilt, crackling and sparking with sinister energy. She knew her metal suit wasn't invincible. One versus nine weren't odds she liked, especially against nine men with powers similar to her own and then some, but she didn't have a choice. She couldn't let them keep shooting innocent people. Bronte saw Athena a few hundred yards away, crouched low over a prone victim. She thought about Athena's rule about dying. She scanned the Ten Romans stalking closer, weapons raised. She hoped she wouldn't let Athena down and if she did, she prayed Athena wouldn't turn around and watch it happen.

Chapter Thirty-three

A thena wiped sweat from her eyes as she did the best she could to stabilize another patient. They had no medical supplies to speak of and were working in the middle of an active battlefield, but she was fairly certain the folks who were still alive would stay that way as long as they made it to a hospital soon.

"I'm going to check on the next group, Galen." Athena stretched as she stood. The soldiers had disappeared which made her work easier but her heart uneasy. She glanced at the stage and gasped, clapping her hand to her mouth.

Bronte was center stage surrounded by a blur of camouflage, metal, and fury. How were Bard's soldiers made of metal? Bronte was being bombarded by wave after wave of attack. Athena nearly screamed when Bronte fell to a knee and three men jumped on her back, fists and weapons raining down on her. However, she managed to throw them off and go on the offensive. She started to glow and two of the men fell and didn't get back up. Athena counted five left. She didn't know how long they'd been fighting or how many there'd been to start.

Despite the metal skeletons and screens, she could see on their uniforms the men weren't fighting particularly skillfully. The metal looked bulky and constricting. It was nothing like the fluidity Bronte moved with when she was suited up.

She wanted to go to Bronte, but others needed her more. If Bronte was glowing, the men on the stage stood no chance. Athena reluctantly moved away from the stage and Bronte. Her heart pulled in one direction while her body walked in another.

There were fewer dead and less severe injuries at the second location. Athena was glad for that, for the people involved and for herself. She'd seen enough terror and trauma to last her a lifetime.

She moved quickly from person to person, assessing and forming a mental triage list. She used clothing, shoelaces, and anything else she could find for bandages, slings, and tourniquets as needed.

After her initial survey, she returned to the most severely injured and began her work. She'd only just stopped the bleeding when a hard, metallic object jabbed into her back. It felt like the end of a pipe.

"Our wayward nurse and Dr. Zepto's special friend. Oh, do I have plans for you."

Athena shivered at the sound of the man's voice. He sounded detached from the words, as if they had a different meaning for him than most of the world. He also sounded like he was enjoying himself. She didn't need to be told the metal object bumping against her spine was a gun.

"Let me save him. It's not too late. I have the bleeding under control. I need to bandage it." Athena held her breath.

"I would worry more about who's going to save you," the man leaned close and whispered in her ear.

"I'm going to, not that she needs saving. She's the strongest woman I know. You don't stand a chance against her, Antonio."

Athena had never been so happy to hear Bronte's voice. The joy was short-lived when she heard Antonio remove the safety on the gun. She closed her eyes, waiting for the shot, the ultimate end to her adventures. Instead she heard the sounds of a scuffle behind her, grunting, bodies colliding and falling. She didn't dare turn around.

When the expected shot did ring out, Athena was enveloped in Bronte's strong metallic arms, her body shielded by Bronte's. Antonio cursed and kept firing. The bullets clanged off Bronte's back again and again. Antonio emptied an entire magazine. The sound was overwhelmingly loud, and each shot made Athena jump.

Each discharge was like an electric shock directly to her heart which couldn't take much more sadness and fear today.

Athena finally dared a look under Bronte's arm. Antonio collected a discarded rifle and swung it around, butt end toward Bronte.

"He's going to hit you with a rifle next." Athena looked at Bronte.

"As long as he's not hitting you." Bronte smiled at her.

Antonio swung the rifle onto Bronte's back. Athena could tell when it connected because it sounded loudly against Bronte's metal exoskeleton, but she also let out a grunt and sharply sucked in air with each strike.

"Get up and fight him. Don't sit here protecting me and getting the crap beaten out of you." Athena poked Bronte in the stomach.

"No. If I'm not protecting you, he can hurt you. I'm not willing to risk it." Bronte pulled her closer.

"I know you're not really bulletproof. I've seen you bleed. How about I carve you out of that suit? Then I'll let your girl watch while I slowly take you apart." Antonio's voice was thick with venomous evil.

Athena peered around Bronte again and watched in horror as Antonio raised a knife high above his head, ready to drive it into Bronte's vulnerable back. There was a blinking box attached to the handle. She didn't know what it was, but she was sure the added tech was specially made for Bronte. She wasn't sure the zeptobots would be able to protect her from Antonio's blade.

Athena closed her eyes and pictured how she might attack Antonio once Bronte was incapacitated. Could she wrest the knife from him? Would she be able to stab another human being? She thought about Bronte bleeding in the dirt. Absolutely she would.

Before the integrity of Bronte's suit was tested, two sharp gunshots echoed through the strangely quiet park. Athena snapped her eyes open. Antonio was on his knees, the knife on the ground at his side. He was clutching his shoulder and chest, two splotches of blood blossoming across his uniform shirt. He fell over in the dirt, his breathing ragged. He caught Athena's eye and his mouth twisted into a maniacal smile. She turned away. The look in his eyes wasn't one of a man who valued human life, even his own.

"Bronte, are you okay?" Athena helped Bronte to a seated position and ran her hands over her face, her shoulders, and her back. She could feel the pockmarks and dents in her exoskeleton. "Sweetheart, how much pain are you in?"

Bronte's eyes were unfocused when she looked at her. "I'm okay. Who took that shot? Where's Bard?"

Athena saw police officers and paramedics swarming the park which was much emptier now. Spero must have been successful in evacuating a majority of the civilians. Bard's soldiers were in handcuffs or rounded up. Antonio was surrounded by three officers, all with their service weapons drawn. She couldn't see people clearly on the stage, but from where she sat, it looked like Bard was one of the ones being arrested. With her escape routes cut off and her security crew dismantled, she'd been hiding, waiting for a chance to run. That chance hadn't materialized.

"It's over. You did it." Athena pulled Bronte to her, intending to give her a celebratory hug, but instead caught her as she slumped and collapsed. She pressed her comms unit. "Galen, I need you." Athena leaned over Bronte, crumpled and vulnerable on the ground. She tried not to descend into panic. She watched helplessly as Bronte's metal skin fell away, revealing the very mortal, very wounded, woman beneath.

Bronte groaned and her body shook. Without the metallic skin, Athena could see the damage the battle had inflicted on Bronte's body. Large angry, black bruises, welts, and one fist-sized scrape covered the skin Athena could see, but she knew far worse likely covered Bronte's back.

Athena took her hand. "You made me a promise, Bronte. Don't you dare break it. I love you too damn much to lose you now."

Bronte squeezed Athena's hand. She didn't open her eyes, but she seemed less pained. That was enough, for now.

Athena heard Galen's approach before she arrived. Athena appreciated how swiftly she'd come.

Galen skidded to a stop next to Bronte and knelt. "Whoa, mate, you look like hell." Galen shouted to a nearby paramedic and commandeered a stethoscope and a few other supplies.

Time seemed to stop while Galen completed her exam. The thought of losing Bronte after Athena had finally found her was too much to bear. She chewed the inside of her lip and silently urged Galen to hurry the hell up.

"All right, mate. You've got your lady pretty worried. I don't have many options with you lying in the grass so I either need you to pull it together and tell me what and where is hurting most or I'm going to load you on a stretcher and haul you to the hospital." Galen leaned over Bronte and spoke close to her ear as if all the fighting might have robbed her of her hearing. "There are going to be questions at the hospital that you might not have figured out answers to yet. I'll be polite this one time. Get up, please."

Bronte was still for a few beats. Athena's heart turned into a metronome, pounding out the rhythm of her rapidly rising panic. Galen looked at her, worry in her eyes. Then, before stretchers were mentioned again, Bronte groaned and moved her legs, then her arms. She moved her hand to her face and rubbed her eyes. She opened them a crack and looked from Athena to Galen.

"Get that away from me, you dirty bird." Bronte pulled the stethoscope from Galen's hand and tossed it across her body.

"Welcome back, metal head." Galen leaned back on her heels, smiling. "It looks like you went through a rock tumbler. As your doctor, I have a few health and wellness recommendations."

"More like target practice and you are *not* my doctor. Where's Athena?" Bronte struggled to sit.

"I'm right here. Please be careful, I've already watched you collapse once today." Athena didn't try to hide the tears freely running down her cheeks. "You scared me."

"I'm sorry. Did you mean what you said?" Bronte looked hopeful with a large helping of nervousness.

"About loving you? Is the metal starting to seep into your brain? Of course I meant it. Don't you know how much I love you?" Athena cupped Bronte's cheek.

Loud gagging noises interrupted their moment. Athena turned and glared at Galen who looked like a cat gawking up a hairball.

"Yeah, I know, I said I wanted to watch, but unless you want to spend hours being questioned about all this, we need to go. Now." Galen pointed around the park.

Athena surveyed the scene. The park was now swarming with police officers and federal agents of every persuasion. Thank goodness all the screens of Bard's men were either disabled or had been confiscated. "Galen's right. We need to go. Are you okay to move, love?"

Bronte stood, somewhat shakily, but after a couple of cautious steps she had her sea legs under her again. "Where's Spero?"

"Were you rolling around moaning on the ground for sympathy? How are you fine now?" Galen was looking at Bronte skeptically.

Bronte shrugged. "I got shot about a hundred times. I needed a minute. Where's Spero?"

"When the cops showed, I told him to hide. Figured he might scare them into doing something stupid. He's on his way to us now." Galen pointed behind them.

Spero was indeed loping over. His suit was the color of Caribbean ocean waves. Athena felt calm and relaxed as she watched him approach. She looked away. She needed focus, not false serenity.

"There's something I need from the stage. We can't leave without it." Athena started walking, but Galen and Bronte held her back.

"Tell me what you need, and I'll get it." Galen looked around the park and her helmet looked for a moment like it glowed.

"Cell phone. It's hidden between two hard cases for some of the sound equipment." Athena chewed her lip. She needed that phone.

"Coming right up." Galen jumped into the air and transformed into a miniature open cockpit biplane. A tiny Galen was piloting the plane. She saluted and flew off.

"She's like a toddler with a new toy." Bronte's words had no bite.

They didn't have long to wait until Galen returned. She transformed back into her human form as soon as she'd made a lap around their heads. She handed the phone to Athena. "What's so important about this phone?"

"It's been recording everything said on that stage since I was able to sneak onstage, after Bronte destroyed the screen. It should have all we need to keep Bard from wiggling out of this horror. We can review it later. How are we getting out of here?" Athena tucked the phone in her pocket and looked at her three friends expectantly.

"You ride with me." Bronte scooped Athena into her arms, much to Athena's surprise. "Galen, Pegasus? Phoenix? Unicorn?"

"Don't be absurd. I don't want to call too much attention to our escape. As soon as the paramedics get all the victims stabilized and carted off to hospitals the press is going to be allowed in. They've got us on their footage already but no need to get too flashy with our exit. I'm thinking dragon." She transformed into a horse-sized dragon and shook out her wings.

"All aboard, Spero." Bronte took a step into the air. "Meet back at the usual place. If anything happens to either pair, leave a message at Spero's dead drop and we'll regroup. See you soon."

Athena held Bronte tightly as they left the ground. She tried not to laugh as Spero casually climbed onto dragon Galen's back as if he rode dragons regularly. As soon as Bronte climbed higher and started running Athena couldn't do anything but nuzzle into Bronte's chest and hold on. It didn't matter that they were far above the ground moving faster than a carpool minivan. Wherever they were, she'd want to be in Bronte's arms. Somehow the worst job she'd ever had, albeit for less than a day, had led to the best thing that'd ever happened to her. Growing to love Bronte hadn't felt like falling. It felt like this moment, speed and wind and freedom and trust. She squeezed Bronte tighter and closed her eyes. Her heart felt at home as she fully gave in to the miraculous feeling of flying.

Chapter Thirty-four

They hadn't discussed what would happen if they didn't die during their bid to save the world, and so for two days after the big battle in the park, everyone stayed at the warehouse, all of them at a loss as to what would happen next. The fight had left them all bruised and exhausted, so the safe place to recover was welcome, but Bronte knew they were all on the same page. Where would they go next? There didn't seem to be a straightforward answer, and given what they saw on Spero's screens, the hunt for the strange beings who had done battle in the park was already in full gear. As soon as she felt up to it Bronte had suggested a romantic picnic, to which neither Galen nor Spero were invited, and Athena had jumped at the idea.

Bronte stopped in front of the building she thought of as belonging to Athena and her. She took the blanket and candle from Athena, adding them to the picnic supplies she already carried.

"After you, beautiful." Bronte held her hand out toward the fire escape they used to climb to the roof.

Athena put her hand on her hip and frowned. "Are you seriously going to make me climb this death trap when you can fly?"

"I hope Dr. Zepto isn't the only one of us you love." Bronte winked so Athena knew she was joking.

Athena didn't seem to find her joke funny. "Bronte Scales, how many times do I have to tell you, there's only one of you and it's made of you and the zeptobots. I happen to love you, all of you. And if you're hoping this evening ends with me naked, you probably don't want me wearing myself out climbing that ladder, do you?" Athena batted her eyes ridiculously.

All the blood in Bronte's body not required for basic life functions detoured straight between her legs. She *had* been hoping to shed their clothes later, but hearing Athena bluntly labeling the plans for the night was hot as hell. She shoved the blanket and candle back into Athena's arms and scooped her up.

Athena squeezed Bronte tightly and trailed kisses along her neck. "Maybe this is why I wanted you to fly. You have to concentrate, and I have your body to myself."

"My body is yours anytime. All you have to do is ask." Bronte was out of breath and she'd only just climbed into the air. Athena was stealing more than her concentration.

"Get us to the roof and put down everything you have for the picnic." Athena pointed toward the roof. Her eyes were hungry.

Bronte climbed faster. She barely landed before Athena threw her parcels on the ground and pulled Bronte's items from her hands and threw them on top of the crumpled blanket.

Without a second look at the romantic dinner they'd planned, Athena shifted so she was straddling Bronte's waist, her arms wrapped around Bronte's neck. "Back in the air, sexy."

Although she would do almost anything Athena asked of her, Bronte wanted to be on the rooftop, removing clothing, and reveling in each other and the fact that they were finally free. She didn't say any of that, of course, as she climbed back into the air. Whatever Athena wanted, she could have.

"You think it's better down there, but I'll show you you're wrong." Athena bit Bronte's earlobe and gave it a gentle tug.

"Are you a mind reader now too?" Bronte shuddered as Athena bit and kissed her way down Bronte's neck. She held her more closely and tilted her head to give Athena better access.

"No. I can't read everyone's mind, but yours is pretty easy to understand right now. You want to rip my clothes off and let gravity worry about getting them to the ground. Am I right?" Athena kissed Bronte deeply, possessively.

All Bronte could do was nod.

Athena broke the kiss and looked Bronte in the eye. "Then do it."

Bronte hesitated and looked around. It was dark and there was almost no light from any surrounding buildings in the mostly abandoned industrial park. They were alone and hidden. If Athena didn't care, why should she? And she wanted her so badly.

Athena smiled slowly, like a poker player revealing the winning hand, when Bronte reached for her shirt. After a few unsuccessful attempts to remove her shirt, Athena batted Bronte's hands away and slowly pulled the shirt over her head.

Bronte's distraction with Athena's breasts nearly caused them both to fall out of the sky. "More, please."

"Your turn." Athena pulled Bronte's shirt off and let it flutter to the rooftop.

The extra work of undressing each other midair made the experience more exciting. They couldn't let go of each other so each new reveal also came with opportunities to build pleasure, grind, caress, and explore. Bronte marveled at the feel of Athena's nipples in her mouth and breasts in her hands.

She loved the moans that escaped Athena's lips and the thrust of her hips against Bronte's stomach. "When you come for the first time, I'm going to be the one to send you over the edge. Don't go there without me." Bronte bit down gently on Athena's neck.

"Don't wait too long. All I have to do is think about your hands on me and I'm close. I need you, Bronte. Now." Athena's thrusting against Bronte's stomach increased in intensity and urgency.

Bronte had no intention of waiting. She put a hand behind her, relieved to feel the same solid feeling behind her as that under her feet. She sat in midair, pulling Athena onto her lap.

She slipped her hand between Athena's legs and ran her fingers back and forth through the folds of her slick, wet sex.

Athena grabbed Bronte's wrist. She tried to hold her hand still over her clit, but Bronte wasn't ready to send Athena to orgasm just yet. "Is sex in the sky everything you hoped it would be?" Bronte kissed along Athena's jawline, her neck and over her breasts. She circled round a nipple with her tongue before grazing it with her teeth and pulling it into her mouth.

Athena threw her head back and moaned loudly. She thrust against Bronte's hand. "You don't want to make me beg."

Bronte released Athena's nipple and kissed her deeply. "You're right, I don't. I want to give you the world." With that, Bronte sank two fingers deep into Athena.

Athena nearly bucked off her lap but Bronte held her tight. She matched the rhythm of Athena's thrusts and soon Athena called out her pleasure loudly into the night before slumping against Bronte's chest, breathing heavily.

"To answer your earlier question, sex in the sky is amazing, but I think it might have more to do with you." Athena ran her hands through Bronte's hair before kissing her tenderly. She pulled away and pointed at the rooftop. "I need you on your back on the blanket. How quickly can we get there?"

Bronte didn't waste time answering Athena's question when she could show her instead. They were on the ground before Athena finished exploring Bronte's pulse point. Bronte set Athena down gently and then was unsure what to do. The blanket was in a messy pile where they'd thrown it.

Athena had no such hesitations. She retrieved the blanket and quickly spread it on a patch of the roof free of rocks and debris. She dragged Bronte by the hand to the blanket and gently shoved her on to her back.

"I love you. I'll never get tired of saying that." Athena crawled along Bronte's body, kissing as she went.

Bronte's breath hitched. She wanted to insist Athena take care of the throbbing between her legs, but she was helpless against Athena's lips and tongue. Bronte squirmed against her arousal. She'd never been so wet or hard.

Thankfully, Athena didn't make her wait long. She shimmied back down Bronte's body and spread her legs. "You're beautiful, every inch of you."

Bronte's instinct was to cover herself and keep the world from seeing what she looked like. The awareness of the zeptobots living within her wasn't something she was totally comfortable with yet. But with Athena, she wanted to be seen. Athena made her feel beautiful. She didn't cover herself, she spread her legs further, inviting Athena in.

Athena needed no further invitation. She wrapped her hands around Bronte's thighs and buried her tongue in Bronte's sex. Bronte arched off the blanket, sure she'd never recover from the ecstasy.

"I'll make it worth your while if you stick around." Athena paused long enough to tease Bronte before returning to Bronte's sex.

"Don't stop." Bronte could hear the pleading in her voice and didn't care.

"Come for me now." Athena increased the pressure of her tongue along Bronte's clit.

Bronte came fast and hard. She was too spent to move after, but Athena crawled up and curled into Bronte's arms. They lay like that, content, tangled naked together for a long time. Bronte briefly wondered where their clothes were but decided she didn't care to move so clothing didn't matter.

"I love you, Bronte." Athena lifted onto an elbow and kissed Bronte's nose.

Bronte pulled her close. "I love you too. Of all the people I could have kidnapped that day."

Athena laughed. "Right? You could be on this roof having sex with a basilisk."

Bronte shuddered at the thought. "It was always you. From the moment I opened my eyes."

"You know things are about to change, right?" Athena looked worried. "We have to leave the warehouse eventually now that Bard's gone and we're not being hunted."

Bronte sighed. "Can we be together?"

Athena kissed her and laughed. "We better be."

"Then the rest will work itself out." Bronte pulled Athena on top of her and kissed her again.

Despite so much still undecided, Bronte had never been happier. Defeating a supervillain and falling in love had that effect. She and Athena, and Galen and Spero too for that matter, had a lot to work out, but they'd already worked through something harder than she thought she'd ever face. She couldn't have done it without Athena, and she didn't want to move forward without her either. How this spectacular woman loved her was beyond comprehension. That alone was worthy of the most epic of tales and Bronte couldn't wait to write the next chapter.

CHAPTER THIRTY-FIVE

B ard checked her watch. She'd been waiting in a conference room at the courthouse for over an hour. Her lawyer was late which was making her more antsy. What was taking so long? Her first pre-trial hearing was supposed to start soon and she'd heard nothing from anyone since being led into this room. She drummed her fingers rhythmically on the table and checked her watch again. When she couldn't stand it any longer, she paced the room, looking at the prints of sailboats, rain-soaked European streets, and hunting dogs that lined the walls. Who was the target audience with these pictures? She guessed the old white men who still comprised the majority of judges and lawyers in the city. Men like her father, who hadn't spoken to her once since she'd been arrested, though he'd made certain to tell the press that he'd had no idea whatsoever about Bard's plans.

All of her plans were to save his company. The one he cared about more than her. The one he'd handed over to her but never truly gave up control of. She'd worked so hard to make him proud and now he was denying her, again. She used to be terrified of his rejection and disdain, but look where seeking his approval had gotten her. No more. She didn't care about what he said. She was a free woman.

After her fifth lap around the table, the door finally opened, and her lawyer strolled in as if he wasn't obnoxiously late. Bard opened her mouth to detail exactly how she felt about being kept waiting when Antonio shuffled in behind him. He was in prison orange and shackled at his ankles and wrists, and there were two guards behind him.

"Sorry I'm late, my errand took longer than expected." Bard's lawyer looked from Antonio to Bard and then returned to the door. "I have a matter to attend to directly outside the door. I trust you two will be okay in here for a few minutes?"

Bard nodded and quickly circled the table to hug her oldest friend. She'd been worried about Antonio after she'd seen him shot by a police officer and then handcuffed to a gurney before they put him in an ambulance.

"I tried to get you released prior to trial, but the judge refused." Bard's heart squeezed as she examined the sling holding Antonio's shoulder immobile. "Are you getting the proper care for your shoulder?"

Antonio pulled out a chair and sat. "I asked that I not be released no matter how many strings you pulled."

"What? Why?" Bard sat heavily next to Antonio. "Why won't you let me help you?"

"Because cutting corners and pulling strings is something your father did and you're better than him. And because it's my turn to help you. Every shred of evidence now looks like I was the one behind the Program, the park, all of the research. Anything you were aware of you were forced to do against your will. Getting me out of jail doesn't help you prove that's true." Antonio leaned back in his chair, a satisfied look on his face. "I've already made a statement to say as much."

Bard's stomach dropped. "Why would you do that? It's not the truth." She'd had hesitations and had questioned some of the paths Antonio had recommended, but at the end of the day, she was the head of the company, and she had the final word. She'd wanted to make her father proud and to continue their legacy. She'd wanted ultimate power. Antonio had only supported and encouraged her. "It isn't true," she said again.

Antonio shrugged. "It is now. The truth is a funny thing. Say something with enough conviction and people will believe it because they want to. Your heart was never in it. It's too pure. You tried to hide it, tried to be like me and your dad, but you're not and that's okay. The world can't handle many people like me. Look, men like me, there's only two places we end up, prison or the ground. You kept me out of both longer than I ever expected. This is my repayment. And now." Antonio leaned forward and tapped his finger on the table, the predatory look that always scared Bard in his eyes. "I have a new kingdom to conquer and I can't wait to get started." Antonio rose and kissed Bard on the top of the head. "Thank you, my friend. And remember, no matter which path you choose to follow, there is plenty of room between the hero of a story and someone like me. You'll find your place and your passion and when you do, don't let anyone or anything stand in your way. Just because I won't be there doesn't mean there aren't other ways to permanently solve your problems." He walked to the door and knocked twice.

Bard's lawyer opened the door, nodded to Bard, and walked after Antonio down the hall. Antonio never looked back.

After Antonio left, the room was unnaturally still and quiet. Bard wasn't sure what to do or think. Was she free to go now or did she need to stay for the hearing? Why was Antonio taking the fall for her? They'd been friends since childhood, but Bard couldn't think of anything she'd done for Antonio over the years that warranted this kind of repayment.

While she sat trying to sort out her feelings, her lawyer returned. "I assume you had a nice chat with your friend?"

"You set this up? Are you paying him off? What's going on?" Bard stood, angry now.

The lawyer held his hands out in front of him. "I had nothing to do with it. Antonio reached out to me. I only facilitated this meeting. He explained that everything was his doing, and the evidence would bear that out."

"It's not fucking true." Bard slammed her hand on the table.

"Okay." Her lawyer looked confused. "We can argue that in court, if you want. As your lawyer though, I would strongly encourage you not to take a position trying to help the prosecutor prove their case. As things stand it sounds like there will be some legal hurdles in the next few months and then you'll be a free woman."

Bard scrubbed her face with her hands. Was it possible to be pulled apart inside? This was clearly what Antonio wanted, but could she live with the guilt of what she'd done and allow Antonio to take the blame? She took a deep breath. "Okay, obviously I'll follow your advice. What do you recommend I do?"

The lawyer smiled. "Excellent. The legal wrangling you can leave to me. That's why you're paying me. As I said, I expect it to be sorted out in the next few months. I'd recommend hiring a crisis management team for your business. There will be considerable blowback once the full details of Antonio's activities come to light." He took rapid notes on a legal pad. "And, Bard, everything will be okay."

Bard sat heavily again and leaned her head on her hands. She wasn't sure that was true. How could it possibly be true? She'd lived in Antonio's and Ludo's morally dark zone for so long now, would she be able to find her way back? She'd been willing to kill people to get what she'd wanted. That wasn't down to the men around her. That kind of evil lived in her, and she'd have to find a way to deal with it.

She thought about her science and those she employed. Did she need to fire all of them and clean up the lab space? She'd already woken the lab subjects who remained on the restricted floor and discharged them. She'd released the emotional response subjects as well. The experiments hadn't taken. as far as she could tell, so there was no reason to keep them out of the real world.

She sighed heavily and collected her belongings. She could find her lawyer on the way out. There were decisions to be made about her research, her company, and her life, but the answers were not in this room of extinct masculinity.

Would she turn over a new leaf or continue down the path of darkness? She didn't know, but she was sure letting fear manipulate her actions was a thing of the past. It had to be or she'd soon be right back where she stood, regretting her actions and unmoored when she considered how to move forward. That thought alone was enough to scare her into behavior change. She said a prayer her new compass would steer her in the direction she was always meant to travel.

CHAPTER THIRTY-SIX

A thena sat on her now familiar spool in the circular meeting
spot they'd dubbed "the campfire." It was family meeting
time, and from the look on everyone else's faces, Athena wasn't
the only one feeling melancholy. It had been three weeks since the
events in the park. Even though the threat from Bard and her men
was gone, Athena, Bronte, Spero, and Galen were all still residing
in the warehouse. None of them seemed to want to leave, and
when one of them broached the idea of moving forward, the rest
shut it down. But the days were empty now that they'd defeated
their enemy. They watched the news and kept up with every bit of
information on Bard's trial, but there wasn't much to say about it that
they hadn't said before. There'd been no mention of the basilisks
and any discussion of Bard's laboratory touched on how Verstrand
did important work and how it shouldn't be shut down over one
rogue employee's actions. Conveniently, there was no mention of
human experimentation or mind control. Someone was still pulling
important strings.

Spero's speech was coming along well, Galen was in full control
of her zeptos and often went into town for supplies that no longer
included the drugs that had allowed her to endure her existence. But
other than that, they were simply waiting. For what, there didn't
seem to be an answer. That's why she called the family meeting.

Everyone took their seats and looked at each other tentatively.

"Are you a-holes going to insist I lose your numbers now that
we saved the world?" The corners of Galen's mouth turned up in a

lopsided grin that didn't hide the hint of vulnerability beneath the words.

"Sure would, but I don't have a phone, so call all you like." Bronte winked at Galen.

Spero looked ready to join in the teasing, but Athena cut him off. "Boys. Enough."

Galen tried to hide it from her view, but Athena saw her point to Bronte's crotch and mime a large penis. She gave Bronte a thumbs-up. It was difficult not to join in the giggling once Galen and Bronte started.

"Grow up, you two. We need to discuss the warehouse." Athena instinctively took Bronte's hand.

"Warehouse, home. Home, warehouse. I don't have anywhere else to go." Galen looked at the floor. "Even Bard and Antonio have nice jail cells waiting for them if everything goes according to plan, but me, I've got nothing."

Spero pointed at Galen, nodding. Despite the fact that he could talk now, old habits died hard.

Bronte looked at Athena. "I've been in that hospital or in here for well over a year. My stuff has probably been sold and my apartment rented. I don't have anywhere to go either."

Athena tapped her chin. "I don't know the status of my apartment, but I'm not eager to return, either way. There's very little I care about there. So the next question is do we stay here or find somewhere else, and if it's somewhere else, do we go together?"

It was silent while everyone took time to gather their thoughts. Athena wasn't sure how to answer her own questions. She wanted Bronte with her, but other than that, she wasn't sure.

"The warehouse has served us well, but I think I'd like something with a real bed, a stove, and a place that doesn't have a room that was once used to torture Spero." Bronte looked around. It was clear from the look on her face how much this place meant to her.

"I'd be interested in somewhere that had a gas line I was more than sixty percent sure wasn't going to explode." Galen popped open a bag of chips and crunched one loudly.

As was still the norm, Spero said nothing.

"A few more walls would be nice too." Athena wasn't sure she'd ever get the smell of a burnt dinner creation Galen had attempted when they'd first arrived fully out of her clothes. She looked at Galen whose eyebrows were sky-high. "That's not what I meant, but you're right, that would be nice too. I've told you plenty, you aren't invited."

Bronte frowned. "So if we're done with warehouse living, does that mean we go our separate ways?"

There was another long stretch of silence. No one seemed to want to voice the most likely outcome.

"What happens if the world needs saving again?" Athena would miss Spero and Galen. Having her superhero to come home to overnight didn't mean she wouldn't miss the rest of the team.

"Eventually, Bronte's going to need to buy a phone. I'll call her if everything goes to shit again." Galen didn't sound at all lighthearted.

The mood in the warehouse was now heavy and sad. Athena looked at her friends, then at the space they'd called home for so long. She remembered what it had looked like the first day they'd walked in. Now it truly did feel like a home. It wouldn't win any interior design awards but when they'd needed shelter and safety, they'd found both here. It would be hard to leave.

"Maybe I could offer an alternative? I believe it would solve both of our problems." Spero calmly looked around the circle as if his declaration wasn't worthy of pomp and circumstance.

"I thought you were still malfunctioning when you tried to talk." Galen was slack-jawed. "How did I not know you're British?"

"I'm not British," Spero said with a perfect German accent. "I'm a spy."

"Do Russian." Bronte leaned forward on her spool.

Athena pulled Bronte back toward her and kissed her cheek. "How about Spero explains his proposal and later he can show off his accents?"

"Fine." Galen leaned close to Spero. "Are you a real spy?"

Spero nodded and then looked at Galen with his finger held over his lips. "I'm in possession of an estate in the historic district. The property covers an entire city block, and it has multiple buildings and residences. The manor house itself boasts nine bedrooms across two wings. We could all comfortably live in the manor house or split between that and the carriage house or one of the smaller buildings and still maintain plenty of privacy and personal space."

"Dude, why do you have that? And why have we been living in a warehouse?" Galen looked like she could strangle him.

"Property records list me as owner. I'm sure Bard checked there immediately. As to how I acquired the property? I'm not at liberty to say, but it is mine and it is empty."

"What's the catch?" Athena searched Spero's face. The deal felt too good to be true.

"No catch. Not in the traditional sense. But it's a dump. We'd have our work cut out for us rehabbing her." Spero flashed the image of a run-down, but beautiful manor house surrounded by a wildly overgrown garden.

"Fixing that will take money and heroing isn't paying much these days." Galen stuck her greasy chip fingers in her pockets and pulled out a piece of blue lint and a wadded up receipt.

Spero flashed a map on his screen, then another, and another. They continued rapidly and Athena lost count of how many there were in total.

"Every one of those is what you and Bronte found in the cemetery. In my previous life I was judicious with my spending and made certain to put plenty away in case my chosen career no longer suited me. Which it didn't, once I became one of Bard's experiments. Thankfully, it's all available to us now." Spero spoke to Athena. "Money isn't our issue. And if we need more I can always go out and get some."

Athena raised an eyebrow. "Legally? And what was your previous job description?"

"Why don't we stick with the money we have and worry about additional funds later." Spero wouldn't make eye contact with Athena. "And perhaps we let the past remain where it is."

"Is the house habitable or should we stay here while we work?" Bronte looked thoughtful. "I think we should do as much of the repairs ourselves as we can. Given who we are, I don't want unnecessary strangers trudging through our home."

"Can we call it a base of operations? A lair? Bat cave? Headquarters?" A blossom of excitement stirred in Athena's chest, threatening to ignite into a cascade throughout her system. There seemed to be no question of the fact that they were deciding to stay together.

"Headquarters, unless Spero tells us it's located underwater, in a volcano, or buried in an ice cave. Then it's a lair." Galen's eyes got wide at the thought.

"We can move into our new headquarters as soon as we like." Spero pointedly looked at Galen. "The carriage house is habitable enough given where we've been living."

"And what about your special talents? Will you be using our new headquarters to hone your skills so you can keep saving the world?"

That question seemed harder to answer, and this time the silence was longer. Finally, Galen looked up.

"I'm still getting used to not having to defend myself against humanity's emotions. Let me tell you, there are some really shitty people out there. And a lot of broken ones, too. I think I need time to work with my zeptobots before I go spreading my special brand of love. But I'm not saying no."

Spero nodded slowly. "At least you guys can pass out there. I'm not exactly incognito. I think if we make that move, we do it when we're all ready. The zeptobots and I have been brainstorming ways I may be able to move more freely in the world. We'll see if any of them work out."

Bronte hugged her knees to her chest. "I was scared shitless throughout that whole thing. We did good, but I think I need a little time too."

They were honest answers, and Athena was glad to see the melancholy and self-doubt lift as they realized they were all in a similar place. "That's settled. We go live like rich people in a mansion with nothing better to do than fix up the house and drink tea."

"I don't drink tea, so I'll need some flexibility on that requirement." Galen made a face.

Athena looked at her two friends, and Bronte, the love of her life. Spero looked happy, a descriptor she'd never have used for him before. Galen seemed unburdened, and Athena would be happy if Bronte never stopped looking at her the way she was right then. It was settled, they were trading warehouse living for mansion living and they were staying together.

She took Bronte's hand and they walked out to the patio. "You don't look torn in two today, about who you are and how the world sees you."

Bronte pulled Athena into her arms and kissed her. "You've been trying to tell me all along, I'm the same person I've always been. The only way I'm a robot now is if I was before, but every very human cell in my body cries in sweet unison how much I love you. Robots don't feel this way. I'm sure of it. My doctor's appointments haven't been replaced by mechanics and oil changes just yet."

"We can set up a shop at the new place, just in case." Athena kissed Bronte lightly.

"From warehouse to mansion. Will you share a wing with me?" Bronte pulled Athena close.

"My terms are that the only part of our wing I'm expected to occupy at the end of the night is your bed." Athena wrapped her arms around Bronte's neck and tickled the short hair at the base of her neck.

"I never want you anywhere else." Bronte rested her forehead against Athena's. "I love you, Athena. Whatever struggles led us to this moment, I'm glad for every one of them because they led me on a path to you."

Athena kissed Bronte again. This time she took her time. She was claiming her, leaving her mark on Bronte's skin and heart. This beautiful woman, super heroic and strong, was hers now. Loving her was the greatest adventure Athena didn't know she needed. And lucky for her, this adventure was only just beginning.

About the Author

Jesse Thoma doesn't have superpowers but wishes she did. She would only use her powers for good and not evil if given the opportunity.

Although she works best under the pressure of a deadline, she balks at being told what to do. Despite that, she's no fool and knows she'd be lost without her editor's brilliance. While writing, Jesse is usually under the close supervision of a judgmental cat or two.

Jesse loves to write what she knows or what she wishes were true in the world. She's thrilled she finally wrote a book where people have superpowers, but there still isn't anyone wearing a cape.

Hero Complex is Jesse's eighth novel. *Seneca Falls* was a finalist for a Lambda Literary Award in romance. *Data Capture*, *Serenity*, and *Courage* were finalists for the Golden Crown Literary Society "Goldie" Award.

Books Available from Bold Strokes Books

Catch by Kris Bryant. Convincing the wife of the star quarterback to walk away from her family was never in offensive coordinator Sutton McCoy's game plan. But standing on the sidelines when a second chance at true love comes her way proves all but impossible. (978-1-63679-276-7)

Hearts in the Wind by MJ Williamz. Beth and Evelyn seem destined to remain mortal enemies but are about to discover that in matters of the heart, sometimes you must cast your fortunes to the wind. (978-1-63679-288-0)

Hero Complex by Jesse J. Thoma. Bronte, Athena, and their unlikely friends, must work together to defeat Bronte's arch nemesis. The fate of love, humanity, and the world might depend on it. No pressure. (978-1-63679-280-4)

Hotel Fantasy by Piper Jordan. Molly Taylor has a fantasy in mind that only Lexi can fulfill. However, convincing her to participate could prove challenging. (978-1-63679-207-1)

Last New Beginning by Krystina Rivers. Can commercial broker Skye Kohl and contractor Bailey Kaczmarek overcome their pride and work together while the tension between them boils over into a love that could soothe both of their hearts? (978-1-63679-261-3)

Love and Lattes by Karis Walsh. Cat café owner Bonnie and wedding planner Taryn join forces to get rescue cats into forever homes— discovering their own forever along the way. (978-1-63679-290-3)

Repatriate by Jaime Maddox. Ally Hamilton's new job as a home health aide takes an unexpected twist when she discovers a fortune in stolen artwork and must repatriate the masterpieces and avoid the wrath of the violent man who stole them. (978-1-63679-303-0)

The Hues of Me and You by Morgan Lee Miller. Arlette Adair and Brooke Dawson almost fell in love in college. Years later, they unexpectedly run into each other and come face-to-face with their unresolved past. (978-1-63679-229-3)

A Haven for the Wanderer by Jenny Frame. When Griffin Harris comes to Rosebrook village, the love she finds with Bronte de Lacey creates safe haven and she finally finds her place in the world. But will she run again when their love is tested? (978-1-63679-291-0)

A Spark in the Air by Dena Blake. Internet executive Crystal Tucker is sure Wi-Fi could really help small-town residents, even if it means putting an internet café out of business, but her instant attraction to the owner's daughter, Janie Elliott, makes moving ahead with her plans complicated. (978-1-63679-293-4)

Between Takes by CJ Birch. Simone Lavoie is convinced her new job as an intimacy coordinator will give her a fresh perspective. Instead, problems on set and her growing attraction to actress Evelyn Harper only add to her worries. (978-1-63679-309-2)

Camp Lost and Found by Georgia Beers. Nobody knows better than Cassidy and Frankie that life doesn't always give you what you want. But sometimes, if you're lucky, life gives you exactly what you need. (978-1-63679-263-7)

Felix Navidad by 'Nathan Burgoine. After the wedding of a good friend, instead of Felix's Hawaii Christmas treat to himself, ice rain strands him in Ontario with fellow wedding-guest—and handsome ex of said friend—Kevin in a small cabin for the holiday Felix definitely didn't plan on. (978-1-63679-411-2)

Fire, Water, and Rock by Alaina Erdell. As Jess and Clare reveal more about themselves, and their hot summer fling tips over into true love, they must confront their pasts before they can contemplate a future together. (978-1-63679-274-3)

Lines of Love by Brey Willows. When even the Muse of Love doesn't believe in forever, we're all in trouble. (978-1-63555-458-8)

Manny Porter and The Yuletide Murder by D.C. Robeline. Manny only has the holiday season to discover who killed prominent research scientist Phillip Nikolaidis before the judicial system condemns an innocent man to lethal injection. (978-1-63679-313-9)

Only This Summer by Radclyffe. A fling with Lily promises to be exactly what Chase is looking for—short-term, hot as a forest fire, and one Chase can extinguish whenever she wants. After all, it's only one summer. (978-1-63679-390-0)

Picture-Perfect Christmas by Charlotte Greene. Two former rivals compete to capture the essence of their small mountain town at Christmas, all the while fighting old and new feelings. (978-1-63679-311-5)

Playing Love's Refrain by Lesley Davis. Drew Dawes had shied away from the world of music until Wren Banderas gave her a reason to play their love's refrain. (978-1-63679-286-6)

Profile by Jackie D. The scales of justice are weighted against FBI agents Cassidy Wolf and Alex Derby. Loyalty and love may be the only advantage they have. (978-1-63679-282-8)

Almost Perfect by Tagan Shepard. A shared love of queer TV brings Olivia and Riley together, but can they keep their real-life love as picture perfect as their on-screen counterparts? (978-1-63679-322-1)

Corpus Calvin by David Swatling. Cloverkist Inn may be haunted, but a ghost materializes from Jason Dekker's past and Calvin's canine instinct kicks in to protect a young boy from mortal danger. (978-1-62639-428-5)

Craving Cassie by Skye Rowan. Siobhan Carney and Cassie Townsend share an instant attraction, but are they brave enough to give up everything they have ever known to be together? (978-1-63679-062-6)

Drifting by Lyn Hemphill. When Tess jumps into the ocean after Jet, she thinks she's saving her life. Of course, she can't possibly know Jet is actually a mermaid desperate to fix her mistake before she causes her clan's demise. (978-1-63679-242-2)

Enigma by Suzie Clarke. Polly has taken an oath to protect and serve her country, but when the spy she's tasked with hunting becomes the love of her life, will she be the one to betray her country? (978-1-63555-999-6)

Finding Fault by Annie McDonald. Can environmental activist Dr. Evie O'Halloran and government investigator Merritt Shepherd set aside their conflicting ideas about saving the planet and risk their hearts enough to save their love? (978-1-63679-257-6)

Hot Keys by R.E. Ward. In 1920s New York City, Betty May Dewitt and her best friend, Jack Norval, are determined to make their Tin Pan Alley dreams come true and discover they will have to fight—not only for their hearts and dreams, but for their lives. (978-1-63679-259-0)

Securing Ava by Anne Shade. Private investigator Paige Richards takes a case to locate and bring back runaway heiress Ava Prescott. But ignoring her attraction may prove impossible when their hearts and lives are at stake. (978-1-63679-297-2)

The Amaranthine Law by Gun Brooke. Tristan Kelly is being hunted for who she is and her incomprehensible past, and despite her overwhelming feelings for Olivia Bryce, she has to reject her to keep her safe. (978-1-63679-235-4)

The Forever Factor by Melissa Brayden. When Bethany and Reid confront their past, they give new meaning to letting go, forgiveness, and a future worth fighting for. (978-1-63679-357-3)

The Frenemy Zone by Yolanda Wallace. Ollie Smith-Nakamura thinks relocating from San Francisco to her dad's rural hometown is the worst idea in the world, but after she meets her new classmate Ariel Hall, she might have a change of heart. (978-1-63679-249-1)

A Cutting Deceit by Cathy Dunnell. Undercover cop Athena takes a job at Valeria's hair salon to gather evidence to prove her husband's connections to organized crime. What starts as a tentative friendship quickly turns into a dangerous affair. (978-1-63679-208-8)

As Seen on TV! by CF Frizzell. Despite their objections, TV hosts Ronnie Sharp, a laid-back chef; and paranormal investigator Peyton Stanford, have to work together. The public is watching. But joining forces is risky, contemptuous, unnerving, provocative—and ridiculously perfect. (978-1-63679-272-9)

Blood Memory by Sandra Barret. Can vampire Jade Murphy protect her friend from a human stalker and keep her dates with the gorgeous Beth Jenssen without revealing her secrets? (978-1-63679-307-8)

Foolproof by Leigh Hays. For Martine Roberts and Elliot Tillman, friends with benefits isn't a foolproof way to hide from the truth at the heart of an affair. (978-1-63679-184-5)

Glass and Stone by Renee Roman. Jordan must accept that she can't control everything that happens in life, and that includes her wayward heart. (978-1-63679-162-3)

Hard Pressed by Aurora Rey. When rivals Mira Lavigne and Dylan Miller are tapped to co-chair Finger Lakes Cider Week, competition gives way to compromise. But will their sexual chemistry lead to love? (978-1-63679-210-1)

The Laws of Magic by M. Ullrich. Nothing is ever what it seems, especially not in the small town of Bender, Massachusetts, where a witch lives to save lives and avoid love. (978-1-63679-222-4)

The Lonely Hearts Rescue by Morgan Lee Miller, Nell Stark, Missouri Vaun. In this novella collection, a hurricane hits the Gulf Coast, and the animals at the Lonely Hearts Rescue Shelter need love, and so do the humans who adopt them. (978-1-63679-231-6)

The Mage and the Monster by Barbara Ann Wright. Two powerful mages, one committed to magic and one controlled by it, strive to free each other and be together while the countries they serve descend into war. (978-1-63679-190-6)

Truly Wanted by J.J. Hale. Sam must decide if she's willing to risk losing her found family to find her happily ever after. (978-1-63679-333-7)

A Good Chance by Ali Vali. Harry, Desi, and Desi's sister Rachel are so close to getting everything they've ever wanted, but Desi's ex-husband is coming back to get his revenge and rip apart their chance at happiness. (978-1-63679-023-7)

A Perfect Fifth by Jaycie Morrison. Streetwise pianist Zara Keller and Lady Jillian Stansfield couldn't be more different; yet their connection brings a new awareness of who they are and what they truly want in their lives—including each other. (978-1-63679-132-6)

Catching Feelings by Ana Hartnett Reichardt. Andrea Foster expected to catch a lot of pitches from the Alder Lion's star pitcher, Maya, but she didn't expect to catch feelings. (978-1-63679-227-9)

Defiant Hearts by Lee Lynch. In these stories, you'll find your lovers, friends, and lesbians you wish you knew—maybe even yourself. (978-1-63679-237-8)

Love and Duty by Catherine Young. All Princess Roseli wants is to marry her three lovers, but with war looming, she must instead marry Princess Lucia to establish a military alliance between their planets. (978-1-63679-256-9)

Murder at Union Station by David S. Pederson. Private Detective Mason Adler struggles to determine who killed a woman found in a trunk without getting himself killed in the process. (978-1-63679-269-9)

Serendipity by Kris Bryant. Serendipity brings jingle writer Annie Foster and celebrity pop star Bristol Baines together, and their undeniable attraction keeps them close, but will their different paths drive them apart? (978-1-63679-224-8)

The Haunted Heart by Jane Kolven. A ghost, a ring, and a quest to find a missing psychic—it's a spell for love. (978-1-63679-245-3)

The Rules of Forever by Nan Campbell. After reconnecting at their high school reunion, Cara and Lauren agree to embark on a textbook definition friends-with-benefits relationship, but trying to keep it uncomplicated is harder than it seems. (978-1-63679-248-4)

Vision of Virtue by Brey Willows. When virtue and desire come together, be prepared for sparks in this next installment of the Memory's Muses series. (978-1-63679-118-0)